Advance Praise

"Cyndi Stuart's *Dressing Room Confessions* is a fun, thought-provoking, compelling ride. The writing is entertaining and offers insight into the female, not to mention human, psyche, and the lengths one goes to hide our true selves. Cyndi offers us an inside look at the essence of female friendship and the complexities of their inner world. Stuart's writing is easy to read while maintaining a sophisticated and nuanced style. Looking forward to the next installment in the Shadyside series!" **– John Homa, Acting Coach & Producer at John Homa Productions**

"Cyndi Stuart masterfully captures the spirit of female camaraderie. The narrative is reminiscent of *Sex and the City* with a tantalizing twist akin to *Fifty Shades of Grey*, all while keeping a refined style, like Truman Capote's *FEUD: Capote vs. The Swans*. The writing is both captivating and stimulating; inviting readers to question the facades people present to the world and the secrets they keep." **– Mrs. Julia Audit**

"You might just end up lusting after your handyman or woman—or really anyone who knows how to hold a hammer. The best page turner since *Fifty Shades of Grey*! Question is, will there be another?" **– Elizabeth Jones**

"*Dressing Room Confessions* is a seductive and engrossing read that will leave you eagerly anticipating Cyndi Stuart's next book in the series. A novel that has the feel of a juicy tell-all with the mystery of untold truths…what is real versus what's fiction…leaving the reader to decide for themselves if the author is really writing about themselves." **– Linda Lloyd**

DRESSING ROOM

Confessions

SHADYSIDE NOVELS

DRESSING ROOM

Confessions

CYNDI STUART

Dressing Room Confessions: A Shadyside Novel, Book 1
Published by Midnight Ink Publishing, LLC
Naples, Florida, U.S.A.

Copyright ©2024, CYNDI STUART. All rights reserved.

No part of this book may be reproduced in any form or by any mechanical means, including information storage and retrieval systems without permission in writing from the publisher/author, except by a reviewer who may quote passages in a review. All images, logos, quotes, and trademarks included in this book are subject to use according to trademark and copyright laws of the United States of America.

While certain story elements were inspired by actual events, this series is a work of fiction. The characters, names, places, and events in this series have been fictionalized for dramatic purposes and no identification with actual persons (living or dead), places, or events, should be inferred.

STUART, CYNDI, Author
DRESSING ROOM CONFESSIONS
CYNDI STUART

Library of Congress Control Number: 2024910967

ISBN: 979-8-9906890-0-8, 979-8-9906890-2-2 (paperback)
ISBN: 979-8-9906890-3-9 (hardcover)
ISBN: 979-8-9906890-1-5 (digital)

BIOGRAPHY & AUTOBIOGRAPHY / Rich & Famous
FAMILY & RELATIONSHIPS / Love & Romance
HUMOR / Topic / Men, Women & Relationships
TRUE CRIME / Con Artists, Hoaxes & Deceptions
FICTION / Romance / Erotic

Publishing Advisor: Timothy Jacobs (jacobswc.com)
Editor: Nina L. Marshall (ramadevinina.com)
Proof Editor: Jennifer Christiansen (JenniferChristiansen13@gmail.com)
Book Cover Designer: Damien Mayfield (damienmayfield.com)
Personal Stylist: Marina Sararo (salonsararo.com)
Photography: Annie Watson (anniewatson.com)
Book Project Manager: Susie Schaefer (finishthebookpublishing.com)

QUANTITY PURCHASES: Schools, companies, professional groups, clubs, and other organizations may qualify for special terms when ordering quantities of this title. For information, email info@midnightinkpublishing.com

All rights reserved by CYNDI STUART and
MIDNIGHT INK PUBLISHING, LLC.
This book is printed in the United States of America.

Dedication

For my husband Thomas, who provides me with unwavering life support. Your belief in my abilities unleashes my super powers, granting me increased courage, confidence, and ambitious dreams. My potential is limitless! Without your encouragement, this book series would remain confined, unable to reveal the hidden stories lurking within my mind.

To my daughter Angela, the ray of sunshine in my life. Everything I'm proud of is because of this remarkable and intelligent woman. You are my inspiration to pursue my wildest dreams.

To my son David, who is the greatest gift in my life. No one has brought so much encouragement and inspiration into my life more than this young man. My love and gratitude are endless.

To all the women who have been a part of my life. I cherish the strong bonds I have formed with each of you. While some friendships have endured the test of time, others have faded away, but know that you are always in my thoughts.

Table of Contents

Chapter One

Forgive Me Father

I sat on my bed and stared at the empty page of my diary, contemplating its potential. I chewed on the end of my pencil. It was my preferred writing tool, at the time, since it made it easier to revise my words. Taking a deep breath, I exhaled a sigh and began to scratch the paper with my thoughts.

Being vulnerable is a scary thing.
Allowing someone to unravel your emotions and explore your soul.
Letting them see beyond your eyes and into the wounds of your past.
Running into their arms, unsure if you'll stumble.
Placing your trust in their hands, uncertain if they'll let go.
But it's also scary to never try.
To never embrace the possibility of unexpected love changing your life forever.

I paused and sighed again. *Wow, that was powerful!* I read the words once more, savoring their meaning. Lost in my thoughts, I continued to muse without writing them down.

I carefully placed the pencil back into the spiral binding of the diary and walked over to my dresser. I hid the journal in the back, behind my collection of trinkets and my panties, keeping it private. I knew love was my drug. Risk-taking fueled my soul, and chasing my dreams was vital to my life's existence.

With a sigh, I got up to prepare for the day ahead. Nora, my cousin and almost-sister, whom I nicknamed Sis for that very reason, would be going with me to a concert that night. The excitement rushed through me.

It was 1980. The day flew by, and before I knew it, we were on our way. As we entered the Civic Arena and went through the security checkpoints, I realized this was our last chance to see Steve perform with the band Kansas. I had adored Steve since I was a teenager, while Sis admitted to being infatuated with the violinist.

Unable to contain my nervous energy, I twirled my curly hair around my fingers. "I can't believe we're actually here, Sis. We're about to see the love of my life! I need to buy a Kansas t-shirt before we go in."

Sis pointed to a t-shirt vendor in the distance, and we quickened our pace. "There's one over there, Sophia. Come on, let's hurry! I want to see the stage! Let's run!"

Although Sis was my cousin, she seemed more like a sister. Our mothers were the youngest among twelve siblings, and although we had countless cousins, we shared a special bond.

She always told me, "We stick together through thick and thin. We ride and die together, Sophia." I loved that we were attending this concert together.

We chatted as we ran. "I really need to use the bathroom! I had no idea the drive to the city would take two hours. I hope I never have to see a lump of coal again once I'm in Miami. Just sunshine and sand."

Sis sprinted ahead of me. "Come on, Miami girl. Get your Kansas shirt. I'll save a spot for you in the bathroom line."

I surveyed each t-shirt, trying to decide which one to purchase with my hard-earned money. I settled on a white one with blue sleeves, featuring the Kansas logo on the front and a list of cities on the back. I handed the vendor a twenty-dollar bill, removing the price tag. "Keep the change. Thanks, I need to go!"

While changing into my new shirt, I walked toward the bathroom line and found Sis waiting for me. "You already changed your shirt? What did you do with the old one?"

Breathless from running, I managed to respond as I adjusted my bra beneath the new shirt. "Yeah, I threw it in the trash. I couldn't stand that ugly thing. You know I can't wear ugly."

Sis pushed me forward in the line. "Come on, girl, hurry up. We need to get to our seats. Nothing matters right now except getting inside. I want to dance!"

Patiently waiting for the next available bathroom stall, I thought about my obsession with fashion and looking put together.

The truth was, I constantly drew inspiration from what others wore. At a young age, my aunts spoiled me by taking me shopping in the city and influenced my fashion sense each time they arrived back home from a summer in the Hamptons with a suitcase full of wealthy women's donations for me.

Sis interrupted my thoughts, urging me to move up and pay attention. I was next in line, and she needed me to be quick. As Sis posed in front of the mirror, flaunting her hourglass figure and perfect teeth, she primped and preened like a runway model. She applied a bold, red lipstick and pouted at herself in the mirror.

She's so much prettier than me. I'm not jealous. I love her unconditionally.

Leaning in toward the girl beside her, she asked, "Excuse me. Did you say we can go down to the floor to watch the concert? We don't have to stay in our seats?"

I smiled, admiring Nora's ability to make fast friends with strangers.

"Yes, it's true. You can walk down to the floor, but once it's full, it's full. You better hurry!"

Sis knocked on the bathroom stall I was in. "Let's go, Miami girl! We're going down to the floor. It's going to fill up soon, so hurry!"

We rushed down the concrete steps, gripping the handrails for stability amidst the crowd. I forgot about our seats, hoping to join the gathering crowd on the floor in front of the stage. The stadium filled with fans wearing Kansas t-shirts, and the air hung thick with smoke from flickering lighters and the obvious scent of weed.

"Excuse me. Sorry, excuse me," we repeated as we weaved through the crowd.

Sis pushed her way through until she found a handsome security guard to charm. "Hello, officer. Is there any way you can get us to the front, right under the stage?"

He quickly fell under her spell, as most guys did. His eyes grew round. "Hey, girl. Has anyone ever told you that you look like Marilyn Monroe? Come on, follow me." Using his authority, he parted the crowd, flirting with Sis along the way. "You're one gorgeous woman. Damn, do you know how sexy you are?"

Sis grinned, accustomed to such attention. "Only you, officer. Thank you."

He positioned himself near the stage, pointing to where we should stand. "I want you girls to behave yourselves tonight. If you need me, just give me a wave, and I'll come over to rescue you. The crowd gets wild down here. I'll be standing at the end of the stage, over there." He pointed to a corner right in front of the stage.

"Thank you so much, officer. We'll wave, I promise. Thank you."

He touched his earpiece and leaned in closer to Sis. "I have to go backstage. The singer needs an escort to his dressing room. I'll be keeping an eye on you girls."

She threw him a super-flirtatious, coy grin. "Thank you, officer!"

We were right in front of the stage, with nothing between us and the band.

"Oh my God, I can't believe we're actually here. I wonder what our mothers would say. We'll have to confess all our little sins at church on Sunday!" My grin was so wide, it felt like it would split my face.

Sis smirked back at me. Although she wasn't raised Catholic, like me, she always accompanied me to church. "Do you think Father John will make me say fifteen Hail Marys and twenty Our Fathers if I tell him we lied to our mothers to come to this concert and flirted with a man in uniform to get to the front?"

We laughed uncontrollably. "If that's our punishment, I'm okay with saying a hundred of each! I'm more worried about my mother finding out than Father John. He's easy!"

"Stop talking! Let's enjoy the music and forget about priests. Screw it all. We're here. Let's have fun!"

Closing my eyes, I let the bass reverberate through my feet as the opening act, Michael Stanley Band, began to play.

In that moment, I felt like I was in heaven. I wished I could live in the city, surrounded by music and art. Graduating as one of the top ten in my class a few days later, I knew I had to escape the coal mining town and move to Miami, where I could be free to pursue my dreams and bask in the sun and sand. I longed to be free from the constraints of my mother.

I tried to quiet my thoughts and simply enjoy the music, but being present in the moment has always proved a challenge for me.

My mind flashed through memories. I remembered the day my mother stood over me and wagged her finger as I comfortably sat in my favorite emerald velvet chair in our living room. I had been reading an *Architectural Digest* magazine from front to back, hoping she didn't take it away from me. She hated it when I read. She glared at me intently while saying, "Only lazy people read. Start dancing with a scrub rag. You need to get to work today; we have things to do."

I looked up at her but remained silent.

She darted glances at me as if I did something punishable by death. "Sophia, listen to me," she said. "Girls don't go to college. If you insist on this crazy idea, you'll attend community college and become a medical assistant. All girls need medical training to raise kids. At least you'll be able to meet a doctor to marry you. God knows you'll need a rich man to take care of you with all your expensive tastes."

I rolled my eyes. Trying to block out the memory, I looked over at Sis, who had her eyes closed while she swayed to the music. I wished I could be simple like her.

I thought maybe she was easily relaxed because she had far less pressure to be the best. Her parents accepted her and her twin sister just the way they were. They tried to get them to read and write, but in our small coal mining town, their teachers said, "These twins are incapable of learning to read and write."

A sad truth. My mother insisted I try to teach them to read on the weekends, but my time would get exhausted with my own studies and activities.

They didn't graduate from high school. Instead, they started working at a local factory on their eighteenth birthday.

Just simple. So much easier. Why can't I be simple? Why can't I just settle for less instead of chasing more? Why can't I be like them and just enjoy the country life and become someone's wife who raises children and supports his dreams rather than my own?

I shook my head, wanting to stop thinking.

Be quiet, Sophia.

The Michael Stanley Band was performing their last song, so I knew Steve would be running out on stage any minute. "Sis, my heart's skipping a beat. I'm so nervous! Steve's going to be right in front of me!"

"I know, Sophia! It's so much fun! I'm so glad we came!"

As Steve ran out onto the stage, a burst of lights illuminated the scene behind him. The crowd erupted in cheers as he began singing "Carry on my Wayward Son." He was a true rockstar, commanding the stage with his presence. As I looked up at him, our eyes met for the first time.

Sis noticed the connection and turned to me excitedly. "Oh my God, Sophia. Did you see him look right at you?"

I couldn't help but smile back at him, engaging in a playful flirtation. I knew he was flirting with me, and I relished every moment of it.

As Steve continued to sing and dance on stage, thoughts of kissing him consumed my mind.

He has the attention of every girl in the audience, so why not me?

A few songs later, our security guard friend approached Sis with an invitation from Steve. "Hey, Marilyn." He smiled at his nickname for her. "Steve would like to invite you and your friend to meet the band. If you want to go backstage after the show, just come over to me."

A massive flood of adrenaline shot through me like a drug and made me feel deeply alive. "Oh my God, Sis. Are you serious? We just got invited backstage to the after-party! I'm going to meet my dream man! I knew he was flirting with me! I knew it!"

Sis and I couldn't contain our excitement as we accepted the invitation to meet the band backstage.

Throughout the concert, I was mesmerized by Steve's performance and his flirty interactions with me. It felt like a dream, and I was as head over heels in love as a child with a puppy.

After the show, we made our way to the security guard.

"We want to go backstage to meet the band." Sis winked. "We accept the party invitation."

The security guard gave Nora a wink back as he led us backstage. "You girls need me, just let me know. I'll be right outside these doors for the next hour. I'll be here."

Nora flirted back playfully raising her eyebrows. "Thank you so much, officer. You're so nice."

The blood rushed to the tips of my fingers, the pulse coming in hot waves that caused everything else to pulse. "I can't believe this is happening, Sis. Can you believe it?"

Sis seemed unusually quiet, which was rare for her. I grew concerned about her sudden change in demeanor. "What's wrong? Don't you want to go to the party?"

She looked pale. "I'm just so nervous. What if someone asks me to write my name or read a song out loud? I'm scared. I'll just die."

I was used to boosting her confidence and calming her nerves. "Just be yourself. Everyone always loves you! Just smile and be Marilyn. Nobody's going to ask you any of those things."

I held onto my cousin's hand to reassure her. "I've got you, girl. Stop worrying about silly stuff. You've got this. Now let's have some fun!"

As we entered the room behind the stage, I scanned the private party gang. The room was filled with familiar faces and a lot of attractive, young women with fair complexions and long, straight hair neatly parted down the middle.

Some of the girls were only wearing thong underwear, allowing their breasts to freely salute the crowd without any inhibitions. I couldn't help but stare. I also couldn't help but notice the group of fashion divas standing together, dressed in flamboyant bell-bottom pants, sexy, tied-up blouses, large hoop earrings, and platform shoes. Their outfits were incredible, and I couldn't help but wonder where they shopped. I wanted to ask them.

I walked toward one of them and stood close by, hoping to get a chance.

With one raised brow, Sis also took note of their flare for fashion. "I've never seen such a scene in my whole life."

As the thick, smoky air filled with the scent of weed, a sense of euphoria crept over me, like golden morning sunlight on a field of sunflowers. Colorful bongs sat on every table next to oversized sofas scattered around the room. It was like something I had read about in magazines but never really believed until now. I stood there, awestruck by the atmosphere. Suddenly, I felt a bit out of place in my Wrangler jeans, cowboy boots, and new Kansas t-shirt.

Steve walked over to me. "Hi, I'm Steve. Have you ever been backstage at a concert before?"

I laughed nervously, tucking my curly hair behind my ears.

As if he needs introducing!

"Of course, I know who you are. Hi, I'm Sophia. No, I've never been to a backstage party before. I've never even been to a concert until tonight."

Meanwhile, Sis had left my side and was standing next to the bar doing a shot of whiskey with the band's violinist. She had always been drawn to musicians and whiskey. That night didn't seem that much different than the many times we chased boys at the skating rink or local carnivals; she usually dumped me for a boy.

Steve moved closer to me, and a mix of excitement and nervousness made my hairs stand on end. I pulled at my Kansas t-shirt, feeling a bit self-conscious.

"I guess my cousin Nora found her way around already! She's so pretty. Isn't she, Steve?"

"Yes, Sophia. She's pretty. But I was flirting with you, not your cousin. Did you notice?"

"I did notice. And I flirted back." I threw him a slightly shy yet coy glance. "Did you notice?"

He laughed, showcasing his pearly, white teeth and charming smile. "Of course, I did. I couldn't concentrate for a minute once my eyes found yours! I told the security guard I had to meet you."

My mind raced with disbelief. "Oh my God. Why would you choose me? With all the pretty girls in the crowd, why me? You can have anyone you want, and I know it."

Steve took my hand and led me toward the stage door. He pushed it open and bowed in front of me. "Enter the stage, Ms. Sophia. Take a bow for your audience."

I stepped out onto the stage. The empty seats echoed the music that had played just moments before, as if welcoming me. "It's magnificent. It's so big! It's much bigger than it looks from down there in the audience."

Steve chuckled. "Yes, it is big. Very, very big. It's an amazing feeling to be on stage. Have you ever performed, Sophia?"

As he held my hand, I couldn't help but think, *Oh God. I'm holding his hand right now. He's here, touching me.*

We held hands and took a bow together, acknowledging the imaginary audience. "Thank you, everyone, for coming tonight," we said in unison. We shared a laugh as Steve tightened his grip on my hand.

I smiled, continuing to feel a mixture of nervousness and excitement. "I'm sorry my hands are so sweaty, but I'm just so nervous. I can't believe you're standing next to me. I can't believe I'm here."

He looked at me with a gentle gaze, his eyes filled with admiration.

"You're amazing, Sophia. Don't be nervous. Just enjoy the moment. You deserve to be here."

He stepped back, staring at me as if he could see right through my clothes. "You're so sexy, Sophia, and you don't even know it."

I felt my cheeks on fire. "I'll bet you say that to all the girls."

He walked toward the large, black velvet-covered box that held the drum set. Then he reached behind the chair and pulled out a bottle of Patron tequila. "Let's have a shot. You're old enough to drink tequila, right?"

I paused for a moment, reflecting on the memories of sneaking a sip of my grandfather's whiskey with Nora. I remembered the warmth the brown liquid brought me and the way it quieted the thoughts in my head. I wanted to enjoy the moment without any inhibitions. I nodded. "I could use a drink right now. I can't believe I'm standing here on stage next to you."

He grinned and looked around for something. "We don't have any glasses, so let's just do it right from the bottle."

We drank a couple of swigs, then Steve grabbed my hand. "Step out to the front of the stage and say something to the crowd."

I hesitated but so desperately wanted to please him. "Oh my God. I couldn't. I'm not a singer."

"Come on, it's easy. You have great stage presence. I can tell. Give the audience what they want. You don't have to sing, just talk."

He coaxed me as if he were my trainer, but my mind raced with the overwhelming thought of being by his side. I still couldn't believe I was there with him. Still, Steve's magnetic presence made me feel at ease, as if we had been friends for a lifetime.

His contagious energy and vibrant personality filled the room, and I found myself drawn to his happiness. I wanted to soak up every ounce of his positivity and bottle it up for future moments when I needed a boost. Being around him made me feel alive, and I craved more of his energy. I stepped up to the microphone, my heart still racing. "Is this what you want?"

Steve grinned, jumped to his feet, and clapped for me. "You got this, pretty girl. Command the room like I know you can. You go, girl. More, more, more. Give me more."

My voice quivered and rattled as I said, "You'll know you're on the right path when the person you dream of being lines up with the person you are today. When the person you visualize as your highest self is who you show up as each day."

He stood and clapped and clapped for me. "Bravo, girl, bravo! Did you write that yourself?"

I wasn't sure if I should tell him the truth. I loved to write, especially when I sat alone in my bedroom dreaming about faraway lands and trying to escape the wrath of my mother. I answered him, "Yes. I wrote it. I'm giving this speech at my high school graduation in a few days."

His eyes sparkled while he sipped on the bottle of tequila. "Tell me, girl. Give the audience more of what they want."

Steve started to laugh as he walked closer to me. Then, as he stood right next to me, our shoulders touched. "You realize you're standing here with a man who is twenty-nine years old, right? I do have some experience when it comes to writing."

I noted a scent of musk in his sweat. I loved his candid banter with me about his music. "You're twenty-nine? I had no idea. I'm so fascinated by your story! I want to know everything about you from the start!" I wanted to assure him I was mature enough to be there with him. "I just turned eighteen a few weeks ago, in case you're wondering. I have my driver's license to prove it!"

Steve clapped and beamed at me. "Tell me more about you!"

My courage grew stronger, and I held the mic up in the air like I was performing with grace and confidence. "Thank you all for coming tonight. When you finally let go of things that aren't meant for you to create space for things that are, that's freedom."

Steve walked closer to me again. He gently grabbed my face to turn it to his, pressed his hands on each cheek, and positioned my lips so he could passionately kiss me. The long kiss made all my cells tingle. Then he whispered in my ear, "You're such an old soul. You should be writing songs. How do you know of such things about life?"

I chuckled and put my head on his shoulder, unsure how to respond. I nuzzled his neck. It all seemed unreal yet totally real at the same time.

"Let's write a song together."

He encouraged me with his words, flirting with my creative side. My thoughts raced again in disbelief. The tequila was clouding my judgment a bit. I felt sure I just kissed a famous rockstar. I already decided never to wash my face again.

I knew for sure that nobody would ever believe my story of this night. I wanted Sis to witness my new friendship with Steve.

Suddenly realizing I had forgotten all about my cousin, I murmured, "Oh shit. I forgot all about Sis." Then I looked into his eyes. "Can we go back inside to the party to find her?"

Steve started walking all over the stage, pacing back and forth like he was still on for the audience.

I felt uncomfortable.

He came closer to me. "Are you nervous, Sophia? Are you scared to be here alone with me right now? It's okay if you are. I understand."

I felt the effects of the tequila and looked right into his eyes with pure delight and excitement. "I just can't believe it's really you, and I'm standing on your stage right now, and you just kissed me."

He giggled at my playful manner. "You silly girl. I am human, you know. Let's walk together. I'm not in the mood for the party, are you? Let's find your cousin."

I felt grateful for his candidness and welcomed a walk with him anywhere. "I don't care about a party. I came here to see you."

Steve pushed the stage door open, and we talked while we searched for Sis.

"Wanna go back to my hotel?" he asked. "We can grab a bite at the hotel restaurant. It looks decent."

One of the groupies came up to Steve. "Yeah, man. Great show tonight. Your girl's friend told me to tell you she left a few minutes ago. She said to tell you she left with Stein. They went back to the hotel."

Steve held my hand as we walked outside to find his driver. "Don't worry. Your cousin will be fine. Stein's probably teaching her how to play the violin. I'll call him and make sure they're together. Will that make you feel better?"

I nodded yes, feeling like I died and went to heaven.

I felt his warm skin against mine. His presence was magical. I understood why he was a rockstar. He had it— the "it" thing I always read about in magazines.

My mind never shut down to just enjoy the moment. I wondered, *Does his mother encourage him? Does she support his decision to be a rockstar? Does she come to see him perform? Does she cheer him on? Does he have a mother who told him she loved him?*

Steve interrupted my thoughts, playfully pulling on my hand. "Sophia, do you want to talk to your cousin? I'll get my driver to get her on the phone."

I stepped into the limo. I didn't know where to sit. The inside was so big. I had never been in a limo before. Some of my friends rented one for prom last year, but my mother said we didn't have the money, so my date drove us in his baby-blue Chevy Van. I hated that van. I hated my date, Gary. My mother insisted I go with him. He wasn't my type at all, but I usually followed my mother's advice.

If she finds out where I am now, she'll ground me forever.

I looked at Steve. "Where do I sit?"

Steve took the lead and pulled me close to him. Our legs twisted perfectly together, like two salty pretzels.

"Stay close to me, Sophia."

The limo driver wore a black, tailored hat like the ones you see in the movies. His tuxedo, the kind with the tails, was topped off with a black bowtie.

He took two long, narrow glasses out from the small bar area built into the armrests next to us. "Would you like to toast to us? Do you like champagne, Sophia?"

Intoxicated by his charm and good looks, I was still in a state of disbelief. So many questions. I'd never had champagne, and I wondered if I should lie.

I answered using my sexy, flirting voice with my eyes slightly slanted up from my brow. "I would love to toast to us! And I've never had champagne with you, so I guess it's our first time for a lot of things tonight."

I thought that sounded more sophisticated than admitting my parents barely had enough money for a six-pack of beer, let alone champagne.

The city lights were twinkling outside the windows, like sparklers on the Fourth of July. I wanted to engage him, allowing him inside my head. "I love the city. I dream about living in Miami someday. I want to own a restaurant or maybe be a designer. All I know is I must live in the city. I gotta get out of the coal mining town we live in now."

Suddenly, I couldn't stop talking. A light started flashing on the console in front of me.

Interrupting my babbling on and on, he said, "Hang tight a minute, Sophia. Stein is on the phone. Your cousin's with him. Do you want to talk to her?" He pulled the phone from the limo's center console.

I grabbed it. "Hey, Sis. How are you? I'm headed inside the hotel with Steve. We're gonna have dinner. Meet me in the lobby at midnight."

She agreed and giggled. "Have fun, Sophia!" I hung up the phone. Steve grinned from ear to ear. "Hmmm. You're meeting your cousin at midnight, huh? I guess that gives us a couple of hours to get to know each other better!"

I suddenly felt shy. "I guess it does. Or should I go? You must be tired."

Steve looked out the window. "We're at the hotel, Sophia. It looks like I have a few fans waiting for me. Just follow my lead. Stay close."

The limo driver pulled over in front of the hotel sign, and then he got out and opened the door. Steve climbed out of the limo and offered his hand to help me out of the backseat. We stepped out in grace and style onto the sidewalk, cameras snapping and lights flashing all around us.

Steve straightened his shirt and jacket while he took a fan's autograph book to sign and pose for one quick photograph with me.

"Smile for the cameras, Sophia. You might just be famous tomorrow! Come on, girl."

I just stood there not knowing what to do other than to watch him. "This is crazy, Steve."

His big, beautiful smile impressed me. His confidence felt contagious, and his charm mesmerized me as I stood and watched him work the fans.

Then he turned toward the entrance. "Let's get inside quickly. Keep walking and smiling!" He continued to hold my hand tightly as we walked away from the crowd.

I floated in disbelief while thinking, *This kind of stuff only happens in romance novels, not to me. I'm just a poor girl living in a slate dump.*

We dashed through the hotel lobby and to the elevator.

"Do you mind if we run up to my room first?" he asked. "I wanna change out of these sweaty clothes."

I didn't think twice. I wanted to run away with him. "Of course. I don't mind. I'll follow you," I said as we ducked into an open elevator car. "That was crazy! Do you ever get used to that?"

He pushed the PH button. We rode swiftly up the building, hand in hand, as he gazed into my eyes until we reached the destination. "All that action is just PR stuff. I gotta do it. You understand? Wait until you see this suite, Sophia! This is heaven on earth to me!"

We stepped inside the most breathtaking place I had ever laid eyes on. It was like entering a scene from a magazine spread, a place I had only read about in *Architectural Digest*. Elegant decor adorned the living room, which was filled with the intoxicating scent of fresh flowers. The oversized windows offered a mesmerizing view of the city's twinkling lights, casting a warm glow throughout the room.

My senses grew overwhelmed as I took in the grandeur of the enormous glass table big enough to seat twelve guests. A sight to behold, it was staged with exquisite place settings and a sense of lavishness I had only dreamed of. In that moment, I felt like I had stepped into a fantasy surrounded by beauty and luxury. My mind drifted off. Dreaming of what our life would look like together, my imagination ran wild.

I could see myself sitting in a modern, cliffside home overlooking the ocean. I envisioned myself laughing amongst friends as a butler poured our wine into fancy Waterford crystal glasses. I felt like I was the queen to his king, or maybe the Eve to his Adam, just naked in a paradise garden together.

I gently ran my hands over the back of the vibrant, purple-colored, velvet sofas, admiring their luxurious texture. They were positioned facing each other, accompanied by mahogany end tables adorned with gold-etched lamps, their long sparkling tassels adding an extra touch of opulence.

The delightful blend of fresh peonies with a hint of vanilla mingled with the rich aroma of his scent. I didn't know where to direct my gaze next. Every corner of the room exuded a sense of grandeur and sophistication, leaving me in awe of the remarkable experience. As I looked around, my eyes struggled to take in every detail fast enough.

The opulent surroundings, the intricate decor, and the stunning views all competed for my attention. It was as if I had stepped into a dream where beauty surrounded me. I wanted to savor every moment and soak in the splendor of it all. I gently reached out and touched the luxurious heavy-paneled curtains. The fabric felt soft and rich beneath my fingertips, and I admired the intricate details of the gold, braided tiebacks.

"I'm in heaven. This place is gorgeous! I love the view!"

Steve watched me slowly slide down into the velvet sofa. "Do you always touch everything you see, Sophia? You're quite the lady, a very interesting character."

In that moment, I realized I was meant for better things—that I deserved to be surrounded by intriguing people and exquisite experiences. This realization fueled a sense of ambition within me, driving me to seek out a life filled with beauty, sophistication, and meaningful connections.

"Do you think I sound crazy? You can tell me the truth!"

Steve stood in front of the fully stocked bar and poured two shots of tequila into fancy shot glasses. "No, you don't sound crazy at all. It sounds like you have a heightened sense of awareness. This allows you to feel and perceive things on a deeper level. Embrace it, Sophia. It's a special gift that allows you to connect with the world profoundly."

My attraction to him grew stronger, hearing his wisdom. "I love that. I do feel my environment. It affects me. I love beautiful things. And yes, I do like to touch everything!"

Steve resumed flirting with me as he walked over to the sofa and stood in front of me so I could see his hardness. "I have something for you to touch."

He had a smug smile on his face as he motioned for me to follow him into the bedroom. "Take my hand, Sophia. Let's go to my bedroom, sexy girl. I want you to see what I've created in there. Maybe you can learn more about me by looking at my bedroom."

I looked up at him, afraid to say the wrong thing. "You're a rockstar. I'm just a coal miner's daughter, a small-town girl who is a virgin." I giggled at the words that fell from my mouth. "I'm sorry, I didn't mean it like that! I'm not an idiot, I just…"

He put his hand over my mouth. "Shhhh, you don't need to explain it to me."

As Steve took my hand, we entered the stunning bedroom suite. I marveled at the oversized pillows and the most luxurious bedding I had ever laid eyes on. The inviting ambiance filled me with a sense of comfort.

"What do you think?" His penetrating gaze revealed he really wanted to know me.

I took a moment to observe the room, taking in the details and the atmosphere. "I can tell that you love comfort and style. These oversized pillows are so cozy! You must enjoy peace and tranquility in this room. It's evident you pay attention to the details."

When Steve pulled back the heavy curtains, the city lights twinkled in the distance, creating a mesmerizing view. "I love great bedding. It's a fetish for me. My manager takes care of it for me before I get here, and it helps me get ready for my performances."

Steve patted his hand down on the bed, motioning me to sit down. "Let's lay down and just rest here for a bit. Give my sheets a try, girl. Come on."

I giggled at his playful flirtation. I loved his slow approach with me. I loved his soft, luxurious bed. "This is gorgeous. It's so sexy. It tells me you love soft, sensual things."

He coaxed me down onto the bed by tapping his hand down on the comforter again. I obeyed his call for my company, and we entangled in each other's bodies fully dressed. He slowly moved on top of me. His body felt warm and inviting as we kissed. His tongue entered my mouth, and I accepted it. "I do love soft, sensual things, like your body, your soft skin, and your warm eyes."

Steve kissed like a rockstar. I loved it. I wanted to kiss him forever. I allowed him to lead the way. He needed no direction from me.

"Let's get more comfortable under these sheets. Just wait until you feel them against your naked body. I think the experience between a man and woman should be sensual, and every detail matters."

I was afraid to get naked. "I told you that I've never had sex with anyone before, right? I'm scared I won't be good at it."

Steve tucked my curly hair back behind my ears, exposing the beauty mark next to my right eye, and gently touched my face with both hands as if he were sculpting a mold of it. "There's nothing I want more than to be with you, Sophia. We can just be in bed together with all our clothes on if you want. I like the smell of you. Just enjoy the moment, girl."

Our eyes locked.

My breath stopped.

I basked in the glory of the moment of pure delight.

I even felt like visions of sugar plums danced in my head. I loved the feeling of his warm body next to mine. I loved the soft, cotton sheets touching my bare feet; the soft sheets felt like my skin was touching freshly cut grass for the very first time, stimulating every sense inside of me.

I wanted more.

He jumped off the bed like a kid, quickly opening the nightstand drawer and pushing around things as if he lost something important. "I love these vanilla candles. I brought them with me on this tour. Do you mind if I light them? I wanna see how the candlelight reflects upon your skin."

He was saying and doing everything right in my eyes. "I love to burn a few candles at night when I'm sitting in my room alone. It's wonderful to escape into the flame."

He lit all of the eight pillar candles carefully placed around the bedroom. "You are my twin flame, sexy girl. I feel it." He made me feel so relaxed. He stood by the window and took off his boots and jeans. I watched him get undressed. "Are you going to take your clothes off, Sophia, or do you want me to do it for you?"

I wasn't sure of my next move, still feeling so nervous and afraid to do or say the wrong thing. Even though he said I could keep my clothing on, I did want him to take them off me. It sounded so romantic to me. I told myself to just tell him what I wanted.

He chuckled playfully as he stepped closer to the bed. "Is this what you like, sexy? You want me to take your clothes off for you? Do you like me to be in control?"

I thought maybe I liked it better in case I didn't know how to do it right. "I want you to do it for me."

Steve offered his hand to help me out of his bed as my heart pounded.

I placed his hand over my heart. "Can you feel my heart beating? I'm so nervous." I gazed into his eyes and whispered, "I'm sorry."

He simply smiled while he kissed me with his mouth open. I felt his tongue on mine, and I wanted to be naked next to his muscular body. My mind was very full, but I decided to let myself rest and enjoy the journey. I felt enveloped in a state of euphoria.

As his calloused rockstar hand rested gently over my pounding heart, a rush of emotions surged through me. "You silly girl. No, I can't see it or feel it. Relax and enjoy this adventure with me."

Steve unbuttoned my low-rise Wrangler jeans, then he unzipped them and pulled them down around my ankles. He stared down, eyeing my lace bikini underwear. I was grateful that I had decided on my sexy panties earlier, my favorite little reds.

I had found those panties with a matching bra in the bag of treasures my Aunt Dorothy carried back from the Hamptons. She probably saved them for herself but forgot they were stuffed inside the bag of jackets. I hid them in the back of my dresser, behind my jeans, so my mother didn't find them. I smiled, grateful.

He grinned. "I like your little red panties. Sexy."

He slowly rubbed his hands down around the cheeks of my ass. "You have such a beautiful ass, my girl, mmmm."

I desired him. I felt an unusually warm feeling between my legs as he whispered in my ear.

"You're such a beautiful woman, Sophia."

He lifted my Kansas t-shirt over my thick head of hair. "I love your curls, so many waves. Sexy."

He tucked them back against my neck and then pushed himself against my warm body. I felt his hardness against me. I pushed myself back against him. I allowed his every move, and his caressing warmth filled my mind with thoughts of sex. The motion came naturally.

Feeling my young, firm breasts against his muscular, bare chest made my panties moist with his words. The thought crossed my mind that maybe I was dreaming, but I knew I'd carry the feeling with me forever. Lovemaking should always be sensual. I thought, *I love being in this moment.*

Our kissing grew more intense; his soft, tender lips were all over my face. They wandered along my earlobes and down along the right side of my neck. My thoughts raced, and every cell tingled. He was an amazing kisser, so passionate and intense.

Lying on the bed with our bodies pressed against each other, I felt his hardness against me once again. I craved his words. I whispered in an innocent voice, "Steve, I'm a virgin."

He stopped kissing me and looked right into my eyes. "I know, my love. I promise I'm going to make this the best night of your entire life. I promise you'll always get wet when you think of our lovemaking."

I was in heaven, wondering how I got so lucky. I was about to give my virginity to a rockstar who loved to make love exactly the way I always imagined it should be. It was a night most girls only dreamed about, and I was the lucky one. *Keep going, my rockstar lover,* I thought. *Keep going.*

He gently pressed himself against me and pulled my silky underwear down using his calloused hand. "I'm going to devour you, Sophia. I promise you'll love every minute of our lovemaking."

I knew he was an experienced lover; I wasn't afraid. I was simply intrigued by his playful manner of tonguing my body, gently and sensually, as though he could taste my skin and read my mind. My body became ignited in a way I had never felt before.

Steve asked my permission with every move he made, and I loved his gentlemanly way of teaching me how to be a good lover.

"Do you like my tongue, Sophia? Can I taste you? I know you must taste delicious."

I moaned, unable to answer him with words. I loved his questioning. Loved his way of guiding my pleasure. *Teach me,* I thought. *Tell me how to be a great lover. Show me.*

"Yes. Please, teach me. I want you to taste me," I finally managed to say between moans.

Steve slowly licked my stomach with his tongue, creating circles around my belly button.

Turned on by his attention, I felt as melted as an ice cream cone on a summer afternoon as he continued with a child-like exploration of my body.

He gently pushed my legs apart, sitting back to look closely at his virgin before he started to kiss my inner thighs. He stopped only to make eye contact with me.

I felt embarrassed but wanted to learn this way of lovemaking,

"You're so sexy, my beautiful girl."

I felt so nervous by his glance but answered his cry for approval. I wanted more. I sighed, not wanting him to stop.

He continued.

"Don't stop. You feel so good on my skin. I love your tongue."

After finding my clit, his tongue wiped over it with one large lick, as if to wait for me to beg him for more. I slightly lifted my spine to the sensation of arousal. I was hot with desire, already very wet.

"Oh my God, Steve. It feels so fucking good. Please don't stop," I begged him.

"Talk to me, lover. Tell me."

My rockstar was begging me to express myself.

My body started to shake from his continuous tongue bath. "Can't you tell by the way my body's moving? I love it."

He laughed as if he knew. "I just want to please you. I want you to forget the world exists. It's just us." He made me even hotter by talking while he lapped up my love juices. "I want you to feel the energy in the room, Sophia. I want you to smell the scents of our lovemaking."

He licked me. He kept on talking and licking me continuously until I orgasmed in his mouth.

I thought, *I just wet the bed*, as I felt the warm liquid flow out of my body and onto his beautiful, luxurious sheets.

He pressed my legs back further, softly stroking my inner thighs. Then, after lapping up the wetness, he dove in for more of me. "I'm going to lick you again. Is that okay with you?"

I had no hesitation for his rockstar licking and lovemaking. "Oh yes, I want more."

He sang to me between his tongue licks. He was a playful lover. A happy soul. He encouraged me to laugh.

"You want me to sing you into an orgasm? Tell me what you want, Sophia."

I couldn't think straight in my dreamy state of euphoria. I'd never felt this way before.

"I want you inside me. I want you to kiss me."

I pulled on his thick, soaking wet hair. I wanted to taste myself on his lips. I wanted to be sure this was really happening.

"I want you to cum inside me."

When Steve finally took his hardness and thrust it inside me, I cried out with such enormous pleasure. I couldn't help but moan. "Oh my God. It feels so good."

He continued to talk to me, our rhythm in sync. "I want my cock inside you, Sophia. I want to be inside you."

We came furiously. I felt his hot cum pouring inside me like a volcano erupting. We collapsed from exhaustion, entangled in each other's arms as he gently twirled my curly hair, taking over my little habit. "My virgin. You were wonderful, Sophia. Did you like it?"

I answered my lover immediately. "I loved every second of it. You're so wonderful."

We stayed twisted in each other's bodies. He murmured, "Come with me to Boston. I leave in two days. Come with me, lover. We'll write songs together. I'll make you cum again. I want you to cum endlessly."

I was in heaven. My rockstar was lying next to my naked body in the most beautiful suite surrounded by city lights asking me to write songs with him. To run away with him. I hesitated to remind him of my obligations but had to tell him the truth. I had to be loyal to myself. "I graduate in two days, Steve. I'm giving a speech, remember?"

He looked at me strangely, like a spoiled child who didn't get what he wanted. "I want to be with you, Sophia. What about after graduation? Meet me in Detroit. I'll send a car for you, a boat for you, a plane for you. Tell me what it's going to take to get you to travel with me on this tour. You're a unique creature, not like the other girls. Come with me, lover. Let me devour you every day!"

While I may have desired the love and affection of my rockstar, I knew deep down that I needed to be realistic. I felt tremendous guilt. I wanted to run away with him, but I doubted his motives to be with me.

I spurted out, "By the time you get to Boston, you'll find another virgin girl and forget all about me. I'm just a little country girl with big city dreams."

He laughed. "I won't forget you, baby, I promise." He kissed me.

Suddenly, Steve sat up in the fluffy bed. He possessed a childlike energy, his eyes wide with excitement. His stage presence filled the bedroom with charismatic energy, like an ocean wave rushing into a cave. "I promised you dinner! Let's order room service. I'm starving, unless you want me to eat you for dessert instead?"

My sexual appetite further ignited. I did selfishly want him to taste me again. I felt something I'd never felt before. I did want more of what he was offering. I felt such a desperate craving for his tongue, more of his sensual, licking pleasure. I felt greedy for it, selfish, but I wanted it.

My hand went over my mouth as if to disguise my guilt. "Yes, please! I would love to be your dessert before dinner!

Who says you can't have your cake and eat it too? I always say, 'Why bake a cake if you're not gonna eat it!'"

Acting like a young schoolboy, Steve jumped up on the bed and started clapping. "Oh, my sexy. I love dessert before dinner. Your wish is my desire. And yes, why bake a cake if you're not gonna eat it?"

His head was under the luxurious white cotton sheets within seconds. This moment marked a discovery of my own sexual fetish.

I was hotter this time than the last time he licked my pussy. I wondered why. This time, he licked me slower and with longer strokes than I remembered before. Just knowing he was tasting our sex juice mixed into our own cocktail turned me on.

He reached up and kissed me so I could taste us. "I really like you, Sophia. You're different. You have *it*. Like me. We're different. You and I could fearlessly conquer the world together! We can cum together endlessly in beautiful suites around the globe!"

He got perfectly feisty. After tossing my body on the bed like a wrestler, he turned my ass to face him. "These sheets are as sexy as you are, my love. I love tasting our body juices mixed together. I'm going to finger you from behind. Do you mind?"

"I'm all yours. Do as you please."

I soaked the sheets with my sex juices. His words turned me on more than before. His finger play grew stronger, and my moans grew louder with every stroke inside my pussy. He played with me.

"Shhhhh, Sophia. Someone's going to call security on us."

He made me feel so comfortable. I liked it. He was a playful lover. He took the lead. It suited me. I loved making love while we laughed together. I thought hot sex mixed with a lot of laughter was the way it was meant to be. The way it always played out in my mind. *Why not?*

Steve stood up and wrapped the cum-soaked sheet around his body to announce his excitement. "I have a great idea! Let's celebrate the loss of your virginity with some champagne and big, juicy steaks. I love to eat in bed!"

I nodded, feeling famished. "Yes, I'm starving!"

I remembered one time when I was sick, I wanted to eat in bed. But my mother denied the guilty pleasure. "You'll come downstairs to the table, Sophia," she said. "I don't want crumbs in the sheets. We don't eat in bed in this house." Her words echoed in my head as a mischievous grin blossomed on my face.

There was a knock at the door. "Come in," Steve called.

The room service waiter seemed uncomfortable while he wheeled in the silver cart covered with a white linen tablecloth. He reached inside the warming drawer to pull out plates filled with the fillets. After shelling the lobsters, he asked, "Is there anything else, Mr. Walsh?"

Steve stood tall and proud still wearing the white sheet soaked with our love juices. "Thank you, sir. Give yourself a big tip and run along. My girl is hungry!"

He insisted we place the room service trays on the bed, and then he cut the fillet into bite-sized pieces and fed them to me. "Open wide, sexy. Let the butter drip all over you. It tastes the best that way!"

We sat with our legs crossed Indian style, eating like two children in bed. I glanced at his sheet getup. "I love your new outfit—a love toga!"

He laughed. "You love my cum-soaked suit, do ya? Maybe it's time for a little dessert!" He grabbed a huge chocolate cupcake from the dessert cart, licking the icing with his tongue while he glanced up at me. "I'm going to smear this icing all over your pussy then lick it off slowly."

"How can I say no to such a sweet idea?"

We giggled like school kids while he smeared the icing on my hot body. "I think I'm going to die from sugar shock in this soaking-wet sheet-suit of mine!"

He licked my sugary lips until I squirmed all over the bed, waiting for him to enter my wetness. We moaned with delight, in sync with each other's bodies. I would have expected to be sore, but I just wanted more and more.

"Run away with me, Sophia. We can live in any city you want! I'll buy you a restaurant. Come on. You're an adventurous and curious creature like me."

My heart swelled with love. I felt the urge to stay with him. I didn't want to leave his side in fear of never seeing him again. "I must go. I'll think about your offer, and I'll let you know after my graduation. Okay?"

He scribbled on a hotel notepad. "Just call Rodger if you decide to meet me in Detroit. He'll get you transportation and take care of all the details. I would really love to see the country with you, Sophia. We are the same humans. We are two peas in a pod."

I kissed him passionately, taking in the scent of our glorious lovemaking. It was hot. We hugged so tight, I could barely breathe. I folded the hotel notepad with his number and tucked it in the back pocket of my Wranglers for safekeeping. "Thank you for taking my virginity. It was such a perfect night. I'll always remember every second of it."

"I wrote my address down on the notepad next to the bed in case you ever tour in Coal Town, USA."

He grinned. "I'll track you down. I plan to see you in a few weeks; promise me!"

As the night came to an end, I shared a bittersweet goodbye kiss with him, feeling a tinge of sadness knowing that it may be our last. I was a small-town girl with big city dreams. "Okay, Steve. I'll try."

My legs felt heavy as I walked to the elevator to meet Sis in the hotel lobby. My head in the clouds, I felt the brisk air of the night against my face as happiness rushed through my veins like a river runs through the forest.

Sis and I drove back to our small, country town in comfortable silence. The sound of the paved roads beneath us served as the backdrop to our thoughts.

Suddenly, Sis turned to me with a huge smile on her face. "I can't believe we lost our cherries tonight. We were bad girls, Sophia."

"We were bad with two rockstars; we're soul sisters forever. It'll be our dirty, little secret, right?"

"We're soul sisters, girl. And yes, I'll keep our dirty, little secret forever."

I stuck my pinky finger out for her to twist. "Pinky promise."

She grabbed my finger. "This was the best night of my entire life, Sophia, and we did it together. I love you."

My heart warmed by her words, and I couldn't help but feel the same deep love for her. "I love you too, Sis. I finally understand the meaning of love; we had such a great connection. I want to go with him, to follow him. I'm scared, but I might just go for it!"

Sis listened to me attentively, understanding me better than anyone.

"I'm happy for you, Sophia. I want you to stay. I'm glad you're here with me. I don't know what I would ever do without you. Just stay with me forever."

I felt a mix of sadness and contentment. "We better say a hundred Hail Marys and a hundred Our Fathers at church next Sunday."

We both laughed, knowing that our bond was strong and unbreakable. "We ride and die together, Sophia."

Chapter Two

Lead Me Not into Temptation
Twenty Years Later ...

My week was chaotic with two big-budget films being produced in the city—*Wonder Boys* starring Michael Douglas and Robert Downey Jr., and *Unbreakable* starring Bruce Willis and Samuel L. Jackson. I scrambled to get an A-list crew for our healthcare commercial being produced by one of the largest advertising agencies in town.

The movies were hiring the best freelancers, and traffic was a mess with roadblocks. My job was getting more stressful by the minute. I needed a break from demanding clients, teenagers with busy schedules, and a husband with an exaggerated handicap in our country club golf tournament this weekend.

I called Leanne on my forty-five-minute drive home.

She answered out of breath, "Hey chick-EE. You getting excited about South Beach? I'm so glad you said yes!" I could tell she was running.

"I can't wait to get to the sunshine state!" I grinned. "Are you jogging? It can't be twenty degrees outside!"

Leanne was a slender, cute, little blonde who reminded me of a young Laura Dern. Her fiery spirit for life, her outrageous disregard for the truth, and her potty mouth were all my favorite reasons to love her unconditionally.

She was so obsessed with having fun. She loved to party, and everyone reveled in her love for life that radiated from her entire being like a light force. She wore her five-carat diamond ring like a trophy, except when she twisted it around to face her palm to disguise the glare from the young boys who would undoubtedly steal the ring for lunch money if given the chance.

Leanne laughed. "I love to run in any weather; bring your tennis shoes so we can hit the streets in Miami."

I was impressed by her fitness routine.

I gave her my signature punch line when the women at our country club asked me to join them in the Thanksgiving marathon. "I don't run unless I'm being chased."

She snorted. "Oh my God, Sophia! You're funny!"

I noticed a call coming through from a producer and ignored it. Leanne stopped to catch her breath. "I'm going to teach you how to relax on this trip!"

I hoped she was right. "I just feel stressed out about going away with a bunch of girls I barely know. And I should be working this weekend…I haven't been on a girls' trip in forever."

Leanne barked back at me, "Remember, all work and no play makes you old and grey!" Her cute little snort laughs and carefree attitude reminded me of Cameron Diaz in the movie *Something About Mary*. "That's your fault. We invited you last month, but you were too busy. Don't you know work is as useless as tits on a bull!"

Must be nice to be a rich girl. I wasn't insulted. "My mother always said, 'Marry a rich man.' I guess she was right!"

Leanne was a bad influence on me from the minute we were thrown together on the fundraising committee for the Firemen's 9/11 campaign a few months before. She encouraged the bad side of my personality to come out to play.

Her voice was shrill as she giggled in between her words. "You're going to have a blast, I promise. What can be bad about wearing bikinis, bar hopping, and chasing bad boys!"

I giggled. "Chasing boys? Isn't everyone married?" *I don't know what to expect.*

I could hear Leanne enter her front door as her alarm system was going off, and she screamed at her nanny, "What the fuck is going on?" She came back to me. "Hang on a minute. This stupid girl. She's clueless. Let me call you right back."

Leanne stopped men in their tracks when she entered a room. It didn't matter if she was wearing tight jeans with a tiny t-shirt revealing her huge nipples, a little black dress, or a skimpy string bikini. Leanne's body said, "Come on over and fuck me." And she knew it.

I admired her willpower. She stayed in great physical condition thanks to her gorgeous, young personal trainer, Philip, and her husband, Markus, who kept the trainer on his payroll so he could also reap the benefits with his trophy wife.

I turned up the volume on the car stereo, listening to the Best of the 80s music, Tina Turner's "What's Love Got to Do with It" blasting as loud as my speakers could handle. I knew every word to every song, and singing made me feel young again.

Our garage doors were wide open, and I pulled my car inside, raced upstairs to my closet, and dragged out my set of Louis Vuitton carry-ons and my passport. This set of luggage was my gift to me for selling my first big job, a commission that put me into the six-figure club. I smiled at the memory. *I earned my own way.*

I knew I had just short of an hour before everyone arrived back home, starving. I quickly sorted through my closet to find a velvet box filled with my favorite swimsuits. I wish I had time to buy a new one—most of mine weren't sexy enough for South Beach. I heard Leanne's voice saying, "Just bring bikinis and the boys will follow." *I've been married way too long.*

I talked to myself as I got undressed, tossing my favorite black suit into the dry-cleaning bag, hoping William would remember to drop it off like I asked him. I had an important interview next week, and I wanted to wear it for luck. He was terrible at running errands unless it was for a golf event. My husband was going to be in charge of our two teenagers for an entire weekend, alone. I tried to suppress the feeling. The whole idea of being carefree and frivolous with a group of girls in Miami stressed me out. I quickly reminded myself, *Guilt's the thief of life.* I just kept thinking about the mess I would encounter upon my return.

William screamed upstairs, "Hello? Anyone here?"

Shit! He's home early! I huffed, "I'll be down in a minute. Hang on." I rang his extension on our house phone, a ridiculous phone system he had insisted on installing. "I told you I needed an hour to pack, and then we'll run up to the club for dinner. I don't have time to cook tonight."

He huffed, "Ugh. I don't feel like getting showered and ready. I'm tired." The tone of his voice told me he wasn't in the mood to be social. I knew a round of golf after a morning at the office would mean an early nap on the sofa for him. I shouted back at him, "Order something then. Take the golf cart to pick it up. You decide. I'm done making decisions." *Jesus. How will he survive without me for the next four days?*

I blocked him out. I wasn't hungry; frankly, I was tired of being his chef, laundress, and business partner. I needed this long weekend away from all my responsibilities.

My luggage waited open on the bed for my final wardrobe decisions. I laughed knowing Leanne had a black belt in shopping. Most of my designer stuff came from vintage stores and aunts with hand-me-downs from the Hamptons.

When I met her for lunch to discuss the fundraising party details last month, she invited me to join her for a private event at Saks Fifth Avenue afterward. While her private shopper served her champagne and handed her the new spring line from Gucci, I sorted through the sales, looking for bargains. I love name brands but never pay full price for over-priced designer labels.

I felt nervous about what the other girls would say. I knew her friends judged a woman by the brands she wore. I continued to pack knowing I would forget all about the other women once I got there. These wealthy women were way out of my league, but if you can't run with the big dogs, stay home with the puppies!

I packed some Sky dresses; they were my favorite fun, party styles. I bought most of them at a cute boutique on our work trips to Vegas. William told me I looked sexy in every one of them since they showed off my hour-glass figure.

I included my favorite hand-woven beach tote made by local artisans in Ecuador. I found this gem at a flea market in New York City. Inside the bag, I tucked away a few of my special Chan Luu wrap bracelets for a bohemian vibe. I was set.

I'll show them what real style's all about, my way. Style doesn't start in the fucking Gucci store; real style comes straight off the streets. Only poor girls know how to create something out of nothing.

Our early flight meant I had to leave home by seven o'clock to arrive on time. I took a private car to the airport because William suggested, "Treat yourself, Sophia. Start the trip off like a queen, you deserve it!"

I knew the truth: William hated driving to the airport, so he made an early tee time to avoid the task. I used the time to call the producer back on the way, approving the overage on the props budget. My job was starting to feel like I worked in an emergency room, always a crisis and someone bleeding out. *God, I crave the sunshine and some girl talk!*

I spotted Leanne and Jayne ahead at the check-in desk. They were hard to miss in the latest trendy Juicy Couture velvet sweat suits with Juicy written across their asses in bold lettering. Leanne's was blue, and Jayne's pink. I already felt out of place in my simple denim jeans with a t-shirt tucked in to showcase my turquoise belt buckle. *It's easy to buy the trendiest clothes, so much harder to show off your own style!*

Jayne ran over to me. "So glad you decided to fucking join us, chick-EE. We're going to have a fucking blast! Come over to the desk. Leanne's working her fucking magic already!"

I liked Jayne even though we only met once before. We had danced the night away with all the firemen at the fundraiser gala last month. She attracted men like bees to honey, but she only had eyes for one, her husband Mike.

She was devious. When she sipped too many martinis, she reminded me of Brittney Spears with her girl-next-door beauty and sassy truck-driver-mouth. Jayne had long, lean legs and no waist, but her huge implants outweighed her lack of booty.

She always wore high-heeled Prada shoes and knew how to strut in them. Her long, mousy brown hair had started slowly falling out due to her constant dieting habits. But it was her redneck wit when she drank too much that made me like her even more. A real hometown girl attitude kept her down to earth.

Leanne was standing next to me, anxious to use her charm with the older gentleman checking us in. She leaned in and whispered in my ear, "Sophia, give me your driver's license. Our new best friend, Charles, is going to upgrade us to first class."

She flirted with the attendant, giving him a come-hither look. "Charles, don't forget my friend Sophia!" She winked at him, then glanced back at me. "See what a little tit will get you, or should I say a lotta tit." She winked. "I guess I still got what it takes to get us into the mile-high club, yes!"

She's proud of the fact she used her assets to get upgraded. I like her style.

Her phone rang, and she answered and put it on speaker. It was her husband, Markus. "You better stop spending money, or we're going to be broke."

She turned red in the face as she covered the phone with her hand, rolling her eyes back in her head. "Okay. See you next week." She abruptly hung up the phone.

I raised an eyebrow.

She laughed. "He's such a bastard. He's just trying to fuck with me. He doesn't want me to buy another pair of Gucci shoes in South Beach. Fuck him." She threw her phone into her carry-on bag, dismissing him completely. We walked through the security line. "He can kiss my white ass if he thinks I'm listening to one fucking word he says. I'm buying whatever the fuck I want."

Markus had many skills. Heading up the list had to be seducing women, and manipulating the law was a close second. His charming Italian personality and round, brown eyes with extraordinarily long eyelashes made him hard to resist. He was a prominent real estate attorney with a skillful tongue that made him easy to trust. Markus was not used to losing battles, especially ones of the heart. So, when he met Leanne by coincidence one night at an oyster bar downtown, he stopped at nothing to lure her into his life.

He pretended to be single, lying to her about being married and having three young daughters. Since he kept a bachelor pad near the airport, it was easy to lead a secret life away from his family responsibilities.

He was a master of disguise; she would be no match for his artful, narcissistic ways. She didn't realize he was married with small children until the day they arrived back at the airport from a week in Paris. Markus's wife had discovered his secret apartment along with his love affair with Leanne. She planned to meet them at the airport with his three daughters in tow.

Leanne was pissed about his lies and deceit, but she agreed to marry him after his divorce, despite the red flags. They built a stately, multi-million-dollar mansion in an exclusive neighborhood of Sewickley Heights, one of the wealthiest and most prestigious neighborhoods in Pennsylvania, accelerated by the establishment of the Allegheny Country Club as a haven for wealthy Pittsburgh residents, celebrities, and professional athletes. Their newsworthy wedding included the wealthiest guests in the city, an extended honeymoon in Lake Como, Italy, and a new life for them.

Leanne pulled out her Gucci wallet, showing us her stack of hundred-dollar bills. "Just enough to tip our way through South Beach this weekend!"

Jayne chimed right in. "We gotta buy some slim cigarettes. I wanna drag on a cig and sip on dirty martinis. Oh, and call your kingpin to get us some somethin' somethin'."

I had no idea what she was talking about, but I laughed along with them. I felt like stress was exiting my body, like a balloon deflating and spinning into thin air.

We landed at the Fort Lauderdale Airport on time. We planned to stay overnight at Leanne's beach house in Boca Raton. She rented it for the winter and wanted to check on a delivery she was expecting. Leanne's private driver, Ray, would be waiting for us outside at the curbside pickup. She called him to say we arrived, her tone jovial. "Hey Ray, we are off the plane and walking your way. See you in fifteen minutes."

Leanne grabbed her elegant Bulgari sunglasses from her handbag, placing them on her slender face as she peered up through the diamond-studded frame. "What goes on in South Beach, stays in South Beach."

We stood like three rockstars waiting for our driver, a stretch limo pulled up to the curb. "Jesus, Leanne. You didn't tell me about the limo, let me pitch in."

She waved her hand. "It's my treat. Forget it, Sophia. You'll love Ray; he's my driver."

A very handsome Cuban guy stepped out of the car. He looked like Dwayne Johnson, The Rock. Jayne was the first to give Leanne her approval. "Oh la-la, he's a hottie, Lea. I like me a little Cuban sandwich."

Ray stepped forward, grabbed her overstuffed luggage, and loaded the trunk with our suitcases. She hopped right into the limo. He poked his head into the backseat and introduced himself with a charming smile. "Hi girls, I'm Ray, and I'll be driving you to Boca and then to the Delano in Miami tomorrow morning."

"What kinda trouble you want to get into this weekend, Ms. Leanne?"

She peered up from her Bulgaris and giggled. "The usual." She smiled back at me. "He knows me! What can I say!"

Ray looked back in the rearview mirror. "Perfect. I got a few things in the works, a big celebrity party on Ocean Drive and a new nightclub private opening."

She punched me in the leg. "I told ya, Sophia. Aren't you glad I convinced you to come with us? You're gonna have a blast!"

Hope I packed all the right clothes, might have to go shopping!

She popped the bottle of champagne nestled in between the seats.

I said, "Ray, has anyone ever told you that you look exactly like The Rock?"

Ray laughed. "I get it all the time and if it helps me to get you girls into the best places, I'll use it to our advantage."

I like him already!

Leanne's rental house was nestled inside a gorgeous, gated community in Boca Raton, Florida. A cascading fountain greeted us. The guard at the front gate asked Ray for the house number and name of the tenant. Leanne handed him a business card with her access code, and the guard lifted the gate. "Third right, second house near the country club entrance."

I was astonished by the perfectly manicured landscaping lining the community's streets; well-appointed lanterns hung tastefully along the natural walkways.

I had never before seen a neighborhood so magical.

As we approached, I noticed that Leanne's home looked just like the one next to it and every one of the houses in that section of the complex.

She talked a mile a minute. "This is not the home of my dreams, but as soon as Markus straightens out his legal issues, we're going to buy a house to renovate in Boca. We decided we'll be renovating and flipping houses together, especially if he loses his law practice. He's such an asshole. God help me!"

Jayne didn't say a word, and I followed her lead.

We settled into separate bedrooms, leaving our suitcases on the luggage rack. I wandered around the extravagant house and peeked inside the guest house while Leanne and Jayne opened a bottle of red wine. I could see them giggling while I admired the pool nestled inside the center of the house. A ceramic fish spit water from his mouth into the seafoam blue infinity pool as a cool mist gently fell over my shoulders. *This is pure paradise. I could stay here all weekend. Just relax and read a juicy Jackie Collins novel by the pool.*

I joined the girls in the kitchen.

Jayne flicked her straight brown hair back off her face. "I'm starving. I haven't eaten a thing all day, anyone else?"

Leanne answered with a big smile on her face, "There's a great pizza place close by. There's a really hot delivery boy. When he delivered last time, my fucking husband answered the door in his underwear." She rolled her eyes. "I tipped him big time on my credit card so maybe he'll forget all about my idiot husband and come in to play with me!"

I teased her, "If you want to reap the rewards of your gratuity, you should answer the door naked. He will definitely come in and come inside your seafood pizza. Go for it, Jayne, and I will eat the pie while he eats yours! Call me Nicola, the Queen's fool, and favorite court jester! I'm here for your entertainment purposes this weekend!"

We belly laughed back on the sofa while Leanne considered the idea. "Pizza and early to bed tonight, but I'll definitely save him for a rainy day!"

Her hearty sexual appetite was no surprise.

The delivery boy was hot, a sexy surfer blonde who was lean and very young. He smiled as she opened the door.

"Thanks for coming by, see you next week when I'm back from Miami." Leanne flirted and winked back at the kid.

He paid very little attention.

She giggled. "I like them young, dumb, and full of cum! What can I say!"

◆

When Ray arrived at the front door early the next morning, we were ready. The hour-and-a-half trip seemed to take longer with all the traffic leading into South Beach. Ray pulled the limo up to the Delano Hotel. I was blown away by the grand white linen drapes billowing in the Miami breeze. I knew I loved the hotel already, it was just as I imagined. I had an addiction to boutique hotels and loved how their design sparked my creative side.

The unique hotel's massive outdoor veranda was absolutely breathtaking. A cool, trendy place with an eclectic Art Deco detail that embraced me like nothing I had ever seen before. I thought about what my life might have looked like if I followed my dream to be an artist living in Miami years ago. A far cry from the coal mining town I grew up in. I knew city living was meant to be part of my life, someday.

Ray stepped out of the limo, and valet boys opened the doors on both sides so we could step out in style. Leanne walked up to the reservation desk. "We have two suites reserved under my last name, and we want to check in to one of them ASAP." It was obvious to me that she had done this many times before.

The handsome young man at the front desk searched for her name and suite number. "We have your suite ready, Ms. Leanne. Just three of you today?" She smiled politely. "Yes, the other girls are arriving later this afternoon; five others are joining us, four of us in each suite."

I wonder who the fourth girl would be joining us in our suite.

The reservation attendant continued, "I see you paid a deposit of five hundred dollars, but there's a balance owing of thirty-five hundred dollars for your stay this weekend, plus the hold for mini bar charges, so we will charge four thousand on your credit card. Is that amount okay with you, Ms. Leanne?"

My mouth dropped wide open in surprise, my heart racing with anxiety. I felt guilty for not contributing, but Leanne had insisted. "Lea, are you crazy?" I asked. "Markus is going to be pissed, so let me give you some money."

She ignored me and immediately spoke in a low tone to the attendant, "Of course, you can place the charge on my credit card. No worries."

She reached deep into her Gucci wallet and pulled out a black American Express card, handed it to the front desk attendant, and turned to Jayne. "I got the suites covered completely; you can pick up the tab for the weekend pool cabana rental later."

Jayne agreed and thus put my guilty feelings at rest. "We got this, Sophia. I told you before, it's our treat this time. You can be our personal stylist—start by choosing our bikinis and be in charge of keeping our schedule with Ray! I suck at both!"

Leanne hugged me. "Sophia, seriously, just let it go, it's all good. I fucking earned this money. I had to fuck an asshole for the past five years. Get over it, already. Let's have some fun."

I felt so awkward, but I knew Leanne was genuine. "Thanks, girl, you're the best. I'll buy dinner all weekend, it's on me."

Leanne laughed and grabbed my hand, then walked toward the elevator, leaving her luggage with the bell boy and pulling my luggage over next to hers. "Just let him bring up the luggage. I want to give him an extra big tip, in case we need him. We might get into trouble, and he'll take good care of us if we do! Hang on, girlie, you're in for the ride of your life!" She opened the double suite doors with the electronic key.

"Oh my God, Leanne, suite number 811—my two favorite numbers on the roulette wheel in Vegas!" I took it as a sign, as I always looked for signs.

The suite was magnificent, with an ocean view and a balcony overlooking the pool and the aqua sea below. A gorgeous white cotton sofa faced the ocean, and a bleached wood dining room table was set for eight guests. The two bedrooms each had king-sized beds covered in white linens with oversized white velvet headboards designed for a queen. There were plush white bathrobes neatly tied and hung in the bathroom, and luxurious spa amenities filled the vanity. *Reminds me of the night with my rockstar!*

I grabbed Leanne's luggage. I wanted to gift the girls for paying the tab downstairs, as my guilty feelings wouldn't allow me to relax just yet. "Let me hang up your clothes; it's the least I can do for you guys. I'll unpack everything then come down to the pool after, it's cool."

Leanne nodded at my generous offer to be her assistant. "We're going to the pool, Sophia, so get your plump little ass into a bikini and you can play stylist later! Fuck it! Just leave the suitcases out on the bed."

I laid my bag out, found my bikini, walked into the large bathroom, and started to change.

Leanne and Jayne were already walking around the room naked, their perfectly toned bodies both holding breasts that looked like trophies. They couldn't decide which Gucci bikini to wear, gold or white. *I knew it!*

Leanne pulled the tag off of a skimpy little gold bikini with a large Gucci logo on the bottoms. A small fringe hugged the top, which barely covered her nipples. "I worked hard for this motherfucker. I had to let my gross husband fuck me before he left for his meeting with the feds, a whole fucking twenty seconds of his pounding was pure fucking torture."

Wonder why she married this guy, Markus. I guess she likes the fringe benefits!

She laughed hysterically and pulled out a box of tampons; she unwrapped one of them, opened the cotton tube, and pulled out a bag of cocaine, then side-eyed us. "It's a pretty sweet idea, right? I learned this little trick from my kingpin last time I came to Miami; he said security would never search inside, and he was right, damnit!"

Leanne shrugged off the crime like she had just run a red light. "Calm down, Sophia. I didn't tell you guys because you would have blown it, been a nervous fucking wreck about it. Kellie's going to meet a guy later, if you want a bag of your own. Let me know. It's the best cocaine ever, really strong. Lasts quite a while unless you're getting your pussy licked by a vampire, then the buzz only lasts until sunrise!"

She laughed and handed me a hundred-dollar bill rolled into a straw. "Here, go for it, girl. Relax. You need a big line to fucking chill out already, Jesus."

I took the bill and snorted one small line, half in each nostril. I choked back the white powder and passed the bill to Leanne, who snorted three lines with the greatest of ease.

"Jesus, Leanne. That's strong!" She giggled. "Don't be a baby, Sophia. This is Miami, for Christ's sake."

We finished getting dressed, I threw a beach bag together, and Leanne searched for a container to put the white magic in. I handed her one of my little white MAC makeup sample containers. "I always have these with me if you want an extra one for your vitamins."

Leanne laughed. "I'll take two!" She gave me a side-eyed glare, showing off her big green eyes. "You know, for my vitamins!" She winked. "Thanks, Sophia."

Jayne walked over to me, holding her tiny white Gucci bikini that looked like a child's swimsuit. "Sophia, can you fix the back of this thing so I can pull it over my nipples? I don't think I should have bought this size. Maybe should have gone up a size? What do you think?"

I tried to tie it in the back and tried to adjust the top, but there wasn't enough fabric to cover Jayne's huge breasts, and she grew impatient with my efforts. "Fuck it, it's South Beach, baby! Let it all hang out."

I agreed with a nod. "I think the Delano Beach is topless, so whatever, nobody really cares anyway. Just go with it, work it, baby. If I had a skinny little body like yours, I'd go naked to the beach!" My head was spinning from the white disco dust and all the chatter, hoping to get out of the room.

Jayne laughed hysterically as she snorted another line of coke with Leanne's favorite hundred-dollar bill. "Topless, baby, topless. I like being topless, so fuck it, my nips will thank me later!"

We headed down to the beach. I felt overdressed in my ordinary swimsuit, it was more like a two-piece suit compared to my new friend's skimpy little bikinis, but I was high, so I let it go. "This place is so fucking beautiful, it's like a heaven on earth, pure paradise." Leanne raced to the door, opened it for us, and waved her hand for us to step out to the red carpet leading out to the breathtaking pool area. "Yes, Sophia! It *is* paradise!"

———◆———

The pool was something out of a movie set, with white cabana tents lined up along the sides of the stunning palm-fringed infinity pool. The floating silver tables and chairs and large outdoor spa and solarium led out to the white sandy beach, and the beautiful people all around made the scene even more stunning. My eyes quickly shifted around the area. Women were flashing more sun-kissed skin than a spread in *Playboy* magazine. The men sported muscular chests and chiseled and clean-shaven faces. There wasn't much left for the imagination. I could see Jackie Collins soaking up the sun while she collected shady side stories for her next best-selling novel.

Jayne walked over to the service bar and flirted with the waiter, tilting her head and acting coy. "We need to reserve the cabana in the corner between the pool and the beach for the weekend. Can we have you…as our waiter?"

She smiled as he looked up, pulling his long silky black hair back in a ponytail. He had piercing black eyes that seemed to peer directly into Jayne's like he was undressing her in front of us. "Of course, I would love to service you girls." His smile glistened and revealed his brilliant white teeth that were immaculately straight.

Are all people in Miami a specimen of human perfection?

Jayne's eyes were open windows to her joy, sparkling like stars on a clear night. "How much for the cabana rental, sexy?"

He handed her the cabana rental card, which read "Daily Rate Cabana: Five hundred dollars without bottle service and one thousand dollars with bottle service." He continued to mix cocktails, never missing a beat while she decided on the menu.

She answered with her right breast falling out of her white bikini top. She pretended not to notice so he could catch a glimpse of her large, rounded breast against the Gucci fabric. "We'll take the cabana with bottle service and you!"

He grinned with delight. "Hello there. I'm Onacona, White Owl. I'm here to service you and please you."

Jayne glanced back at us. "I'd like to tenderize his red meat, what a juicy steak!"

She smiled from ear to ear. Leanne stared him down from top to bottom and glanced over at me. "Oh my God, an Indian chief. A rich man, a poor man, a baker man, a thief, a doctor, a lawyer, an Indian chief."

I whispered to her, "He's our Cherokee, a little secret name for our White Owl; he's a hottie."

Leanne liked the nickname and whispered back to me, "I sure hope he takes me into his teepee and marks my face with some of his war paint. I'm wearing a wet suit over this Cherokee."

Love her sense of humor.

We laughed as we walked over to the cabana and dropped our bags to settle in the oversized bed. Leanne was still in la-la land over The Cherokee. "He's so hot, and I can't stop staring at his long black hair. I can only imagine what fucking him feels like. God, I hope I get the chance."

She was obviously high and extremely relaxed. Jayne handed over her black American Express card to our new friend, The Cherokee, and he brought it back with the receipt and our first bottle of Cristal champagne.

Suddenly, I felt so out of place amongst my new friends. I nervously tucked my hair behind my ears and started to make jokes about growing up in the boondocks. "I wasn't born with a silver spoon in my mouth. I was born with a wooden spoon on my ass!"

Leanne stood up to adjust her gold bikini bottom. "Girlfriend, I wasn't born with a silver spoon in my mouth either. I married my silver spoon, and I've been forked ever since!" She snorted. "Markus is probably going to go to federal prison, I'm raising a two-year-old son by myself—well, with the help of my Polish nanny, who, by the way, is an idiot. I wish I had a wooden spoon; I would spank that Cherokee's ass with it right now!"

We belly laughed back onto the bed.

Leanne grew serious. "Let's just change the fucking subject. I'm here to forget about life and all the bullshit. I don't want to get fucking depressed about it; I can do that at home."

Jayne was on the phone. She muted the call and looked up at Leanne. "Can you believe Kellie and Crystal are on their way down? They already checked in. I told you she would have the fucking nerve to show up. I told you!"

Leanne tried to calm Jayne down, rubbing her arm and then pouring more champagne into her empty flute. "Why did you invite Kellie? You know she likes to stir the pot!"

Jayne frowned, pissed. "I can't fucking believe Kellie invited Crystal, the woman who's fucking my husband. She thinks I'm the only one who doesn't know!"

Whoa, my head's spinning! What! What the fuck?

When Kellie blew through the doors to the pool area, she strutted toward the cabana, swinging her arms like she was on a catwalk. Kellie was wearing a slutty swimsuit from Victoria's Secret—a solid black one-piece suit cut out on the sides, exposing her tiny waist and barely covering her ass cheeks. "Hello, my girls, I'm here and ready to play with you!" She kissed everyone on each cheek twice.

She was bombed out of her mind already.

She leaned in to kiss me, then stepped back with a smirk on her face. "Aren't you something special? Who are you?"

I immediately noticed her powdered foundation was caked on, wearing more makeup than a drag queen on a Saturday night.

Kellie was a petite Lebanese woman in her early forties with a protruding overbite that she seemed to use to her advantage. Her implants were nestled high on her small frame, which gave her even more confidence to lure in new prey for special favors. She preferred looking at people using her side-eye glance. She was overly friendly, in an untrusting way.

I only met her briefly at the charity event but had heard enough stories to know she was a spoiled bitch married to a fat gold dealer. She was also drawn to the allure of a jealous boyfriend, Carl. I already found her quite demanding.

I smiled as she prowled over. "I'm Sophia, Leanne's friend. We met at the Firemen Fundraiser a few months ago, remember?"

Kellie frowned, unimpressed, and turned to the bottle of champagne, which was empty. "Where's our cabana boy? I need a glass of bubbly ASAP."

I felt puzzled by Leanne's friendship with her as she was obnoxious, so unlike her other friends.

Kellie introduced her friend Crystal to the group, who stood patiently outside the cabana as she waited for Kellie to stop talking. "Hi, everyone! Today's my birthday, so I'm super excited to be celebrating with you girls!"

Kellie leaned into Leanne. "I invited my cousin, Monique, but she had to cancel at the last minute. Crystal wanted to come. I figured, why not?"

Jayne was burning mad and threw her a hot glare. "I think you could have asked me first, Kellie. What the fuck?"

Crystal was extremely fit, naturally, from being a yoga teacher, and nothing on her body was fake. She was rather simple, with a long blonde ponytail that fell to the middle of her back, exposing the little white ribbon tightly securing the braided twist. She wore a matching little white bikini. She was understated, except for the tattered, straw cowboy hat that complimented her swimsuit and added a stylish flare to her freckled face. She scanned a glance at us all and said, "I think I'll celebrate with a shot of tequila; anyone want to join me?"

I was surprised Crystal acted so comfortably around Jayne.

She flung her hands in the air. "Let's celebrate my birthday! Come on, girls."

Leanne whispered in my ear, "This should get really interesting."

I rang the service bell for our sexy waiter. "I'm in, and I'm buying, it's your birthday!"

The Cherokee came over and took our order for five shots of tequila and took my credit card, but Kellie pushed mine aside, saying, "Take my card and give Sophia her card back; she's not buying, I'm buying. I invited Crystal, so the shots of tequila are on me!"

So competitive, she already one-upped me. Like I care!

We did the shots of tequila and toasted to Crystal's birthday celebration. Crystal was singing, "Happy birthday to me, happy birthday to me!" Leanne handed Crystal the small white container and said, "Do a line to celebrate; my little treat to the birthday girl!"

Hopefully she finds a new place to sing! I poked Leanne. "What the fuck Lea, she doesn't need coke, she needs a tranquilizer!"

Crystal did two big snorts from her fingernail. I was surprised but didn't react.

She smiled. "I'm going to give myself a birthday present, something wrapped up with a real big ribbon—a boy toy!"

Kellie's phone rang. "Oh hi, Helena. Yes, we're all at the pool in a cabana. Stephanie's on her way from the airport now; when will you get here?" She hung up and looked pissed but tried to act like it didn't matter. She announced to the crowd, "Helena won't be here until after dinner; she's delayed in LA and couldn't get a flight, so she's flying private."

Oh God!

Helena. The queen of the High Society Rich Bitch Club, a polished group of wives with designer clothes, flawless facelifts, and narrow ethics. Helena wrote for the scene column, painting picture-perfect stories about the rich and famous living in glass houses, wearing masks to hide their secrets.

So many last-minute guest changes. *I had no idea she was coming!*

Just then, another girl arrived in the cabana. "Hi everyone."

I barely knew Stephanie except for an occasional wrap party when she would show up on the arm of a celebrity. She was picture perfect, wearing her tasteful Louis Vuitton red bikini, showing off her new cosmetic enhancements, and bragging about her speedy recovery just in time for this debut vacation. We all nodded a welcome.

"I'm so thrilled you girls thought I was worthy enough to be here with you this weekend!"

She slipped Leanne a hundred-dollar bill, whispering, "Do you mind if I take a line of your white powder?"

Leanne pushed her hundred-dollar bill back in her hand. "Steph, keep your money. Be my guest, silly girl; your money's no good in this cabana."

She took a fingernail full and then another one in the next nostril. Her eyes lit up wide and open from the strength of the Miami delight. "Jesus, your disco dust is really strong!"

Stephanie looked breathtakingly beautiful. She was the kind of girl who stopped men and women in their tracks. I often witnessed heads turning to stare at her striking appearance. She had long, silky black hair with an unusual set of slanted, sexy brown eyes. She possessed a movie star quality—a blend between Katherine Zeta Jones and Angelia Jolie.

She had been to several wrap parties and occasionally invited me back to her place for an after-party, which I never attended for fear of being the ugliest one in the crowd, having nothing sexy enough to wear. I had overheard her whispering on the elevator one night about her sex work and medical research, as she called it. "I use my client's fetishes as ways to learn about the male psyche; it's all fun and games until it's not." She intrigued me. I should have considered this as a career when I was so broke and alone. Fucking to pay the rent seemed easier than scrubbing the floors in a hotel bathroom.

Leanne discreetly whispered to the group, "If anyone wants a little powder of their own, I'm collecting orders and money. Kellie is going to meet our kingpin at five to buy us some more of this yummy white magic."

Stephanie smiled. "I'm in. Here's my money." She handed Leanne a stack of cash.

Jayne followed her lead. "I want a little somethin' somethin', but only half an eight ball. Anyone want to split with me?" She looked around the cabana.

Leanne smiled. "I'll take your other half. I'm staying in Boca this week. I'll need it."

Crystal was obviously drunk and high as she danced around the pool, swinging back and forth and then into the cabana. "It's my birthday, it's my birthday."

Kellie enticed her friend by teasing her with the endless possibilities, saying, "You should have whatever you want on your birthday, girl. What do you want? You know I can help you get it."

She laughed. "I want him, that hottie over there." She pointed at the preppy man across the pool. He was perfectly put together, wearing navy blue swim trunks with a matching white polo collared shirt and blue and white flip flops, carrying a striped navy towel. His blonde hair was cut close around his ears with a fluffy swooped-back top, and he had large blue eyes and shiny white teeth.

He was like something out of *GQ Magazine*. Crystal pointed to him. "I want him, he's my birthday present to me. Happy birthday to me!"

She's acting like a four-year-old; enough of this shit!

I looked at Jayne, who looked back at me with shocked surprise in her eyes. "What the fuck? This whore's going to cheat on my husband. She's out of control."

Wait! If she's married and cheating, can she cheat on her lover?

Leanne joined the conversation now. "What the fuck's she doing? She's going to cheat on Mike. Isn't it enough that she's cheating on her husband, but now she's cheating on her lover? This is fucking bullshit, just so much fucking drama."

Jayne reached over for the white container and snorted two lines with her fingernail. "This bitch needs to be put in her place. I want to knock her imaginary birthday crown right off her fucking head!"

Kellie insisted we let Crystal do whatever she wanted. "Who cares, if she wants to fuck the hunk for her birthday, who gives a shit? None of us are innocent; mind your own business." As if Crystal was given the green light to freedom, she was all over the blonde tennis pro, flirting, fondling, and French kissing him at the pool. "It's my birthday, I can do whatever I want today."

We ignored her and continued to drink and snort lines in our cabana. Stephanie entertained us with her sex banter.

"I had a very rich client spank me last night. He was so into it. I almost missed my flight this morning!"

Whoa! This script's starting to get even juicier by the minute!

The time passed by quickly with all the conversation. We lost track of the whereabouts of the birthday girl until Kellie interrupted us. "I gave Crystal my room key so she can have her cake and eat it too for her fucking birthday! No word from any of you!"

Jayne rushed in, speaking in her thick, red-neck language, about how she was so angry about Crystal cheating on her husband, Mike.

What a strange plot twist!

We all listened to her rant on and on.

"I can't fucking believe she came to Miami. She fucking knew I was going to be here, and now she's acting like a fucking whore with this poor tennis pro; it's embarrassing!"

We all just looked at her.

Jayne lit a slim cigarette, dragged on it, and ranted on. "I'm going up to our suite to grab my phone to call the guys. Don't you think our husbands have the right to know she's cheating on both of them with a tennis pro in South Beach? I'll be right back."

Leanne barked back, "Just let her go, who gives a fuck? I'm sick of all this drama between you bitches; you're fighting over men like any of them is a fucking prize." She was in a mood. She wanted to dance and party, and she couldn't care less about drama.

I tried to calm her down with a glance, pleading with Jayne to stop talking. "Just relax, Jayne. Let Crystal do whatever she wants. I think she's all talk and no show."

Jayne put out the skinny cigarette, pulling her long hair into a messy bun on top of her head. "I'm not letting it go, Sophia. It's fucking bullshit. She's a whore. I'm tired of her shit. She wrecked my marriage, and now she's fucking cheating on my boyfriend."

I whispered in Leanne's ear, "We have ringside seats in a bare-knuckle brawl, right here in paradise!"

She giggled back, keeping pace with my sarcastic wit. "I'm going to give everyone the 'blow by blow' on this big event." She winked, pulling out the disco dust for another whiff up her nose.

We watched Jayne pace back and forth in front of the cabana, lighting another slim cig. "I'm out. I gotta call my boys, or I'm going to lose it on this fucking bitch." She walked inside the hotel.

Leanne rolled back, holding her stomach as she laughed, back on the cabana bed, throwing punches in the air and singing the theme song to *Rocky*. Leanne grew feistier. "Betcha never thought you would be in the middle of all this bullshit in Miami? You might be front and center of a chick fight in a minute!"

I rolled my eyes. "Just when you think you've seen it all." I threw a punch back at Leanne and she pretended I knocked her out cold. "I'm getting in the pool; fuck these bitches."

Leanne and Kellie agreed with me and followed me into the infinity pool, which faced the blue ocean. I was high but I was grateful to be surrounded by beauty. "How can you be angry in Miami? This place is stunning. Who the fuck wants to fight over a man? None of them are worth it."

Leanne high-fived me. "Now ain't that the fucking truth, not a fucking one. These bitches are stupid little cunts!"

Kellie frowned at us for talking shit about our girlfriends. "We do not throw our girls under the bus, no matter what they do; take it back, Sophia." I looked at her. "Take what back? My opinion? I won't do it."

Stephanie interrupted the chatter amongst us while she dipped her toes into the warm water. "I fucked this guy last night and left my jewelry on his nightstand. Shit! He just called to tell me."

Leanne gave her a stern *fuck you* kind of look as she snapped back at her, "What the fuck, Steph, don't you know that's one of the oldest tricks in the book? I mean, all guys know you left shit on purpose, just so you can go back and see him again. How fucking stupid are you?"

I could see this girl's weekend was going to be filled with drama. I joked with her, "Maybe he wants to hold it as ransom just to get your sexy ass back in his sex dungeon!"

Stephanie pouted like a first-grader who wanted to play in the sandbox. "I'm never irresponsible. I don't know what came over me. Oh, wait! It was definitely his Harvard college paddle that made my mind go to *Jell-O;* he placed holes in the wooden spanking toy to sting me in the ass like a wasp!"

Leanne was never letting her get away without a lecture. "I sure hope you charged him more than the jewelry was worth because you might never see it again! How could you be so stupid?"

Kellie barked back at Leanne, "Be nice. Why are you being so mean today? It's bullshit." She stormed away, grabbed her beach bag from the cabana, and went inside the hotel.

Leanne laughed. "Hey, three girls down, only two more to go, then we'll be here alone, Sophia, in peace. We should have come alone. Next time."

Stephanie wasn't offended. "I think you girls are cool. You're right. I don't give a shit about the jewelry, it's all fake shit so no big deal. I never wear my real diamonds on first calls. If he takes it to a pawn shop, he might get fifty bucks tops! I charged him double my regular rate, so I don't really give a fuck!"

Leanne offered her a high-five. "Good job, girlfriend. I hope he tries!"

We ordered more cocktails from The Cherokee and floated around in the swan rafts like we were queens. Stephanie beamed from ear to ear. "So much fucking drama, I just can't do it all weekend. I'm going to reserve spa treatments for tomorrow morning. Anyone else want to join me?"

We shook our heads up and down. "Absolutely!"

Finally, my kind of vacation! A spa day!

The sun was beginning to set in the distance. We decided it was time to get back to the room to take showers and prepare for our late dinner reservations at a new restaurant in the lobby. Ray was able to secure eight seats at the sushi bar, telling us that Madonna might make an appearance since she was a major investor in the swanky Miami establishment.

Leanne opened the suite door to the living room. We could hear groaning coming from the bedroom, a voice moaning with pleasure. "Oh fuck, fuck me harder, oh yes!"

We stayed close to the door. Leanne called out, "Hello! Hello, who's here?"

I looked over at her. "Is that Jayne? Who's screaming?"

Just then, Crystal came running out to greet us. She was naked and holding her cowboy hat on her head. "Oh God, what are you guys doing here? Kellie said this was her room. I'm so sorry!"

Leanne frowned, furious. She turned around, grabbed my hand to follow her out, and screamed at the suite door next to ours, "Hey, Kellie, open the fucking door, what the fuck?"

Kellie came to the door holding a bottle of wine with curlers in her hair. "What the fuck Lea, what's up?"

Leanne screamed, "Your fucking girlfriend is fucking in my suite. She's fucking the tennis pro in my fucking bed; go get her out of my fucking room right now!"

Kellie looked surprised and clueless. She didn't like being out of the loop of the drama, and you could tell she was offended that we knew more than she did about the situation. "I have no fucking idea. How the fuck would I know? Nobody tells me anything."

The suite doors flew open across the hallway, and Jayne and Crystal came out swinging fists. Crystal was still naked, Jayne still wearing her white Gucci bikini and screaming, "I got the whole fucking scene recorded on my phone. While you were fucking your little tennis pro, I was in the closet getting all the fucking and sucking recorded on my phone, you stupid fucking whore."

Crystal was screaming and crying uncontrollably. "I'm going home to tell Mike before you tell him. I'm leaving, Jayne, does that make you happy? Now you can have my husband and your husband too—you can fucking have both of the assholes."

God! Wonder how this story would be written in the social scene column!

My head spun like a whirling dervish. I wasn't sure what the fuck was going on right now, but it was all happening in the hallway of the beautiful Delano Hotel in Miami. Leanne jumped right in. "Get this stupid fucking whore out of my fucking suite and take your fucking tennis ball boyfriend with you."

Leanne just wanted to get inside her suite and be left out of the drama. "Let's go, Sophia, we gotta call housekeeping and have them change these fucking sheets. Fucking in my suite, bitches are so nasty." She was more pissed off about the sheets than any of the crazy drama.

She dialed the house phone, covering the receiver like she was telling her story as she waited for an answer. "I need a maid as soon as possible; someone shit in my bed." She laughed at her own joke as she waited then politely requested maid service.

Crystal went into Kellie's suite and called a taxi. She took the next flight back to the city. Jayne bragged, "I took care of that nasty situation, didn't I? That bitch really had the nerve to show up this weekend."

Leanne just ignored her chatter as she sorted through her suitcase and did a line of coke. "I frankly don't give a fuck, Jayne."

But Jayne couldn't stop talking about it. "If Mike doesn't want me, I don't want him to have anyone else. Now he's alone, I'm happy. End of story."

I learned a lot about Jayne that day. She loved to play games. She was a master at cock blocking. She wasn't interested in fucking any of the men who chased her, except Mike. I could hear her bragging about her marriage on the flight. "I'm married to a star football player, the quarterback; he's such a star athlete. Mike is my hero."

But Mike cheated on her, so revenge was now her master. She wanted revenge against her husband and his mistress and would do anything to get it, including fucking his mistress's husband, Clinton. *So complicated. I came here to relax, not get caught up in a soap opera—a swap opera!*

Leanne grabbed her phone and threw it into her Gucci clutch. "I told you once you spent a weekend with these rich bitches that you would appreciate your own life! You have the world by-the-balls!"

The restaurant was set up as a pop-up inside the lobby. We ordered all kinds of sushi, seaweed, and sashimi, and we ate and drank cosmopolitans, talking about sex and love. No sighting of the queen, Madonna. Or Helena either. Kellie reported on her flight schedule every twenty minutes. We didn't care, honestly.

Leanne laughed. "She's a blow-hard! Who invited her anyway?"

Kellie interrupted, "Stop, Leanne. What's gotten into you? Be nice. You've been angry all day. It's not cool."

Just then, two handsome men approached the table wearing neatly pressed white jeans and cool-toned blue t-shirts. The taller, dark-haired guy flirted with Leanne. "What's all the girl talk about? Can a guy get in on this conversation?"

She flirted back with a wink. "It will cost ya!"

He grinned, indicating he liked her sass. "We wanna buy you girls a round of drinks. A couple of cosmopolitans for the table."

She winked at him and accepted immediately. "Of course you can. But will you?"

She was always a smart ass. Most men enjoyed her sarcasm, as she was a challenge for them.

"Well, we already paid the waiter for your dinner so thought we could get you another round of cocktails and finish it off right for you girls."

He's trying to impress her. Guess my credit card isn't going to get used again tonight!

I felt surprised. I had experienced complimentary first-class upgrades, and now our dinner checks were getting paid. The check had to be at least five hundred dollars. Leanne patted the guy's chest with her hand. "Well, aren't you special? What's your name, big guy?" She kept the sarcasm going as she lured them closer to the table to tease them with the girl talk. "You see anyone you like here, who's your pleasure? Who pleases your eyes the most, as if we can't guess; just fucking say it already."

The leaner, more handsome guy went straight for Jayne. It was so obvious. His friend liked Stephanie. I noticed she appeared to be sluttier looking tonight, wearing a top that didn't cover her freshly created nipples. She leaned into Sophia to offer her approval. "I like him. He's a hottie. I don't give free samples very often but tonight might be his lucky night!"

She has more self-confidence than anyone I have ever met.

Leanne and I decided to leave the girls behind with their new boy toys. "Thanks for the drinks, boys!" Kellie said as she left to meet the kingpin. He was three hours late but who was going to argue with a drug dealer? She felt comfortable going alone and, quite frankly, I felt glad to see her go. She was a drain. I looked at Leanne with a serious glare as Kellie walked out to the valet. "That girl's not energy efficient; she completely sucks the life out of me."

No Helena yet. No surprise.

Leanne walked and talked a mile a minute. "It's funny how drinking eight glasses of water a day seems impossible, but four cosmopolitans go down like a fat kid on a seesaw! I gotta level out with a line. Let's exit to the bathroom before we go to the bar."

We walked into the white-tiled bathroom; everything inside the hotel was white, and this room was no different. I glanced around at the bland décor. "God, I'm kinda craving some color!"

She agreed, pulling out her new accessory—my MAC container holding her white magic. "We even have white disco dust, a white container, and now a white fucking toilet tank to snort a line!"

I laughed. "Yeah, maybe this hotel is a movie set for an insane asylum, and the nurses are coming with a couple of white strait jackets for us!"

We giggled as we snorted lines off the tank, rolling the hundred-dollar bill back into Leanne's clutch for later.

She washed her hands and reapplied lipstick. "Let's go to a Cuban restaurant tomorrow night—get out of this hotel and see some fucking color." I nodded and swiped three packs of matches with the Delano logo stamped in gold. "A gold digger's dream bathroom!" Her laughter echoed through the cavernous room, a boisterous sound that seemed to bounce off the stone walls.

Leanne snapped, "All that glitters isn't gold, my friend. Don't ever forget it!"

Leanne held my hand as we wandered into a swanky, wood-paneled room filled with golfers who must have just finished dinner after playing eighteen holes. I laughed. "I can't get a break from boys with tee times and girls with matching visors. I thought so much more of Miami until today."

I looked around at the golfers thinking about how much I hated seeing grown adults dressed in similar clothing. I said to Leanne, "Why do golfers wear matching clothes like kids in first grade wearing *grrr-grrr-grr-animals?*"

She growled back at me, "*Grrr-eat* question, Sophia. No imagination! We gotta get out of here right now! I can't take any more bullshit today!"

We walked out, hand in hand, just to stir the pot and get the attention of the men. "These fucking men couldn't turn me on if they had perfect handicaps and big balls! And these girls are so full of fucking drama. Next time we come to Miami, we must come alone."

She pressed the elevator button to the suites. "Yeah, I agree. A bunch of drama queens!"

I smiled. *She's my kinda friend.* "I'm so glad we booked massages tomorrow morning. I need it after a day of happy birthday bullshit and a night of being ringside at a catfight!"

———◆———

The tranquility of the pristine white spa was everything I hoped it would be. White billowing drapes gracefully blew softly in and out of the gorgeous veranda facing the ocean in the distance. I knew the experience was going to be just what I needed to relax and unwind.

The masseuses came out to the relaxation lounge to gather us. One very handsome young man with a muscular body and long hair could have been a model. Leanne stood up immediately, taking his hand to lead her back to the massage room.

She smiled from ear to ear. "Enjoy!"

I giggled.

Stephanie walked into the lounge area in her robe. "I'm so glad we're here this morning. I saw the girls having breakfast. Helena just arrived with her friend Meg."

I rolled my eyes, grateful for our choice. "Oh God Steph, I hear she's a handful."

Stephanie leaned in to whisper in my ear, mocking Helena's greeting to her earlier with a sly smile. "Oh yeah, I think you're right. She called me cupcake! Seriously!"

My name was called. I winked at Stephanie. "See you in two hours, cupcake!"

I was given a beautiful young Cuban woman; she spoke very little English as we walked back to prepare the suite for my massage.

I took Leanne's suggestion and upgraded my massage to include the hot stones, which proved the perfect way to complete the wonderful time I had allowing the Cuban woman to touch my body in every crevasse. *I daydreamed about what my life would have looked like with my rockstar.*

The woman shook me lightly, waking me from a blissful state of mind. I had finally closed off my thoughts, but the massage was over. "Thank you, it was wonderful." I lay quietly on the bed, hoping the day ahead would be peaceful.

Leanne looked like she just gotten laid, her thin blonde hair standing up like Phyliss Diller's, and I wondered if she attacked the young guy. "Please tell me you fucked him in there. You did, didn't you?"

She laughed and let me think she might have taken advantage of the sexy young man. She smiled and admitted, "Trust me, if he had made the first move, I would have spread my legs for him in a second; his hands were amazing!"

We sat quietly in the relaxation lounge, listening to the sound of the waves crashing upon the beach in front of us. A nice lunch was served with fresh fruit and finger sandwiches filled with salmon and goat cheese with sprinkles of dill and chives.

Stephanie joined us. "Do we have to go? I want to stay here all day instead, it's so much better than sitting at the pool with those drama queens."

I giggled and tried to keep my voice low while I played with Leanne's hair, trying to pat it down. "Let's save this memory for when the snow is blistering cold in the city; oh wait, you'll be in Boca all winter getting your delivery boy toy to eat your seafood pizza pie! I forgot."

She gave me the evil eye, which I knew was a signal to be quiet and not remind her of her reality. "You know Markus is on his way to trial. He might do time for his crime."

Stephanie leaned in closer. "I have a full-time client who is a judge. Maybe she can help your hubby."

Leanne leaned her head back against the back of the lounge chair. "Thanks, girl. It's too far gone at this point. He is in deep, kinda too late for favors. But thanks."

God, it's true, everyone has a shady side.

Stephanie gave her a warm glance. "I'm here for you if you need anything, Leanne. I'm in my first year of medical college studying relationships, so I'm all ears— confidentially, of course."

Guess she wasn't lying on the elevator that night after the wrap party! No judging, Sophia!

Leanne turned up her confidence. "I'm just going to enjoy life. If he goes away to prison, I'm moving to Boca full-time. Maybe I should put a spell on him, a little hocus-pocus full moon magic shit."

I smiled. "Oh, hell yeah! I love full moon magic tricks! Let's do it!"

Stephanie nodded. "Let's plan it for the next full moon. I'll host it—in my city loft. You girls will love my pad, it's super fun and very sexy! Say yes!"

We got giddy from all the silly talk about full moon wishes. "I think it's bikini and Cherokee time at the pool. Let's get out of here and grab a line in the bathroom while we get dressed so I can forget about my asshole husband."

She's relentless.

We strutted our sexiness by the pool, sipped cosmos, and made plans to go to a new disco tech that was holding a special VIP grand opening. I said, "Ray's getting all of us access to this new nightclub; it's closed to the public until next weekend."

I went on and on; I felt better when I was able to deliver the details. Leanne had put me in touch with Ray, and I enjoyed the planning. "This fucking place is supposed to be off the charts with enormous cages hanging from the fifty-foot ceiling. Dancers get hoisted up inside the metal cages and then spun around while in the air. Ray said it's unbelievable!"

Leanne immediately smiled a huge smile, revealing her gums. "I gotta get in one of those fucking cages."

I smiled back at her. "I already have Ray working on it for you. I knew you would want to go up!"

She was psyched beyond words all day, and couldn't talk about anything else besides dancing in a cage. "Sophia, we gotta get in one of these cages. I'm doing it tonight, I'm telling you it will be an amazing experience."

We had dinner reservations at a trendy Cuban restaurant close to the nightclub so Ray could drive us directly to Cages Nightclub right afterward. I reminded everyone at dinner, "Remember, it's a one-hundred-dollar cover charge per girl, and bottle service is five hundred for our table. I'll pay for the table service; it's on me."

The waiter brought the check for dinner. I paid it and reminded the girls of our obligation to Ray. "I'm collecting cash for the club entry; let's have it ready for Ray."

Helena spoke up, "I don't think Meg and I are going to join you, cupcake. We want to check out a place on Ocean Drive. Our friends own a home there."

Leanne frowned. "We reserved a table for eight. Since Crystal left yesterday, we're only seven now. Ray did us a big favor by getting us on this list. You're coming!"

Helena looked down; she wasn't confrontational, just sneaky. She was the founding member of The High Society Rich Bitch Club, and she wore a mask to disguise her hidden secrets. Helena never wore colors, she always dressed in black shorts with knee-high boots and black halter tops revealing her large breasts. Her shiny mid-back-length black hair was a signature. She flicked it back with a constant motion, distracting eyes from her slightly blemished skin. Helena wanted to be famous more than anything in the world.

Helena's friend Meg called herself Megabucks. The nickname suited her pursuit of a wealthy husband, and she preyed on anyone who held a black American Express card. Meg's parents financially supported her when Helena ran low on funds. There was no doubt the duo had only one mission—to find suitable partners to invest in their gold-digging expeditions.

When Megabucks had asked me if she could borrow a dress from me earlier, I was caught off guard. She had said, "I lost my luggage at the private airport. I think your style suits me best. Do you mind?"

I responded, "Sure. I guess so. Come over now so we can be ready to leave." I had loaned her my least favorite Sky dress in case she forgot to return it.

We finished dinner and Jayne followed us to the bathroom to snort a line of coke.

Leanne scurried her out of the stall, applying a fresh coat of lip gloss. "I think these girls are users. They cling to whoever's willing to pay their tab. I'm sick of it."

Jayne chimed right in, "Helena's husband is in big trouble; word on the street is, he's being investigated for something."

So many secrets. So many lies. So many shady sides.

Ray arrived on time and had the limo prepped with champagne and sparkling water. "You girls look hot as fuck tonight; you're all gonna have a blast." I collected the money from everyone except Helena and Meg, then approached them. "Do you girls have your money for the entry? I gotta give it to Ray before we get there."

Helena scrambled through her YSL crocodile-skinned clutch like she was searching for a long-lost treasure. She pulled out a wrinkled one-hundred-dollar bill and then found a second one for Meg. "Here's our money, cupcake. I hope they have Cristal Champagne." She finished her glass of bubbly and poured another. "I get a headache from this stuff."

Megabucks held her *Chanel* lambskin-quilted clutch so tight against her thighs, she was either hiding something between her legs or thought one of us wanted to steal the rented bag from her. "I can't drink cheap champagne either, Helena. I must only have the best!"

Leanne rolled her eyes back in her head.

We headed out, and when we finally arrived, Ray opened our door. "Check it out, girls, it's the hottest place in Miami right now!" He was proud of himself, shoulders squared and face beaming. Leanne handed him a hundred-dollar bill, and I handed him our collection of cash.

Cages Nightclub was one of the most innovative nightclubs that you could find in Miami. It was a unique theme and vibe from Ian Scharger from Studio 54. There were private green rooms for celebrity guests, bottle service for parties who wanted tables, an enormous dance floor, and gigantic disco balls suspended from the fifty-foot ceilings—where, in between, hung large custom-made cages, which locked exotic dancers inside while they twirled and twisted their way up into the ceiling.

I had not seen a space like this one since I had toured a film studio in Hollywood back in the early nineties.

"Oh my God, Leanne, it's amazing!" Stephanie whirled around the dance floor. "I love this place! Oh my God, it's fabulous!"

I lost focus for a minute until Leanne pulled me out to the dance floor. "We can't sit at a fucking table all night, girl; let's party out there with these crazy fucking people."

Jayne spun around wearing her favorite strappy Prada shoes. "I'm in heaven!"

Amazing she can dance in those four-inch stilettos!

Kellie was already out dancing around with a guy in a wheelchair, spinning him around. He was loving every minute of the attention. Jayne was back at our table flirting with the waiter, who was mixing us cosmopolitans.

Helena sat quietly at the table while her young friend, Megabucks, poured them glasses of Cristal champagne. The music was so loud, it was impossible to talk to anyone. The bass pounded through the concrete floors, up into my feet, like primal tribal drumbeats. Ray stood to the side, watching us.

Leanne walked over to the first cage being lowered to the floor. As Ray walked over to her, she screamed, "Ray, I gotta get in this cage." She wasn't taking no for an answer. She grabbed me by the upper arm and pulled me over to stand close to her, making it clear she wasn't going up without me. "It's you and me, girl, we're going on the ride of our lives. Get fucking ready!"

Ray stood talking to the bodyguard standing next to the cage as it lowered, then he turned away and walked back to us with red ribbons in his hands, which he tied around our wrists. "You girls are going up. Are you sure you're ready? It's pretty high up. Once you're in, you are in."

I wasn't sure. Stephanie smiled and held out her wrist for the ribbon, but I wasn't as excited about it as they were. I hesitated. "I'm scared of heights, I'm not sure I wanna do it."

Leanne snapped around, and I knew she wasn't going to take bullshit excuses. "You're going with me. Don't be a fucking baby."

We all stepped into the cage with the other three exotic dancers. "Hi, I'm Gina. Let me shackle your right foot to the cage for safety." Gina was sexy as fuck, wearing a skimpy black lace bikini with stockings and a garter belt to match. Her breasts were perched high on her chest; nothing was left to the imagination.

She took Leanne's right foot and placed the shackle around her ankle and a handcuff around her right wrist and cuffed it to the bar in the corner to secure her in tightly. "Don't be worried. It gets a little rocky going up, but once we're locked into the ceiling we don't shake around much, so just don't dance until we tell you to move."

Gina shackled me and Stephanie in. "It's fun, you'll see. You'll be glad you did it once it's over; it's such a rush!"

I wanted to step out of the cage, but we were already being hoisted up. Gina gave the thumbs up to lift us off the disco floor. The hoist made a chain-like sound as the links clicked, one at a time, while the cage began to lift off the floor. Everyone below started to look smaller and smaller as we went further up into the ceiling.

A sudden click into the lock secured the cage, and a huge smile appeared on Gina's face. "Dance girls, dance!" Leanne danced and grinned while she threw her head back singing. She found her bliss, and exclaimed, "Oh, girl, I'll never forget this moment—never."

I thought it was pretty awesome watching the scene from so high up. I screamed, "Oh my God, cupcake!"

She snorted.

I noticed people pointing up at us and saw Jayne and Kellie giving us big applause below. My heart was still racing, but I felt so alive and so powerful. *I defeated my fear of heights, at least for tonight!*

❖

We spent our last day by the pool with a reservation planned at a swanky Mediterranean restaurant across the street. Ray got word that the private celebrity party on Ocean Drive had been shut down due to a raid at the neighbors the night before. The night would be quiet.

Helena and Megabucks left early in the morning. Kellie and Jayne were going back on the noon flight so they could attend the Steeler game. Jayne had club seats; her husband, Mike, was playing his final game as the quarterback. Leanne and I were finally alone. Stephanie took the other suite across the hallway so she could catch up on some medical research for her upcoming presentation on sexual fetishes. She promised to give Leanne and I her perspective on the subject.

Leanne and I relaxed by the pool. The Cherokee flirted. "You girls come here often?"

She giggled, giving him a serious cat-eye glance. "We do come often." I slapped her lightly on the thigh. "We come often, oh yes we do." The cosmos felt stronger. The sun, hotter. Every time she laughed, she would involuntarily snort at the end of it, a quirky habit that only made her more endearing to me.

We noticed a good-looking guy sitting close by who looked familiar. "Isn't that the same guy who liked Jayne last night? He bought us drinks after dinner?" I turned my head to peer closer. I wasn't sure.

"I have no idea, really; all the boys are beautiful here in paradise. I couldn't wait to get away from that table last night. I don't know."

Leanne stood up and walked over to him with her pink fizzy drink with a flamingo popping out from the rim—the Cherokee's special cosmopolitan with a shot of champagne, making it fizzy. He had said the drink was his interpretation of us.

She abruptly asked, "What's up, buddy?"

The guy peered up over his book. He looked out of place reading a gift store novel with his leather briefcase oddly sitting next to his lounge chair. Nobody worked next to the Delano pool. Leanne grew suspicious the minute she spotted him.

He jumped. "Hi, Leanne."

She sipped the special cocktail. "You remember my name? What's up with you? Come sit with us. I insist."

The guy followed her over like a lost puppy. "Hi, I'm Dimitri."

I stood to shake his hand and moved over in the cabana so he could sit with us.

Leanne waved to her potential redskin lover. "Can you bring us a bottle of Cristal and three of your pink fizzy drinks?"

The Cherokee smiled. "Of course, Leanne."

Leanne, secure on coke, smiled. "Whatcha looking for, Mr. Dimitri?" she asked, finishing off her pink drink with one slurp, giving him her side-eyed flirty grin. He looked at his watch, nervously touching it on both sides.

She snuggled closer. "You got any ID? My friend Sophia and I don't trust you!"

She blurted it right out!

The Cherokee carried over a bottle of bubbly and three pink fizzy drinks, sat them down on our table, and placed the Cristal in a white bucket with the Delano logo engraved on the side. His big white teeth glistened in the sunlight. "Anything else, ladies?"

Leanne said, "Bring us lunch, lover. I'm starving!" She waved her hand over his tray. "Enough for all of us. You choose, love—bring us everything!"

She winked at me. Dimitri looked strained. *So unlike last night at the table with the girls,* I thought.

She dug deep into her large tote bag. searching for something. I was distracted but made small talk with our new friend. His pale alabaster skin turned pink from the sun. "I better get under an umbrella, it's my first day at the pool."

Leanne tugged on his shorts. "Stay." I noticed her slip a pill into his drink while he turned to address her demand. "Let's play, Dimitri. Don't go. Stay for lunch. I insist. Sit under our cabana. Don't leave us!"

I knew something was going on. I played along. Lunch came. We devoured the cucumber finger sandwiches and sweet potato fries and left the Caesar salad half-eaten.

Dimitri seemed suddenly loose-lipped. "You girls sure know how to party!"

Leanne went in for the kill. "Sophia, wait here while I give Dimitri a look at our suite." She winked and clicked her cheeks to make a snapping noise, flirting with me. "We'll be back shortly. Wait here."

He obeyed like a well-trained dog waiting for a treat from his master. "I'd follow you anywhere, Ms. Leanne." She walked away, hand-in-hand with the alabaster-skinned Dimitri, carrying his brown leather briefcase next to his side.

Stephanie called me, saying, "I'll be down in fifteen minutes. Is our Cherokee still working?"

I smiled. I couldn't wait to catch up with her and learn more about her thesis on fetishes. "Oh yeah, he's here. Leanne isn't though. She's up in the suite with a very young white boy!"

She giggled. "Good for her. Jayne and I struck out with those boys last night. They were not interested in sex. They never stopped asking us questions. A real drag."

I finished the Caesar salad, licking the bowl like a child, then sat back against the lounge chair to soak up the beautiful sunshine. *I love this place!*

I noticed Leanne and Stephanie walking through the doors together. Leanne's smile was bigger than a full-sized rainbow. "I got his phone and left him naked on my bed in the suite!" She snorted a loud laugh, proud of her accomplishment. She paced back and forth. "Ask the Cherokee to bring us more fizzy drinks and hand me the blow!"

Leanne's fired up!

"My husband hired him to spy on us. I found his notes in his briefcase, and I have his phone." She threw the phone into the pool. It sunk to the bottom. She laughed hysterically. "I put a note on top of his dick saying, 'You're fucked,' and left him there passed out!"

Just like a synced chorus singing for the church, Stephanie and I both sang the same word: "What?"

Our eyes met, and we laughed. The Cherokee offered us his specialty fizzy drinks, and she slurped hers down. "Bring me another, keep them coming!"

He grinned. "Whatever you please, Ms. Leanne."

She smiled. "Really? I like you, White Owl."

She's extra feisty! I couldn't contain myself. "Tell me everything. You fucked this guy? What's Markus going to say when he finds out?"

Her face grew red with anger. "He can go fuck himself. Mr. Dimitri won't say a fucking thing now, will he? And I went through his phone—it had photos on it of me dancing at Cages the other night, but it's at the bottom of the pool now. So, fuck him."

She pulled out her disco dust and snorted another line with her fingernail, then another. "I'm so fucking sick of this motherfucker. He'll be in prison soon and I'll be fucking whoever I fucking wanna fuck, including this Cherokee."

Stephanie leaned in closer. "Let's just relax and enjoy our last day here. Sophia and I have to leave early tomorrow morning. Is Ray coming for you?"

I loved how she gracefully tried to change the subject.

Leanne pulled on her gold Gucci bottoms, tearing them out of her butt crack without a care in the world— so unlike her. "Ray. Yes. He'll be here. I can always count on my Cuban boy."

The Cherokee walked over with more pink fizzy drinks and the phone from the bottom of the pool on his tray. Leanne plopped it into her beach bag, sipped the pink drink, and glared up at him. "I'll be back next weekend just to see you, White Owl."

She giggled, spilling a little pink fizz on her chest and quickly wiping it away in a way so he would pay attention to the motion. "Just to see you!"

Chapter Three

Praise & Worship

T he early morning light glistened on my sun-kissed body, and my Miami tan still glowed. My head cleared and my mind felt ready to get back to work after all the South Beach fun one girl could handle.

I tip-toed through our kitchen, carrying my Mui Mui strappy heels and wearing my favorite black Prada suit with an Eileen Fisher white tank underneath, grateful William had remembered to pick it up from the dry cleaners. My confidence skyrocketed in the designer suit, and these platforms were my Cinderella shoes. I had found the suit on the clearance rack at Saks Fifth Avenue and altered it to fit me perfectly.

I slowly opened the side door leading out to our garage. The dew on the fresh-cut grass reminded me of one of the many reasons I loved the early morning hours. I was trying to be quiet to not wake anyone, as today was the last day of the long holiday weekend.

My oversized Louis Vuitton tote, filled with makeup bags, a change of panties, and my favorite little black book of notes, was already in the passenger seat. I was never late, and today wasn't going to be the first time.

I had been preparing for this interview with the newspaper since the day the editor called to offer me an annual award given to businesswomen who went the extra mile by doing something extraordinary in their field. I could hear my mother's voice in my head, saying, *What does this woman think, you're a brain surgeon? Such ridiculous trophies, so worthless for someone like you.*

The editor, Patty, scheduled an interview for eight o'clock on a Tuesday morning in the city. I should have said I had a prior commitment, but I accepted her invitation. *What was I thinking? I know better.*

The seat in my white BMW 7 series was all the way forward, telling me that my husband had been offering driving lessons to our son last night after I went to bed early. I hated when he left the seat returned to this position. And the gas tank was nearly empty. Hope I had enough to make it to the city. *Fuck! I hate pumping gas more than anything!*

I fluffed my hair in the rearview mirror. My long, silky brown hair was perfectly blown out by my favorite stylist, Vanessa. She knew exactly how I preferred my locks after years of weekly blowouts—bouncy and not a curl in sight. I laughed thinking about the girls' trip to South Beach. A weekend of drama that gave me a new perspective on my life. I was proud of my mistakes, for a change. *Being honest is far better than hiding the truth.*

The radio was set to The Best of the 80s music. I yielded at the stop sign in the neighborhood—a "moving stop," knowing nobody was out on the roads this early—except maybe a golf cart full of neurotic men who couldn't resist an early morning tee time.

I turned up the volume. I needed to relax and chill out on the forty-five-minute drive to the city, where I had to find the newspaper's office where I was meeting the reporter. In my ten years of working in the city, I had only seen the soaring building from a distance.

The radio DJ announced his morning playlist, and I grinned when he selected the band Kansas. I turned up the volume even higher, catching the lead singer's mesmerizing voice, which set me back to my night of bliss. I sang to "Carry on Wayward Son," as loud as my raspy vocal cords would allow.

Fuck! My rockstar's singing to me this morning! I took it as a sign, a message from my rockstar lover.

The steering wheel took control. I was so used to driving this freeway, it was like an extension of my body. I felt one with the road, granting me the ability to drift back to the night of the concert. *I should be focused on my notes for the interview, not that glorious night of pleasure. Fuck it!*

It was 1980, and I was preoccupied with my curls as I got ready. I wanted to iron them down, try to make them flat so I could look like the rest of the girls, and part it right down the middle. I struggled with the idea, uneasy with how to place my head down on the ironing board without burning my neck.

My mother said girls with curls were wild and wicked. I wondered if she had any proof. I secretly loved my bouncy brown locks with sunlit streaks. I never wanted to blend in, but my aunt said I should try to be more like the other girls, maybe try harder to fit in, especially in our small coal mining town. *I guess she was wrong!*

My attempts to tape down my newly plumped breasts haven't worked out for the best either. It's not helping me keep the boys away; it seems boys like girls with bigger breasts and smaller waists. I wore my favorite worn-in Wrangler jeans and a pair of tattered cowboy boots that I lifted from the bag of donations my aunt carried back from a summer job in the Hamptons. *God, I loved those boots!*

The real crime is being ashamed of the beauty you've been gifted. My mother said it was a curse, not a blessing. I needed to disguise my beauty since that's all the adults ever talked about when I was around. I wanted them to applaud me for being smart.

Steve had said I wasn't like the other girls as he stroked my curls behind my ears, gently kissing me down onto his luxurious bed, exposing my nakedness to the moonlight beaming through the hotel's expansive windows. I had surrendered to him. *God, I want to repeat that night over and over again.*

I slammed the brakes at the red light and my right arm slung firmly across my Louis Vuitton bag on the seat next to me, barely staying out of the crosswalk with my abrupt stop. The sudden halt jolted me out of my dreamy state. *Shit! There's a cop standing across the street!*

Thankfully, the cop must have been looking the other way. I pulled into the parking garage, and the attendant guided me to the reserved interviewees' spaces. I had plenty of time.

I reapplied a coat of MAC Rapturous lipstick, my go-to red shade, a hue of red to capture attention. *Calm down, Sophia. Just tell the truth. Be honest, that's what people say they like most about you.*

I pulled my scribbled notes out of my designer bag and quickly reviewed the reporter's list of questions. What college did you attend? *Shit. I hate that question. University of Life. School of Hard Knocks.*

I heard my friend Leanne's voice in my head, saying, *Who gives a fuck about college credits? You've earned this fucking recognition. Tell this reporter, a girl can use the casting couch to easily fuck her way to the top, but I used my common sense instead!* I wasn't taking Leanne's approach, but I loved her way of thinking. *She's right.*

The reporter, Thomas, greeted me at the reception desk with a nod. "Hello. You must be Sophia. How are you?"

I smiled. "Yes. I'm good. Nice to meet you, Thomas."

He was handsome. I felt grateful. He wore a starched, button-up white shirt that held a gorgeous Pucci print silk tie. His wire-rimmed glasses sat neatly upon his slender nose. There was no doubt his chest was ripped into a muscular torso as his shirt buttons revealed a pull only caused by pecks created at the gym. I noticed his shoes were polished. He had a manicure. *I like him already; Leanne would approve of my sexy reporter!*

He walked slightly ahead of me, and I followed him into the conference room. He offered me coffee. I placed my tote bag on the chair next to mine and pulled my little black book out. The notebook held my most guarded secrets but brought me comfort during stressful situations. I walked to the window where there was a spread of pastries, bagels, and a silver canister of coffee, and I poured a cup for myself.

I offered Thomas some small talk, saying, "What a gorgeous view from the twentieth floor! You must be so inspired to write from here!"

He grinned. "I don't get to spend a lot of time in this room except during interviews but yes, it's a wonderful landscape."

I'm sure Stephanie could get him to admit his hottest desires!

My eyes glanced quickly around the room, I wanted to take in the energy around me. I shifted in the brown leather chair and then took the lead as if I were the reporter. "So, where should we start?"

He grinned, peering up from his legal pad. "I often wonder how anyone breaks into the entertainment industry, especially in this city. Did you study filmmaking or script writing in school?"

Oh no, here we go. The school question I wanted so desperately to avoid.

"Well, Thomas. Let me be honest." I let out a sigh. "I wish I had a body double standing in for me during my twenties. A cast of characters to play both the leading lady and the supporting roles. A director who might have offered me some good advice. Instead, I was left on stage with no script, little direction, and a sequel."

He looked puzzled. "Not sure I follow, Sophia."

I giggled; I knew he wouldn't get my sarcasm. "I got pregnant at eighteen, had a baby at nineteen, and a divorce at twenty. Then, to make matters worse, I repeated the performance. I was desperate for a job, nothing more."

He glanced up from his legal pad. "Well, I guess the sequel turned out to be a box office smash!"

I liked him. I smiled. "I agree. I got lucky, getting a paid gig without experience. Maybe my writer wrote in a sub-plot for me."

He laughed, enjoying my comparisons to my life and the movie business, but then he changed the subject. "Were you into any sports? Just curious about your hobbies."

The silence in the room grew deafening as he waited patiently for my response. A drop of sweat rolled down my waist. My armpits were drenched in wetness as the stories of my abusive ex-husband number one rushed through my mind like an avalanche crushing down upon me. *Wonder if a shotgun wedding could be listed on my resume as a big-game sport.*

I laughed, furiously pushing my past down into my belly. "I sucked at sports, every single one of them. I tried volleyball, softball, soccer, gymnastics, and even a day of track. When my mother said I ran like a duck, I stopped running, even though I liked running that day!"

My head dropped, covering my face and the beauty mark that sat on the right side of my face. I glanced up at him in a flirtatious manner. I knew I was disguising my pain with humor; I was good at it. I set him up for the climatic phrase and waited.

"Now, I only run if someone is chasing me." I waited for his response like a comedian on stage delivering a punch line.

The handsome young reporter laughed at my joke. "You have a great sense of humor, Sophia!" He grinned. "Let's skip the details about the less important stuff and get right to the meat of your story. Tell me about your first day in the entertainment industry. How did you start?"

Fuck yeah! It's about time. Get to the plot twist and forget about the character development.

I was excited to share my story with him. "If there was an industry in the world that was carved out just for me, the film and television business was it."

His radiant smile stretched from ear to ear.

The room suddenly seemed like a warm blanket around my shoulders. I wasn't nervous anymore.

"I started at rock bottom, first as a secretary answering phones and serving coffee. Then I learned how to do actors' makeup. Set design came next, naturally."

Thomas glanced over at me, giving me a pleasant smile. "Wow! That's exciting! How did you learn those skills? Is there someone who teaches makeup application here in the city?"

I smiled. "I wish. There should be. I invested in a MAC make-up kit. I studied the craft through some online courses. And I made a whole lot of mistakes on set. Best way to learn, right?"

He nodded. "Yeah, absolutely! But set design. Really? You must have had a knack for it. I know some friends of mine who are still trying to get a chance, and they have degrees in film. They can't even get a call back, let alone an offer to work on set."

I shook my head up and down, agreeing with his analogy. "I guess I was in the right place at the right time."

He grinned. "Isn't that the truth?"

I continued, "My addiction was born in the process. I became so obsessed with the details. I didn't sleep much, at that time; for me, producing projects was like sugar to a kid or wine to a wino. I was addicted!"

The lights in the overhead fluorescents flickered. "What an exciting time in your life, Sophia! Sounds like you found your dream job!"

My head turned slightly toward the window facing the offices. I offered him a childlike grin. "It was so exhilarating! I loved working more than anything in the world." I spotted Patty at the door. She entered, and I stood to shake her hand. "Hi, Patty. How are you?"

She grinned. Her crooked smile, despite its imperfection, was endearing. "I hear you're causing trouble again! I hear things, you know. You can tell me."

Thomas went back to his legal pad, writing notes while he continued to listen to his boss poke me for answers. "You know I'm a troublemaker! If the truth fits, wear it, right?"

If she only knew the half of it!

Patty was a stern older woman with an extensive background in journalism. She had been the editor for over thirty years, so she knew where all the bodies were buried in the city. "The word on the street is your business just bought some animation equipment for over a million dollars; that's a healthy investment for anyone in the film and television business in this city."

She stood over the table of pastries, grabbed a bagel, and spread cream cheese over one side of it. "I want to see it for myself. Do you have time to show it to me on Friday?"

I nodded my head. "Of course, stop by around lunch time. I'll have our chef prepare something delicious for you! What's your favorite?"

She grinned. "Don't make me anything special, I trust you! I'll see you then, Sophia."

Thomas took the lead. "A chef? In your business? There's an unusual twist!"

I continued with my story while I stared up at the ceiling. "Yes, exactly! I designed a commercial kitchen and hired a full-time chef. I regret to say, I am a perfectionist! I insist he creates masterpieces rather than just a burger for lunch. I strive to be the best."

He laughed using his hand to disguise his wide-open mouth. "There's nothing wrong with going above and beyond for your clients. Sounds like you wanted to offer them a great experience."

I smirked at the thought. "Our clients are sometimes difficult and demanding. I have one client, Philip, who claims he can tell if his coffee is more than twelve minutes old! The creative world is filled with crazy creatures!"

"Wow! Sounds bizarre yet so fascinating! You are such a driven woman." His voice sounded deeper than before.

I continued, "Success comes from sleepless nights, personal sacrifices, struggles, and outsmarting your competition."

His reassuring smile encouraged me to continue. "Ever meet anyone famous?"

I grinned; everyone was always impressed by celebrities. *Guess it's name-dropping time.* "We met Michael Douglas and Robert Downey Jr. at an awards dinner a few weeks ago, and Harvey Keitel, Dennis Hopper, Ted Levine, and even Sharon Stone, who was a bitch."

I peered up to make sure he was paying attention, and he was looking at me with wide eyes.

I continued, "Michael loved parking his limo under my office window late at night, with girls in and out of that car for hours. I got my picture taken with Robert and met his mother, who warned me to stay clear of the star, as he didn't need any more distractions."

I stopped for my grand finale and gave him a sly smile.

Thomas smiled back, clearly impressed.

"Thomas, always remember, all that glitters is not gold."

He smiled. "Good point, Sophia."

I was never impressed by Hollywood stars; they had more issues than the extras.

I couldn't resist the need to continue. "We worked with former athletes like Jerome Bettis, Andy Van Slyke, and

Kevin Stevens. We even held the Stanley Cup in 1992 and passed it around to our staff to snap photos!"

His eyes lit up with excitement. "Sounds like a glamorous life, Sophia. What do you remember the most about it besides the celebrities and special perks?"

I thought about it for a minute. I wanted to tell him I thought these Hollywood stars and athletes weren't any different than any one of us, they just had more attention. They had more money, but the wealth brought them bigger problems. Their shady sides were darker shades of grey. They needed water but many times nobody was there to quench their thirst. I answered differently instead. "I saw the need for change. I wanted to bring much-needed change to a stale industry."

My husband says I'm the change-maker, like the rainmaker. I am determined, that's for sure. I noticed his list of questions written down on his notepad.

He glanced at it and then asked, "This is a small town, and most people don't like change here. Did you have pushback? Were you met with any obstacles?"

I tucked my bouncy hair back behind my ears, realizing my nervous habit was part of my natural way of being me. "Oh my God, so many obstacles. One competitor actually called me recently to tell me he owned this town! He said I needed to ask him for approval before we bought any new equipment!"

Thomas raised an eyebrow. "What did you say?"

I giggled, clearly remembering my response. "We need your approval to buy new equipment. Oh sure, I'll call you, when hell freezes over!"

He laughed. "Sounds like you are feisty, Sophia!"

I smiled, knowing he was right. "I am very outspoken. I have to be. I'm told the industry has an 'old boys club,' and I wasn't invited to join it. I showed up to meetings uninvited and told the old boys club, 'I have more *chutzpah* than anyone in this room. You have no idea what I've been through and what I'm willing to do to get my own way and to make a difference.'"

He laughed, covering his mouth with his hand in a way that surprised me. "I guess feisty is a nicer word than aggressive. You got the job done! I guess this is the reason our editor, Patty, thought you would stand out in the crowd of corporate nominees. You don't have to follow the rules in this industry, and you definitely need to color outside the lines, by the sound of it!"

I looked down at my watch. I had a meeting at my office in twenty minutes. "There's always a crisis in this business. Like someone is being kidnapped and held for ransom."

His broad smile showed all his teeth and he nodded sagely.

"The key to success is simply to do exactly what you say you will. Give clients more than they expect and always tell the truth, even if the truth gets you into trouble!"

Thomas's smile stretched from ear to ear.

I hoped the interview was over soon, as we had been in that conference room for nearly an hour already. I waited for him to speak.

"So fascinating, Sophia. I could listen to you talk all day, but I think I have what I need to write your story."

We shook hands. "Thank you, Thomas. I enjoyed our talk. Will you send me your story before it goes to print? I'd really like to take a look at it first."

He nodded and handed me his business card. "Yes, of course. My direct line is on my card. I'll call you when I'm finished."

◆

As I drove through the city side streets to my office, I reflected on a strange memory weighing heavily on my mind since the question about attending college. I had sacrificed those early years meant for studies for a hard road instead. All the years I spent learning valuable lessons at the Real Life, Hard Knocks College earned me a master's degree in tenacity.

I should be proud. Most women would have failed the course, but I was a valedictorian. I had run away from ex-husband number one in the middle of the night with a fierce determination burning in my belly.

I remembered walking down the country cow path, knowing I had to be careful where I stepped because of the holes in the dirt road, while my baby girl cried and screamed with colic. I eased her pain by stopping to rub her belly along the way. I sang a few lyrics from John Denver's song, "Take Me Home, Country Roads." I was convincing myself as well as my baby girl; she had no choice but to go along with my plan to exit my marriage to abusive ex-husband number one. It was my only chance to escape the farm boy's wrath and change my destiny.

The truth was that I knew the minute that bastard dragged me by my long, curly hair that I would either kill him using rat poison or use it on myself—*not an option*. I would watch him swell up like a balloon and die in a corner alone or I had to plan to leave him.

I wasn't about to tolerate this farm boy kicking me while I was pregnant and punching me with his fists as though I was one of his eight brothers. I had only fucked this farm boy twice and I got pregnant with his baby, but that didn't earn him the right to fucking abuse me.

I had to escape since orange wasn't my color and prison jumpsuits didn't fit into my stylish wardrobe. I laughed at my wit, grateful for my sense of humor. It calmed me down through the tough times.

I reminded myself what I loved most about William. Tomorrow was our fifteenth wedding anniversary and we agreed not to exchange gifts. I walked inside our glorious production offices, greeted by the forty-foot stainless steel bar as our reception area. Hung above the structure were twelve televisions serving as entertainment for our clients during breaks from their long days in dark edit suites.

We created this place as a team. A well-oiled machine. And I was his leading lady in an original film written and produced by me. The credits were rolling. It was my time to take the stage. I bowed for my audience. I was grateful.

Chapter Four

Adam & Eve

William hadn't put a trumpet to his lips in over twenty years, even though music had been part of his life since he was born. A blister had busted open during his incredible performance as the opening act on The David Letterman Show, leaving his treasured upper lip permanently flawed. The imperfection made his mouth sexier than usual. I loved that scar, especially when he shaved his facial hair to reveal the marking.

I had accidentally (and purposely) married a musician. I remember the attraction from the moment we met and the way his plump lips moved so eloquently when he spoke. His somatosensory organ was soft and pink. Hidden behind a thick brown mustache, a scar cut through his facial hair like a river cut through the forest, exposing his pain. He dragged on a Winston cigarette. He promised to quit. He hated his smile. He was adopted. He blamed his birth mother. He called her Betty. He carried a chip on his shoulders. I remembered every little detail about him.

William's long hair brazed the top of his collared shirt. His leg hairs, exposed against his short white tennis shorts, covered his muscular calves. He played tennis, loved to paint, loved art exhibits, and loved to write music. He knew every word of every movie ever made. He told awful jokes. He stuttered in large groups. He was brutally honest. He loved to play poker. He was competitive. I clung to the way he protected me from my judgmental mother.

He proposed after an important dinner meeting. He had hired me a year earlier. We worked together like a pendulum clock. He was the reliable swinging weight that regulated my speed. I was the ticking hands that made the clock move. I needed the balance. He brought out the best in me. He pushed me forward. I trusted him.

He adored my two young children. I loved him just for that very reason alone. I finally said yes to his proposal of sixteen years earlier. Time had passed so quickly. I felt grateful he wasn't an ordinary man. He was complex. We had that in common.

I heard the clock. Tick. Tock. Tick. Tock. *Does everything in life have an expiration date?*

I think so. I hoped not. Until now, everything good in my life had eventually come to an end.

Love on one hand. Hate on the other. Good versus evil. Both weighed heavily on my mind.

I craved the mechanical equilibrium of the scales, starving for balance like food to the malnourished.

As William drove through the Santa Monica mountains, I drifted off, staring out the window at the breathtaking views of Los Angeles. We had decided to take an anniversary vacation rather than exchange the mundane anniversary gifts or the standard fancy dinner at an overpriced restaurant to celebrate our victory.

I gathered travel experiences like kids collected baseball cards.

Our first stop along our journey was a short stay with his childhood friend, Ethan, and his wife. He was a big-shot Hollywood talent agent, emerging as a leader on the comedy talent side with a growing list of in-demand players, including Jim Carrey. His bride, Hannah, was an up-and-coming screenwriter with a long history of producing top box office films.

William had reunited with Ethan at their twenty-fifth high school reunion a few months ago. Ethan threw out an invitation for us to come out to LA and stay with them in the fall. His polite invitation was merely a kind gesture, but William demanded his friend own up to his offer, longing to witness his friend's success, as if he needed proof.

The landscape was magical along the way to an exclusive mid-century house perched high upon the hillside. A sight to see, especially for a girl like me coming from a coal mining town with slate dumps as mountains and black soot as clouds. Mulholland Drive was everything I ever read about. I was in awe.

William had spent weeks planning the itinerary for our great escape. First, a night in Los Angeles, and then we would spend a week at Shutter's on the Beach in Santa Monica, where we would attempt to rekindle our love on the white sandy beaches, the sun reflecting off of the Pacific, and a gentle ocean breeze to calm me. William insisted on splurging on a luxurious cottage resembling one of Cape Cod's, with shuttered doors opening onto breezy balconies and a sun-drenched pool deck.

He knew my love for boutique hotels was my muse. He loved to please me.

William reached for his pack of Winston cigarettes, and I barked, "Please don't smoke in the car. I don't want to stink like stale cigarettes."

He huffed and placed the cigarette between his lips unlit.

I leaned my head against the glass, smashing my bouncy curls against the window, peering out on the horizon. I fantasized about my rockstar lover taking possession of my virginity so many years ago. He claimed he would devour my curvaceous body forever. He had begged me to run away with him to Los Angeles, but I was only eighteen and torn between my need to please my mother and my desire to chase my own dreams.

My rockstar had a sense of humor. I chuckled silently to myself recalling how he had said, "If you turn the world on its side, everything loose ends up in LA."

I often looked back on those carefree days as the happiest times of my life. No pressure. No worries. Sometimes I wondered what happened to my rockstar. I followed his tours all over the world and read the press releases about his success. I kept his manager Roger's phone number locked inside my journal. I wondered what life would have looked like if I would have gone with him that very night. *Most men are easy lays. And who needs easy?* I giggled. I preferred a challenge.

William's deep voice interrupted my daydreams. "We're almost there, Sophia. I don't think Ethan thought I would ever take him up on his offer for dinner. Remember, he booked our band as the opening act on The David Letterman Show. My lip still hurts every time I think about that night."

He said it like he needed to remind me of the story. I smiled, silently rolling my eyes back in my head. I had heard this story a million times before. "I know, William. I know."

I giggled to myself, thinking, *Every woman should be so lucky to be with a horn player at least once in her life.*

I marveled at William's ability to find all eight thousand nerves of my clitoris. When we first met, I had researched the art. It seems the word embouchure, or lipping, is the use of the lips, facial muscles, tongue, and teeth in playing a wind instrument. This includes shaping the lips to the mouthpiece of a woodwind instrument. *My pussy is his trumpet.* I tucked my curly hair nervously behind my ears, a habit I had grown to love.

"How did we get so lucky to have friends in all the right places?" He grinned. "Be grateful, Sophia. We've created a wonderful life together."

I sighed. "Why do I feel so lonely then? I just don't get it."

His voice was soft, each word a gentle caress that calmed my restless heart. "You're surrounded by interesting people, yet you feel alone? You need to consider my idea; swinging is something a lot of married couples do, it's a way to bring some spice into our marriage again. You need to be passionate about something besides work."

You're just that…. the swinging pendulum. I giggled. *Wonder what my new friend Stephanie would say about his fetish.*

Peering over at him as he drove, I continued, "I told you; I can't do it. I'm not into it at all. I want romance and sensuality, not porn and fucking for fuck's sake."

He frowned. "Let's just relax and have fun with our friends. We're here to celebrate and forget our worries."

We arrived at the magnificent mid-century house off Mulholland Drive. Situated behind a gate up a private drive, this architectural property looked like something out of a Tarantino film. We could see the pool through the double front doors, which were open to an oversized deck looking over the hills and into the valley. The dramatic views and beautiful light flowing throughout the home showcased the incredible design, magical walls of glass, privacy, and grand open spaces.

Ethan greeted us at the open double front doors, immediately taking William's hand and pulling him into his chest for a manly hug. "So nice to see you, man."

They caught up with small talk for a minute. "We schlepped here all the way from The Steel City just to see you, you schmuck!" William loved to get a rise out of his closest friends; his dry sense of humor stunned many people, but it was charming to some.

Ethan immediately stepped back from William. He glared over at me as if to ask for my permission to hug me. "You must be Sophia! So nice to meet you. What the hell is a woman like you doing with a putz like him?"

I smiled.

He laughed. "Let's go inside. We've prepared some nosh and champagne to toast my new client!"

I smiled at Ethan but continued to stand in awe of my surroundings. I wanted to take it all in. I could see all the way to the ocean and Catalina Island, as it was a clear day. The sunset was just beginning to paint streaks of tangerine and cantaloupe across the skyscape.

We walked inside. Hannah was preparing champagne glasses and holding a bottle. "Hi! You must be Sophia." She side-kissed me.

I said, "I love your dress! Your home is exquisite. So beautiful."

She smiled. "This old shmatte. Let's celebrate your anniversary, congrats!"

Ethan poured us champagne, and we lingered in the gleaming kitchen with exposed wood on the ceilings and a streamlined wall of built-in cabinetry that both divided the space and offered plenty of storage. I looked up, taking it all in. I must have looked like a tourist in a celebrity mansion tour, but I couldn't hide my surprise.

I felt as overwhelmed as a country girl on the New York City subway. My eyes couldn't take in all the beauty.

Ethan turned to Hannah. "I can't believe you didn't have time to dust my CD collection today. Can you grab the dusting cloth from the maid's quarters?"

Hannah ignored his request and poured more champagne into her already-emptied flute. "Please, Ethan, enough. I'm going to take Sophia to see the observation tower; it's nearly sunset, so we must go now."

Hannah and I walked and talked a mile a minute, immediately making a fierce connection as women who worked in a male-dominated industry. She had just written and produced her first movie. I remember being so impressed by her willingness to be so open with me. I envied her style.

She was pretty, like Demi Moore—feminine and strong at the same time. She was feisty and spirited, and I liked her immediately.

Hannah was still pissed off. "Ethan came home from his production meeting with Jim Carrey early this afternoon, and we argued because I hadn't dusted off his CD collection. He's crazy about this stupid fucking collection. Ethan thinks he's holding the largest horde of gold in human history, like it's the New York Federal Gold Vault, for Christ's Sake."

I nodded, agreeing with his ridiculous behavior. I smiled, hoping she was exaggerating. "Come on, really? Don't you have a housekeeper to do that for you?"

She giggled. "Ethan insists I do it; he doesn't trust anyone else to touch it, just like his dick, a precious jewel." She laughed wildly, spilling her champagne, exposing her wide sensual mouth as she gasped, "He's neurotic."

Hannah showed me her new spinning wheel while she sat on the bohemian-style cushions laying around on the floor of the observatory. I was mesmerized by the view and captivated by the wealth of these two people and their childish arguments. I thought to myself how all people, rich or poor, share similar issues.

Isn't it funny how we all have shady sides and love to confess them when given the chance?

She leaned in closer to me as if to share a secret. "Are you willing to sneak my Prada luggage into your rental car so I can exit Mr. Chow's restaurant after dinner? I'm planning to stay in our suite at the Beverly Wilshire; it's the perfect place to finish my next script and get a much-needed break from my crazy, narcissistic husband."

My smile grew large with excitement. I was glad she was a take-charge kind of woman. "Of course, I would love to be your accomplice. What's your new script about?"

Hannah smirked and suddenly looked like a shining star. "I'm having an affair with my figure-sculpting instructor. He's a man half my age with hands meant for molding malleable dust into shapes until he met me. Now his artfully skilled hands have a new purpose other than warming them in my kiln."

She giggled like a schoolgirl. "My new script is about our love affair—a sensual and erotic romance."

"I'm so jealous!" The words just fell out of my mouth like a rotten tomato, leaving me with regret.

She glowed with such a force as if she was snapped like a light stick to shine in the darkness. "Jealous? Of what? My awful marriage or my hot fucking lover?" She giggled. "Don't be envious, love. Remember, all that glitters is not gold!"

Leanne told me the same thing!

I felt an overwhelming need to share my innermost fears with Hannah inside the observatory. I think the champagne had given me loose lips.

Their home reminded me of what I imagined my home would have looked like with my rockstar—if only I went to shake things loose in LA with him— a ticket to freedom. I felt very vulnerable.

I blurted out without thinking, "William's begging me to have sex with other couples."

Hannah sat back against the wall. "He's into swinging? Interesting. I have a lot of friends into the lifestyle. I think it's just a phase. He'll get over it."

I frowned and sipped the rest of my champagne for a much-needed boost of confidence. "He can't get a hard-on unless we're watching porn—about orgies, of course. Oh God, please don't say anything."

She turned, hesitated for only a second, then smiled dazzlingly. "There's another bottle of bubbly in the fridge behind you. Grab one!" She frowned. "Men. They think they know how to please a woman. God. If just one of them would watch a chick-flick, what a fucking education they might get!"

We laughed. I opened the second bottle of champagne, and I poured her glass full and mine.

The sunset glow glistened all over the concrete floor in the conservatory, casting shades of orange and yellow everywhere. I allowed my curls to cover my face and I dropped my head in shame. "I feel so pressured. I feel so ugly. Why am I not enough for him?"

Our eyes met unexpectedly. "I'm so sorry, Sophia. So many men disappoint us in life. I never count on one man to satisfy me."

Is she encouraging me to find a lover?

We got up and walked her suitcase outside to the rental car, placed it in the trunk, and walked inside through the double front doors, left open to accept the cool evening breeze so gently rolling through the valley. We walked past the sunken living room. The sprawling structure embraced me in a welcoming manner. I could hear roaring laughter coming from the kitchen.

The smell of weed filled the room. I noticed someone coming out of the butler's pantry carrying a bag of pretzels; it was Jim Carrey. He looked as average as the next guy, wearing a navy blue hoodie with a white t-shirt underneath with a Visit California logo on it—well, except for his exceptionally large grin. Jim extended his hand to shake mine. "HELL-O."

I smiled and passed on taking a puff on the joint by waving my hand in front of it. "No, thanks." I feared what might fall out of my mouth as I talk entirely too much when I smoke weed.

Ethan's phone rang; it was the concierge from the restaurant. He answered while coughing from the inhaled smoke. "We're leaving now. Hold the table. Prepare a bottle of Krug Clos d'Ambonnay 1995 for us." He looked at Jim. "Do you want to join us for dinner?"

"No thanks, man. Maybe I'll stop by later."

William and I waited patiently in our rental car, leaving Ethan's driver standing in the peat driveway, holding the car door open for Hannah while Ethan spoke briefly with Mr. Carrey, his demeanor confident as he walked to the black car waiting for entry.

Ethan shook his hand, gloating from ear to ear. "Thanks for trusting me; you won't regret it, Jim."

Upon arriving to Mr. Chow's restaurant in the heart of Beverly Hills, it was obvious Ethan was a regular with a lot of clout with the staff, including Mr. Chow himself, who greeted Ethan and Hannah at the door. His signature round black glasses so neatly perched on his face, a bubbly personality so engaging, he was captivating. The staff waited on us like we were royalty, immediately bringing more champagne and a bottle of Ethan's favorite wine before we ordered from the extensive menu.

The place was abuzz with clients from the art, fashion, music, and entertainment business. I could feel the creative energy filling up the space like a swarm of bees in a hive full of honey. Ethan took the liberty of ordering for our table, a combination of old authentic Beijing and original recipes such as Chicken Satay, Mr. Chow Noodles, and Ma Mignon, all carefully created by their passionate and skillful chefs. Ethan spared no expense with us; he was a generous host who treated us to the best prepared Beijing Duck in the world, one of Mr. Chow's house specialties.

The night was magical. William was impressed by his friend's success, and I was in awe of their mysterious shady sides.

As I sipped the fancy champagne, I watched Hannah laugh and smile as if nothing was wrong with her marriage. Allowing the bubbles to filtrate my sanity, making me tipsy, I pondered, *Not often do we conceive of women giving into their darkest urges, celebrating the wicked and depraved sides.* I wanted to scream, "Congratulations, Hannah."

After dinner, I insisted Ethan and William grab a cigar at The Mayborne Hotel next door. William thought we should spend the night close by rather than drive to Santa Monica after a night of drinking. I agreed, and this time would give me a chance to get Hannah's luggage from our trunk. She kissed me on both cheeks and walked away into the darkness of the cool autumn night.

We went home to our chaotic lives. I didn't stay in touch with Hannah, although I thought of her so often.

Silence was now my response to everything, especially my pain. I worked longer hours. I gave him space to change his mind. Silence is not empty; it is the loudest noise. I thought Hannah was right about him getting over it. Unfortunately, she was wrong.

William made two calls the previous evening. One, a complicated business conversation regarding a scene in a bowling alley with the producers of the movie, *King Pin,* starring Woody Harrelson. And the other to tell his new lover, Diane, that he had a fabulous time watching her fuck his friend, John, while he fucked John's fiancé.

I gagged, unable to process the thought. *How dare he ruin our lives?*

My stomach churned with nausea as my fingers continued to scroll through his unopened phone messages. I waited on our bed for him to exit the shower, a white towel wrapped tight around his bronzed skin exposing the golf tan he had worked so hard to achieve. I reached for his phone. "I know all about your little rendezvous with Diane. I read your fucking messages."

Jayne was right, all men were lying pricks!

William stood tall with a smug look of confidence on his face, without remorse. "I admit my guilt, Sophia. I can't lie. But I won't apologize. I did tell you. I told you in Santa Monica but you were not listening. I told you I needed to live this lifestyle, with or without you."

My ears felt ringing like a grenade thrown onto a battlefield with an explosion of particles scattered everywhere.

He continued, "Join us. Diane's open to taking you as her lover."

How dare you suggest who my lovers might be? I'll choose.

I didn't blame William for cheating on me. I was a workaholic and he sought after his swinging fetish as if it consumed him, like a serial killer's need to find the next victim. *She's so unlike me. I can't wham-bam, a fuck for fuck's sake.*

I only had one wish.

I just wished he would have found a stranger as a swinging partner, not Diane, the married events coordinator at our country club. She was an over-made-up Barbie doll. She looked a lot like Debbie Harry but with far less femininity. Diane rode a Harley Davidson motorcycle. She was sarcastic. She loved to golf. All of the ladies at the club were gossiping about her bad behavior, claiming she was too friendly and flirtatious with their husbands.

I wasn't worried. I should have been.

I guess I figured you can't lose what you don't have, so what's the difference? Their affair shredded my life into bits and pieces, like a woodchipper spits out mulch. I couldn't write a better script myself until the plot twist came crushing down upon my head. *A man will seek whatever he is missing.*

The cheating was the easy part.

Our once warm and welcoming home stood in silence as we navigated through the following weeks. I drove into our city production offices alone. He left the office early for tee times. My workload had been far greater than his recently. I needed to create space between us as I tried to figure out our next move. I thought time and distance were a cure for our severely damaged marriage.

The next morning, as if we weren't living under the same roof, William entered my office and fired me, just like I was one of his twenty-two employees. Oh wait, I was just that, an employee.

After all these years of trust, I had never become a partner. *Even Truman Capote couldn't write a better plot twist even if his "swans" handed him the juicy scandal on a silver platter!*

That night, he packed his clothes into suitcases, like nothing happened earlier. "I'm going to stay with John for a few weeks. I'll call the real estate agent to sell the house."

I cried, "You're a loser. A nothing. A lousy lay." I had a way with words. We didn't part on good terms, to say the least. I pressed him to get a rise. "One last fuck for fuck's sake? What do ya say, William?" I poked him harder. "Oh, wait. You can't get your limp dick to work unless you wind it up with some porn. Maybe your new swinging partners will learn how to get you hard!"

He walked out.

I called Stephanie. "I can't believe he left. He fired me. What the fuck will I do now?"

She offered me sound advice. "You'll surround yourself with your friends. We'll help you get through it! Do you think William will give me an interview for my thesis? I would love to write your story!"

The best and worst moments in my life seemed to fall on holidays. Valentine's Day would be no exception. A day set aside for a bouquet of red roses, a heart-shaped box of chocolates with a velvet ribbon tied neatly around it, a sparkling diamond ring to ask for her hand, a memory for your loved one.

My day of love wasn't so sweet, as Cupid delivered an arrow right through my heart instead. He was very naughty and not so nice. My little angel, Cupid, had a shady side.

The final court decision on my marital assets with William was delivered on that special holiday meant for lovers. I felt anxious as I muttered to myself, grabbing fists of my curly hair as I cried, "I gave him fifteen years of blood, sweat, and tears, built an entertainment empire with him, and he let a judge determine my fate. He must suffer in some way. I hate him."

I was no cactus expert, but I knew a prick when I saw one—it just took me years to see the bastard.

To make matters worse, William's partner, Robert, was a clever accountant who should have been a master chef, as he took care of cooking the books to disguise their profits into losses. His attorney, Joanne, skillfully manipulated the truth about his expenses from the court. A judge decided my settlement was zero. I looked up at the ceiling as if to thank God for his gift.

I had to confess: my shady side was ignited, as potent as a rocket launch.

I wanted to hunt him down and kill him with my bare hands. I could see the scene play out in my mind. I chased him with a hunting dog by my side, tracking his scent. I caught him by grabbing his neck with my hands, like Catwoman might torture her victim in Gotham City. I imagined strangling him to death, gazing into his eyes as he begged me for mercy, but I ignored his cries for relief. My razor-sharp retractable claws cutting his throat, my peak human physical condition was no match for his weakness.

The scene continued unfolding in my mind. I slowly dragged his body out to the woods and hung him up in a barn, like a deer, letting him bleed out until I could gut him, and then deliberately cutting him into lean chops. As a kid, I had watched the hunters in our neighborhood hang deer in the barn, so I felt confident I could do it.

I knew ex-husband number three would run scared as hell if he saw me chasing him.

I called Leanne, looking for someone to be my partner in crime. She was my one and only friend who would agree to conspire with me. She had *chutzpah*. I searched inside my closet for my knee-high black leather boots, tossing around the black turtlenecks and leather pants as if I could create a catsuit suitable for a midnight kill.

I laughed. "MEOW!"

I waited for Leanne to pick up her phone, anxious to be talked down from the ledge as if I were a cat waiting to jump. I sat on the floor inside my walk-in cedar closet, choking back the tears. My mind raced with evil thoughts. I hated revenge but he had pushed me to the edge.

She answered, "What's up girlfriend?"

I laughed. "MEOW!"

She giggled. She understood me. "MEOW!"

I stopped; grief enveloped me like a wet blanket, heavy and smothering.

I began to pace, knowing my fate. "I'm thinking about renting a Chevy pickup truck to tie ex-husband number three's sorry ass down in the back. I'll torture him for days before I'll gut him like a deer, make his ass into a rump roast!"

She laughed. "That's a horrible idea. What time? I'm in."

My spirit shriveled and sank like a deflating balloon. I disguised my sadness with humor. "Girl, that fucking redneck judge just granted me a big fucking zero dollars as a settlement. I lost my job, and now I'm about to lose my house. All vanished into thin air—a horror movie, and I'm the leading lady!"

Leanne wanted to go on the hunt with me. "I say we destroy him. He's a pussy, so easy to fucking scare. He'll probably just get in the truck with us and not even ask questions. You know he's as sharp as a marble! Let's do it, Sophia."

I laughed at her willingness to commit a crime with me. "Be serious, Lea. I can't kill the fucking man. I called you to talk me out of it. Let's make a full moon wish instead. Come over on Tuesday. We'll brew up a stew. It's my last week in the house so let's destroy the kitchen!"

She laughed, covering the phone to scream at her nanny. "Hang on a minute, this stupid fucking bitch. I'm in. My son's running through the house with a water gun! I'll see you on Tuesday."

Just like that, we brewed a karma soup for ex-husband number three. The karma soup recipe included lots of vegetables, chicken, and fresh herbs, but the secret ingredient was a wicked spell—a powerful spell made under the full moon.

As Leanne stirred the soup, it bubbled with an aroma that filled my house with the scent of chicken and onions. "Let's ask the moon to make his dick fall off. I think that's his punishment—life without a dick."

I giggled at her idea. "His limp dick is already like a slinky; it isn't worth the energy. Why fuck with his already dysfunctional organ? No, we need a better one. Think. What's the worst thing that could happen to him?"

Leanne jumped up and down like a schoolgirl jumping rope. She clapped her hands with excitement. "I got it! I got it! Let's wish for his new lover to drop dead! Yes!" She laughed hysterically while celebrating like the Munchkins cheering the death of the Wicked Witch. "Ding. Fucking. Dong."

My mind raced back to the dreadful memory.

The new lovers eloped to Vegas to tie the knot the minute the divorce papers were delivered. Their lavish wedding was held at our country club with all our country club bitch friends in attendance, just a few weeks later. Their love was displayed for all the world to witness, written up in the society pages. She wore an iconic Vera Wang strapless sweetheart mermaid gown with an asymmetrically draped bodice and cut organza blossom hem with blizzard beading. They moved into their custom-built home just days after returning from their romantic honeymoon in France.

A love story beautifully written using the blood he drained from my body as the ink to write this horror script.

Leanne and I were both so high from drinking vodka martinis and snorting lines, we wrote the wish down on paper. I placed the paper under a glass of milk on the windowsill facing the moon. We howled like two werewolves and continued singing like munchkins.

"How old are we, Lea? We're so stupid. But I love you!"

We sipped on the soup while we jarred the rest for another day. We marked the mason jars using ex-husband number three's name, *Kill Bill Batch, 02.14.*

I woke with a hangover that felt as if a tornado from Kansas whirled in my brain overnight, spinning Dorothy and Toto around in my head and destroying all the common sense inside. Leanne had arranged for her driver to pick her up at midnight, as she had to be in court the next day with her husband.

I made a pot of coffee, reread the judgment, and noticed the attachment in the last page. I was entitled to relinquish my investment in the building his business was in, an investment opportunity I took before we were married. He wanted me out. I took the offer, surrendering the investment for my next chapter, a chance to reinvent myself.

I lost my sanity by locking myself inside our once-sacred palace, demolishing bottles of champagne we had saved for celebrations. The gossip whirled all around me, promising to carry me out into the high winds to shred me with a fierce burning sensation.

I called Leanne, seeking comfort. "Why's he acting like an idiot? He cut me off at the club and won't even let my son continue his golf lessons this summer. All for a bimbo who forged my fucking name on our country club deed to steal my membership. She's fucking me, just like she wanted to…"

Leanne took my pain into her own heart. "I'll fucking shred that bitch into a million fucking pieces if you give me the green light, Sophia! Say the word!"

I cherished her friendship, grateful to lean on our relationship for comfort.

William continued his extravagant lifestyle, flaunting it in my face. I withered away; no food could satisfy my emptiness, no amount of sleep could cure my need for rest, and there was no way to stop the bleeding inside my heart. I felt lifeless and numb, unable to process the pain.

His attorney, Joanne, gave me a week to move out of our home nestled conveniently on the fourteenth tee box of the signature golf course. I called William to plead with him. "Please wait until I move out to strut your Barbie doll wife past our living room window. I'm sick of seeing the two of you wearing matching golf clothes like two fucking kids wearing Grr-Animals!"

He barked back, "You're just jealous."

I wasn't envious of a bimbo who loved to sport around in visors and spikes. I shouted back to him, "She married a guy with a handicap, a hacker, a whiff."

William slammed the phone down.

I laughed.

He forged my name on our deed to surrender our house to the bank, and all my attempts to prove his signature wasn't mine had been exhausted. I sold most of our furniture, including a custom-made dining room table made from antique doors and the twelve chairs that held memories of glamorous dinners.

I found buried treasures inside our attic, sports memorabilia that had filled our home with joy until today. I tossed out his hand-written anniversary cards declaring his undying love for me. His sexual fetishes would destroy those notions.

I slurped down my afternoon vodka martini while I continued to bubble-wrap my collection of vintage glasses. My thirty-ninth birthday would not be my best. I ignored multiple calls from Leanne and Stephanie begging me to celebrate with them. I couldn't bring myself to celebrate.

I spent the night crying amongst the weeping willow tree outside our bedroom window while packing my designer shoes away into storage containers. I lit all the candles in the bathroom, filled the jetted tub with bubbles, and let it bubble over onto the floor, knowing this night would be my last in our beautiful home meant for a queen.

My new business would be my distraction, a way to mask my heartache and renovate my soul.

And, just like that, I decided to chase my dream to open a retail store. I had to get as far away as possible from the entertainment business and away from ex-husband number three and his new wife in this dreadful country club neighborhood. I had been dealt a new start.

Chapter Five

Deliver Me from Evil

I found comfort inside my shady sides but knew I had to step out from the shadows. I felt the familiar feeling of survival rear its ugly head, yet I felt powerful again. He couldn't rob me of my tenacity. I had a master's degree, and nobody could ever steal it away from me.

My warrior side appeared as I prepared the last-minute details for the grand opening of my store—The Garden of Eden. The new logo would be the symbol of a confession, the forbidden fruit—in my eyes, an apple core carved out to the shape of a very curvy woman to signify the core of the female body, a temptation.

My friend Violet called me, out of breath. "Sophia, I'm at my son's football game, and the school just put new AstroTurf on the field. There's a huge hunk of it in the garbage, so I'm going to go dumpster diving for you!"

"Oh my God, girl! That's awesome! The grass for my garden. What a great idea!"

A few minutes later, Violet walked in with a huge smile on her face. She was strikingly beautiful with straight, long, brown hair; large, brown eyes, and a welcoming, wide mouth with big, white teeth. She battled with her love for sugar, but when she was at her best weight, she rocked her slender body with her tomboy personality and funky bohemian style.

I understood the reason the producers of *King Pin* chose her for the role of the farm girl in the opening scene. Violet was a simple woman, yet she was naturally gifted with beauty.

She was the woman we all counted on to help us with handyman tasks, since she taught herself to rewire lighting, paint, install flooring, and repair furniture. She was always ready to take on new adventures as long as there was a meaning behind the destination, like hiking through the woods to find exotic mushrooms, exploring a cave to discover what lives inside it, or walking the beach to find shark teeth.

For Violet, life was all about purpose and the end results, especially when it came to her two teenage boys. She lived for them and for creating art. There wasn't anything else—well, except for her obsession with professional athletes.

We spent hours placing the AstroTurf between the cracks in the concrete floors. "Unreal, Violet. This is exactly what we needed to make this garden grow!"

She smiled, proud of her creativity. "I hope the Steelers show up at your party! I'll wear a fig leaf to tempt them!" She giggled.

I hired an ironworker artist to design custom-made twenty-foot metal trees that were sculpted to form branches to hang the clothes on. The thick, twisted branches were stretched out, creating a dense canopy to provide an ambiance of The Tree of Knowledge in an open field. We placed apples in the oversized windows underneath the voluptuous mannequins wearing colorful wigs.

The Garden of Eden would be as sexy as possible so that women were not only tempted to shop but would long to confess their secrets to me from behind the dressing room curtains. This way, I could put a bandage on my wounded heart and find peace by knowing I was doing it my way.

My shop girls had to be beautiful and smart enough to follow my strict instructions on everything from how to greet a customer to how to place white tissue inside the bag with a perfectly tied red ribbon—no matter the size of the purchase. I expected each customer to feel special. Violet offered me a list of names from her previous interviews. "We thought these girls were qualified, just didn't need any more help at the store this summer. Call all of them!"

I had a hot, young bartender create a list of tempting cocktails and a sexy chef create tapas for the menu, as every detail mattered to me. I invited my South Beach friends down to the store for a taste-testing night. "Just stop by for a bite. Let me know what you think!"

Jayne rolled up with her boyfriend, Clinton. "Hey, Chick-EE. I love the spot! So sexy!" She brought a smile to my face.

Leanne arrived late, as she had a previous date with a new young boy toy who was fancy on her cherry bomb. She whispered to me, "My new boy tells me my lips taste like wild cherries! I can't wait to see him naked!"

She fucked the young culinary boy in my stockroom. "I had to get the best of him for you, Sophia; add a little hot sauce to his love muscle before your party! It's like training before a big game! You can thank me later!"

She never ceased to amaze me with her hearty sexual appetite. There was a time when she might have fucked a couple of different young men in a week—if they were attractive and prepared for her "Don't call me, I'll call you" dismissal.

She was my single married girlfriend. I loved her unconditionally.

I held a casting session. I had to find eight beautiful women to walk down the street wearing sexy dresses with their hair teased up into avant-garde, beehive hairdos with birds carefully placed inside the wigs.

I expected people to stop to pay attention.

Helena showed up with a few girls of her own.

She smiled in her usual provocative way. "Cupcake, I love your ideas. Once these girls hit the catwalk and the men go crazy, you'll make the scene column, I promise!"

I hired her girls, of course. She grinned. "Meg is here. She's dying to model your clothes in the reality series she's being cast for next week. Wanna loan her a few dresses?"

I rolled my eyes at Leanne. "A cupcake is full of sugar, and she's full of shit." We laughed as I pulled a few dresses for Megabucks.

In Hollywood, bodyguards held the crowds back using velvet ropes, guarding the entrance as if royalty was arriving. I wanted to create the same hype at my party, leaving mystery stirring in the minds of my guests while they waited outside to enter the garden.

I was reminded of an assignment given to a young production assistant I knew in Hollywood—to find a young woman who was willing to follow Eva Longoria around at the Golden Globes. The girl's only assignment was to repeatedly tell the star how beautiful she was as she cascaded down the red carpet. Eva needed the boost of confidence. *Such a life, a desperate housewife indeed!*

Jayne's lover, Clinton, helped me with the bodyguards. He convinced two security guards at his nightclub to take the role by the door. He waited for them to show, and said, "Sophia, one of them is a student at the medical college, and the other is a trainer at a boxing gym. Both great guys and willing to do it for a few bucks!"

I insisted they wear only the tightest pairs of jeans, no shirts, and no shoes—just a smile. They would check the guest list carefully to ensure only the private list of attendees entered the secret garden.

I didn't mind that the snooty country club wives called us all sluts. I thought, *Sluts stands for sexy ladies under tremendous stress.*

<hr/>

The night air was warm with an August breeze that filled the streets and casted shadows of orange hues with an early fall sunset. As I peered over my garden creation inside my beautiful boutique, I realized I was an idea person, a rare breed who could only be recognized by the creatures who walked this earth with the same grace as me.

I brought The Garden of Eden to life.

My invitation list included one hundred people, and two hundred showed. I felt exhausted from all the small talk but was thrilled with the turnout for the grand opening party.

I walked back to the dressing room area to escape the crowd and check on customers who tried on trendy clothing behind the curtains. I was excited about the great attendance and wanted to offer my personal touch to clients in the dressing rooms.

I called out, "Does anyone need any help?"

One customer peeked from behind one of the curtains. She smiled, extending her hand to me. "Hi, I'm Donna. I could use your help."

Donna was a petite, young woman who was probably in her early thirties. Her over-processed, thin, blonde hair was not flattering to her pretty face. She was so skinny, but her breast implants enhanced her boyish figure. I remembered her looking like the paintings of the girl with the oversized eyes, as she hid a sadness inside herself.

I immediately felt uncomfortable with her gaze focused on the floor. *What's she afraid of?* I would soon find out.

"My boyfriend, Ted, gave me his VIP ticket. I hope that's okay." Her tone of voice betrayed her insecurity.

I felt sorry for her. She seemed like a battered dog in need of rescuing, so I replied, "Of course it's okay. What can I help you find?"

She didn't lift her eyes but stared at the floor while she said, "I'm not sure. I'm the national rep for Adidas Athletic Wear. I'm unsure about sexy stuff to wear. I need your guidance."

Her lack of ease felt uncomfortable for me, but I listened.

"I met Ted at his athletic store," she continued. "It's all I ever wear, but I wanna look sexy for a change."

I stepped in to get a better look at Donna and try to extract some life. "Hi, I'm Sophia. I own The Garden of Eden. Nice to meet you, Donna."

She extended her hand. "Hi, Sophia. My boyfriend Ted said I would like you. He also told me that I should buy something sexy but not too sexy."

I smiled while I tossed the large, leopard pillow from the chair so she could sit down. "Well, you've certainly come to the right place. Would you like some champagne?"

My mind raced around the expansive dressing room while she talked, my eyes scanning the details of my creation. I stepped to the curtain, pulled it back, and motioned for one of the girls to come closer. "Can you get me two glasses of champagne?"

The girl handed Donna one of the glasses, and I clicked mine to hers. "Enjoy your champagne and relax while I gather a few pretty dresses for you."

When I returned to the dressing room, Donna was still sitting on the leopard chair, crying.

She gazed down at her cell phone and then peered up at me, a tear rolling down her face. "Ted flew to New York to ring the bell at the stock market, and while he was there, he hired a prostitute."

I couldn't hide my surprise—not of the story but of her revealing the intimate details to a stranger. "Are you sure? Who told you such a tale?"

She reached for the glass of bubbly while she stood to take the dresses from my hand.

I motioned for her to continue to sit in the sexy, leopard chair. "Relax, Donna. Let me do this for you. We aren't in any hurry."

She cried into the long, slender champagne glass. I watched a tear plop down to expand the bubbles inside the glass. Her words were almost incomprehensible, as she sobbed between the sips. "I just don't understand why he would tell me. Why did he tell me? To hurt me. To rip my heart right out of my chest? Why, Sophia?"

My mind raced. I had my reasons, but I wanted to step gently with my new friend. She wouldn't be ready for my brash answer. "Oh, Donna, I'm so sorry. Men are so immature at times. He's not thinking clearly. Maybe he had too much to drink after his day of celebration. Why not wait until he returns, so you can talk face to face?"

Still crying, she undressed so she could try on one of the dresses. "He's still married, Sophia, and he refuses to tell his five children about our relationship until his divorce is final. And now this." She sighed. "I don't think I can forgive him for this."

I took the next dress off the velvet hanger. I handed it to her after she took off the first dress. "Why don't you finish that glass of champagne and let me get you another one? I need another one too."

I stepped out to get two more glasses of champagne, and then I peeked back into the dressing room. "Donna, stop looking at your phone for just a few minutes. Don't answer his text yet. Sometimes silence is the best answer. Let's chat about this before you answer him."

I couldn't stop my mouth from moving. I had fury in my soul, as I hated cheaters. "You have a great body, girl.

Forget those gym clothes for a while. You need to show off your sexy, little body, girlfriend."

I could see that Donna felt embarrassed and lacked self-confidence, so I thought to reassure her with compliments. "You're so young and pretty. Don't hide it. Show me what you're hiding behind those track pants, sexy girl."

Donna whispered, "Ted's so jealous that, if I wear this dress with him, he'll fight with me all night about being too sexy. He prefers me in golf clothes. He has a lot of rules."

I didn't like the direction this conversation was going. I hated rules, especially from powerful men like Ted. I had known him for many years. We were members of the same country club, and our kids went to the same school.

Just then, I heard a voice from the next dressing room. "Excuse me, Sophia! It's me! Your old neighbor, Katherine!" A tall, blonde woman dripping in diamonds tucked her head out of the stall. She wore tailored pants and a cute blouse——conservative yet full of spirit. I wondered if she would like anything in my store; it didn't seem to be her style.

She stepped out to show me the dress she chose. "What do ya think of this little number? Do ya like it?"

Katherine held a sophisticated look with her oversized body; she was probably a beautiful woman before the sun captured her youthful skin. I remembered drinking dirty martinis with her and her ladies' golf league. They kept her skills sharpened on the course while bartenders kept her chilled martini glass ready for happy hours.

I recalled feeling so awkward inside the country club. It was such a different lifestyle than mine—and one I obviously didn't blend into very well. The traditional, wood-paneled walls felt cold and unwelcoming, a world so unfamiliar to mine. Intimidated by the country club atmosphere, William insisted my internal struggle to fit in came with the unwillingness to be friends with women I had nothing in common with. I agreed.

Katherine welcomed me into the group one Friday night, saying, "You look fabulous! I love your suit! Were you working today?" She giggled as if to poke fun at me for being a working girl. "I did. Just left the city. It's been a long day. I need a big dirty martini!" And, just like that, I briefly felt oddly part of this group of women who wore matching clothes and visors.

I greeted her, reminded of my feelings of insecurity so long ago. "My God, Katherine. How are you? How's Alex?"

Her husband was a retired gynecologist, and she loved to tell us wild stories about his weird requests in the bedroom. "He's good. I left him outside with the models. He's getting his rocks off staring at the young girls. That was the hottest fashion show, almost like a striptease! Such a great event! Thank you for including us!"

I handed Donna her dress while I tried to wrangle Katherine down a bit. "Let's get you in this sexy dress, Donna. It's going to look amazing on you. Try it on with these luscious kitten-heeled shoes. What size are you?"

I started to look through the stack of shoe boxes I kept in each dressing room, and then I handed Donna a gold, strappy shoe with a four-inch heel. "Try it on. It's going to look so hot on you."

Katherine's voice was loud. She never cared who heard what she had to say about her sex life with Alex. "I'm buying all five of these dresses. They all look fabulous, Sophia. My husband said, 'Buy it all, baby, as long as you know we're having girdle sex tonight!'"

My mind raced back to the night Katherine explained her husband's crazy fetish of fucking her while she wore a tight girdle. He said it made her pussy feel tighter while he was inside her.

I recalled a drunken party after a big golf tournament at the club. Alex whispered in my ear, "Katherine's not the greatest in bed, too damn ladylike for my tastes. But she makes a great wife if you like tasteful parties, knocking a ball around the course, and hot cookies out of the oven."

So many shady sides locked up inside those wood-paneled walls in the country club…

I was shocked at her willingness to share the intimate details of her strange sex life with a group of friends. I gave her credit for being so open about his request, and I must confess, I ran home to google the weird fetish. *I'll ask Stephanie, she'll know all about girdle sex fetishes!*

Donna tried on the next dress. She stepped out to show me, rolling her eyes into her head. She pointed slightly at Katherine's dressing room, making a crazy sign with her hands. "I love this one, Sophia. It makes me feel so pretty and sexy." She looked right into my eyes. "I don't look like a hooker in it, do I? Ted will say I look like a hooker."

I nodded, smiling at her. "You look so pretty in it, Donna. I'm not just saying that, either. You really do look amazing. I think you should tell him to go fuck himself if he says you look like a hooker. Pretty hypocritical, don't ya think? Or maybe you should ask him if you look like the hooker he had sex with the other night?" I hesitated, too late to take it back. "Sorry, that wasn't very nice of me."

Donna looked at me. Her eyes filled up with tears she couldn't hold back. "Ted said the whole time he was fucking that hooker he was thinking about me. He said she made him realize how much he loves me. I'm so hurt. I don't think I can ever forgive him."

"Forgiveness is a difficult thing to understand, isn't it? The human heart is the only thing in this world that weighs more when it's broken." She pondered. "I have to find a way to forgive him, I just have to…"

I handed her a tissue. She looked like a kid who needed a hug. "Why don't you sleep on it? I always feel better about things after a good night's rest."

Katherine stepped out of the dressing room holding the dresses she was ready to buy, interrupting my conversation with Donna. She had obviously been eavesdropping on our conversation. "If a girl wants to marry a man with money, she better be willing and able to fuck on command and tolerate a lot of bullshit, including girdle sex and cheating."

I giggled to be polite but wanted her to leave as soon as possible. "I suppose. I wouldn't know. I don't tolerate cheating, as you know! Thanks for shopping with me, Katherine. I hope to see you again." *What balls she has coming here to remind me of my cheating husband, take her money…*

She smiled. "We miss you at the club. Why don't you stop by for a martini, and I'll tell you all about my new boyfriend? He's our tennis pro, a sweetheart of a boy. It's a dirty martini kinda story!"

I grabbed her credit card. The only reason these bitches were included on my party list was to extract their money from their wallets into my cash register to get my sweet revenge on them for their betrayal. I was the evil one now. *She won't be back. Shadyside's out of her zip code!*

We kissed on both cheeks as though we were long-time girlfriends. I had no intention of returning to that awful place surrounded by dark-paneled walls that reminded me of an overpriced casket. I despised these imposters, who pretended to be my friends until ex-husband number three invited them to his fancy wedding, and they all forgot my name.

Donna obviously came into the store looking for advice and was not willing to leave without it. "I'm helping Ted design our new home in Sewickley Heights, but he won't tell his children he has a girlfriend. We've been dating for three years already. Isn't that weird? I just don't understand."

I wanted to tell Donna my true feelings about cheaters. I had strong opinions about a cheating man.

Fuck him and move on. I cut cheaters loose. I'm a runner.

I decided to take a slow approach with her instead. "Maybe you should give him some time, Donna. Everybody needs their own time to work through things at their own pace. This sexy dress will certainly get him to pay attention to you."

Her eyes were ginger-brown. When she looked sad, they darkened and dimmed. "A prostitute, Sophia. Why would he tell me about being with a prostitute? He coulda kept it a secret instead, just jumped on his jet without telling me." A tear ran down Donna's tiny cheek, and she brushed it away with her hand.

I felt sorry for the innocent girl. "Why do you think he betrayed you? Why even tell you all the little details about his private session with the prostitute?"

When the Kinsey report on male sexual behavior was published in 1948, it revealed, among its then scandalous findings, that up to sixty-nine percent of American men had paid for sex at some point in their lives. I laughed to myself as I recalled the research. Sixty-nine percent. Sixty-nine seemed like an ironic twist for the percentage of men.

Does a cheater's mentality come with wealth and power? I hate these women who tolerate their unfaithful husbands.

I knew so many of them.

They would discover the affairs and just sweep it under a rug of denial. I was reminded of one woman, especially; she told me she preferred not knowing the details about her fiancé's multiple rendezvous. Lauren was a petite woman who worked as a designer, and she had told me, "I know he has a wandering eye. I'll wait. He'll grow out of it!"

I barked back at her over a plate of pasta, twirling my fork vigorously around the linguine as the steam poured out of my body. "Dave's forty-five years old. When do you think he'll grow out of it? Maybe when he's too old to get it up! You must be kidding me, right?"

She married him even though he cheated the night before their wedding. I ignored her calls. So tired of the nonsense.

How do those women sleep next to the bastards knowing their dirty, little secrets? Do they smell the lover on his beard? Do they tolerate the cheating to buy a Gucci bag? What a price to pay.

"Sleep on it, Donna. Here's my cell if you want to call me. Why not join me for dinner some night? Do you have any girlfriends to talk to about your love life? I couldn't live without mine!"

The dressing room banter was starting to grate on my nerves. I immediately regretted giving Donna my number, but I wanted the conversation to end. I needed to get back to my other guests.

She continued talking on and on, while she finished trying on the other dresses. "I don't have time for girlfriends. Ted's so strict with me. All these stupid rules about what to wear just because he's the CEO of a big retail business doesn't mean he has the right to tell me what to do. I'm so sick of it."

I couldn't take her chatter and hated her lack of confidence. "You really let him tell you what to wear? Do you tell him what to wear? What makes him an expert in women's clothing?" I giggled. "I'm sure he listens to you, right? What's good for the goose is good for the gander, right? He takes your advice about his wardrobe, right?" I was burning mad inside and trying to keep my cool with my client, but I had a hard time biting my tongue. *I need a mouthguard!*

Donna stepped out of the dressing room and held the dress up against her body as she looked in the mirror. "What is it about men that makes them so jealous?"

I just couldn't stop myself. I couldn't resist the opportunity to help another woman, especially one who lacked self-confidence. "Jealous men are men with something to hide. Sorry, it's just true. Ted had something to hide. You just found out that he wanted to fuck a hooker."

She pondered but didn't answer as she changed into her track pants and t-shirt. I thought, *What an odd outfit for a grand opening party! I guess her CEO told her what to wear tonight. CEO should stand for Coldhearted Egomaniac Oaf in this case.*

Though afire with anger, I wanted to boost her ego. "Ted's secret obsession for a prostitute was something he shared with you before he did it, right? My ex-husband told me he wanted to swing before he did it. I admit, I hated that cheater, but I knew it was coming. I dumped him after sixteen years, lost everything except my integrity."

Suddenly, Donna's tone shifted as if I'd lit a fire in her belly. "You're right, Sophia. He did have something to hide. Now he's told me his secret, and I hate him for it. All this time he's been accusing me of fucking my ex-husband, fucking my golf coach, fucking my trainer, fucking the garbage man, and fucking the mailman. Yet, he's out fucking hookers!"

I knew it was time to reveal my truth. I talked as she tried on the next dress. "I remember Ted from my country club. He had a lot of strict rules for his soon-to-be ex-wife. Where are you going with a plain man like that one? He's a saltine cracker without salt!"

I was joking but trying to get her to see my point of view about him being so boring. "If you allow Ted to dictate your behavior, then he will continue to do it. I would rather be single than put up with a man telling me what to do."

"I know he's boring, and he's a picky eater. Did you know he only eats burgers and pizza? He won't even try pasta, let alone fish. He's boring, for sure, but I love him."

She's a vanilla wafer and he's a saltine without salt, yuck!

I knew she wouldn't change her mind about him. She loved his power and influence. It didn't surprise me how Donna quickly reverted to her old way of thinking, defending Ted's strange eating habits.

I grew tired of her banter, knowing she wasn't going to change her feelings for Ted. "Love. It's a complex word, isn't it? Do you want to try on any other dresses tonight, Donna?"

She gathered her purse and handed me one of the dresses. "No, I think I'll just take this one dress for tonight. The sexy one. I'll wear it for Ted tomorrow night when we're alone."

She's never going to change. "Sounds good, Donna. Thank you for shopping with me." I handed the dress to the girls to wrap and ring up the sale.

That's a lot of hard work for one dress. I need a stiff drink after that one!

Donna paid for her inexpensive, sexy dress, acting like she just purchased a Chanel dress from Saks. I thought, *She needs a lesson from Jayne about the art of giving a wealthy man her famous Chanel blow job for the exchange of fancy gifts!*

Her resentful smile was a clear indication of her frustration. "Thank you for helping me and for all the great advice. I appreciate your honesty."

I realized I was more than a boutique owner. I was going to be a full-time therapist who listened to all these dirty, little secrets coming from the dressing rooms. I wasn't just selling dresses but discovering that most people have a shady side. *If Stephanie could analyze them while they undressed, what a story we could write!*

I was exhausted from the unexpected confessions and nonstop conversations, but I was also impressed by my ability to once again earn a living doing something I truly loved. I had reinvented myself so many times, and this was just evidence that I could do it again.

I stepped outside for a breath of fresh autumn air. I noticed Jayne and Clinton in the distance. I had been so busy, I hadn't had a chance to spend time with them.

A moment passed by, then Kellie appeared out of nowhere and approached me. "Hey, Sophia. I'm Kellie. Remember me from South Beach a few months ago?" She pursed her lips, giving me her signature side-eyed smile. "Thanks for inviting me. Great fucking fashion show!"

Suddenly, she wants to know me!

I tried to be polite by offering her a seat on the stoop next to me. "I'm glad you could be here, Kellie. Yes, of course I remember you! Sit next to me. Tell me what you liked about the fashion show and the party. I want to know everything and what anyone had to say about it."

She sat down, carefully moving her dress under her hands before sitting on the alley seat. "I loved the sexy men at the door. Nice touch. My friend Margie has a hot date with one of them tonight!"

The crowd was thinning, and I felt the need to say goodnight to my guests. "Let's get together for lunch this week, and you can tell me all about it. My treat!"

She smiled. "You got it, Sophia. I had a great time. By the way, some hot, silver-haired fox wants to take you out on a date." I walked back inside the store, ignoring Kellie's comment about the potential hot date.

I invited Kellie and her cousin Monique purposely. Leanne insisted they both had to be on the guest list if I wanted to secure a write-up with Helena. She rarely missed a party, but when she did, she sent Kellie for the scoop. Kellie and Monique. The darlings of the scene column. If the world only knew their shady sides!

The women walked out together, swinging their Chanel quilted clutches and screaming for attention. They nicknamed themselves the cockroaches. I wanted to extract their stories and listen to all the juicy details about their torrid love affairs, scandalous rendezvous, and wild parties, but Leanne convinced me to play it down and wait for their invitation.

They giggled while their friend Margie strutted out with one of the bodybuilders who flaunted his nakedness at the front door. He was finally wearing a black t-shirt to cover up his bare-chest debut. "Hope you don't mind, Sophia. I dick-napped your friend!"

Kellie waved and said, "Come with us, Sophia! We're going to the new after-hours nightclub down the street!"

I wish I had the strength. I smiled. "I'll take a rain check. Don't do anything I wouldn't do!" I shouted. *I have them now!*

"Oh, Sophia, you have no idea!" She smacked her ass and quickly licked her fingers with approval.

I was finally alone in the store. While turning off the lights, I realized how much I loved the darkness of the night with the stars twinkling bright enough to light a path. I walked without fear, so proud of myself.

Leanne rang me and left a voicemail, saying, "How was the party? I want all the details. I wish I could have been there. Did the cockroaches show up? Call me."

She would have to wait until tomorrow.

I wanted to take in the twinkling city lights, sniff the autumn air, and listen to sirens in the distance while I walked back to my new home. I knew my mattress was waiting for me on the concrete floor, a smokestack on my horizon. I fantasized about my rockstar as I walked the streets. I was exhausted in a way that made my heart race. I was finally home.

Chapter Six

The Forbidden Fruit

I stood alone in the hallway of my beautiful city loft staring at all the boxes just delivered by the moving company. I wasn't looking forward to unpacking everything, but my goal was to have it all put away by night.

I knew I was overly ambitious, especially if I wanted to keep up my strength for something better than unpacking boxes. I had a hot date the next night with a gorgeous, young doctor who was going to teach me a few things about city life—hopefully from the comfort of my king-sized bed. I decided he would be my treat for finally taking a step toward creating my dream of living in the city.

We had met at Whole Foods earlier in the week. I had spotted him getting out of his sexy little red Porsche Turbo S Cabriolet with a beige interior. I had been a Porsche enthusiast since my high school crush on a rich boy who had gotten one from his parents as his graduation gift. He was wearing pale green scrubs. I hoped his untamed facial hair might be the hallmark of a wild spirit.

He snuck up behind me in the produce section and quietly whispered in my ear, "You look so beautiful grabbing those peaches. Are you new to the city? I'll bet you're juicy in bed." He had extremely penetrating eyes, blue as the sea.

I felt anxious for the touch of a masculine hand and longed for passion. I smiled at him as he intoxicated me with charm.

"Let me take you to dinner Friday night. Those lucky peaches are getting all your attention."

I knew he was a flirt, but I liked it and played along. "You love my peach-grabbing skills, do ya? I should add that to my resume."

He leaned in, smelling incredible as his body touched mine. "Can I have your number, Peaches? Give a guy a chance to pick you up, say around six tomorrow night? We can make a peach pie if you want. What do you say?"

I nodded yes. I couldn't resist his charm.

I smiled as I recalled our initial interaction and the tingles of anticipation I had before our date. The truth was, I liked the chase game and the attention from my lovers—an innocent brush with foreplay. I saw the chase as part of the act of lovemaking, a heated desire to find the right kind of lover—a lover who could gently soothe my aching heart and rid me of the painful, heartbreaking memories that still lingered in my soul.

I hadn't been out on a date in over fifteen years. That opened me to the idea of taking on a new lover—a little present to me! I hated sexual hypocrisy, it outraged me. Who thought a man who slept around was a stud, but if a woman had a lover, she was a nymphomaniac?

I giggled as I walked toward the box marked "bar" and dug through it to find an unopened bottle of Grey Goose vodka. I decided to have a martini to celebrate my accomplishment. I had thought dating was going to be difficult after my divorce, but Cupid had proven me wrong!

I was finally home, in a place I had only dreamed about until then—a city loft with soaring, factory-style windows, original brick walls exposing twenty-five-foot raw ceilings, polished concrete floors, and an exceptional view of the river in the distance with factory smokestacks blowing steam into the sky. The residents had access to a marina for docking boats, a beautiful infinity swimming pool, grilling areas for barbecues, and green space for gathering family and friends for picnics.

I absolutely loved it.

Listening to the sensual music of Barry White while I enjoyed my cocktail, I sang along and twirled around in my eight-hundred-square-foot loft; it felt like a luxurious penthouse in the sky!

I was grateful I had decided to pay the Geek Squad extra money to connect my soundbar when they mounted my television in the living room. I danced over to the stereo control with the martini in my hand, smiling from ear to ear, knowing life was about to get a whole lot better.

I did it. It's not Miami, or even Los Angeles, but Shadyside is going to be where I create my new life as a single girl in the city.

My kids were grown. I had my first baby when I was nineteen years old, so life had been complicated until now. My turn arrived to find happiness, find peace, and get a piece—a sweet, young piece of ass. I laughed as I walked to the window to gaze at the river swiftly flowing beneath my loft, smokestacks in the distance.

Heavenly.

Shadyside was young, growing, and still developing as a neighborhood. Trendy shops, swanky restaurants, and cool nightclubs opened almost daily. These suited the quaint upper-middle-class area with well-educated residents who had plenty of disposable income.

Gazing out the window, I continued to reflect on my new situation in life. I couldn't wait to get laid when I felt like it, no hassle of a relationship.

Shadyside was exactly what I wanted in a city, and I knew it immediately. I had caught city fever on my first glimpse of urban life with my favorite Aunt Audrey so many years ago. Until then, I had sacrificed that dream for raising a family in a country club in the suburbs.

I sipped my martini, twirling the olives to stir the bottom with the stick. I loved to watch the vodka meld with the blue cheese from the olives. I embraced my time alone, thinking about my life. I didn't have regrets. The first few sips of the martini went straight to my head. I loved the feeling! I had put myself in my own rehab—a January dry month in October, a hiatus from alcohol, or whatever you wanted to call it. I often decided to take a break from partying while I spent time re-evaluating my life.

My empty martini glass and the calming buzz inside my head let me know I needed another. I had to admit that I thought I had mastered the art of martini-making when bartending at the hotel in my twenties, but it was time to create a city girl martini, just for me!

I started my martini research by reading the sides from the James Bond movies. I quickly discovered that Ian Fleming invented the Vesper martini for his character James Bond. *So, why can't I have a special martini, shaken not stirred?* Bond's special martini was named after his lover, Vesper Lynd. I needed my own cocktail.

My recipe for a perfect vodka cocktail included my preferred Grey Goose and a splash of Riccadonna Vermouth from Italy, expensive but worth the splurge. Then, after a light shake, a perfect, blue-cheese-stuffed olive served as the perfect garnish—the salty olive and the creamy blue cheese made the martini.

Maybe the name should be a tribute to the man who took my virginity, a wet and wonderful night of cumming with a rockstar. That's it—my Rockstar Martini! Yes, that's it!

I ever so gently shook another Rockstar Martini. I had bought blue cheese olives at the state store while in the checkout line, but I would walk to the Italian specialty market to buy real olives and blue cheese the next day. Then

I would stuff my own olives. Mine were far better, and the young, Italian deli counter boys were the sweetest eye candy!

I caught a glimpse of myself in the full-length, silver mirror leaning against the wall. I stopped and posed before slapping my own ass. "Not so bad for a single thirty-nine-year-old woman," I said aloud.

A squeeze of a peach and a slap on the ass sounds like a country-music song, Sophia.

❖

I laughed, spilling the martini down the front of my t-shirt. I figured I would be talking out loud a lot now that I lived alone. Although it felt strange to be alone, I knew I was going to love it. "Oh well, Sophia. I guess you better just get used to it. It's just you and the pigeons now."

Just then, I heard a knock at my door. Peeping through the little hole, I spied my crazy friend, Leanne. I had been hoping she would stop by. I hadn't spent much time with her since we brewed that evil full moon wish ritual in my kitchen.

I opened the door to find her holding a magnum of Cristal Champagne. Her favorite appetizer at any affair, she thought the bubbly just added a twist before a cocktail. "Hi, Chick-EE."

I threw the door open. "Oh girl, get your ass in here."

We hugged so tight while standing in the doorway with Leanne's heavy Gucci tote bag falling to the floor as she lifted me off the ground to embrace me even tighter. "I missed you, sexy mama. Sorry I had to fuck and run the other night. My nanny had the night off and my fucking husband was babysitting!"

Leanne leaned back, gazed at me, grinned, and hugged me again. "You look fucking hot as hell, girlfriend. Fucking sizzling hot! Whatever you've been doing, keep it going!"

I missed Leanne so much, but I had avoided her on purpose during my divorce from ex-husband number three. Admittedly, Leanne and I had proven to be bad influences on each other. "I'm sorry I didn't call you back. I know you get it. Sometimes a girl needs some time to reset her algorithm."

She laughed, and it sounded like the clinking crystal of a running brook. "It's cool, Sophia. I had a lot going on as well. I missed you though! No more of that shit. Reboot with me next time!"

Leanne looked up at the ceiling as she walked around the loft. "Oh my God, girl. This place is a thousand times better than you described it on the phone. You got yourself a city crib."

She loved to listen to rap music and knew all the lyrics. She turned the dial on the stereo to play a Ludacris song. As it was emanating from the sound system, she began to sing along. She memorized the song as if she was the artist, thrusting her hips like Elvis Presley, grinding around the room and holding the bottle of champagne in the air.

Leanne could have been an entertainer; she knew how to work the crowd. Her eyes glistened like a sparkler. Her smile extended into the heavens. She loved rap music and begged me to fly to Detroit to see Eminem perform live in concert last month. I regretted turning her down, but I had been searching for a new place to live in the city, and I didn't have time to be frivolous and carefree.

I laughed at her comment and knew she felt genuinely happy for me. "Thanks, girl. It's sweet, right? I can't wait to play in the city and walk home to this beautiful place." I giggled. "No reason to be sad here."

Leanne couldn't stop looking around, gazing out the enormous windows. "I love the graffiti all over the walls. I can relate to these artists. Did you see this graffiti on the windowsill? It says 'love.' How appropriate for you, right? It's an amazing home, Sophia. What a place to play!"

I wanted to tell Leanne why I really chose this building over all the other ones. I was fascinated by the history, built circa 1901 and designed by architect Frederick J. Osterling. In 1860, Thomas Armstrong, the son of Scottish-Irish immigrants from Derry, joined with John D. Glass to open a one-room shop carving bottle stoppers from cork by hand. His company grew to be the largest cork supplier in the world by 1890.

I was a history enthusiast, but I kept that little secret between me and myself. I liked it that way.

The building was abandoned before its renovation. The homeless people and drug addicts who made this their home for nearly a decade were the ones who created the graffiti and brought a new energy inside this once-vibrant cork factory. I had visited once, during that time, when I led a team of volunteers to deliver food, blankets, and basic necessities to homeless people. My mind raced with the details of that week-long mission to make a difference in the city; it felt so good to give back.

I kept that part of the story to myself. She would never relate to such a strange way of thinking; she wasn't the girl who stopped in the streets to offer a homeless person a dollar. She truly didn't know there were homeless people in our city because her world didn't see that side of the tracks—the side I came from. The wrong side.

She walked toward the box next to my painted patina cocktail bar and touched the vintage martini glasses so neatly perched inside the box waiting for my attention. "These glasses are sweet! Are you using them or just looking at them? Mama needs a big martini; we have so much to catch up about."

She pulled out a little baggie filled with white powder, knotted tight to keep the magic inside. Then she rolled her trusted hundred-dollar bill into a straw-like vessel and poured the white fairy dust onto the counter. She never hesitated to snort a line anywhere, as if cocaine was just part of the food triangle—something everyone did to survive.

She did two lines and handed the bill to me. "Come on, girlfriend. Have a little bump to help you get started. You big baby, you need to lighten up a bit. Don't you know it's time to party? You fucking deserve it."

I took the bill without hesitation, snorted a line, and choked it back into my throat.

Leanne laughed loudly and shouted, "Oh-la-la! You're such a lightweight! Do another line, you big baby! It's the South Beach disco dust, the magical powder! There's a story for another day!" She winked.

I rolled my eyes. "Oh, girl. I'm just so fucking happy right now. It doesn't take much for me."

Leanne wore the cute little shit-eating grin she used to get attention. She played it using her big green eyes to lure you in. She took a sip of her martini and ambled toward my bedroom to see what it looked like. "Oh God, Chick-EE. Now this is what I'm talking about!" She scanned the horizon and gasped. "The view of the city is breathtaking! Those smokestacks are unbelievable. It's like something out of a fucking movie!"

I grinned and nodded.

She pointed out the window and then back to the wall facing the smokestacks. "You gotta face the bed in this direction and hang that sexy chandelier above your bed so you can wake up to its beauty every morning!"

I loved hearing what she had to say about design with her traditional, well-trained designer eyes, although we had very different styles. She was fortunate enough to be properly trained at the Parsons School of Design. The four-year BFA degree earned her the right to charge clients high rates and buy expensive fabrics.

Her compliments meant so much to me since my experience in interiors came from dumpster diving, producing commercials for clients with little to no money, and spending an enormous amount of time in thrift shops.

I smiled. "I thought the same thing, especially in the morning when the sun rises, right?"

Leanne took my hand and led me over to the mattress on the floor. Squeezing my hand as we dropped down to sit, she said, "You're the early bird. This toot fairy prefers crashing at four a.m., not waking up at that hour!"

I giggled. "The early bird catches the worm!"

She always had a comeback for my silly clichés, and we shared the love for them equally. "Who cares about the fucking worm unless it's on the very bottom of a bottle of great tequila!"

I laughed. I loved early mornings. She wouldn't understand, especially since she had been through four nannies already, and a housekeeper prepared breakfast for her son so she could rise from her luxurious linen sheets any time she felt she was ready.

She popped the cork. As the champagne bubbles spilled out over the top, she licked the bottle's rim, trying to catch the bubbles down the side before they dripped on the mattress. She glanced at me and laughed hysterically. "Your mattress is wet! Now keep it that way!"

Leanne sprinkled a little white powder on her wrist for me. I snorted it. My mind was racing, but it was worth the buzz to reconnect with her. "This is exactly why I had to keep you away from me; you're a bad influence." I threw her a conspiratorial glance. "I love you for it."

She giggled. "Oh sure, blame me. I don't give a fuck. I have big shoulders!"

Leanne couldn't stop talking, and she was squirming all over the mattress with anticipation. "I met this guy. I call him the vampire because he only comes after dark!"

I raised an eyebrow.

She had the most sophisticated giggle except when she was high and talked about sex with me. During those times, she snorted with excitement, unable to keep herself intact. "If you think the vampires in the *True Blood* series are hot, wait 'til you meet my vampire! Last night, he told me my pussy tastes like a sweet, red cherry! Now he calls me his Cherry Bomb. That's love to me!"

We belly-laughed back on the mattress, remembering how much it meant to us to be real when we were together. Our sassy sense of humor made our friendship so special, unlike any other.

"Cherry Bomb. Jesus. He's a keeper!" I tickled her. "I have a date with a guy who says he likes my peaches! It must be fruit season!"

She giggled. "Yeah, the forbidden fruit season!"

She grabbed my left ass cheek with her hand, squeezing it so hard it hurt. "Here's a peach for ya. You're a juicy peach. I'm so happy you're here in the city and back in my life, bitch!"

I missed her laugh so much. "Lea, does Markus have any idea where you are right now? He was so pissed the last time you were with me, remember?"

Leanne got dead serious as she sat straight up on the mattress. She faced me with her lips tight. Anger fueled her soul when it came to talking about her husband. "Markus can go fuck himself. I'll do whatever the fuck I want from now on. He's such a dick."

I nodded. She was pissed at Markus for being investigated for tax evasion. Maybe he tried to extort money to keep up with their expensive lifestyle. There had to be reasons for his manipulation of the law.

I wondered what he was thinking when he obviously knew what he was doing. It's easier to steal from an anonymous, large organization, like the government, than from an individual.

"He's probably going to serve time in federal prison and lose his law practice. He's such a fucking idiot with no consideration for our new baby boy or my interior design business, let alone my fucking reputation in this town."

I was feeling high from the cocaine but felt sympathetic to her dilemma. "I'm sorry, Lea. What are you going to do? Fuck the vampire and hope he turns you so you can live forever with him as your maker? You'll be just like our girl, Sookie Stackhouse, in *True Blood*."

She laughed but then grew serious for a minute. "I'm going to stay in Florida for the winter. Markus claims he'll put a million dollars in my account if he goes to prison. He's so full of shit. But if he does it, I'm moving full-time with my son and nanny to Boca Raton—The Mouth of the Rat. Sounds sexy, right?"

I smiled. "The same house with the fish spitting water into the pool? The house with the hot, young delivery boy?"

She smiled. "Not that one but one in the same neighborhood so my pizza guy can eat my seafood pie!" She giggled.

Leanne snorted another line and passed the little baggie to me. I pushed it away, knowing I already had enough. "I'm high as a kite, girl. I can't snort coke like you do; you're the nose when it comes to coke. Follow the nose, it always knows! Or should I call you Sookie Stackhouse?"

She sipped the last few drops of champagne from the bottle and then licked the rim. "You're such a big baby. Just take one more line. Be a man, for fuck's sake."

I snorted another line with the famous one-hundred-dollar bill. "Remember when we were on the 9-11 fundraising committee for the firemen fund?"

She did a bump and smiled. "Oh, fuck yeah. I remember. I remember those country club bitches we nicknamed that night, remember? We called them all The High Society Rich Bitch Club. Those fucking cunts with their snooty noses so far up each other's asses."

"I remember them well."

Leanne rambled on, "We certainly gave them something to talk about, didn't we? Whatever happened to Helena?"

I shook my head.

"I have no idea, she doesn't tell me shit, cupcake! She sent Kellie and her cousin Monique to my grand opening party, remember? The cockroaches had a blast, but the queen was nowhere in sight."

I laughed at the memory. "My husband was pissed that we danced with the firemen all night and wore their big red hats while we danced on the bar! Oh my God. I totally forgot about it!"

She frowned, growing angry from all the memories. "Yeah. Those fucking bitches were really pissed when they found out how much fucking money we raised for charity! Shocked the shit out of them. Didn't we, Sophia? Those fucking high society bitches!"

We loved our little secret nicknames, especially the one for all the wealthy women who thought they were comparable to Capote's swans. This was the little town of Shadyside, for Christ's Sake, not Hollywood or Washington. These snooty bitches barely climbed out of the boondocks, let alone climb a social ladder of elite status. Get real!

I poked her. "Maybe we should have nicknamed these elite bitches 'the Swans.' You know, like Capote's swans?" *Even though Leanne was one of them, at least she owned her imperfections, so she was different. Her infidelities were part of her healing.*

They so wanted to be unguarded. They appeared to have everything a trophy wife could ever want—big homes, unlimited access to money, wealthy husbands, and all the glitz and glamour a princess could dream of having—well, until you got a peek inside their drama-filled lives.

They had shady sides, just like the rest of us; they all had dirty secrets and sins. We knew they did.

"Yeah, those bitches only wish their husbands didn't want to fuck us, but they did and probably still do, motherfuckers," she continued. "Do you remember how many phone calls you got after your divorce? I just know you kept the list in case we ever need it. Right, Sophia? You kept a list of names?"

"I did keep the list of names. I wrote them all down in that little black book you gave me. I wrote the stories with the names and pushed the little black book behind my lingerie collection for safekeeping. Their names are all nestled among my panties. Appropriate, right!"

Leanne's phone rang and she answered. I could hear Markus screaming at her. "Where the fuck are you, Leanne? I'm in court early tomorrow morning, and I wanted to have dinner with my wife. Remember, you're still my wife."

I laughed, covering my mouth with my hands as I whispered to her, "You are the only single wife in the city."

She punched me, putting her hand over my mouth.

She barked back at him, "I left you a fucking note. I'm out for a few hours. Dinner is in the fridge, and our nanny has our son in his room. Go up and say hello to your son for a fucking change."

She hung up without saying goodbye, and Markus rang her right back, shouting, "What the fuck, Lea? Don't you ever hang up on me. You're a fucking bitch. Get your ass home, right now."

I was used to the colorful conversation between the two of them. They often argued in front of me, even before his trouble with the feds. "Just go home," I said. "It's the night before his court hearing, so give the big baby what he wants."

She frowned, not easily persuaded. "Fuck him. I'm not going home until my vampire licks my pussy. I want to hear him tell me my pussy tastes like a sweet cherry again. It keeps me going during this shitstorm investigation."

"Oh my God, girl. A sweet cherry? What a line. You're a sweet cherry, and I'm a juicy peach. I think we're both fruitcakes for falling for a line of bullshit."

We both laughed so hard. Leanne was holding her crotch, so she didn't pee in her pants. "I can't take it, Sophia. I missed you so much. I hope that bastard gets a life sentence so we can be together forever!"

Leanne got up off the mattress, spilling the rest of her martini all over the floor. "Whoopsie Daisy. Remember when we used to say 'Whoopsie Daisy' every time we spilled our cosmos?"

I got up and twirled around the bedroom and into the kitchen to find the paper towels. "I say fuck it. Whoopsie Daisy, I guess my new cleaning boy will have to lap it up off the floor."

I walked over to grab my phone and pretended I was talking to my hot, new housekeeper. "Hello, cleaning boy. Can you come over? I just had a Whoopsie Daisy. Oh, and by the way, I like it when you're naked on your hands and knees, rubbing and scrubbing up all my dirty, little messes. Now be a good boy and fuck me."

Leanne added, "Make sure you like to lick a cherry pussy. We don't like little boys who don't like cherries! Oh, and peaches!"

She's just as naughty as me. We share a naughty mind. We like to think we have golden pussies!

She pushed open the large, eight-foot windowpane in the bedroom overlooking the busy street below. A cool, autumn breeze blew in, further brightening her mood. "Hey, everyone," she shouted out the window, "My girlfriend has the hottest fucking loft in the city. There's a party going on right here."

Someone screamed back at Leanne, "Hey, sexy. Want some company?"

She loved the chase as much as I did, which was one of the many reasons we were so dangerously bad together. "Sorry, I already have a hot date with a vampire tonight. I'm Sookie Stackhouse."

I chuckled. "Let's drink another Rockstar Martini!"

We belly-laughed into the kitchen where we poured another martini. "These are going down real smooth. I love this bar, and I love your new Rockstar Martini. James Bond style."

Leanne reached into her oversized Gucci tote bag, pulled out a brown envelope, and handed it to me. "I want you to have this, from me."

I opened the envelope, and there was a stack of cash inside—a lot of cash. "I can't take this, girl. You're gonna need it."

She threw me a stern look with pursed lips. "I won't need it. I have plenty; my idiot husband gave me twenty thousand for my birthday a few weeks ago. I want you to have half of it to use to buy merchandise for your new store. I'll take a credit and use it to buy stuff. I might not have access to cash in a few months. Just take it to get you started. I love you, and I'm so proud of you." She hugged me. "You're my soul sister, girl."

I hugged her back. I couldn't believe her generosity. "We're like sisters from another mother." I choked up and could barely get the words out to thank her for her gift. *I have two younger sisters, but neither were close to me.* "I love you, girl, and now you have a gorgeous city loft. You'll always have another home as long as I'm alive."

Sometimes, friends become family. And, in my case, it was true.

Leanne got a huge grin on her face and then looked at me seriously for a change. "You better fuck some young, beautiful man in this bed this weekend, or I'm going to do it for you. Promise me—pinky promise me, girl."

My eyes lit up with enthusiasm about my secret meeting with the doctor at the grocery store. "I have a hot date tomorrow night—a guy I met at Whole Foods." I smiled. "He's a smart guy who is actually taking me to dinner—a real dinner date. And he drives the sexiest little red Porsche ever! You know I love a great car to match the intelligent man who drives it!"

She was not interested in boring conversation over a plate of pasta. "Fuck dinner! Bring him up here and fuck his brains out; that's what you really need. You need to get fucked in this bed, damnit. Just go for it! How long has it been already?"

"He's young, and he's handsome. And better yet, he's smart. You know I can't fuck stupid. I'm a sapiosexual. I love big brains, and I cannot lie."

Leanne started singing the lyrics to "Baby Got Back," by Sir Mix-a-Lot. She thought she was a rapper, and we busted out laughing because she knew all the words.

"How long since you fucked a man, Sophia?"

"It's been a year, big deal!"

"Why do you need smart? So, you can talk about world politics during sex? Or maybe you want to discuss the female anatomy? Please. Smart is so overrated. I married smart and look where it got me. Smart enough to go to prison for tax evasion. Yeah, real fucking intelligence there."

Leanne's phone rang. She answered abruptly, assuming it was Markus again. "What the fuck do you want already? What?"

But it wasn't Markus. It was her new lover, the vampire. She leaned in close to me so I could hear his voice saying, "Where's my cherry bomb? I'm waiting for you, baby."

We giggled like schoolgirls.

She smiled so big her gums were showing. "Oh my God, babe. I'm so sorry. I thought you were my husband.

Yes, I'm on my way down. See you in a few. Ciao, lover boy."

Leanne looked at me with a huge grin on her face.

She lights up when she talks about her young, hot boy toys. They bring out the best in her now.

"On your way then?" I tilted my head and reflected her grin right back.

"I gotta run, girlfriend. I'll see you tomorrow. Mommy needs a tongue lashing from her vampire. Let's use that as our code name if you text or call me. We can pretend we're talking about the hot series, *True Blood.* I'm sure Markus has my phone tapped."

My face was glowing from all the laughter. "I can't wait to hear all about it, Cherry Bomb!"

She tied her Gucci bag together and kissed me on the cheek. "I'll tell you all about it when I see you next time. Remember, no sex-texting me. I don't want my fucking husband finding out about my sexy vampire. You know he's always creeping on my phone."

I knew all about Markus's spy work after he hired a private detective to follow her on our weekend girls' trip to South Beach. "Oh, God. I can't believe you fucked that detective just to steal the evidence he had on you! Thank God the guy was hot!"

Leanne laughed. "Fuck him and his fucking detectives; he'll see it all the next time. I'll fucking let him watch me fuck the next detective."

I knew I was Leanne's alibi tonight; she had the perfect night planned with her vampire. In the last few months, Leanne had several boy toys, and we nicknamed every one of them. There was her youngest boy, a nineteen-year-old who had thick, black hair. And because he fucked like a rabbit and flopped around in the back seat of his daddy's white Rolls Royce, we called him Flopsy Mopsy. There was the fireman who had a long, skinny dick that reached her most erogenous zones. We called him The Hose.

I knew her betrayal to her husband would get worse if Markus was sentenced to prison.

We kissed on both cheeks, and she poured out a puddle of white powder on the countertop. "Swish it up with your bill or save it for a rainy day, like your fucking boring dinner date with the doctor guy tomorrow night."

Leanne was a ball of fire, and tonight she was exceptionally hot. She was out the door in a flash and on the street below, calling my phone. "You better be proud of yourself, chick-EE. This is a brave move, on your part. None of us girls have a set of balls like you. Nighty night. Love you."

I grabbed the stash of cash from Leanne and tucked it inside my Louis Vuitton duffle bag in the back of my closet. I piled a stack of shoeboxes in front of it and threw a coat over it. I would take it to the bank on Monday. I went back to unpacking the box of alcohol and began setting bottles on the new piece of furniture I had just bought from my friend, Violet's, furniture store.

I thought about my struggles. I had worried about money since I had been a single mother. *God, I wish I had someone to have my back. It sure would feel good for a change, but I also know nobody hustles harder than a woman who doesn't like asking people for anything.* I was that kind of woman.

I could always count on Leanne to help me escape my worries.

Wish I could be her for a week, with a million bucks in the bank, all my bills paid, a live-in nanny for my baby, and a gorgeous mansion with a full-time maid and a sexy vampire to lick my pussy.

◆

When my phone rang, it startled me. It was Violet. She was close by and wanted to stop in to say hello and see the new furniture in the loft. The bar collection looked amazing on the sideboard. I couldn't wait for her to see it and share a Rockstar Martini with me.

In the background, I heard her trying to start her big, white Hummer. She screamed, "Fuck. I hate this fucking car. I'll be there in about fifteen minutes if this fucking truck starts. It's been acting weird. Can I park in your parking lot?"

I smiled while I swooped up the cocaine from the kitchen counter and put it away in a small, white MAC cosmetic container. I saved the coke for a rainy day.

I love hanging out with Violet but would never dream of doing drugs with her, especially coke.

"Let me know if it starts. I can bring my jumper cables if you need them. And yes, pull next to my car. I'll leave the door unlocked. I'm in loft 1711."

She walked in carrying a gift bag filled with tissue. Violet lit up. "Oh my God, girl. This place is incredible. The concrete floors are killer!" She walked past me and into the bedroom. "Shit, look at this closet! It's big enough to be a room. You gotta put a dresser in here, Sophia."

I loved collaborating with Violet. I appreciated her funky approach to design; she was a gifted artist. I knew I made the right choice by my friend's overwhelming reaction.

"I know, right? It's truly all I ever dreamed about. I'm so excited to put everything together. And thanks again for dumpster diving for me. I love the Astroturf in the store, it looks great, right?"

We went straight to the vodka bottle. "Let me make you my famous Rockstar Martini!"

She smiled. "Yummy! Sounds sexy! Yes!"

I poured the Grey Goose into the shaker over ice, added a dash of the vermouth and two blue cheese olives to both glasses, then gently clicked our glasses together.

"Cheers, girlfriend. Here, I brought you a little something—a housewarming gift."

I opened the bag. "Oh my God, girl. I love them. Thank you."

She had wrapped up two ceramic pigeons, which were so unique.

She giggled; her large smile illuminated her face. "I figured it's just you and the pigeons now! I love you, Sophia."

Violet immediately started to cry. "I think Kennedy is stealing from me. I found bank charges for stuff she bought for her beach house. I didn't know she was paying for her beach house furniture through our business account. What should I do?"

I felt surprised but comforted her, exclaiming, "Oh no, Violet. Are you sure?"

Kennedy was part of the High Society Rich Bitch Club, which meant she wore a prim and proper mask disguising her dirty, little secrets—except from us girlfriends of course. We had her all figured out, or we thought so, anyway.

She was a Southern girl who used her charm to get her way with her very handsome husband, who we all believed was hiding his homosexuality. She convinced him to buy her a beach house on the outer banks of North Carolina. He believed she wasn't cheating on him, and she played the game so well. She loved fucking on the side but lied to all of us about her bad behavior; being shady wasn't part of her perfect country club lifestyle. We hated liars.

She didn't fool me. I recalled one Sunday morning when I walked to their store early and caught her in the act on the store's loading dock. She saw me walk through the back door to discover her in the middle of her nasty, sex play. "Sophia, what the fuck?"

I looked at Kennedy and her city cop still dressed in his police uniform. Her cropped, black hair was tangled around the cop's fingers while he stood behind her, fucking her rapidly. The sweat poured down over his face as he pounded her skinny, little body.

"Oh God, fuck me, Mike. Arrest me. Fuck me."

I was so pissed at her irresponsibility. "The fucking door was unlocked, Kennedy. You're lucky it was me and not a customer."

As I walked out, I could hear her crying out, "Fuck me harder, Mike. Fuck me harder. Arrest me for fucking you in public."

Mike the cop couldn't pass a fitness test if his life depended on it. His big belly was evidence of all the donuts he must have consumed while strolling along the city streets looking for thugs. He wasn't attractive either—no charming personality to disguise his obesity. We all wondered what it was about the guy that made her willing to cheat on her handsome husband. Was it a big donkey dick? Maybe fat lips perfect for pussy licking? God, we giggled so hard as we made up reasons to explain the weird attraction.

Later that night, I ignored Kennedy's calls. She begged me to hear her out. "Can this be our little secret? I really need to save my marriage. My son is addicted to drugs, and my daughter is fighting an eating disorder. I'm trying to be a better wife. I can't resist a man in uniform though. Please call me back."

I ignored her messages, knowing she was a liar and a cheater. We all wrongfully accused Kennedy of being a slut, but we had our reasons. She wasn't any different than the rest of the women who openly cheated except she denied her infidelities making her far worse than any of the other sluts.

She insisted we were wrong about her sexual romps, accusing us of exaggerating these nasty sex stories as if we were insane to think she would be a cheater, a manipulator, and a slut—absolutely! We committed the girl-on-girl shaming, a revenge against a trader, she needed to confess her sins but refused so many times. She was our victim.

There was no turning back no matter what. It wasn't fair, no doubt, but her denial made her guilty of a crime far worse than cheating. The betrayal to us was her crime.

A man in uniform? Why not choose a fucking mailman, an army sergeant, or someone else less gross? I went back to my work and turned off my phone. She wasn't worth my time.

Violet's phone rang, breaking my recollections.

She rushed to answer it. "Hello? Oh, hi, Jerome. What the fuck?" A smile turned her face into a glowing globe of happiness. "Where did you go last night? I was waiting at the bar for you, but you didn't come back inside after your call."

The last time we had been out in the city, we spent the night drinking vodka gimlets with a new recruit, Keyaron, and a retired Pittsburgh Steeler, Jerome. They smoked a joint inside her Hummer, Jerome claiming this kind of weed wasn't traceable in their blood tests. She claimed they were only friends, but I wasn't so sure.

Violet hung up the phone and turned to look at me. "Do you remember the night we went out with Jerome and Keyaron and he introduced us to his friend, James? Well, I met James for drinks last night. He's so dreamy, and now we're hanging out."

I remembered James. I thought he was a big dummy. I wasn't ever impressed by professional athletes. James was four times stronger than his teammates, and so fierce on the field. He was large and in charge, and he knew it. I just didn't get it, but Violet loved athletes. James was the leading linebacker, known for his hard-hitting styles during games. Sure, he was a talented athlete, no doubt. But lovemaking didn't seem to be his thing, more like a "wham-bam" thank you ma'am kinda guy.

I pressed Violet for more details. "Hanging out? What the fuck does that mean, Violet?"

We laughed, but she knew exactly what it meant.

Violet was like a giddy schoolgirl telling me the story. "James is the same player in bed as he is on the football field—aggressive. Just last night, he ripped off my jeans and my thong underwear with one hand, lifted me off the floor, and threw me against the wall to fuck me like a defensive tough guy. I liked it!" Violet covered her mouth to hide her smile while she giggled. "He's such a bad boy. Ferocious, my James."

I walked toward her, looked her in the eyes with all seriousness, and handed her the fancy Rockstar truth juice, saying, "Jesus, Violet, just be careful. I worry about you. Just make sure he wears a condom."

She giggled. "Oh God, Sophia, really? I know. He wore a rubber!"

I turned to her. "Good. God knows how many girls he's fucking at the same time. I'm sorry, just being honest with you. Those guys are like fucking rabbits, fucking for fuck's sake, you know what I mean."

Violet looked surprised by my reaction. She knew we both loved great sex, but I was dead serious about the condom stuff.

"Really, Sophia, please don't tell anyone about me and James. And forget what I said about Kennedy and the beach house furniture. I need to ask her about it. She'll be so pissed if she knows I told you." I felt bad keeping my discovery. "Your secret's safe with me, girl. No worries. This sweet little HOHO has turned into a spongy, cream-filled Twinkie."

I busted out laughing, and she laughed so hard, her cocktail came spitting out.

"Yes! She's a fucking Twinkie. She must have a golden pussy, a snapping gyro. She gets fucked more than I do, and I'm single!"

I winked at Violet. I knew she needed to laugh. "The HOHO is officially nicknamed the Twinkie! Thank God that's settled! Now, promise me you're going to use a condom with James. These guys are HOHOs. Trust me."

"James just asked me to meet him at a new nightclub grand opening party tomorrow night. Will you come?" Violet seemed excited to change the subject and raised both eyebrows, her eyes wide. "Have you heard about the place called Sanctuary?"

I smiled but hesitated to answer. I walked around the large box holding the bar collection and started unwrapping glasses. "Girl, I gotta get my loft put together, and I have a hot date. I really can't go. Maybe you can take Rondaya. She's always game for a party. I'll call her now, okay?"

Violet frowned like a little kid. "Okie Doke, Artichoke! I want you to come too. I like hangin' out with you the best!"

I giggled. "That's because I'm the boss, applesauce!"

Violet and I felt so connected as friends. She lacked confidence, and I needed someone to trust. *We make a good team.*

I would make a great business partner for her artistic talents. I would never dream of stealing from her, as I longed for someone to trust. She was a friend who was so easy to love. *Stop thinking. Listen to Violet and enjoy the moment.*

Rondaya never answered her phone. She always claimed she had a reason for not answering the first time. She told me a while back that it was just a thing. "You know, to make everyone believe you're too busy to pick up on the first call."

This time, she called back seconds later. "Hey, girl. What's up?"

The sound of musicians tuning guitars and talking in the background let me know Rondaya was in a recording studio. *Her happy place.*

"Violet has two VIP tickets to a new nightclub party, Sanctuary, tomorrow night. She wants you to go with—can you?"

I heard the muffled sound of covering the phone while she asked the musicians to turn down the volume. "Yeah, sure. About what time?"

Her guitarist, Jimmy, called hello to me, so I added, "Say hi back from me! Violet's here now. I am going to order some food. Can you come over, and you two can talk about it? I'll order some french fries just for you!"

"Okay, will do. See ya soon."

She hated talking on the phone, and I understood. I welcomed the chance to catch up with Rondaya, as it had been months since we had seen each other. I wasn't sure if she knew I left the business and got divorced. "You gotta date, Violet. Rondaya will go with you."

Violet was unpacking boxes while she sent text messages to James. "Cool. Thanks, Sophia. I just hung up with James. He mumbles his words so bad that I can't ever understand his jive talk, so just let me text him so I know what he said." Her eyes glimmered to match her silly girlish giggles as she texted her lover.

She looked down at her phone and texted him back while I started to unpack boxes again. I was laughing so hard as I walked over toward her. Her laugh was so contagious, her mouth so big, and her teeth glistening white. She was gorgeous because of it.

"James wants to see me tonight." She giggled like a schoolgirl. "He called me his honey pot! Can you believe it!" I rolled my eyes back in my head. "Oh God, there's a line! I guess he's your Pooh—Winnie the Pooh, a big teddy bear!"

I dropped the packing paper to the floor and walked over to my nightstand. "Please use a condom. I'll give you a few of mine if you promise to use them. Promise me, Ms. Honey Pot!"

I opened the next moving box. I tried to stay focused on unpacking while Violet told me more sex stories about

James being large and in charge. I giggled; I couldn't believe it. I teased her, "He's as ferocious as Winnie the Pooh!"

"He loves fucking but isn't into oral. I tried to push his head down there, but he refused to go down on me. What's up with that, Sophia? You're the sex-pert. What do you think? It seems so weird to me. What guy doesn't like to lick pussy?" I smirked. "Winnie the Pooh doesn't like pussy licking! I think I read that in *Playboy* magazine!"

Violet was serious. She wanted my opinion, but we both started laughing so hysterically. I couldn't answer because I was laughing too hard.

When I caught my breath, I replied, "I guess he doesn't like honey, Ms. Honey Pot!"

Violet stopped laughing and got right back to the topic at hand: licking pussy. "I just can't get over the fact that he hates oral. What guy doesn't like to go downtown to lick pussy?"

I had my own opinion about why, but I didn't want to disappoint Violet with my answer. "Maybe James doesn't like it downtown. Maybe he likes the countryside better, or maybe he prefers the East Side. Maybe your bush is too bushy for his taste. You better ask him, Ms. Honey Pot!"

We busted out laughing again, and Violet spilled her Rockstar Martini all over the concrete floor, just like Leanne had earlier in the evening.

"I see this floor is going to get a lot to drink," I said. "I think I need a hot boy to scrub my floors naked. What do you think?"

She nodded. "I love that idea! Let's get resumes!"

Violet's expression grew serious for a minute, her brows knit. "I really needed to laugh, Sophia. My stress level is really off the charts with the thought of the Twinkie stealing from me. We don't have twenty thousand dollars to spend on her beach house furniture. There are months I can barely make enough money at the store to pay my mortgage."

My blood was boiling, but I tried to remain calm and listen without interrupting. I felt so bad for her. When she paused, I said, "Jesus, Violet. You need to get to the bottom of this tomorrow. You are fifty-fifty partners, right?"

She wiped up the martini from the floor and lifted her head up with the rag still in her hand. "Hell, yes. I put my hard-earned money into the store when I bought it a few years ago. She's stealing from me. I just know it. And to make matters worse, I think she's cheating on her husband. I think she has sex in the loading dock. Elaine and I found evidence."

I acted surprised by Violet's comments. "Why would you say that about the Twinkie cheating? Do you know for sure?" I pressed her to share her story, hoping I could share mine afterward.

Violet put her head down as if the shame was hers. "Elaine found two condoms in the loading dock hidden behind a dresser. And there was a used one in the garbage can." She frowned with disgust. "It's so gross!"

She continued to talk and wipe the floor. She shook the martini shaker for more of the Rockstar ingredients, filling her glass to the top again.

Violet's eyes got big as she sipped her sexy drink to birth more liquid courage. "I walked into the store on Sunday. I forgot the paints I needed to paint a new canvas. I found Twinkie sucking on Mike the cop's big, black dick in the loading dock. She's a HOHO. It was going in and out of her mouth, and I couldn't stop my eyes from seeing it. I saw it for myself. The Twinkie is a liar and a cheater."

My hand covered my mouth, and then I started to laugh. "Oh my God, it's kinda funny. What did he do? What the fuck did she do when she saw you?"

Violet made funny, animated motions in and out of her mouth with her tongue pushing out her cheeks like she was giving a blow job. "She didn't stop. She kept sucking him off. The cop had been hanging around lately, so I suspected he wasn't just walking the beat. You know, our store isn't in his zone. He's so disgusting. She's just so gross. She'll fuck anything with a dick. She kept pumping her face with his bushy hot dog."

Violet was finally getting it all off her chest by making fun of it. She laughed until she started to cry. "She's gross, just like a Twinkie, all spongey and fake. I can't get his bushy dog outta my mind!"

We both laughed, but Violet quickly stopped and looked at me with all seriousness. "I hope she doesn't get a disease like herpes. I could catch it off our toilet seat. I'm grossed out. I went into the store early the next morning and washed the toilet and the sink with straight Clorox." She sighed. "I'm losing my mind."

I knew I had to share my story. "I have to tell you something, Violet. I walked in on them fucking last Sunday. I went to the store to shop early, and the door was left unlocked. I walked in, and I heard moaning coming from the loading dock. I walked back, never thinking she would be back there fucking!"

Violet scowled. "She's such a lying, fucking cheater. I gotta watch my back, Sophia. Thank you for telling me."

An hour passed by when we realized we had all the boxes unpacked, but the contents were scattered all over the loft—on the floor, on the furniture, and all through the kitchen. It was an even bigger mess, but it was progress!

The vodka had taken over my head, and I was getting tired of talking about her lover's oral issues, bushy hot dogs, and the Twinkie's disgusting sex stories. I asked Violet to call Rondaya again to see why she was an hour late. Rondaya was typically late, but I felt tired of waiting. "We gotta get some food, Violet, or I'm going to faint. I'm starving, aren't you?"

I started to dial one of the local restaurants.

Violet looked down at her waist, grabbed her love handles, and smacked her ass. "I'm starving, but I'm trying not to eat anything fattening this week. I'll have some hummus and veggies if they have it. Oh, wait. No, change that hummus thing, as I'm meeting James later. I'll just have the veggies with some ranch dressing on the side."

I giggled and grabbed Violet's ass cheek while the restaurant rang through. "James will have you eating collard greens soon enough, Ms. Honey Pot!" Then the restaurant answered, and I ordered.

Violet's giggles were contagious as she walked around making sounds like a gorilla. "Did I tell you about the night he challenged an escalator? I'm not making it up! I watched him take on an escalator like he was going to outsmart it. I think he's all linebacker and no logic!"

I paced back and forth with silverware and utensils, placing them in all the right places. "Leanne always says, 'Go for the fuck, not the fucking intelligence.' He sounds like a winner, winner, chicken dinner! He reminds me of a buffalo." She giggled. "Oh my God, Sophia. You're funny!"

<hr />

Rondaya knocked at the door, startling us both out of our conversation. We were snorting, tears running down our faces laughing. Violet put her phone down and answered the door while I finished with my silverware mission. I was barely able to compose myself.

She appeared a mess, her hair pulled into a floral silk turban. Her mascara was smeared in streaks all over her face, and the black circles under her eyes showed she hadn't slept in quite a while. Her rich ebony skin, usually vibrant with a warm glow, now appears ashen and dull. The dark circles under her eyes are stark against her complexion, highlighting her exhaustion. Her full lips, typically a deep lively hue, are pale and chapped. Her eyes, though still holding a hint of their usual warmth, are heavy and shadowed, reflecting the weariness that had sapped her vitality. Her cheekbones, normally prominent and striking, seem hollowed, and her overall expression is one of profound fatigue, marked by the subtle yet unmistakable signs of wear and tear.

I knew she had lost her husband, Robert.

Rondaya ambled in, walking like a zombie. It was so unlike her. "I've been writing a love song about how I met Robert."

"Come and sit." I tried to console her with a brief hug before she plopped on the couch. "Are you going to be okay, Ronnie? We're so worried about you." Everyone called her Ronnie except her dad. She looked down to the floor, shaking her long, chocolate brown hair loose from the tightly bound wrap. It fell down around her face. "Does everything have an expiration date?"

I thought about how different she appeared this day. When Ronnie entered a room, she was recognized throughout the city as one of the best female singers—not only for her amazing voice but also because she looked a lot like Jennifer Hudson.

She always had a huge smile on her face, showcasing her wide mouth and big, white teeth like a prize she just won at the county fair. Ronnie grew up as the only daughter of four siblings, granting her with five supportive men in her life, including four older brothers and a father who adored her. She was spoiled by her parents, who proved very supportive, both financially and emotionally.

I was so envious of Ronnie's relationship with her parents. I longed to have it. I wanted to go to Sunday brunch with my mother like Ronnie did every Sunday. I would give my left arm for a dad like hers, so proud of her even when she fucked up. She had four brothers who would kill someone to protect her from harm. In my eyes, she had it all.

Do I penalize our friendship because of my jealousy? Be honest with yourself, Sophia, you feel most comfortable in the shady sides.

Ronnie worked in the radio business and was executive producer at a top radio station for ten years. She owned an advertising agency and was a hardworking artist. Her dad was a well-known hair stylist, always dressed in a tailored suit, tie, and matching silk pocket square. He was handsome with a movie star-like quality. He reminded me of Idris Elba with a sophisticated elegance about him. Ronnie adored him. Her mother was attractive but quiet and reserved. Ronnie outshined her mom but loved her just the same.

She whispered her words while her big, round eyes peered up from her hanging head. Her signature melodic voice radiated through her lips as she whined, "I miss Robert so much. He was my soulmate. Why would he kill himself and leave me? Sophia, were you with Robert the night before he killed himself?"

I walked over to my turquoise-colored bar and found her favorite coffee-flavored Patron tequila. I poured her a large helping of the thick liquid. I handed the glass to her as she looked up at me, waiting for my answer.

My expression had to show surprise. I turned back to make eye contact with her. "What? I wasn't anywhere near Robert's place that night." I extended the glass toward her, adding, "Ronnie, what are you saying?"

Ronnie took the tequila from me. She frowned. "Robert's note said he saw you and that you told him we belonged together."

I regretted not telling Ronnie sooner but feared she wouldn't like it. Plus, it was never the right time to tell her such a story. "I did see him days before when he stopped by the store while I was working on the renovation. I told him to be patient with you. I was sure you would return home to him soon. I'm so sorry, Ronnie. I didn't know you were living with someone else. I lost touch with you, and I was so caught up in my divorce." I let out a deep huff of regret. "I'm sorry."

Ronnie started to cry, turning her mascara cheeks into Jackson Pollock-esque art. "He broke my heart. His drinking and drugs were out of control. I had no choice but to leave him. I fell into the arms of the drummer in my band one night after practice, and…well, one thing led to another. I killed him." She moaned. "I killed Robert, my soulmate."

Violet jumped up and hugged Ronnie. "No, girl. You didn't do any such thing to Robert. He was sick; he had a terrible disease—an addiction to drugs and alcohol."

Robert was a creative director in a big ad agency in New York then transferred to our city. He was briefly my client. I suspected his addictions but valued my business relationship, so I didn't interfere. I recalled Robert's producer once telling me she found his hidden fifth of whiskey, a bunch of random pills, and a bag of cocaine in his desk drawer. She suspected his addictions were worsening.

I tried to comfort Ronnie with a soft smile. "You weren't to blame. Stop punishing yourself. I agree with Violet, he had some serious addiction issues."

Ronnie cried so hard, her big, brown eyes drowning in sorrow. I admired her willingness to be so open and vulnerable. I sat next to her and put my arm around her.

"I'll never get over it. I'll never be the same." She leaned in and put her head on my shoulder, moaning again. "I'll never be able to write —or love—again."

My heart broke. I searched for her CD and placed the disc inside the stereo. I wanted to ease Ronnie's pain by turning up the volume on her new release, "Counting Minutes."

Her mood immediately changed, and some light returned to her eyes. "Will you girls please come to my release at Whisper next week in the South Side, please?"

The South Side in the city was known as the blues part of town, like a little SoHo Village in the early 1990s filled with hip clubs and seedy dive bars. Whisper was a new nightclub in the South Side with an open format, which simply meant that any night of the week you could be treated to anything from Top 40 to a live singer like Ronnie who wanted to debut a new album.

"Of course, we'll be there. We would never miss your opening night."

I hugged Ronnie again with a tight squeeze. "We'll always be here for you, Ronnie. We're here to help you. Just ask, any time. Come here to visit me whenever you want."

Her eyes lit up with excitement. "The newspapers interviewed me and wrote, 'Ronnie's new CD *Daydream* seems like the work of another musician altogether. It's as if Jennifer Hudson went to sleep and woke up the next day as Sade.'"

We stood up and clapped for her. She beamed.

She loves being the center of attention.

It changed her mood instantly. Ronnie was smiling again. She was happiest when she was writing and performing. "So cool, right? And I've invited a new guy as my date. You'll meet him next week."

She took off her worn, black, leather jacket and placed it on the sofa next to the pillows. Her bruised copper-brown arms revealed the reckless moments when she drank herself into oblivion to ease her troubled mind, exposing them to the moonlight. She was drained from spending so much time in the recording studio without sunlight. Her nails were bitten to tiny, little nubs, showing the worn-off petal-pink polish barely lingering near the cuticles.

Violet stood up in a panic. "Oh my God. I gotta call James to see if we can get an extra ticket for you, Sophia. You're comin' with us. No is not an answer!"

"Violet, I have a date tomorrow night. I can't go."

"You must bring your date or change your date to Saturday night instead." She threw me an insistent gaze. "Please, Sophia. It just won't be any fun without you."

I did want to go with my girlfriends, but I felt excited about this date. "I'll text Shawn about changing it to Saturday. I don't want to take a date to a party, that's like taking a pig to a pig roast."

We giggled while I texted Shawn. Violet's tone became playful as she added, "Tell him your friends come first. If he can't accept us, he's not your man."

He texted me a message back immediately: *No worries, peaches. I understand. I'll save Saturday night for you. I'm looking forward to it more than you know. Have fun with your friends.*

The doorbell rang, and I got up to accept the food delivery.

"Mmmm, smells grand!"

We ate right away. Violet and Ronnie chatted about the music industry while I drifted off into a dreamy state of bliss, knowing this was going to be a wonderful life in the city.

Violet licked her lips and put her napkin down. "I gotta eat and run. James is waiting for me downstairs, and my boys will be home soon. I like to be there for them before they go to bed, even though they are teenagers. I just like to be there to say goodnight."

I loved the way Violet loved her kids, who were both awesome teenagers and respected their mother. "I understand completely, Violet. You're a great mom." I beamed at her with unabashed admiration. "Take some of this food with you."

Ronnie took the opportunity to leave with Violet. I knew she never liked being one-on-one with any of us, so I wasn't offended. She glanced at me as they exited the front door and called out, "See you tomorrow, Sophia. Thank you for changing your mind and coming with us."

Alone again.

The solitude felt like a cozy, warm blanket. I had a feeling my loft was going to be a busy place. I reached for the vodka but decided against it. Instead, I poured a bubbly glass of Pierre and kicked off my shoes.

I need a break.

I thought about Violet and Ronnie.

A perfect match for each other, both single and both intrigued by professional athletes and musicians.

<hr>

"So, girl," I uttered to the empty room. "What are you going to wear on your date?"

I walked around the loft, thinking I better get my bedroom put together, so I had a comfortable bed to sleep in. I found my sheets and pillows and threw them on top of the box spring, thinking about my rockstar and how he had raised my standards for great bed linens and orgasms so many years before. I dragged my mattress on top of the box spring, made the bed, and fluffed the pillows just the way I liked them.

My rockstar would be so proud of my bed-making abilities.

I felt finally home. I couldn't believe it was only seven o'clock; it felt more like midnight.

I heard a knock at my door.

Shit. Wasn't expecting anyone else.

I walked over toward the door, trying to be quiet, slowly creeping up on my tiptoes to peep through the hole on the door. "Jayne, is that you?"

I peeked through the door hole. Jayne's bare ass was perched high into the air, screaming as she placed her tongue between her fingers and licked them around and around.

She's so crazy. "Hi, chick-EE. I'm here."

She swung around with her hair flying and catching in her lips, and she didn't bother to take her straight, brown locks out of her mouth. "Hi! Leanne said you were home unpacking, so I stopped to say hi on my way to Sanctuary. Let me in."

I opened the door. "Come in, you silly girl. How are you?" I hugged her, feeling happy to see her.

"I'm out prowling tonight, collecting sex favors from Clinton." As usual, she rolled right in, holding nothing back from me. "You know Crystal dumped my husband? Oh yeah, now she's trying to win her husband Clinton back. Good luck!" She spun around. "You know he's opening the sexiest nightclub in the city tomorrow night, right?"

"Yes, of course I know. Violet and Ronnie are going to be there. Violet is taking her new boy toy, a linebacker for the Steelers. They begged me to go."

Jayne loved professional athletes as much as Violet did. She was married to one and adored the fame. "Ooh la la. I like me some dark choc-o-late like James, he's a hottie. Of course, you're coming. I won't take no for an answer. What the fuck, Sophia?"

She laughed hysterically while walking around the loft, touching stuff, and gazing up at the height of the windows. "This place is pimping, girl. So fucking sexy. I'm jealous—jelly as hell. Sophia, do you remember when we were at the Firemen Fundraiser with Leanne, and we were chasing after Michael Jordan?"

"I remember. And I remember Michael Jordan was chasing you, not us. He was in love with you."

Her trademark shit-eating grin lit her face. "Yeah, it was driving everyone, including my husband, completely insane. I loved every second of it."

Jayne had graduated from college with a degree in childhood education. She taught kindergarten for a year, then met her husband, Mike. They got married immediately, and she quit her job to raise their two children. He was quarterback handsome. She worshiped the ground he walked on, and everyone knew it. She would delight in sharing that Mike was the best quarterback, the perfect husband, and a great dad. Mike, Mike, Mike. Her whole world revolved around him. He was her purpose.

Mike treated her like a queen. He custom-built her a beautiful home in Sewickley Heights, not far from Leanne and Markus's home. He took care of their children so Jayne could sleep until noon after endless nights of partying. The early morning duties took a toll on him, so he finally hired a full-time nanny for her after finding his children running around the neighborhood while Jayne laid in bed recovering from a hangover.

She wasn't the best housekeeper either, with dirty laundry scattered all over their bedroom and toys tossed around their entire house. Their dirty dishes were always piled high in the sink. Mike hired housekeepers, but Jayne always found reasons to fire them, making excuses about their demands on her to give them direction.

She just never measured up to Mike's hopes to have a wife who could entertain and maintain the good wife reputation he desired. Jayne was a bad drunk, often fighting with him in front of a large group of friends with a cigarette hanging out of her mouth, saying things like, "Fuck you. I guess I'm not the dream wife after all, huh? I can't take you calling out orders to me like I'm one of your stupid teammates. Go fuck yourself!"

I winced at the memory. *She really is a handful.*

Jayne stood at the bar, admiring my collection of glassware as she found herself a shot glass. "Do you mind if I do a shot of Patron? You're coming to Clinton's party at Sanctuary tomorrow night, right, Sophia?"

I walked toward her, poured the shot of tequila, and smiled up at her. "Well, I wasn't going to go. I had a hot date tomorrow night, but Violet and Ronnie convinced me.

I didn't know it was Clinton's new place. I wasn't putting it all together."

She threw the shot back with one swallow. "What the fuck, Sophia? You weren't coming to my boyfriend's launch party tomorrow because you had a hot date? Are you completely insane? Sanctuary is the talk of the town right now. Clinton has taken an old church and turned it into a fucking disco—something out of a magazine, it's so fucking hot. I'm the only one who has seen the inside besides the contractors. I'm going over there now to fuck Clinton in one of the church pews."

Jayne licked her fingers and put them on her ass, making a sizzling sound, then laughed about it. "I want you to think about that later—all those guests dancing in there tomorrow night after we fucked in the church pews. Can you imagine what the priest might say about our dirty, little secrets? Ooh la la."

She loved naughty talk, reminding me why I loved her so much. "Oh my God, Jayne. You're crazy. I want to hear all about it."

Jayne pulled out her phone and scrolled through to find my contact information. "Sophia, don't even wait in line tomorrow night. The VIP line's going to be a mile long. We invited like two hundred guests. Just text me when you're there, and I'll have Shad bring you through the line. You're VIP-VIP-VIP with me. You're my VEEP, girl. You and Leanne."

I felt glad I had changed my date with Shawn. I couldn't disappoint my friends, and I was dying to see what Clinton had accomplished with the church renovation. "Sounds good to me. I can't wait to see what he did with the place. Sounds like it's going to be a great place to party."

Jayne walked over to the white powder mark on the kitchen counter, licked her finger, and swiped it across the mark. "Leanne brought you a little somethin-somethin, Sophia?"

She didn't like to admit she liked a little cocaine sometimes, so she nicknamed the party favor "somethin-somethin" instead of coke. But we all knew what she meant.

"Yes, of course she did. She's outta control as usual. Do you want a line?" I raised an eyebrow at her. "I put it away, but I have plenty to share."

She raised both her brows back at me. "Do you mind sharing? Get my motor running for the church ceremony." She gave me a conspiratorial grin and added, "Don't tell Clinton."

I threw her a mischievous smile. "Of course not. Be my guest." I reached inside the silverware drawer, pulled out the white container, and spilled a puddle of coke out for her to enjoy.

She took a swish on her finger and rubbed it across her teeth. "Yummy, it's perfect for my little romp around the pews with Clinton."

"All thanks to Leanne." I winked.

Jayne loved Leanne as much as I did, but she usually tried to play it down. "Yeah, she's still as crazy as ever. Do you think she can bring me some somethin-somethin tomorrow night? Will you ask her for me, Sophia? I can give you the money now if you want. I just hate asking her to get it for me."

I hated being the go-between for Jayne's coke and knew I had to have this boundary set with her. "I'll let Leanne know, but you guys can figure out the money thing together. I don't want to be in the middle of it."

Jayne always played innocent and didn't want a trace back to her little secret. "Cool. Thanks, Sophia. I just don't want Clinton to ever find out. Promise me."

She grabbed my phone and entered her new number into my contacts. "I'm putting my number in as VEEP, so you remember. It's my new private cell phone number for tomorrow. Clinton bought this phone for me so we can keep our little affair a secret."

I smiled.

So many secrets in this world of crazy girls. How do they keep it all straight?

The second line of cocaine still lay on the counter, like a penny on the sidewalk waiting to be picked up. She walked over, grabbed the straw, and did the line. "Did I tell you Crystal is trying to get her husband back, even after she admittedly cheated on him in South Beach with the tennis pro? I guess she's desperate!"

My head was spinning, amazed at how nonchalant she was with sharing such secrets.

Thank God I'm not snorting lines.

I threw back a shot of tequila and just listened to her rant. Then I responded, "What? This is insanity! So, let me get this straight. She admitted to Mike she cheated on him, so he dumped her, and now she's chasing her husband, your lover. My head is spinning off like a top, Jayne! I can't keep it all straight!"

Jesus, Jayne sounds like a fucking soap opera. Better yet, a reality show, desperate housewives!

Pissed, Jayne threw her truck driver mouth into high gear. The coke invoked her redneck tongue. "They're fucking mother fucking fuckers. Yes, it's all fucking true. I'm sick about it. Why the fuck couldn't they find new fuck buddies? No, they had to fuck each other just to fuck us over." She huffed and then added, "It's just so fucking creative. Right, Sophia?"

Jayne's phone rang. She licked her finger and wiped the white dust off the counter to rub it across her teeth while putting the phone on speaker with her other hand. "Hey, baby. Yeah, I'm leaving now. Meet you there. Make sure the door's unlocked, you know I hate standing outside. Why don't you get naked for me?"

She was transitioning into trailer park girl in front of my eyes. I gazed at her, amazed.

Jayne had the white line courage she needed to tell me the truth. "I fucking love my life right now—fucking and forgetting! See you tomorrow, Sophia. Don't forget to text my new phone so we get you to the front of the line. Shad'll be there to let you in." She grinned. "He loves you. You remember Shad, right?"

I smiled. I loved her unconditionally, unlike her husband. "You got it, girlfriend. Love you. And, yes, of course I remember Shad. I'll text you."

She grinned. "Love you too, girl. Kiss-kiss, and thanks for the somethin-somethin. Oh, Helena's invited, by the way. She claims she'll write a story for the society pages; Clinton is thrilled!"

"Oh God, cupcake! I hope she doesn't let him down, she's not reliable."

She giggled. "I know, cupcake, I know!" She walked out.

My head was spinning like a laundry machine. I ate whatever was left of the cold french fries and chicken pieces while I leaned back on the counter to take it all in again.

My crazy friends. All in one night and with so many crazy stories. So many wild men to match these wild-ass women, yet we're all still happy with our little secrets.

Leanne was fucking a vampire while her husband was being sentenced to prison.

Violet's man refused to lick her honey pot.

Ronnie's husband was found sprawled out naked on his sofa while holding his guitar.

Jayne was fucking her college sweetheart, and his wife was fucking her husband.

The Twinkie…well, she was just a HOHO.

I couldn't make this shit up. It's better than a romance novel written by Jackie Collins.

Laughing out loud, I continued talking to myself as I ate whatever was left of the roasted veggies. "Oh, God! And to think this was my first night in the city! It's gonna get interesting!"

I felt glad I was single and had control of my own life. I repeated my new mantra to myself while I gathered the take-out containers and the garbage and tossed them all down the trash shoot in the hallway.

I'm not intimidating, you're intimidated. I'm not mean, not aggressive. I'm honest and assertive, and that makes you uncomfortable. I will not be less for you to feel better about yourself.

Shawn texted me: *Sweet dreams, Peaches.*

I giggled as I walked into my bedroom, flopped myself down on my fluffy bed, and texted him back: *Sweet dreams!*

I fell deep asleep, only waking to the sound of the train below me at four thirty, thinking about my mantra. I embraced my feelings and felt grateful.

I'm learning to accept my authentic self as an asset. Gratitude welled in me like ocean water filling a cave.

———◆———

The morning sun came through the enormous loft windows early, and it felt good against my face. My phone had a text from Shawn that read: *Wish I was waking up to your sexy body this morning, peaches and cream.*

I wanted him to wait for a response. I knew the game we were playing, so I teased him with a tongue emoji.

I dashed over to my store to receive a delivered box, hoping it was a shipment from my favorite designer, Rachel Pally. I wanted to wear a new dress to the party with my girlfriends tonight, something I sold in my store. The box was sitting at the front door. I picked it up, walked inside, turned on the lights, and ripped open the package to find the perfect little black dress I had ordered months earlier. I quickly steamed it, threw it on a hanger, and locked the door.

My phone rang. Shawn's voice was so sultry and sexy. It was the first time I talked to him on the phone since I met him. "Hey, whatcha doing right now?"

"I just left my store. I came in to pick up a new dress to wear to the party tonight. What about you?"

Shawn paused for a moment. "I'm thinking about how hot you looked at Whole Foods the other day." He sighed. "Why are you so sexy?"

I stopped walking and sat down on a bench along the sidewalk so I could listen carefully. I whispered, "Are you being naughty? I doubt I looked sexy fondling peaches…"

Shawn teased me by letting me know he was a serious hunter. "I was thinking about you and just wanted to tell you, nothing more."

I could hear music playing in the background. *Wonder where he is?*

"I'm thinking about you too. Wish we were having dinner tonight."

I could hear road noise in the background as I continued to whisper to my potential new lover.

He whispered back, "Are you okay with me planning a special night with you? More than just dinner? I don't want to assume anything."

I was having a hard time holding my dress off the ground. "I want you to plan whatever you want. I'm adventurous, so surprise me."

"Mmmm…you have no idea how happy you just made me. You won't regret it, sexy. I promise. I feel like I've known you forever, and we just met. I really like you already, and we haven't had our first date yet."

I liked his game-playing. I wanted him to take the lead and guide me into submission. I had longed for this exact feeling for so long. I could barely remember what it felt like to feel so desired again. "I can't wait. I wish we were going tonight."

He never missed a beat in the conversation. "I knew I liked your peaches. Mmmm…I'm having a hard time concentrating on driving."

I wished I was going to see Shawn instead of the party at Sanctuary, but I held out making him want me even more. "I'll text you later, no matter what. You better pay attention to the road, if you're having a hard time."

I laughed a girly giggle as I started walking back to my loft. The concierge greeted me at the front desk, pointing to a guy in a blue jumpsuit holding an arrangement of flowers wrapped in a gorgeous, natural parchment paper disguising the bouquet of beauty. "Someone is here with flowers for you, Ms. Sophia. They want you to sign for them."

When I opened the wrapping, I discovered a large arrangement of white roses with my name written on the card. It read: *My dearest Sophia, White symbolizes new beginnings. I'm looking forward to seeing you tomorrow night, Shawn.*

My heart fluttered with excitement. I knew he played the game exactly the way I preferred it, getting my heart racing with anticipation for our date. I placed the roses on my dresser in my bedroom so I could see them from my bed.

I read the card again while I undressed, and then I smiled while I laid down on the cozy bedding. I thought about Hannah and her young pottery instructor in LA. *Wonder if she felt this way.*

I let the bright sunlight shine through the windows onto my naked body. Still exhausted from moving in and successfully holding a fabulous grand opening party. I covered myself with my white, luxurious sheets and fell asleep until six o'clock—an hour before Leanne was supposed to arrive. I woke up in a panic.

My phone was blowing up with messages from Leanne like, "Call me, girlfriend. Please call me ASAP."

I dialed Leanne's phone, still groggy from the nap, and walked naked into the kitchen to find a snack before taking a shower. "What's up, girl? Are you okay?"

Leanne sounded like she was crying. "Markus was sentenced to three years in federal prison today. He leaves immediately."

"Oh my God. Oh my God, girl. Are you okay? Do you need me to come there?" Leanne's voice quivered, and she could barely compose herself as she said, "I would love to come to your place and get ready for the party there. I can't be here in this house."

"Of course, Lea. Come here, of course. I told you that this is your home now too."

She sniffled and seemed to be holding back her tears, but one sob came out.

My refrigerator looked bare except for a few green apples, some yogurt, blueberries, and a peach. I cut an apple into quarters, found a jar of peanut butter, and dipped while I comforted my friend. "Of course, come down any time. I'm here for you."

Leanne started sobbing out of control now. "I'm already in the car with my driver. I couldn't bear to be alone. My son's nanny is taking care of him tonight. Markus has gone, and I just couldn't…"

Feeling almost speechless, I took a deep breath and repeated, "My home is your home, girl. I'm going to jump in the shower, so I'll tell the concierge to let you upstairs."

Leanne was still crying. "Thank God I have you, Sophia. Thank you."

"I'll see you when you get here,"

I jumped into the shower, shaved my legs, quickly dried off, and rolled my long, curly hair up into a towel to dry. I felt so grateful I had time to take a two-hour nap earlier, knowing I was in for a very long night.

My phone buzzed—another text from Shawn: *White roses are a symbol of purity and romance. You are my peaches and cream.*

Maybe this is going too fast, but I like the attention.

He's already so entangled in my daily thoughts.

I want passion in my life.

I loved it, but I wasn't sure what I should say back to him without sounding desperate. I decided I shouldn't answer him right away. I dried my hair by scrunching the curls to dry naturally and threw on my dark blue, satin robe until it was time to get dressed.

I didn't want a boyfriend in my life right now, and I certainly didn't want to let anyone into my complex head again.

The truth was that I was scared to love again. I thought love brought me trouble, and I had enough chaos to last a lifetime. So, I thought it best to ignore his text for a bit longer, talking to myself as I walked over to my vintage bar. "Silence is the best answer."

I poured myself a glass of Grey Goose over ice, pondering my response as I swished the vodka over the large ball of ice, second-guessing the silent treatment as an answer.

Maybe I should play with him…but why play games? I promised to be honest going forward.

I preferred to be honest with both him and me.

His text message had grown so serious suddenly. So, I decided to give him a funny response and turn the conversation back into a playful one. I texted: *Do you like your peaches fuzzy, hard, or juicy?*

Shawn sent me back an "LOL" emoji and a text: *Juicy. I love my peaches juicy.*

I already loved his sense of humor, and I liked keeping our talk light and flirtatious. *Well, juicy is what you will get then.*

The next text read: *You're my juicy peach. I can't wait to take a bite of you.*

I was intrigued. I thought our date would be a one-night stand filled with passionate foreplay during dinner followed by a heated session of romantic fucking. I was open and ready to receive whatever he had planned for our date.

I knew Leanne was due any minute, and she would consume my entire night. I texted Shawn back, knowing I needed to end our fun, little banter soon.

I wish we were on our date tonight instead.

Shawn sent an emoji of hearts with the next text: *Soon enough, sexy. Now, go have fun with your friends, and don't forget to send me a text when you get home. I wanna know you're safe in your bed.*

I immediately loved his attention to detail. *You're driving me crazy.*

He texted back: *Oh, you have no idea. Have a good night. -Shawn.*

My heart raced with pure delight as I fantasized about his masculine body rubbing up against mine. I hadn't been with a man in so long. I hoped I remembered what to do with him—how to kiss with my mouth open.

As I sipped my vodka, I ran my tongue along the rim of the glass, absorbing the feeling while I drifted off into a fantasy about our date. *Will he be passionate like my rockstar? Will he tease me until I beg him to enter my wetness?*

The front door swung open, and Leanne dropped her suitcase to the floor. "Oh my God, Sophia. I'm so fucking happy to be here. I need a hug."

I lunged up, ran over, and hugged her as tight as I could, squeezing her with all my strength. As I looked at her face covered in tears, I said, "Everything will be okay. I just know it will be."

I walked over to the bar and poured Leanne a large glass of her favorite Grey Goose vodka over ice.

Leanne pulled out her trusted baggie of white-powdered comfort and pressed a one-hundred-dollar bill for a snort. "I just can't believe it. The fucking asshole had the fucking balls to tell me to keep his hair pie free from predators while he's away! He's actually nuts, thinking I'm not going to fuck for three fucking years. Is he crazy?"

She looked pale, drained from crying all day. "I hate Markus so much. I truly hope he dies in prison. How could he do this to our son?"

She wasn't disguising her true feelings of anger, and she was not ashamed of telling me how much she was hurting. I sat close to Leanne on the sofa, trying to comfort her with words, but I knew I was going to need more than just my words right now. I hugged her.

"It's so awful," she said. "Everyone in our neighborhood is staring at me. I'm going to go to Boca and live where nobody knows my name."

Leanne's bullheaded and unrealistic.

"I understand, girl. It's not going to be an easy three years, but we'll get through it together. Be grateful Markus left you money in the bank and you have a nanny to help you. You'll be okay. He actually used the words hair pie?"

She busted out laughing. Her dark, angry side was out in full bloom tonight. "Of course he said hair pie. You know he's an asshole, but he thinks he's cool. I'm going to fuck everyone and anyone I want to fuck, and Markus can go fuck himself."

I stood up and tried to change the subject. "Jayne stopped by and said the renovation of the church is off the charts. Let's get ready for Sanctuary; it will be fun to get ready together like we're on vacation, like us in South Beach."

Leanne pulled her suitcase into the bedroom and threw it open. She had packed enough clothes to stay for a month.

I wasn't surprised but tried to make her laugh. "Where the fuck are you going with all those clothes? It's a party, not a vacation! I still can't get over the hair pie. Honestly? He said that to your face?"

She was such a terrible packer; she always overpacked. She told me she paid a woman to pack for her long vacations with Markus when they first started dating. The personal stylist organized her closet so many times, trying to help her pull together outfits suitable for luxurious resorts.

I knew she would be one of my best customers at the store; even though she had access to Gucci, she loved trendy clothes even more. *She's a shopaholic with an addiction to spoiling herself to get revenge on Markus.*

"Stop it, Sophia. Stop talking about him. I couldn't make any choices, so I just brought everything! You know you're going to dress me, so what's the difference?"

I sorted through her clothes and chose a black Chanel mini dress with her favorite Gucci shoes.

She always looks great in this dress.

Leanne snorted another big line of coke.

She's sniffing too much disco dust.

"I'm worried about you, Lea. Don't get all blown out on coke tonight. Clinton will be pissed. You know he hates it when his girls are high."

With such an angry look on her face, she barked back, "Fuck Clinton. I don't care."

I decided to stop lecturing her and just focus on getting myself ready for the party.

She'll dance it off.

◆

We walked up the busy street past all the restaurants until we reached the long line of people twisted around the corner. I texted Jayne on her VEEP phone line: *Leanne and I are outside. Should we jump the line?*

Jayne texted back immediately with: *Pass the line to the front door. I'll send Shad out.*

We walked past the line of people to the front doors of the church, and a good-looking security guard looked Leanne up and down. "Where do you think you're going?"

Leanne smiled at him and pointed her finger at his chest, tapping it a few times like she knew him. "Wherever the fuck I want." She reached for the large door handle made into the shape of a guitar. "I'm going inside."

The security guard stood in front of her, blocking the entrance. "I don't think so, young lady."

Just then, Shad opened the door. Shad was Clinton's brother. He wasn't as handsome as Clinton, but he had a great personality. "Hi, sexy girls. Come on inside. Jayne's waiting for you."

The security guard smiled and opened the door for the girls. "Why didn't you tell me that you're friends with Jayne? She's my girl."

Leanne didn't let him get away with being a smartass, so she sassed him back. "Well, maybe I'm your girl now." She winked at him as if to say fuck you, but I knew she wanted to keep on his good side for future favors. "See you later, sexy security boy!"

We stepped inside the church. Sanctuary was an adaptive reuse of the old Saint Elizabeth's church into a dance club. It introduced high-energy design into a dramatic environment with great acoustics and lighting. Dimly lit, it possessed a sexy discotheque vibe and a mysterious ambiance that brought the place to life.

The troves of artwork and symbolism relating to the spiritual life of the church were still intact. The day-to-day fixtures such as the font, pulpit, reredos screen, and lectern were all lit by the disco ball streaming down across the stained-glass windows.

The odd mix of religious artifacts and discotheque somehow seemed to blend. There was a mysterious ambiance of temptation everywhere.

My eyes didn't know where to look next. "Wow, Clinton really outdid himself with this place."

Leanne danced onto the empty dance floor and spun around and around. She was high as a kite, and it was obvious.

Jayne ran over to her on the dance floor and tried to stop her from spinning so she could talk to her. "Hey, chick-EE, you look so fucking hot tonight. Welcome to Sanctuary! Let's party."

Jayne was dressed in a skimpy white dress that barely covered the cheeks of her ass. It exposed her long, lean legs and her Prada stiletto heels. She was dragging on a slim cigarette, which meant she was already drinking vodka martinis.

She grinned at Leanne, then turned toward me. "Sophia, what the fuck are you doing over there? Get your ass over here and dance with us."

I danced over, and we all spun around the disco ball together. "Let's find a place to snort a line. I need a little somethin-somethin." She whispered, "Don't tell Clinton."

Don't want Clinton to know I did the lines either, but she's so paranoid.

"No worries, girl. Your secret's safe with me."

We walked to the back of the church altar, and Jayne directed us into the church's old confession room.

Leanne raised her eyebrows at the location choice for their dirty, little secret. "I'll confess my sins while I do a bump, feels pretty fucking naughty to me."

Jayne giggled. "It's sexy as fuck, right?" She was on the lookout for Clinton, already feeling guilty about her secret somethin-somethin bullshit. Leanne poured out a huge amount of white powder, laid it out across the prayer bench, and then cut it into three enormous white piles she called lines.

I blurted, "God, Lea, that's pretty creepy. Right on the prayer bench, really?"

Leanne was in rare form tonight. "Who fucking cares? Just do the fucking line and give your fucking confession, if it makes you feel less guilty."

Her face turned redder by the minute, and I decided to just go with the flow. I snorted half the line and passed the bill to Jayne, who finished it, leaving a line behind for Leanne.

She snorted it, then twirled around. "Let's fucking go. Mama needs to go back to the disco." She danced back out to the dance floor, leaving us behind.

I wanted to warn Jayne so she could help me keep an eye on Leanne. I wasn't sure if she heard the news about Markus yet. I said, "Leanne is in quite a mood. Markus was sentenced to three years in federal prison today."

Jayne's eyes grew round, and she nodded sagely. "Shit, Sophia. Shit. It's gonna be a long three years! Shit!"

We walked out to the dance floor to find Leanne dancing on top of one of the ten-foot speakers on the altar. Waving for us to join her, she screamed, "Get your asses up here!"

We both climbed up the stairs leading up to the top and jumped up on the big speakers next to Leanne. "Get Down on It" was playing as loud as the amplifiers could handle. I could feel the vibration of the base under my feet. Spinning from the high volume and twisty moves, we jumped down after the song was over, leaving Leanne, and decided to go to find Clinton.

Clinton is a fair-complexioned Irishman with an innocent, boyish grin, and a generous manner. It was clear he loved Jayne and her girlfriends. He grinned from ear to ear in his powder-blue t-shirt with a local band logo on it.

Clinton gazed over at Jayne like a schoolboy with a crush on his first girlfriend in the playground. He grabbed her hand. "Hi, baby! How's my girl?"

She batted her eyes. "I missed you, baby."

He's always so casual.

I smiled at him.

"I know you beautiful women will keep the men flowing and spending money, so you drink for free at Sanctuary." He winked at us.

My mouth must have been hanging open with surprise. "Are you serious? Why would you do that for us?"

Clinton looked confident about his decision. "Like I said, Sophia, you girls are my best customers. When the men see beautiful women partying and having fun, they'll spend money here. Besides, I love you girls."

Clinton kissed me on the cheek. I knew he was genuine and kind. I had hired his catering staff for large parties when I worked in the entertainment industry, so maybe this was his way of thanking me for the years of business.

Either way, I gratefully accepted his gift. Jayne and I stood in the upper balcony of the church. The DJ nestled in the choir area, overlooking the dance floor from high above the crowd.

Leanne was still singing and dancing on the speaker.

"What are we going to do with Lea?" I looked over at Jayne, but she already moved next to Clinton, and they were kissing and not paying any attention to me.

"Just let her dance the night away," Jayne screamed, pausing her kiss. "She'll be okay; she's a tough one." She resumed the kiss. They acted like they were the only ones in the room, cuddling and kissing as if teenagers inside a car at a drive-in movie.

Their public display of affection is making me uncomfortable. Should I watch or turn away?

I spotted Helena walking across the dance floor. She looked up at us and waved. Then she pointed to Clinton to ask for his approval to come upstairs to join them.

Clinton motioned for her to come up, then he turned to me with his typical devilish grin on his face. "Helena. She's a real treat. Isn't she, Sophia? I wonder what story she has for us tonight!"

I started reflecting on how Helena had acted so distant in South Beach. She was always so provocative. Her very long, silky, black hair looked longer since we were in Miami, probably extensions. She is constantly flicking it back off her face, just like Cher did while on stage. Her skin was pale, and her cheeks lifted. She preferred YSL Rouge Volupte Shine Lipstick to grace her thin lips, nothing else mattered.

I smiled, recalling how Helena called everyone "cupcake" and always gave us her signature kiss-kiss on both cheeks. She was recently in hiding, ever since her husband Don's investigation for mortgage fraud started a few months ago.

She pretended to be surprised about his illegal activities, but investigators were naming her in the lawsuit alongside him. She was trying to save her reputation and prepare for financial ruin.

Jayne said she delayed the launch of her intimate lingerie and sex toy boutique until after her husband's sentencing. The erotic panties she designed were sixty-five dollars a pair. A string of pearls slid gently across your clit, and the decadent strands offered women foreplay all day! Helena's way of seducing men was mastered beyond belief. She talked with a whisper unless she was laughing, a seductress queen.

Helena made her signature kiss-kiss to everyone standing in our group. "Hi, cupcake. How are you, Clinton? What a fabulous place! It's so decadent! Wanna grab a cocktail and step into your office to talk about the renovation?"

Clinton grinned from ear to ear, surely knowing he made the right decision to include Helena on his guest list, as she could make or break his news release story. "Helena, it's always a pleasure to see you. Yes, of course."

She kissed Jayne on both cheeks, as usual. "You look fab, Cupcake. Is this a Gucci?"

Jayne grinned as she stroked Clinton's back. "My baby bought it for me. Isn't it sweet?"

She kissed me as well. "Hello, Cupcake. I want to talk to you about your upcoming fashion show, maybe next week. I might be back in Tuscany with my boyfriend. I'll let you know soon."

"It's okay, Helena." I smiled.

A boyfriend already? Her husband's being indicted. She moves fast.

She only lightly stroked the arm of Clinton's brother, Shad. It was noticeable, but we ignored it. I wasn't surprised by her change in greeting his brother without the traditional cheek kisses.

She dares not kiss a peasant.

I listened as she dished out her scripted dialogue as if she were an actor in an episodic. "Tuscany is so gorgeous this time of the year. I'm hoping we can fly back next week."

Helena never gave me a chance to get to know her better, since I wasn't part of the High Society Rich Bitch Club, and she wouldn't approve a working girl into the group. I didn't want to be a member. I needed air and was growing tired of the nonsense of small talk with Helena. I suddenly felt nauseated.

I whispered to Jayne, "I'm going to go back downstairs to hang with Leanne. I can't take this cupcake shit any longer. I might be in sugar shock." I kissed Jayne and Clinton.

Helena barely lifted her arm away from the side of her body as she gave me a half wave, as if she was the Queen of England.

Farewell, my fair maiden.

I laughed to myself as I carefully took each step down the spiraling staircase to the dance floor.

I thought about what a wise man once told me. "Don't play rich to impress people. Play broke to test them."

My mind filled with thoughts as the coke ran through my veins; the drug induced a spark of dopamine that triggered my intense feelings of euphoria. I allowed my mind to wander as I walked to the dance floor. The disco was screaming with lights flashing and music blasting. Leanne was still dancing to the music, never skipping a beat.

I needed a cocktail and a break from the action. I ambled over to the bar. "Can I get a Grey Goose vodka over ice with a big squeeze of lime?"

The handsome, young bartender leaned in. "You're Clinton's friend, Sophia, right?"

I recognized him from another bar I frequented with ex-husband number three, so I smiled. "Yes, hi. I'm Sophia."

"You have an open VIP tab on Clinton. No charge." I handed him twenty dollars as a tip.

"Thank you."

I walked to the end of the bar to take it all in, feeling amazed at the transformation from church to nightclub. It was gorgeous. Clinton thought of every detail, leaving all the rich, vibrant design elements of the original church but allowing the disco ball to take over the altar. The twirling lights refracted off the stained-glass windows in psychedelic arabesques.

A rather twisted theme to mix religion with the sinner. It felt right.

I texted Shawn, feeling unguarded after a line of cocaine and a cocktail: *The disco's so hot. I want to dance with you under the disco ball.*

He answered me back quickly: *I'll bet you're the hottest disco girl.*

Clinton and Helena approached me at the end of the bar, interrupting my playful texting. "I'm headed to my office to chat with Helena."

She smiled. "I'll ring you next week, cupcake. I have another party to attend tonight, so I'll be sneaking out the back door after my little talk with Clinton. Nice to see you, cupcake."

Of course, she has to remind me just how important she is. She is the social queen invited to all the best parties.

I smiled and tried to hide my true feelings. "Nice to see you as well, Helena. Have fun at your other party."

She walked out, flicking her long, black hair all the way out the door.

I laughed to myself. *She's got a shady side, just like the rest of us. I can't wait to find out what it is, Cupcake.*

I turned back to my foreplay with Shawn. I had a new text: *I can't wait to smell you again.*

I answered him back with a naughty message, thinking he must be home alone: *I smell like a peach.*

He played back like a cat with a mouse: *Did I tell you how much I love peaches, especially juicy ones?*

I wanted to go home where I could play in the quiet sanctuary of my own luxurious bed. *This peach is tired of the loud music. I'll text when I'm naked and under my sheets.*

I looked up from my phone to see Violet and Ronnie walking in with James and another Pittsburgh Steeler. The crowd turned to watch the athletes strut across the dance floor.

Ronnie didn't dance unless she was on stage, so she continued to walk upstairs to the VIP section while Violet turned and spun around.

James looked surprised by his date's actions with his friend. "What the fuck, Violet! Thought you were with me, tonight." He gently grabbed her hand and led her up to the VIP area. His unhappy frown informed me he was jealous.

Violet spotted me and rushed over. Holding my hand tightly, she led me to the staircase. "Come upstairs with us! Come on, Sophia. Come with us."

"I'll be there in a minute. I promise." I reached out to grab Leanne's hand and squeezed it to let her know I was leaving her for a bit. "The cockroaches are here with their entourage. Can I leave you with them while I visit Violet and James?"

Kellie glided over to me. "Hi, Sophia. Don't you look pretty tonight! I'm dying to sponsor one of your fashion shows. Let's have lunch next week and talk about it! By the way, I love your window display, sexy as fuck!"

I agreed quickly to get rid of her annoying persistence. "Sure thing. Call me. Keep an eye on Leanne. She's in rare form."

Kellie's overbite revealed her dissatisfaction with my motherly request. "Lea's a big girl. She can take care of herself. We're going to go to the wrap party at the after-hours club down the street. I'll take good care of her, no worries!"

I walked away, turning to Leanne as if I needed approval to leave her alone with Kellie and her group of over-processed friends.

Leanne was high; she didn't care what I did. "Fuck yeah, Sophia. I don't need a babysitter. Do whatever you want."

I wasn't in the mood for drama tonight.

I walked up to Violet and hugged her. "Hi, girl. You look so pretty tonight."

James's friend, Hines, interrupted me. "Don't you live in my building? I live in the loft right next to yours. I've seen you in the hallway."

I didn't recognize him. I shrugged my shoulders. "I'm not really sure."

I looked Hines up and down. He was dressed in full camouflage from his ball cap to his tight t-shirt with an Army logo on the center. His parachute pants were neatly tucked into his combat boots. He was donning a little ice around his neck. A dollar sign medallion, larger than his actual face, was a piece of jewelry acting as a reminder not only of his success but also of his journey to get here. He obviously liked shiny things.

"I'm wearing my sports gear 'cause I'm out on a hunt tonight. Hunting for pussy." He laughed, pausing for my response. "Sophia, where's your girlfriend Stephanie tonight? MEOW! She's my kinda lady, even if she wants me to pay to play with her pussycat!"

I didn't find him amusing. I kept walking away and talking without thinking much about what I was saying. "Good for you. Excuse me, I wanna talk to my friend, if you don't mind moving over."

James overheard my chatter. "Bust his balls, girl. He's such a dick. Give him shit, girl."

Hines laughed at James, clearly not offended, and moved over so I could stand next to Violet.

I hated these pro athletes' privileged attitudes. "How do you tolerate their childish behavior? They are so fucking stupid, such childish bullshit." I rolled my eyes.

Violet laughed, but she truly liked their antics. "James is so cute, though—right, Sophia? He's just a teddy bear, my boo."

I laughed. "You mean your Winnie the Pooh! Ms. Honey pot!"

I was high from vodka and lines of coke. Unable to keep my mouth shut, I muttered, "I think he looks like a big dummy—but if you like him, then I guess I like him." I really didn't like arrogant athletes. "James, what size shoe do you wear?" I gazed at him with one eyebrow raised in challenge.

James pulled off his velvet Gucci slippers and threw one over to me. "Try it on and see if you can guess my size, smartass."

I tried on his big slipper; it was twice the size of my shoe. "I'm guessing a size fifteen, maybe a sixteen."

James smiled. "Ha! Try an eighteen baby! By the way, my dick matches my shoe size. Ask your girlfriend." He laughed hysterically. Hines gave him a high-five for being so funny.

I had their attention, so I took full advantage of putting them in their place. "You know you can tell what kind of man you are by the kind of shoes you wear?"

Hines grinned at my sarcasm. "Oh, please do tell…tell us, Sophia."

"Well, a construction boot is a bad boy who fucks like a dump truck—just dumps his load and backs out." I waited for their reaction. Violet covered her mouth to laugh.

I continued my comedy act. "A penny loafer's a momma's boy who's all flash and no fuck. A tennis shoe is a gym rat who prefers to fuck himself."

Hines barreled over laughing, his dollar sign bouncing off his forehead. "Good one, Sophia!"

I smiled. "A flip-flop is a beach bum who's too lazy to fuck. A leather-tasseled shoe is an attorney who will sue you for fucking him."

They laughed at my sense of humor. "Well, Sophia, then what the fuck do you call a man who wears a size eighteen velvet Gucci slipper?"

I tried to carefully select my words, so I wouldn't sound foolish or insult Violet's man. I wanted him to feel good about himself. "I guess I would call him a large and in charge linebacker who has good taste in women—and tastes good, according to my friend."

James smiled, pleased with my answer. "Yeah, I do have good taste. And Violet said I taste good. You got that right, Sophia. You need to have your own radio show   a comedy sex show like Howard Stern, only from a woman's point of view. We should make that happen."

The lights came on inside Sanctuary, and it was now two o'clock in the morning. I had no idea where Leanne was. Clinton tried to find her, but the bartenders said she left with Kellie and her entourage of friends. "I think they said they were going to the new after-hours club down the street."

I hitched a ride with Clinton and felt grateful to be home. I texted Shawn: *I'm home. All tucked in my bed, naked.*

He texted back immediately like he was waiting for my text: *How was your night with your friends?*

I wanted him to know I was thinking about him: *I had fun, not the same kind of fun I would have had with you though.*

Take good care of my peach.

I yawned as I texted: *Good night, sexy.*

He texted: *Good night, can't wait to see you; sleep tight.*

I felt glad the Sanctuary party was over, and I could spend the morning in bed.

Hope Leanne gets home at a reasonable hour, probably early morning.

My phone rang, and I answered, half listening to Kellie screaming while music played in the background. "We're all at Blue Diamond. Come over. Come on, Sophia. We need you here with us tonight."

She continued to scream over the music, "There's a hot, silver-haired fox here who has a mad crush on you. He looks like Richard Gere. He said he spotted you at the Steeler game and said he can't get you outta his mind! Come on. Come get your halo dirty! Play with us!"

Kellie was always persistent. She hated being told no. She rang my phone ten times until I hung up on her, dropped my phone, pushed it under my pillow, and then drifted off to sleep.

Chapter Seven

The Act of Contrition

Shawn arrived, just on time, and texted me from the car: *Come down when you're ready, Sophia. I have a surprise for you.*

I decided to wear a gorgeous, black silk blouse, the top two buttons left open to reveal the little leopard-patterned bra I was wearing underneath. My tight-fitting pencil skirt showed the shape of my rounded ass and curvaceous, hourglass figure. I always said my body was like the Amalfi Coast, a curvy coastline that could be dangerous if you drove the roads too fast.

I laughed as I chose my lingerie. I wore the matching thong underwear in case I got lucky. I wasn't into couture or fancy name brands—Gucci, Prada, and Chanel—like my girlfriends.

Even when I could afford it, I preferred shopping in boutiques. Since my daughter was living in New York and discovering new designers with fashion-forward styles, she pointed me in the right direction.

Shawn was driving his sexy, red Porsche. The convertible top was down, exposing the classy beige interior. He jumped out of the car, rushed over to open the passenger door for me, and said, "Hi, sexy. You look so beautiful. Do you mind if we drive with the top down, or do you prefer to have it up?"

"Please leave it down. I love driving *topless*."

He understood my flirtation and chose to play back without hesitation. "I'm sure you do. I would love to see you driving topless."

We drove through the tunnels, out of the city, toward the mountains.

"I hope you don't mind; I took it upon myself to make a reservation at Nemocolin Woodlands. It's kinda far away, but it's worth the drive. Have you ever been?"

I grinned in approval of his decision to go outside the city. "Yes, wonderful. I used to produce all their television commercials. It's gorgeous there."

I remembered the quaint ambiance of the resort so warmly designed in a traditional hunting lodge with stunning, natural surroundings. Shawn glanced over at me as he shifted gears, turning up the music of Norah Jones on the stereo. "Come Away with Me" was playing, and I wanted to sing but just sang to myself in my mind.

I love this artist.

I soaked it up with the sound of the road beneath us and the scenery passing by, like flipping through pages of an old photo album filled with memories. The wind in my hair, the scent of fresh air, the vibes of desire from my co-rider—all felt divine!

When we arrived at the resort, he insisted I take a seat in the lounge with a cocktail while he walked to the restaurant to check on our reservations. "Just relax here for a few minutes. I'll be back soon."

When he returned, I smiled up from my martini. "Hey, sexy. Are you here with anyone tonight?" I loved flirting with him, feeling a tingling in my cells.

"Oh yeah. I'm with a very sexy woman who has the juiciest peach in the city. She's a beautiful woman who agreed to have dinner with me." Shawn extended his hand to me. "Let's go inside and enjoy our dinner, Sophia. I have a few surprises for you."

He ordered a great bottle of red wine, carefully selected from the wine list so the flavors would pair nicely with our meal. "We need to relax so we can enjoy our first night alone. I hope you like my selection."

Dinner was fabulous. I enjoyed our flirtatious banter and the play of candlelight on his expressive face as much as the delicious food and fine, fragrant wine. The décor was exquisite too. Couldn't have been more perfect. Afterward, he surprised me with a room key.

"I hope you don't think I'm assuming too much by reserving a room for us. I just wanted our first night together to be very special. Will you spend the night with me?"

I smiled, hoping that was part of his surprise. "Of course, sexy. I would love to, but I didn't bring a change of clothes."

Shawn motioned for the waiter to bring the check. After signing the check to our room, he looked up at me with a smile. "Do you mind playing a little game with me tonight?"

I blushed a bit. I wasn't shy, but he caught me off guard. "I'll play with you. Sure, why not?"

He slid the key across the white, linen tablecloth while staring into my eyes. "Go upstairs. Our room number is on the key. Take your clothes off and wait for me on the bed. I'll meet you there."

I entered the suite. My heart was racing with anticipation as I obeyed his request. I stripped off my skirt and blouse, allowing both to fall to the floor. Then I picked them up and folded them neatly over the high-back, winged chair in the corner.

My sexy, leopard-patterned, lacy bra with the matching thong undies were a perfect choice.

Thank God I chose this sexy matching set, just in case I got lucky!

Shawn walked into the room with a bottle of champagne and a shopping bag from the hotel's boutique. "Let's celebrate our first night. I want to make it special for us—a night for us to eat, relax, and enjoy together."

He popped the cork of the champagne and stepped close to where I was sprawled out on the luxurious bed. "I like your choice in panties, leaves little to the imagination."

He placed the shopping bag down on the chair next to my clothes. "You are so sexy, girl." He poured some of the champagne over my lace panties. "I want to taste the champagne from your peach. Do you mind?"

He talked while he leaned in closer to my panties. I could smell his inviting, natural scent as he continued to talk to me. I sighed in anticipation, desire heating me up like an electrical coil heats water.

"I can't resist you. I've been thinking about you since we met. I just want to taste your skin."

"Mmmm…"

He slowly took off his shirt and pants, keeping eye contact with me while exposing his young, muscular body that smelled of musk and vanilla. He sat down next to me and gently pushed me back on the bed so he could lick the champagne from my panties. He licked my belly, around my navel, between my breasts, and through my lace bra until I moaned with pleasure and my nipples grew hard.

He moaned, "Why'd you leave those panties on? You want me to eat right through them?"

The champagne soaked my panties, but I was also wet with desire for him. "You're making me so wet. You're teasing me."

Shawn stood over the bed as he reached inside the nightstand. "I drove to the hotel yesterday so I could prepare for our date with a few surprises for you."

My only response was a moan, knowing I wanted him to taste me now. I loved how he wanted to please me. To make me feel special. He gently closed the nightstand drawer holding up a silky, white blindfold. "I'm going to blindfold you, so you're only going to feel my tongue, not see me."

He tied it around my eyes. I squirmed with excitement as he closed the back of the blindfold so tight, blocking out the remaining light shining in from the window. "You're my naughty little girl, aren't you?"

I trusted him.

Shawn pulled my panties down. I felt them against my thighs first, and then past my ankles and off. He gently pushed my legs back. He licked my shaven peach while slowly pouring the bubbly champagne over my clit. I could feel him lift off the bed.

I heard the drawer open again before he placed a drop of warm liquid over my left nipple, then the right one. I moaned as he licked it off one and then the other.

The air grew thick with the scent of honey mixed with the aroma of our sweat, like a bakery filled with the ingredients of passion.

I felt comfortable with him, like we had been lovers forever. I trusted his touch. His lips were close to my ear as he whispered to me, "Take a bite. Taste it. Let the juice drip out of your mouth."

I bit the end of the fruit, and he touched my lips with his fingers. "I'm going to make you cum now. Are you ready?"

I could feel the juicy peach sliding across my pussy back and forth while he licked me at the same time. "Your pussy's so juicy. I love licking your peach. You taste so good."

I moaned with his movements. I was thrusting myself back and forth against his mouth begging him to fuck me, but his voice offered me no comfort. "Not yet…you're not ready yet, my love."

Shawn untied the blindfold, exposing my eyes to the warm glow of the room and his rock-hard cock waiting for me to enjoy.

"Oh God, is that hardness for me?"

He stood up, took my hand, and turned me around so my ass was perched in the air. "I'm so hard for you. I want to fuck you, Sophia. Can I fuck you? I want you to tell me to fuck you."

I responded to his cry for release, knowing I was ready to have him inside my pussy. "Please fuck me. I want you inside me."

He groaned with every thrust, allowing himself the pleasure of feeling satisfied. I focused on the feeling I waited so long to experience again. He lifted my hips closer to his motion so he could get deeper inside my body. I danced on the edge of orgasm, waiting for my lover to join me in the pleasure.

We came together before collapsing on the bed, entangled in each other's skin as if we were one.

"I knew the minute I saw you squeezing peaches. I could see the passion in your eyes. I could feel your need for pleasure."

I slightly moaned a simple, humming noise of approval with his awareness to fill my void. "Thank you for rescuing me, Doctor Love."

We laughed, enjoying our playful attraction for one another and a wonderful first date.

The morning sunrise came through the windows. I opened my eyes to see a large coffee canister and a basket of fruit set up on a table covered in a white linen tablecloth next to the bed.

Shawn walked in and greeted me with a smile. "Good morning, beautiful. How are you this morning? How's my juicy peach?"

I gave him a lavish smile, still wet from the previous night's adventures. "I slept like a baby. I had such a wonderful time with you last night."

He poured me a cup of coffee. I stared up from the cup as I took a sip. His scruffy beard showed signs of overnight growth and red hues as he grinned from ear to ear. "You're quite the lover, Ms. Sophia."

I smiled, noting his fascination with my body. As he gazed at me, I giggled. "You're not so bad yourself, sexy."

He was tender—a gentle yet dominating lover that turned me on. He asked for my permission for every move he made with me, like he worshiped me already. Later, he asked, "Can you spend the day with me? I'm not ready to leave your side quite yet."

I had the entire weekend to myself for the first time in many years. I felt guilty about spending time away from work, but I craved the attention from him. It fulfilled something in me that had felt empty.

I tilted my head and gazed at him, feeling young and innocent. "What do you have in mind?"

Shawn stood, removed the cup from my hand, and announced his grand idea. "I want to make love to you all day long, then get room service for dinner and repeat the performance. What do you think?"

I couldn't imagine a day in bed with him—a dream come true for me. I smiled. "I'm all yours."

"You liked those peaches all over your pussy, didn't you, baby? They tasted so good against your body."

I felt fascinated by his love for food and fucking, and how he loved to tease me with his food fetish. His naughty, little secret intrigued me. "They were wonderful. My new favorite fruit!"

"I'm craving peach pie—your peach pie."

He walked over to the shopping bag that had sat on the chair all night. I had forgotten all about it.

"I picked up a little something from the boutique downstairs. I hope you like it." He handed me the bag.

I peeked inside. My eyes grew wide at the perfectly wrapped box with a beautiful, red ribbon tied around it.

"Open it, Sophia, and save the ribbon—we might find ways to use it later."

Shawn grinned like a little kid anxious to open presents on Christmas morning. "Open it. Come on."

I opened the box. I went slow, glancing at him while untying the ribbon. "You really shouldn't have bought me anything, you know. I do own a clothing store!"

I pulled out a luxurious, pale-pink, cashmere robe and gasped. "Shawn, it's so beautiful!" I gave him an admiring and grateful gaze, then added, "You really shouldn't buy me gifts."

He was a thoughtful man, which I could tell by the way he planned this weekend with us. I marveled at how considerate he was being.

"I want you to relax for dinner tonight, so I ordered room service for us," he said with a graciousness that melted me. "Are you okay with it?"

I loved the idea of just staying in and relaxing with him. *We just met, but it's like he can read my mind.*

"I love that idea. Thank you."

He walked over to the bed, offering me his hand to help me out. "Try it on, Sophia. Let me see how it looks on that voluptuous body of yours. It's gotta be amazing on you."

I stood naked in front of him, feeling no inhibitions about my body. "It's so soft and sexy. I love it. Thank you, Shawn."

He grabbed my hand and led me back to the bed, then untied the robe so he could see my body. "I'm going to devour all of your sexiness until dinner." He looked pensive for a moment and then asked, "Do you like it when I talk dirty to you, Sophia?"

Shawn shoved his fingers inside my already wet pussy, still moist from last night's orgasms. He slid two fingers in and out slowly. With intention to reach my pleasure areas, he stopped only to taste his fingers in between the strokes. "You taste so good. I could lick your pussy all day. Would you like that?"

He entered my wetness and fucked me slowly this time, looking into my eyes as he rocked over me. "You're so fucking wet. Is that for me, baby? Is all that wetness just for me? Tell me."

I had arched my back to meet his rhythm in sync with his motion. "I'm so juicy wet for you. Fuck me deeper, as deep as you can reach inside me. It feels so fucking good."

We came together furiously, then collapsed on the bed. We fell fast asleep for hours, twisted in each other's bodies. The phone awakened us. Shawn pressed the speaker button, and a voice said, "Hello, it's room service calling to confirm your special dinner menu for this evening."

Shawn confirmed his menu with the waiter. "Just please be sure to save the dessert cart for later, after our dinner is removed. Thank you."

I looked at him with curiosity and surprise. I touched his chest with my hand and slowly moved down toward his hardness. "Your attention to detail is pretty impressive, doctor. Is this how you treat all your new patients?"

"I've never been with a woman who could come multiple times like you do for me, Sophia. Is it me? Or do you do this for all your boyfriends?"

I felt somewhat embarrassed but flattered. "You know exactly what to do to me. You drive me crazy. Did you study the female anatomy in optometry school? Eyes and pussy classes all day?"

He smiled from ear to ear, pleased with my satisfaction and notably grateful for my compliment. "Oh, Peaches, I knew my appetite was starving for your juiciness, and I was hoping you would be a girl who allowed herself to come more than once. I had a feeling…"

We stepped into the shower, washing each other's bodies with the resort's sensual, cucumber-scented body wash. We kissed under the waterfall shower pouring warm water over our naked bodies.

I couldn't get close enough to his skin. I wanted more. I leaned on the wall while Shawn pressed his body against mine. He gently kissed my lips while the water dripped inside my open mouth. Our hands savored the sensations of the warm water beading into the crevices and curves of our bodies.

I toyed with him, slowly stroking his hardness while my head was back against the wall.

"You better behave yourself, Peaches. I'll have to fuck you again."

I leaned in, ready for more of his lovemaking. "I'm wet from all your naughty talk, doc."

"I want you to be hungry for more. We better get dressed, baby. Our dinner should be here any minute."

Shawn stepped out of the shower, wrapped a towel around his hips, and then handed a towel to me. I dried off and slipped into my new robe, my back still slightly damp from the shower.

"I love my new robe, Shawn. It's so soft and pretty. It feels so wonderful."

He grinned back with sincerity and charm. "You deserve it and so much more."

I felt so appreciative.

If he only knew just how much I needed this weekend.

The room service dinner arrived on time. I felt famished from all our activity. "This is a great idea. Dinner in our pajamas."

Shawn signed the room service check and gave the waiter a cash tip for all his help with the details. "Thank you for going the distance for my beautiful girl. She deserves it."

The waiter smiled back at me as I sat at the table covered in a white, linen tablecloth. "You're welcome. Enjoy your dinner and let me know when you're ready to receive the dessert cart."

Shawn lifted the silver dome from the dinner plate, revealing a filet mignon with a lobster tail neatly perched next to a baked potato with butter and chives. I laughed while I peered over the top of the plate. "Oh my God. I'm starving. Are you a mind reader?"

He knew exactly what to say to make me smile. "I am starving—for more of you."

Shawn was already pouring the red wine and smiling at his ordering accomplishments. "I hope you like everything. I ordered it last night after you left to come upstairs to get naked for me."

We ate and barely talked except to moan over the tasty flavors of the dipping sauces and juicy filets and lobsters.

Shawn insisted on feeding me some of the buttery lobster, cutting small bites, rolling it deep into the creamy melted butter, and holding the palm of his hand under the fork to save the creamy delight for licking. "I love watching you receive pleasure. You soak it up like a child who eats candy, so innocent and hungry."

I was amazed we made it through dinner without having sex. "I love receiving pleasure from you, doc. You seem to read my mind when it comes to making me happy. It's like we've known each other forever, right?"

Shawn smiled in his devilish way. "Yes, Sophia. I feel like I've known you forever. I now know every curve of that sexy body of yours. Let's relax and enjoy the rest of our wine. I have another surprise for you."

The room phone rang, and Shawn answered. "Yes, we're ready. Just leave the cart outside our door." He grabbed the "Do Not Disturb" sign and wheeled the dinner cart out into the hallway.

Then he pulled the dessert cart inside, pretending to be a waiter. "I'm here to serve you, madam. Would you like to be fed naked in bed?"

Shawn pushed the cart into the bedroom and stopped it next to the bed. Then, he lifted the cover to reveal his dessert creation, which included an assortment of homemade ice creams with a variety of toppings.

His hand waved over the delightful treats as though they were crown jewels. "We could indulge in whatever flavors you prefer. Lickable from a spoon or your body. What do you think, Sophia? Wanna join me?"

I smacked my lips in delight then circled my lips with my tongue. "I scream, you scream, we all scream for ice cream!"

Shawn reached over and untied my robe, allowing it to drop to the floor and expose my naked body. "You are so hot, Sophia. As hot as this hot fudge."

He seduced me by spilling a small drop of hot fudge over both breasts, letting it slowly run down and around my right nipple. He teased me with his tongue, rubbing the liquid from my already erect nipple. I slightly squirmed around from the heat of the hot fudge. His tongue licked my nipple into a blissful state.

His touch brought a welcoming warmth inside my body with every stroke. My erect nipple was rescued only by his slight tongue stroke across the center before pouring more liquid over my breast. "I'm going to make you very sticky. You're my favorite ice cream cone."

Shawn added the whipped cream and layered on the hot fudge, mixing it together with his fingers. Then, he licked it while he circled the fudge around my nipples.

I moaned. I felt addicted to his movements and suddenly wanted to pleasure him. "I wanna taste. I think it's your turn. I need your hard ice cream cone inside my mouth."

I rolled off the bed sheets, still sticky from his foreplay, and peeked over the dessert cart. Hot fudge and whipped cream remained smeared on my nipples as I gazed over the cart's delights. "I'm thinking strawberry syrup. It's fruit season, ya know!"

I laughed while pouring the strawberry syrup on his rock-hard dick, then used my tongue to slowly lap it off. As his erection grew larger between my lips, I gently allowed it to flow in and out of my mouth while I talked to him, saying, "I love the taste of strawberry against your skin."

He moaned with desire, holding my head gently against his body, allowing me to take his hardness deep into my throat. "We are a sticky mess now. I want to fuck you in the shower. You want me to fuck you?"

I followed my new lover into the shower, his body pressing hard against mine, the sticky fudge molding our bodies closer together. I wrapped my legs around his hips, balancing myself against the wall. He fucked me as hard as he could until I screamed, and he came inside me with force. I could feel his come filling me up.

When we returned to the bed, we fell fast asleep in each other's arms. I fit perfectly within the space between his chest and his hips.

I woke up in the early morning, and he made mad, passionate love to me again amongst the chocolate-covered white sheets. "I'm going to need to leave housekeeping a pretty hefty tip for this sundae delight." This time, he whispered in my ear, "I love watching you squirm around the bed while I lick your pussy, Sophia. I love hearing your moans, and listening to you have an orgasm makes me come."

I enjoyed his dirty talk. "You lick my pussy like you can't get enough of my sugar."

His smile surfaced as he rocked back and forth and leaned back so I could take all of him. Shawn was much younger than me, but I only realized his youthful energy in the morning. I was exhausted, but I loved the feeling.

I loved feeling connected to him as we drove back to the city in silence, holding hands through the winding, country roads as we listened to the sound of the road beneath us. I drifted off, thinking about how I had longed for this kind of connection for so long. I couldn't remember the last time I felt this satisfied.

Why did I wait so long?

We arrived back at my loft parking lot sooner than I hoped. I kissed Shawn in the street, not caring who saw us as lovers. "I can't wait to see you again, sexy. Call me later. I want to hear your voice in my ear like last night." I smiled. "Kiss me, I'm delicious!"

He leaned in, pulled me close, and he French kissed me. "Good night, Peaches."

I walked into my loft, still amazed at the beautiful place I called home. I looked at my phone for the first time all weekend. I had twenty-two messages, including six from Leanne, four from Violet, and one from Ronnie.

I started with Leanne, who answered, "What's up, girlfriend?" She was obviously running—I could hear her panting. "Where the fuck have you been, Sophia? I was worried about you."

Feeling starved, I searched my refrigerator for something to eat. "I'm sorry, girl. I was on a date with Shawn—a weekend date. We went into the mountains, and I didn't have cell service."

She giggled with approval. "Oh, God. I thought it was just a dinner date, but you were gone all weekend. Fucking amongst the bears, I hope? At least tell me you were fucking his brains out. Right?"

I cut an apple into fours and breathed in the aroma. *Smells like autumn.*

"It was an amazing weekend…and, yes, fucking amongst the bears." I couldn't wait to share my weekend with her but wanted to change the subject. "What's up with you? Have you heard from Markus since he got to prison?"

Her voice turned to angry tone. "Of course. The big, fucking crybaby is already bitching about me going to Boca for the winter. He thinks I should stay here and play with myself until he gets out."

"When are you leaving? You know I don't want you to go, but I understand why you're going."

"I gotta get out of here. I already had someone offer to buy my design business, so I'm going to take the money and run!"

I knew how much Leanne loved her business, but she was tired of pretending she wasn't married to a criminal. And all the snooty women had stopped calling her. "I know you're tired of those women and their gossip…"

"Those bitches can go fuck themselves. What they don't realize is that this could just as easily happen to them. Wait until karma delivers them a bowl of shit soup."

Leanne was angry for a good reason. The women in this city were cruel, and most of them were hypocrites who turned their noses up at Leanne now that Markus was in prison. I consoled her, but I knew she had enough of the gossip.

"Fuck all those skinny-ass bitch girls." I laughed. "You have more talent in your pinky finger than they have in their entire bodies."

She laughed. "I know, girl. Trust me, I know."

I understood the feeling of public humiliation. "I can't wait to watch these women crumble. It will happen!"

She grew angrier, her face flushed. "I lost it today…in yoga class at the club this morning. This bitch kept staring at me. I told this fucking cunt that she can go fuck herself."

I laughed. I could see the scene unfolding in my mind. "Oh my God, really? I hope she was mortified!"

Leanne giggled. "Yeah, she was promoting her husband's new movie about his days as a music producer. I couldn't stomach another fucking word out of her mouth and her side-eyed looks at me, so I said, 'Fuck your husband. He always said there's an ass for every seat. I'm not one of his asses! You are!'"

She laughed hysterically at her own sense of humor, but I knew she was hurting.

I grabbed a glass of water and laid down on my bed. "I wish I was there to witness the look on her skinny sunk-in face!"

Leanne screamed, "Wait one minute. I gotta run. My crazy son's trying to slide across the dining room table. Where's the nanny? I swear, she's gotta go. Talk to you tomorrow, Sophia. Love you."

Violet and Ronnie would have to wait until tomorrow.

I stripped off my clothes and slipped under the sheets naked; his scent was still heavy on my skin. I felt grateful I paid such close attention to the details of making a luxurious bed. No matter what financial condition I was ever in, I promised myself that I would always have luxurious bedding. My bed was my warm embrace, my unconditional love nest. I basked in my own self-love for a moment.

Shawn texted: *Sleep well, my love. I wish I was next to you and your juicy peach.*

I texted him back: *Thank you for the wet weekend.*

Chapter Eight

The Fires of Hell

Violet called me at six o'clock in the morning, waking me out of a dead sleep. She left a voicemail message saying, "The Twinkie was in the store working with me this weekend. She had an abortion. I think it was the cop's baby. I'm sick in my stomach. Call me ASAP."

I called Violet while I started the water in the tub. I wanted to soak my sore thigh muscles; I was feeling the after-effects of the wild, sexual positions of the weekend. "Oh my God, Violet. Tell me everything. Sorry I didn't answer your calls. I was away with Shawn for the weekend."

She was walking and talking. I could tell by the sound of her breathing. "It's okay, Sophia. I understand. Did you have fun? He better be nice to you, or I'll kick his ass."

I smiled. "He was wonderful. I'll tell you all about it later, but what's going on with the Twinkie?"

I lowered myself into the steamy, hot tub and poured Epsom salts into the water as I listened to Violet go on and on about the discovery. The view from my bath was of the smokestacks. I could see them in the distance, and I suddenly didn't regret a moment of my life.

I knew I would have died in that coal mining town, just withered away into a bitter woman. Just the thought of it made me sick! I felt content as the steam glistened my eyelashes, leaving me floating on a cloud.

Violet was ranting, interrupting my thoughts. "She was in the bathroom at the store, and then she came running out to tell me there was blood all over the toilet seat. I was like, 'Kennedy, what the fuck do you want me to do about it? Is it your blood?'"

I tried to be attentive but wanted to drift. I was having a hard time keeping up with Violet's chatter since she was going so fast. "Oh! Then what did she answer?"

Violet was panting. "She's like, 'Yes, it's my blood. I just had an abortion, and now I'm bleeding like crazy. Do you think I should go to the hospital?'"

I was in shock but wanted to calm Violet down so I could get the rest of the story. "Are you serious, Violet? Are you okay?"

She continued, "I just said to her, 'I guess, if you're scared, but don't ask me to go with you to the fucking hospital. I can't be involved in your shit.'"

"So, what did she do, Violet? Did she go to the hospital? What happened next?"

I heard Violet inside her store turning on the lights and music. "Yeah, she went. She said it was normal to bleed after an abortion. They told her she was supposed to rest for a few days after the procedure, but she didn't. So that's why she was bleeding."

I knew Violet wasn't one to judge other people's behavior, but she was truly concerned for her own health and safety. "She's going to get a disease, Sophia. I'm telling you, watch and see. I just want to be safe and not sorry. Do you think I can catch herpes from the toilet seat?"

I soaked deeper down into the tub of bubbly, hot water. It felt so good against my sore muscles, and the lavender scent was so soothing.

Shoulda lit a candle...Wish I was kinder to myself more often. I must soak and drift again tonight...

I had to reassure Violet about her problem. "I'm pretty sure you can't catch herpes from the toilet seat, but why don't you get some of those toilet seat protectors like they have in the airports?"

"Oh my God, Sophia. I can't even work in my own store without thinking about catching herpes, and the Twinkie is fucking a city cop who fucks prostitutes. What the fuck? She's out of control. I can't take much more of her bullshit."

I should zip my lip. But I can't.

"She's such a HOHO, you won't ever change a HOHO. Just go to pee across the street at the cigar store. He'll let you use his toilet if you tell him yours isn't working." *She's been extra paranoid about the whole situation lately.*

"I gotta run. I'm getting a shipment of heavy furniture in today, and since the Twinkie is out resting, I gotta unload it myself."

I had a busy day at my own store, as I was preparing for a large shipment arriving from a new designer, Walter Baker. The Garden of Eden was being featured in Real Simple Magazine's holiday edition, so I wanted the display to be perfect.

Violet was a survivor. She was strong and used to pulling her own weight, but she said, "Thanks, Sophia. I'll let you know. Thank you for listening. I love you."

Ronnie was supposed to meet me at my store this morning to try on some new dresses for her big CD release party, but she was always late. So, I didn't rush to be on time. I sipped on my coffee and reflected on my weekend of bliss. I felt so good. His attention to detail turned me on.

God, that man knows how to make me shiver, shake, and shout. I love peach season! And to think, we just met!

I walked to my store, smiling from ear to ear. *I got fucked by a young, hot doctor this weekend.*

I should call my mother and share the juicy story with her.

I can just hear her saying, *"Oh my! No way, it just can't be true. What doctor would want to be with a woman who's been divorced three times? No decent man would ever be with a woman with so many shady sides. Don't tell him the truth. He'll go running for the hills!"*

Ronnie finally walked into the store an hour late, as predicted. She brought my girls her new CD and a t-shirt with her logo on it. "Sorry, I'm late, Sophia. You know I hate being late."

I smiled and hugged her. "It's no biggie. Really, girl." I glanced around the room, conjuring excuses for the unpacked boxes still scattered about the store. "We're in the thick of it this week. I'm trying to get all the clothes steamed and out on the floor today because I have a fashion editor coming in to see this new line."

I asked the girls to play Ronnie's CD. It was so sexy and seductive. Then I turned toward Ronnie and said, "Your music is so awesome, girl. I really love it. Do you mind if we play it during the day at the store?"

Ronnie smiled. "I would love that, Sophia. I'll sign a bunch of them, and you can sell them if you want."

We walked around the store together, gathering dresses for Ronnie to try on.

"How have you been?" I asked.

"I'm so exhausted. I just can't sleep since Robert died. I can't get the thought of finding him sprawled out naked on his sofa, dead, out of my mind. Did I tell you he was holding the guitar that I bought him? I'm sick about it."

I hugged Ronnie, and her eyes filled with tears as she allowed my embrace to comfort her for a minute. I could sense the pain coursing through her veins like molten lava.

I wanted to ease her mind. "Let's get you in the dressing room."

She smiled. I knew she needed a change in subject. "I can't wait to see this Sky dress on you; it's so sexy and perfect for your big release party!"

Ronnie finished trying on dresses, then tilted her head at me. "Wanna grab some lunch across the street at Thai Me Up? It's the new Thai place. Their food's so good. I was there for their opening night. I took my drummer. It's really special."

"Sure thing. I'll grab my bag."

I asked the shop girls if they wanted some takeout, quickly took the orders, and headed out with Ronnie.

We devoured the delicious Thai food and enjoyed the thematic décor, especially the carved sandalwood chandelier and the large paintings of fishing boats, Thai women, and statues. Soft Thai music complemented the scene perfectly. I enjoyed talking with her about the music business during our meal. I walked with her to her car—a white Audi station wagon she had bought right after Rob died. "What the fuck, Ronnie? What on earth is all this stuff? Did you go on a shopping spree?"

She turned red with embarrassment, as she must have forgotten her station wagon was heaped full of hundreds of bags from TJ Maxx, Home Goods, Pier One, and Marshalls. I had never seen anything like it before.

Ronnie started crying. "I shopped and shopped and shopped after Robert died. I returned and returned, bought more and more, and then tried to return things again—so much so that the store managers forbade me to shop in their stores. I need to take this stuff back, but I'm not allowed in any of the stores, in any location." She heaved a huge sigh. "My dad is so fucking mad at me."

I felt at a loss for words, as if my tongue had turned to wax. I had no idea Ronnie had been doing all this crazy shopping. I stared at the bags inside the car, finally putting together all the excuses Ronnie made for not wanting to drive to meet me in the city.

She had these bags in her car for months…

"Do you want me to take some of it back for you? It might take weeks to get all this stuff back to the stores. Do you have the receipts?"

She wiped away the tears streaming down her face. "I lost it after Robert died. I couldn't control myself. I drank bottles of espresso vodka and shopped for shit I didn't even need. My dad is so mad at me right now. He scolded me like a child, and my mom took away all my credit cards and refused to give them back to me until I figure out how to get this stuff returned."

I recalled the day I begged my father for a two-thousand-dollar loan for my divorce. He forced me to count out twenty-dollar bills in front of him, claiming it was my punishment for being financially irresponsible as he stood patiently above me, scolding me for such bad behavior. I had run away in the middle of the night and knocked on their door, hoping my mom would answer this time. My bruises were tender to the touch. I held an ice pack on my swollen lip with my left hand as I counted with my right. My baby girl played with her baby doll next to me on the floor. I was only twenty.

My heart ached for her. "I'll help you, girl. Why didn't you ask me? Us girls, we must stick together in good times and bad ones. It's unconditional love. Your dad will forgive you. He always does."

Ronnie held nothing back as she opened the passenger side door for me to peek inside the car. "I charged over five thousand dollars on this carload alone. I'm so lost without Robert; I feel so guilty."

I hugged her as tightly as I could. I felt so bad for her. *Grief strikes us all so differently.*

"Let me take some of the bags. I'll ask my girls to help us too. I'll just ask them to do it for me as a favor. I'm sure

Violet will help you. We help each other. That's what friends are for. We have to stick together; we got your back, girlfriend."

She leaned against her car and placed her black Sophia Loren sunglasses on her face to mask her tears. "My dad hasn't scolded me like that in so long, other than the time I brought home my five little puppies. I love those dogs. He never liked my dogs because they pee everywhere. He's just so mad at me."

None of us liked those little dogs, either. Her condo reeked of dog urine, so none of us ever wanted to go to her place, even though her city view was incredible.

"Your dad will forgive you. He always does. He loves you, girl. Just focus on your big release party. It's gonna be great!" My heart felt heavy as I carried bags back and forth from her car to my loading dock and into my store.

Wish my father loved me with such force. Wish my mother showed one-tenth the love as Ronnie's mother. They are stern but their love is so apparent.

I felt so envious of my friend. Although she felt tremendous loss, she had incredible support and unconditional love from her family. The city streets were busy. I watched the cars pass by, knowing life was short. I had made good decisions for my children. I hoped I was a good mother. *I try my best.*

Ronnie reached inside her bag and gave me four backstage passes to her opening release party. "Thank you, Sophia. I love my new dress. I'm sorry for being a pain in the ass."

She handed me the last twelve heavy bags of merchandise from her car, and we walked them over to my loading dock. "No worries, girlfriend. We stick together, thick and thin—remember that forever." I hugged her. "Can't wait to hear you sing at the club later."

I leaned against the building, not wanting to go back inside my store yet. I peered up into the sky, scanning the rooftops of the skyscrapers in the distance. I loved the scents of the city. *I'm home.*

◆

The day flew by. I changed into a sexy black jumpsuit from Rachel Pally and added a pair of swanky hoop earrings. Satisfied with my choices, I walked to the club where swarms of reporters waited to get inside the release party. The place buzzed with as much energy as a hive full of hungry bees. The anticipation was palpable, and I felt my hairs stand on end.

Everyone wants to write about Ronnie's new release.

I overheard one of them say, "She's always been the love child in our city; she's our rockstar."

I met Violet outside the club, and we made it to the front door with little hassle. Ronnie hired young, sexy party girls to work the crowd. They all dressed in micro-miniskirts with black garters and stockings and little button-up plaid vests barely covering their breasts. Their ruby-colored, satin, high-heeled shoes made them look eccentric and hot as hell.

I snapped a picture of three of them standing together and sent the sexy photo to Shawn. *Every man's fantasy.*

He texted me back immediately: *They have nothing on you. You're my fantasy, Sophia.*

I smiled. *He always says the right thing.*

I called him and said, "Stop by. We're at Whisper in the South Side. You know the place, right? I'll get you in the side door."

"Okay, finishing paperwork. See you in twenty."

I felt grateful his office was close by. I got to see him at the last minute, which was better for me lately. I never knew how late I would stay open at the store.

I looked over at Violet, who was dancing to the music and stirring her cocktail while she looked around the crowd. "Shawn's on his way. Hope you don't mind a third wheel."

Violet didn't mind; she had her eye on Hines. She gave me a side glance. "Look what the cat dragged in!" She nodded. "I want to find out where James is tonight."

She didn't get out much, lately, so I didn't mind if she dumped me for Hines. She was carrying the store responsibilities while Kennedy was recovering from her abortion. "Sure. No problem."

Hines spotted us, breezed over, and kissed us on both cheeks like he was one of the girls. He was wearing a pair of tight-fitting skinny jeans with a starched white collared shirt holding a silk floral tie and a matching vest. His large diamond earrings covered his earlobes and caught my attention. "What's up, Sophia? Got any juicy stories for me? I've been outta town and miss seeing you girls. Tell me something, girl."

I smiled and let my gaze scan the room. I tried to ignore him but knew he wouldn't let me go without an answer. I shrugged my shoulders. "Nothing juicy to report here."

His slanted grin was devious. He was trying to pry information out of me. "Your friend Stephanie always has something going on in her loft." He caught my eye and added, "What's up with that, girl?"

I wasn't about to throw Stephanie under the bus. "I have no idea. Why don't you ask her yourself?"

Violet tapped me on the back to remind me she wanted me to be nice to him.

I gave her a dark sideways glance.

"Sophia, be nice to Hines. He's just asking you a question."

I stirred my drink and kept my stern look to affirm my feelings. "If you wanna know, ask her, not me." I nodded toward Violet, then turned to leave. "Nice to see you, Hines. I gotta go, catch up with you later."

I walked backstage, thinking about my rockstar night so many years before. Ronnie was standing near the stage waiting to go on, and she approached me. "Hey, Sophia!"

I smiled. "Wow!" I looked her up and down. "You look amazing!"

"Thanks. I love my dress. Thank you for helping me pick it out!" She posed like a supermodel and grinned.

I was happy. I said, "I invited Shawn. Hope you don't mind. I'm gonna meet him at the side door."

She smiled. "Of course! I can't wait to meet him!"

I kissed her on the cheek. "Have fun tonight, Ronnie. You're going to be great." I rushed to the side door, opened it, and found Shawn waiting for me. I ran up to him, and he kissed me passionately.

He glanced up at me with his big, blue eyes twinkling like a galaxy. "Hi, Peaches."

I couldn't resist closing my eyes to receive his kiss. "Let's get inside. Ronnie's about to start!"

Ronnie wrapped both hands around the mic and said, "Hi, folks. This song is 'Lost Inside Your Love' written for Robert by me." Her voice softened, the gentle lilt carrying a tender affection that warmed the room. She sang, belting out the words like she was singing it to him.

I felt a tear run down my cheek. Shawn stepped up behind me, slipped his hands around my waist, and whispered in my ear, "Hey, sexy. How's my girl?"

I leaned back into his chest. I didn't need to say anything, but I did. "I'm better—now."

The next song she sang was Ronnie's favorite song. She dedicated it to her father, who was sitting in the front row. She beamed at him. She spoke slowly, her measured pace reflecting the weight of her words. "My dad, he's my rock. Thank you for always encouraging me to write. I love you."

I felt the energy between father and daughter. *Wow!*

It was so desirable. I felt such a pang of sorrow. I felt emotions creep up from deep within my soul when I watched their eyes meet to confirm their love. *She's the luckiest girl in the world.*

She sang "Melt" while Shawn and I wandered off to the bar to grab a drink. My eyes couldn't hide my sorrow tonight. "It's been a tough day with Ronnie. My heart's broken for her. I'm sorry I'm not good company tonight."

He comforted me by staying close by my side. "I'm here for you, lover. Whatever role you want me to play, I'm here."

We decided to walk back to my loft, hand in hand, past the busy restaurants and people walking the streets. "I would like to stay the night. I'm worried about you."

"I would like that."

We laid down on my white, fluffy bed. Kissing my forehead, he gently removed my dress, untying it while he stroked my belly with his artistic hand until I was almost naked. "Let's just be here together, relax and unwind. I'll turn on some music. You stay right here."

He walked to my stereo and played Ronnie's new CD. "You can truly feel her soul in the words. She's quite talented. You must be proud of your friend." Her voice was velvety, a soft timbre that felt like a warm blanket on a cold night.

Shawn came back into the room and removed his clothes while his gaze remained focused on me. Then he wrapped himself around me, twisting his legs around my legs, just spooning under the moonlight shining in from the city. The silence was a welcomed change, with the rhythm of the music surrounding us with an old, familiar comfort. I just melted.

"You have so much pain in your heart. I can almost see it tonight. I wish I could take it all away."

He read my mind…

We dozed off in a cloud of comfort. When he left early in the morning, I didn't notice. I was in such a deep, sound sleep. A note lay by my bed with a red heart drawn around my name. It read: *I made coffee. Have dinner with me tonight.*

I called Leanne, looking for her advice. "I know you don't want me to be in love, but what if I'm falling in love?"

Leanne wasn't the best friend to call about the subject of love. She was still recovering from her husband's prison sentence, and her young lovers were more than she could handle right now. "Love is for babies. Not for us old ladies. He's probably looking to get married and have kids. Are you ready for more kids, Sophia?"

I walked naked through my loft, peering out to the city view. "I already have two kids, grown adult kids, and he knows it. I can't even have kids anymore. Oh my God, Lea, I never thought about it. There's no doubt he wants to have kids."

She laughed. "Just fuck for fuck's sake, Sophia. Get out of this stupid love bullshit. He's a great fuck. Enjoy it!"

I tried to think about something else all day, but I became consumed with wondering about whether I should ask him about it at dinner. I decided to let it go. It was his choice to be with me. He knew I had adult children. I knew my time with him was limited. I needed to prepare myself to be let down, eventually.

He's a doctor, after all. Surely, he's smart enough to figure out my age.

My phone rang and interrupted my thoughts.

It was Helena, who said, "My husband, Don, was sentenced to five years in federal prison for mail fraud and mortgage fraud. I'm calling my friends, so you'll hear the truth from me instead of strangers."

She sounded mortified. I knew she was worried about what The High Society Rich Bitch Club would say about the story. "I'm sorry, Helena. I'm sorry."

She upped her tone to sound more professional. "Yeah, the feds are making an example of Dan because he sent mortgage papers through the mail. They gave him more time for the mail fraud than any of the other charges."

I was sympathetic and tried to comfort her as best I could. I barely knew her. I wondered how she even got my number, but I wanted to act like a friend. "Oh God, Helena. I'm so sorry. Are you going to stay in town? What about your kids? How are they?"

She avoided my questions and got right to the real reason she called me. "I just wanted to tell you why I wasn't at Ronnie's CD Release Party last night and to let you know I won't be able to attend your fashion show. I'm sorry, Cupcake."

I cleared my throat. "No worries, Helena. I understand. If you need anything, just let me know."

Helena suddenly turned up her public speaking voice. Low and seductive, it suggested she was on top of her game. "I'm fine. My boyfriend's taking me to Italy for a few weeks to recover from all this nonsense. I must get out of the city to let the gossip die down a bit."

And, just like that, Helena fell off the face of the earth for a few weeks. Just enough time for The High Society Bitch Club to forget all about her. I said goodbye and went about my day.

◆

My phone rang. I answered, startled by the call, just realizing I had slept the day away. I was exhausted from the fashion show preparation. *Thank God I gave myself the weekend off.* The shop girls had it covered so I could rest and recharge.

Violet's voice was filled with anger as she rattled her story off without coming up for air. "Our employee, Auburn, is here at market with us in New York. We're sharing a room to save money. Auburn walked in on The

Twinkie while she was wearing a black strap-on dildo and fucking this guy from behind. The Twinkie was screaming, 'Tell me you want me to fuck you. Tell me.'"

I wanted to laugh but held it back instead. I walked into my closet to get my robe, suddenly cold. "Jesus Christ, Violet. This woman has a problem."

"What the fuck, Sophia? What is this whore's problem? She had an abortion less than a month ago. The fucking Twinkie is out of control! Maybe she's a sex addict."

I could tell she needed to tell me every detail about the incident. I put my phone on speaker and stared into the mirror at my face. *I need a facial.* I tweezed an unruly eyebrow hair. "Tell me the rest of the story."

"Auburn was mortified. She ran out of the room and right up to me, saying, 'I want to get out of here, Violet. I'm never walking into that room again. You must go in and get my suitcase so I can get another room.'"

"Jesus. And then…?"

Violet continued to rant. "This whore is out of control. She's fucking vendors in the same room I'm sleeping in. Jesus. She's such a slut."

I felt curious and wanted to make Violet laugh, so I said, "I guess she packed the black strap-on dildo in her suitcase. I wonder if security saw it in her luggage at the airport. Did you know she liked to wear a strap-on with guys? Why didn't we know this about her before? How big was the thing?"

Violet couldn't help but laugh at my questions. "It's just disgusting, if you ask me. She needs to go home and fuck her husband. He told me they haven't fucked in over two years."

I chuckled. *I'm going to have a hard time looking her in the face after hearing all these stories.*

"You gotta stop telling me these stories about this HOHO. I can't stand listening to them anymore. She's disgusting."

Shivering from being naked and walking on the concrete floors, I tied my robe even tighter. "I gotta run, Violet. I'm starving. I didn't eat a thing at the party last night, and I slept all day; I gotta get some dinner."

I hung up and noticed I had three missed calls from Ronnie and a text message from Shawn: *Gonna need a raincheck for dinner tonight. Sorry peaches.*

He canceled our dinner plans because he had an early morning eye surgery scheduled and preferred to do dinner tomorrow. I understood and welcomed the evening to myself so I could enjoy some self-love, but I was starving.

After ordering from the place across the street, I put my jeans and sweater on, and I called Ronnie back while walking. Her whispering voice held a note of mystery, a secret waiting to be revealed. "I'm having some journalist friends over for cocktails on Friday night; you'll love them, join us."

I smiled. She sounded happy. "Thanks for thinking of me. I'll be there. What can I bring?" I could hear her musicians in the background, a voice filling the air with a soulful melody.

Her voice emerged as a hoarse whisper—the aftermath of hours spent in the recording studio. "One of my restaurant clients is catering for me. Just bring your smile."

I grinned. *I'll take her a beautiful candle.* "I returned four bags of merchandise to TJ Maxx yesterday. Let your mom know you'll be getting credit to your card for twelve hundred dollars. I have the receipt."

"Thank you so much, Sophia. You have no idea how happy she will be. My dad too. He's going to stop by on Friday night to say hello. See you in a few days, love you. I gotta run. The guys are waiting for me."

I walked into the bar to wait for my dinner. I was greeted by my favorite bartender, Sergio.

"Hi, Sergio. I'll have a Grey Goose dirty martini with blue cheese olives while I wait. Thank you."

While I was there, I caught a glimpse of a man I thought I knew. Peering more closely, I saw it was Gary. He was Margie's soon-to-be ex-husband. I hadn't seen Margie since she had come to my grand opening party and left with one of the door handlers, my bodybuilder friend. *I wonder if they fucked. Maybe Kellie will confess. Heard he was a great lay.*

Remembering Margie's dressing room confessions, her voice echoed in my head. "I know damn well I'm not giving my husband my ass to fuck. I can handle Gary's desire to be spanked and let him fuck me with his limp dick, but he's not getting in the back door. Anal is not my thing. He's such a butt wipe. I told him to get a hooker."

I hated knowing all these dirty, little secrets about people; knowledge made it hard to look them in the face.

Gary approached me with a huge smile on his face. "How are you, Sophia? How's the new store?"

"I'm well. Thank you for asking. The store's good. I'm excited about an international designer who offered me his new resort line. I'm being featured in Real Simple Magazine's holiday issue."

He seemed eager to share his news, not hesitating to be open and honest with me. "I'm back in the dating scene. Margie and I finally started our divorce."

I knew Margie was already over him, she had dick-napped a man half his age. "I'm sorry, Gary."

"It's okay. She's going to be well taken care of, and that's all that really matters to me. I care for her and our kids."

"She's a lucky girl; not all of us are so lucky."

I had not wanted to sound negative, but it was too late. The words just fell out of my mouth before I could stop myself from speaking. I had forgotten Gary went to high school with my ex-husband number three. *Shit! I hate that I sound so weak!*

Gary waved at the bartender to come over, then leaned in, gesturing for Sergio to get closer to him. "I want to pick up this lady's check."

Suddenly, I felt stupid. "That's not necessary. I didn't mean to sound like I was unlucky. Don't even think about it. It's okay. I don't need you to buy me dinner."

"I just got a huge promotion and don't have anyone to celebrate with tonight. I usually rush home to tell Margie, but I'm rushing home to emptiness these days. Do you mind if we share a cocktail?"

I didn't mind. I welcomed his company and kind of felt bad for him. I knew he was a generous guy and a gentleman.

Besides, I rarely hear the man's side of the story.

"You'll get used to being alone. It can be rather nice at times."

"I don't know about being alone. I've been married for thirty years, as of yesterday. It will be an adjustment. Do you want to have a bite to eat with me?"

"I already ordered a take-out order, but if the waiter wants to bring it out, I'll eat with you instead."

Gary made sure of it by waving Sergio over to change the plan. "Can you please bring her take-out order to the bar and add the same dinner entree for me as well?"

He smiled. It seemed he needed to impress me with his kindness. "Let's keep each other company tonight."

I got to know more about Gary than I ever knew about him before. I learned he was friends with my ex-husband number three and Ethan. They grew up right next door in their little neighborhood, playing the trumpet and going to football games together. He asked me a million questions about my life, like, "Where did you grow up?" and, "How many kids do you have?" and, "Are you happy, Sophia?"

Gary was a dark-haired, Jewish man with a bit of a potbelly that he blamed on fine dining in restaurants all over the world, not having enough time to exercise, and simply prioritizing work over everything else. He had strong, family values, an aggressive attitude about his career goals, and a rock-solid plan for his retirement in a few years.

He trained young executives all over the world, so he traveled four out of five days during the week. His schedule was grueling and especially hard on his family. Neither one of us lacked for words about business. He seemed to like my fresh approach to my new single life, and he was curious about every detail.

"I hate being alone. I really don't think I'll ever get used to it. Do you think you can share your girlfriend Stephanie's phone number with me? I met her briefly outside on the street during your grand opening party. I didn't come inside because I was running late for a business dinner. I'm sorry!"

I agreed and shared it with him. I never gave it a second thought. I knew his sexual fetishes were one of the biggest reasons for his divorce. "You don't need to explain. I understand. Stephanie's awesome. She's one of my favorite humans in the world! Have a great night, Gary, and thanks for dinner."

I walked home texting Shawn: *Wish you were here with me. I'm walking home after dinner with a friend's husband.*

He texted back: *Does your friend know you're having dinner with her husband?*

They just started their divorce. I felt bad for him.

Feel bad for me. I'm all alone in my big, king-sized bed.

I loved the way he flirted with me. I texted: *I think you better go to sleep, so you're rested for your morning patient.*

You'll soon be my morning patient—I'll need to examine your peach. Sleep tight, Sophia.

Stephanie texted me while I was going up in the elevator. She sent me seven big heart emojis along with: *Thank you for the referral, girlie. Call me!*

I called her, and she answered giggling. "Gary just called me and said you gave him my number. Thanks!"

"I hope it's okay. You said it was okay to do it the last time I saw you, so—"

"I'm taking you to dinner." She cut me off, reassuring me of my decision. "You pick the place, love. I charge double my normal rate for his kind of pleasures; not everyone accepts anal, you know, so dinner is on me."

I wasn't surprised but laughed out loud. "He didn't wait a minute! I just left him. You don't have to do that, girlfriend, but I would love to have dinner with you. Let's make a date."

Stephanie wasn't shy about her profession as a high-end escort; she justified her way of earning a living. I didn't judge her decisions and certainly valued her friendship. She is the definition of drop-dead gorgeous, and she knows it. I liked that about her the most.

We decided to meet on Wednesday night after Stephanie's first performance with Gary, so she could share all his little, dirty secrets with me.

"I can't wait to tell you all about our little anal rendezvous. This is going to be so much fun sharing secrets with you! Now you're part of my little circle—my Sinners Club, love. Welcome!"

I grinned at the thought of Stephanie spanking him and allowing him to enter her Greek-style, giving him pleasure in exchange for her tuition.

Wonder if Stephanie would keep the curtains open and lights on? She'll probably beat Gary's ass red. After all, she aims to please, especially crazy fetishes. Would he be turned on even more?

I admired Stephanie's drive to chase her dream of becoming a psychiatrist one day. When we shared secrets one night over a firepit and a few dirty martinis, I finally had the nerve to ask her what her favorite position was, and she giggled, peering up at me over her olives. "CEO baby! CEO!"

I opened the door to my city loft, stripped off my clothes, and poured a glass of red wine left over from the night before. I craved my friend's insights. I was looking forward to dinner with Stephanie.

Chapter Nine

The Secret Garden

My heart raced with anticipation knowing Shawn was on his way over to visit me later that night.

I called Leanne for a boost of much-needed confidence after a terrible call with my mother. She knew how to make me laugh and briefly take away my pain. "My mother told me my ex-husband number one just had a baby with my cousin, Nora."

She giggled. "He married your cousin?"

I sighed. "Oh yeah, a bunch of rednecks! Remember our full moon wish?"

Leanne laughed loudly. "Oh no. Another one comes true! We really are evil witches!"

I continued, "The baby was born on my birthday! Yes, another one of our full moon wishes just came true!"

She laughed so loud. I could see her bent over with laughter as she sang her favorite song by 50 Cent, "In Da Club." She stopped singing to fill me up with feelings of happiness. "Fucking karma. It's a bitch! I love it!"

The knock at my door startled me out of the dance scene with Leanne. "I gotta run, girl. Shawn's here. Thanks for the boost of head juice! Just what I needed! Love you."

I opened the door to find my doc standing there with bags of takeout and a bottle of wine. *He's so fucking handsome. I dare not share my news of the birthday boy or all the dirty, little secrets about my redneck family. He probably had the perfect Hallmark card kinda family, not like mine.*

He showed up wearing his green scrubs. He looked so sexy. *My doctor lover's far better than any lover other than my rockstar.*

Shawn was such a master in the art of seduction and pleasure, so I teased him with my naughty flirtation, tilting my head and coyly saying, "Wanna play doctor with me?"

He didn't hesitate to play right back with me, with wide eyes and a beaming grin. "Of course, I want you to be my nurse. Put those pretty, little white garters on for me."

I grew wet with anticipation.

He spanked my ass lightly. "You're a naughty little peach." He grinned. "I need to wind down for just a bit. Let's watch a movie and play later, after I tease you for a while."

I liked his need to relax after a long day, no pressure.

He pulled out the takeout containers filled with healthy Greek salads from our favorite deli, plus a large container of seaweed and sandwiches. "I felt like a pastrami on rye. Don't know why, just in the mood."

I opened a bottle of red wine while he searched for a movie. "What's the latest dressing room confession? Any juicy stories to share with me?" I rolled my eyes.

I turned to face him while I popped the cork on the wine. "Oh yeah, of course. So, today there was this girl named Camilla, who is a stripper who came to buy a Sky dress—you know, the sexy ones. She said her boyfriend threw her off the balcony at Sanctuary nightclub last weekend."

Shawn's eyes popped with shock as he turned his face away from the television so he could hear me tell him more details. "Obviously, she survived. But she dumped the boyfriend, right?"

"Of course not, and she was telling me the story like it was no big deal. Her idiot boyfriend was jealous of some guy who tipped her a hundred dollars for showing him her muff. He said her twat looked like a hot pocket, so he got into a fight with her and tossed her right over the railing."

"Oh my God, Sophia. Why do these women stay with these guys? And better yet, why do they feel they can confess all these ugly secrets to you? It's crazy stuff. She told her boyfriend what the man said about her cooch? That's crazy!"

"Yeah, I know, right?" He coaxed me to share more confessions while he pulled out his pastrami sandwich and kissed me gently on the cheek. I played with him. "You better be careful; I'll have to attack you! Make you beg me to get naked!" *He even bites his sandwich in such a sexy way.* I loved every move he made.

"Here's a funny one—a woman in her late fifties, she told me when her plumber came to her house to fix her leaky sink, she fucked him because he was cute and she was so horny! He never looked at her leaky sink pipes! So, her plumbing problem was never fixed, so she called the company back to get someone else to return to fix the leaky sink. But he showed up, and they fucked again. She didn't get the fucking sink fixed. She said her beaver was working overtime, but her dam was still backed up! She still needed a plumber!"

Shawn laughed. I noticed his eyes were tearing from all the laughter. "You must be making this shit up. Do women really fuck the guy who comes to fix the plumbing? I thought this was shit I only read in *Penthouse*."

"I'm dead serious. I told her she must be pretty fucking horny to fuck a guy who comes over to fix her leaky sink—a guy with a dick and a wrench!"

He laughed at my sense of humor. "She bought all five dresses and matching accessories after I said that to her. I think they like my sassy answers. I'm like their therapist, I swear. I'm a sex-pert!"

I moved about the loft, putting our food onto plates and pouring the wine as I continued on with my stories about the dressing room confessions. "This girl, Teri, came into the store. Remember the girl who left her powerful husband? The one who's the CEO of the public utility company? You met her a few weeks ago at my store."

He nodded. "I think so. She's the one with the awful nose job and nipples going in opposite directions. Right? Don't ask me how I remember!"

We laughed. "Yes, that's the one! She took a bunch of crazy pills and started climbing out a bedroom window naked. When her neighbor spotted her on the ladder, ass perched high in the air, he called the police. The fireman had to rescue her like a cat in a tree. She was embarrassed telling me the story, but she told me all the nasty details today while she tried on dresses."

Shawn placed the salads on a plate while I poured the wine and continued my story. "Rich women have a lot of issues, more issues than fucking *Vogue*!"

He nodded in agreement. "You should be writing a book, Sophia. You can't make this stuff up!"

I laughed. "I should write a book. I'll call it Dressing Room Confessions!" He smiled, pouring me another glass of wine.

I said, "Here's one more confession for ya. This woman comes walking in, she's dressed in golf clothes, and she has long, over-processed, blonde hair. She introduces herself as ML. I never trust women who have two letters as a name. Anyways, her dentist boyfriend, Charles, cheated on her fifteen times with fifteen different women, all of them patients!"

Shawn stops dead in his tracks. "Seriously? She admitted that to you? Jesus."

I shake my head up and down, realizing the code of ethics issue. "Yeah! And she forgives him every time. How does a woman lack so much self-confidence? I just don't get it."

I sip my wine and sit back on the sofa as he rubs his head in confusion. "I've had enough of the confessions for one night! I don't know how you do it every day, Sophia. I would rather do surgery!"

Our night unfolded, quiet and relaxing, and we fell asleep on the sofa wrapped up together like two salty pretzels. He woke me up at midnight by shaking me lightly. "Let's move to your bed, sexy. Let's get comfortable."

The warmth of his body felt inviting as I curled up with my ass cheeks neatly tucked along his crotch.

"I'm so hot for you. Can you feel my hardness, Sophia?"

I sure can.

I wiggled closer.

The tenderness of our lovemaking felt intimate in the darkness, probably the most intense passion we ever shared. There was no air between our skin, our bodies in rhythm with the stillness of the night. He didn't speak a word, just kept his fingers light to the touch of my flesh. I moved with his hands as he stroked my hair lightly. I moaned as I inhaled his scent. Neither of us spoke a word; we just moved with each other.

His hands were warm and comforting, radiating a sense of security. A faded scar ran across his palm, a memento from a childhood adventure gone awry. I circled the memory with my tongue.

Shawn's hands were surprisingly delicate, incongruent with his rugged exterior. Each finger was slender, the nails well-manicured. His fingertips danced lightly over my clit as if his hands spoke a language of love that only we understood. I shook with feelings of pure pleasure.

He didn't say anything. His eyes focused on mine as he softly massaged my peach. My head was back against the pillow, eyes closed, knowing he preferred to watch me cum for him. He lifted himself on top of me to enter my wetness. My eyes met his, and I could feel his hardness deep inside. His body rocked back and forth. Our rhythm was a tumultuous symphony, full of passionate crescendos and soft and tender interludes.

I touched his face with my hands; our lips locked while his muscular chest brushed against mine. He leaned back so he could see my pleasure. I felt his cock expand inside me. I pulsed. My cum spilled out around his rock-hard cock, bringing him to completion. He smiled. We stayed locked in each other's embrace, no air between us.

He stood above my bed, gazing at me as I opened my eyes. "Good morning, sexy girl. Can I confess a little secret to you?" He laughed. "I loved every second of our passionate lovemaking session last night."

I grabbed his thigh gently with the palm of my hand nestled inside. "Was I dreaming about a sexy man in my bed last night?"

"I hope the sexy man was me. What was your dream about?"

"I had a dream that you seduced me at midnight—made mad, passionate love to me."

"Oh doll, that wasn't a dream. It was real. Do you need a reminder?"

Shawn slipped under the sheets until he reached my morning wetness. "I am really hungry for breakfast."

I spread my legs to welcome him into my juicy peach and pulled his head into my body, moving my hips with the motion of his tongue until I came into his mouth. "I'm such a spoiled girl. It feels so fucking good."

He liked my response. His lips touched mine gently, and I could taste my juices on his mouth. "It's the way it should be. You deserve it. I gotta shower and go, babe. I hope you don't mind I have to eat and run."

I stayed in bed a bit longer. I was looking forward to my dinner date with Stephanie, so I called her to ask if it was still on. "Oh, hell yeah!" she said. "I gotta run, sweets! See you later!"

◆

I walked to my store with a warm sensation between my legs, hoping the day would pass by quickly so I could hear Stephanie's confession about her hot sex.

A tall, beautiful blonde walked into the store and began touching the cashmere wraps and admiring the metal trees holding the Rachel Pally dresses. She smiled at me. "Hi, I'm Taylor. I love your store. It's so beautiful. I'm looking for pretty things to take on a weekend getaway to Naples, Florida."

"Hi, Taylor. I'm Sophia. I own The Garden of Eden. Why don't you look around while I grab a few of my favorites for you?" I chose a couple of Sky dresses, Nicky Hilton tops, and a Rachel Pally jumpsuit and placed them in a dressing room. "Thank you so much for coming in to shop with me. Let me know if you like my choices! I'll pull a few other pieces in the meantime."

Taylor stepped inside the middle dressing room. "Come out, Taylor, and let me see how gorgeous you look in the dresses. I love to see how they fit."

She assured me she would do as I requested.

The doorbell rang again; to my surprise, it was Stephanie.

"Hi, Sophia. Sorry I was short with you on the phone this morning. I was with a client. We partied all night, and he stayed over. I'm here to buy up a storm with his black Amex card; we're going to Vegas this weekend!"

"Hi, Steph! No worries. I'll pull a few things for you. Some sexy stuff I know you'll love."

I searched for all the sexiest Sky dresses and a Nicky Hilton disco jumpsuit, and she walked back to the dressing room next to Taylor.

Stephanie dropped her oversized Louis Vuitton bag to the floor, flipped off her Chanel tennis shoes, and pulled her long, brown hair back into a messy bun. "I love these leopard chairs, Sophia. You thought of everything. Do you have any champagne? Maybe three shots of espresso were too many this morning! I'm dancing on the ceiling right now!"

I smiled and uncorked a bottle.

She continued, "I have a bit of a hangover from last night. We started partying at Sanctuary and ended up fucking in my loft until an hour ago. I'm surprised you didn't hear me screaming! You're loft 1700, right?"

I was trying to manage both women and pour champagne while I listened to Stephanie go on and on about her hot date. I wished I had one of the shop girls in early. I should have known better.

"Steph, here's a glass of champagne." I started to whisper so Taylor couldn't hear me. "No, I'm in loft 1711. I'm quite a way down the hallway from you. Loft 1700 is Hines; you know, the Steeler guy. No wonder he's so hot for you…he can probably hear you fucking all day and night."

She giggled. "Oh, well. Hines will have to get over it. I'm not into giving free samples to football players. He can beg me, but I'm not a sampler platter, for Christ's sake. These pros all think they can get their pussy for free; not this kitty!"

I wanted to include Taylor in the morning treats. "Taylor, would you like a glass of champagne?"

I placed the sexy Sky dresses, Nicky Hilton jumpsuit, and a Young, Fabulous, and Broke t-shirt embellished with gold studs in Stephanie's dressing room. "Just throw out the ones you don't like, and I'll hang them up. I think you're gonna love this Young, Fabulous, and Broke line from LA; it's super hot and trendy!"

As the two girls tried on their clothes, I tossed the rejected ones on the chair and fetched new ones with matching accessories. I was spinning around, busy keeping up with the girls in the dressing rooms, but I loved the chaos.

Stephanie just kept talking and talking. "So, this guy from last night, he was throwing money around like he was going to die the next day! He was buying expensive champagne, nonstop, and he even bought us a couple of eight balls! Then he tells me he's flying to Vegas on his private jet, and he's taking me with him. He's paying, of course, and he's giving me shopping money!"

She stepped out of the dressing room wearing the first turquoise-colored Sky dress, and my mouth dropped open with delight. "Wow, Steph, you must buy this one. It's absolutely gorgeous. You are hotter and sexier than the model who was walking the runway in this little number!"

Stephanie agreed and fluffed up her breasts tucked tight inside the top of the dress. "I love it, Sophia. Add it to my pile. Of course, I want the necklace and earrings to match. I want to try on more of the Young, Fabulous, and Broke stuff, it's so hot!"

I smiled. "I knew you would like it, and I love the name. I have a dress with the name written across the front. I'll grab it for you!"

She rambled on, bragging about her new client, Junior. "Can you believe Junior called my pussy his juice box? I swear he's a child. A juice box, really?"

I started her an exclusive holding area and added the dress to a Garden of Eden garment bag while Stephanie continued her chatter about her date.

"So anyway, Junior—that's my client's name—he's kind of a fat, jolly kinda guy, but he has a great sense of humor, and he loves to spend money. He's definitely in the mood to party. I think he's getting divorced—not sure, and it doesn't really matter. I have his black card, so I'll take all the dresses, the jumpsuits, and the Young, Fabulous, and Broke items you have in my size and the matching everything to go with them. After all, I'm his little juice box."

I wasn't surprised. Stephanie had told me before I opened the store that she would definitely be one of my best clients as long as I was willing to use her clients' credit cards to pay for her play clothes.

I didn't care where the money came from, so I told her, "Yeah, sure, girl. As long as you bring the credit card with you." Then, I said, "You sure are a juicy one! Throw me that card, please..."

Stephanie tossed the black Amex card out through the curtains. "Of course, doll. Junior left it on my nightstand this morning. He said, 'Go shopping for whatever makes you Vegas-ready, my little juice box.'"

I picked up the credit card from the floor. "Thanks, girl. I'll get everything together, and you just let me know when you're ready."

I wondered how Taylor was doing in the dressing room. *She's so quiet.* "How are you doing, Taylor? Are any of the dresses working for you? Do you need any sizes exchanged for other sizes?"

She answered in a very low tone. "I'm good, for now, Sophia. Thank you. I'll come out in a little bit. Sorry, I'm still trying on."

My gut instinct told me she might be offended by Stephanie's conversation, so I walked over to Stephanie and whispered, "I have another client in the dressing room next to you. Just FYI, girl."

She didn't care about Taylor. "Oh, honey, what's my total? If it's less than five thousand, bring me a few more dresses and anything else you have in my size. I'm planning to give Junior the best blow jobs of his life, so I might as well be rewarded for my hard work—get it? HARD work."

Stephanie was laughing at her own joke, and then she started singing, "I work HARD for my money, so HARD for it, honey!"

I pulled everything I had in Stephanie's size, including lingerie and shoes. "Here ya go, Steph. Try these things on."

While I was pulling merchandise, one of the shop girls came into the store. I felt so grateful, as I needed some help this morning.

Barbie saw me running around. She said, "I'm a little early, but I thought you might be busy, Sophia."

"Oh my gosh! I'm so glad you came in, Barbie! Can you start hanging up the dresses in the back? I have two dressing rooms going right now."

"Sure thing, Sophia. I gotcha covered."

Stephanie walked out of the dressing room wearing only her red, thong panties and matching lace bra, which barely covered her very large breasts. "I'm famished, doll. Do you have anything to eat?"

My shop girl Barbie blushed with embarrassment. "I'll look in the fridge. We probably have something in there."

Stephanie walked around the store like nobody noticed her nearly naked body. She picked up the necklace that was on the mannequin up front. It was designed to be over the top to grab attention. "Sophia, throw this gorgeous necklace into my bag. I'll wear only this beauty when I'm fucking Junior's brains out in Vegas. I usually go commando, so these babies will look good against my big nipples!"

"Of course, Steph. It really is a beauty, isn't it? I designed it myself. I simply love it." The pink pearl Lee Angel necklace was held together by black Lucite link chains. It was a combination of feminine and tough biker girl. I loved the way it looked over a casual white t-shirt or an elegant black dress.

Stephanie did not seem interested in the details, as it seemed she was just looking to buy the most expensive stuff in the store.

She put on the necklace and walked back into the dressing room. She slipped on a pair of shoes and strutted around the store in her red panties and lace bra like she was on a runway. "Darling, don't hate me because I'm beautiful. Hate me because I'm fucking your husband for money."

She laughed as she walked the runway. "I gotta run, Sophia. Time to get to the library to study the male brain before I examine the male anatomy! A girl can never be too smart or too rich. Don't forget dinner with me tonight."

I helped Barbie gather Stephanie's items to get her out quickly. "Barbie's going to wrap up all the accessories and place the dresses in our new garment bag. You'll be all set in a few minutes."

Stephanie stepped back into her dressing room and tossed out the dresses that didn't fit. "I must take a nap before our dinner tonight. Do you mind dropping my stuff off at my loft later, Sophia? I'm right down the hall from you."

"I don't mind. Just sign the receipt, and I'll see you later!"

Stephanie signed the receipt. She spent four thousand eighty-five dollars; I was surprised but very happy. "Not my total, love. Junior's total. He said he's going to fuck my brains out this weekend, so it's the least he can do for me. And I wanted to pay it forward to my girlfriend—we girls have to stick together!"

She kissed me on the cheek and waved. "I gotta run. Bye-bye, darling. See you later."

Taylor stepped out of her dressing room wearing one of the cute, silky, lounge shorts. With the matching tank top, she looked as white as a ghost. "Sophia, I'll take you up on that champagne if you still have any left after that client."

I blushed as I walked to my wet bar, set up conveniently near the register. "Oh my gosh. I'm so sorry. Stephanie is not shy. Some people should use a glue stick instead of Chapstick! She really means no harm, though."

Taylor sipped the glass of champagne until it was gone and handed the glass back to me to fill it up again. "I'll take this set in both colors if you have my size. I must be honest with you, Sophia. Junior is my soon-to-be ex-husband. Stephanie was talking about my husband; I just know it."

The look on my face had to express my shock. "Really? Are you serious? What are the chances?"

She smiled. "Trust me. How many Juniors are there in this city? Fat ones? With a lot of money?"

I shook my head up and down, agreeing with her assessment.

Taylor continued, "We're in the heat of a terrible divorce and fighting over alimony, child support, and my house." She sighed. "His billionaire father, Senior, pays all our bills, so I'm basically negotiating with my father-in-law and all his powerful attorneys. Can you believe it?"

I felt shocked, and my eyes grew round with embarrassment. "Oh my gosh. I'm truly sorry, Taylor. I had no idea."

Taylor reached for the handful of clothes I was holding. "These are the things Stephanie was trying on next to me, right?"

"Yes, they are."

"I want to try them. If they fit, I'm going to take all of them. I still have Daddy's black Amex card, so I'll take all these clothes and all the matching accessories."

Why not? I'm here to earn a living. Ring the register, girl. Cha-ching!

I gathered more merchandise for her to try on. "Taylor, these Rachel Pally dresses would look amazing on your incredible body. You're so elegant and classy. Did anyone ever tell you that you look a lot like Elle McPherson?"

"Thank you, Sophia. You don't have to say that to me."

"I mean it…really, I do. You're a naturally beautiful woman. Junior doesn't deserve you!"

Taylor stepped out of the dressing room. She handed me twelve Sky dresses, a Nicky Hilton jumpsuit, a few of the Young, Fabulous, and Broke t-shirts, a pair of shoes, and four necklaces. "I'll take all of these, and please find me a Chan Luu wrap bracelet, an expensive one with pearls on it."

I pulled my favorite pearl bracelet by Chan Luu from the display case. "Your total is thirty-nine hundred dollars. Is that okay?"

She grinned. "Please add this gorgeous candle with the pearl embellishment as well."

I smiled. "I love these candles; the leather strap can be reused once you burn it down. Your new total is forty-five hundred dollars." She smiled.

Taylor gave me a black Amex card with her father-in-law's name on it. I took the card. "Do you know his zip code?"

She grinned. "Of course, Sophia. Don't worry about it. Senior won't question the purchase, and Junior will think his hooker friend charged it. Wait until I tell him the story about me meeting his little juice box!"

I rang the sale, and it was approved. "I don't want to get mixed up in the middle of your divorce. I just opened. I'm a single woman just trying to earn a living. I don't need trouble."

She laughed and then got very serious. "Should I forgive him because his daddy built a hospital with his name on it?

These men are ruthless bastards for arguing about how they pay me. I'm supposed to keep my mouth shut about my kids' school tuition and child support payments going through their businesses as a tax write-off, a conspiracy to hide the truth."

Taylor signed the receipt and then looked up at me with a smile on her face. "I want you to keep this card on file. Call me when new merchandise arrives…whatever you think I will like. And will you deliver it to me? I'll pay extra for delivery."

"Of course. It's my favorite way to shop with my clients. I'll order new merchandise with you in mind and pull your sizes as they come in. And again, I apologize for Stephanie."

"No worries, Sophia. She gave me plenty of great ammunition. These motherfuckers think I'm stupid. They try to intimidate me, but I'm done with their nonsense. She did me a favor. I want you to thank her for me, but only after she returns from her sex weekend with my husband in Vegas. Will you promise me? You will do it for me, right?"

"Of course. I'll tell Stephanie she helped another woman gain power—she'll love it! She's a girl's girl."

Taylor left the store. My head was spinning, and I felt exhausted from all the stress. I already had enough drama, and it was only eleven o'clock—still hours yet to go until closing. I needed some air, some lunch, and a walk just to absorb all the confessions.

I wondered if every day was going to look like this one.

I called Shawn, expecting to leave a voice message. But he answered, so my voice quivered as I responded to his sexy hello. "What's a sexy guy like you doing on a morning like this one?"

He answered quickly, "Hey, pretty lady. I was just thinking about you."

I whispered, "Dressing room confessions. Wait until you hear this morning's dirty, little secrets!"

I heard his sexy laugh. "I can't wait to hear about these naughty women."

I giggled. "Oh, you have no idea. These girls bite back!"

<hr>

I walked home carrying Stephanie's garment bag full of Vegas attire. She was waiting for me in her loft. I opened the door. "Hello! It's me, Sophia."

She answered immediately. "Come in, girl. I'm in my boudoir. Come in!"

She was wearing a sexy pair of lacey thong undies and a matching bra that barely covered her large nipples. "Did you take all the sexiness from every woman in this city? What the fuck, Steph? Nobody gets this much sex into one body!"

She giggled, wrapping a silky black Chanel dress around her curvy body as if it were a simple peasant dress. "You're too kind, love, too kind. Let's go; we have the two best seats reserved at the bar. My favorite bartender, Jules, is there tonight; he's waiting for us!"

Stephanie and I walked hand in hand down the busy street to happy hour at Eddie V's Steak House. The hip, swanky bar, decorated in purple and silver accents, set the cocktail lounge up as a sexy place. The barstool was heavy, but I managed to pull one out just enough to sit down.

Jules handed us each a cocktail menu; I was surprised by the fifteen-dollar drinks. Stephanie smiled at him and ordered a bottle of Opus One to share with me. "I owe you big time, Sophia. My new anal client—your friend Gary— is going to be one of my regulars. He's willing to pay top dollar for his anal play and domination fetish."

"Oh my God, Steph. Do tell. I'm glad I could be your pimp—sorry! Just kidding, girl."

"No need to apologize. You are my pimp, girly. Let's negotiate our partnership. When he comes over for a spanking, we will go to dinner, and it's my treat. Promise me. Let's promise to spend some of his butt money on eating delicious food together. Let's indulge!"

"You got it, girlfriend. Now, tell me all about his spanking! I've been waiting all day!"

Jules poured a small taste of Opus in a glass for Stephanie to try. She swirled it around in the glass and nodded her approval while talking to me. "He asked me to whip his ass with my leather riding crop, which I did with great pleasure. I love that piece of leather; it makes me feel powerful."

Jules was listening as he poured our wine glasses full, nearly taking it to the rim. He was obviously trying to act like he didn't hear her tell me the sex story. "Let me know when you're ready to order."

While the bartender walked away, Stephanie got into her story. "Gary can only get an erection from getting his ass whipped first." She grinned. "He likes fucking in the ass but only after he's turned on by the spanking. I joked with him about his fetish just to put him at ease with me."

She continued with her story, her eyebrows raised, anxious to get it all told the way it happened. "I said to him, 'I hear anal helps reduce fat.' He thinks I'm funny, even though he's so straight. I think he's kind of boring—except for the spanking part. Maybe he'll loosen up after a few sessions."

I was following along, listening to every word she used to describe their sex session. "What did he say about paying more for anal sex and domination? Did he agree?"

She giggled like it was a game. "Oh yeah. He said he's willing to pay me whatever amount just because he can't meet anyone who understands his domination fetish. I told him, 'I'll spank your ass until it's beet red with welts if you want me to. I'll walk on your ass with my stilettos, fuck you in the ass with my dildo, whatever you want, baby. Nothing's too kinky for me!'"

I smiled. I loved hearing about her sexual fetishes. It fascinated me. "Go on. What else did he say?"

Steph could tell I was into the conversation. "He asked me if he could see my rosebud. He enjoys just playing softly with my asshole before he enters me."

Stephanie smiled when the bartender Jules arrived back to take our order. She flirted with him, "Hey baby, we're ready." She was a pro at reading the menu. "We'll have the filet mignon crusted in cumin and black pepper with a platter of assorted grilled vegetables. Make sure our meat is beaten, you know, love tenderized."

She paused until Jules walked away. "I know the world has gone butt-wild ever since Kim Kardashian launched her big, round ass to the world."

We laughed out loud, sipping our wine while she ran her hand around the rim. "He's quite the man. I told him a rim job is in his future! I'm really going to enjoy teaching Gary about the best ways to get the most fun from his little fetishes. Then he won't be boring! Thanks again, girl."

She kept no secret hidden from me, and it made me feel special. I nodded.

"I love studying human sex tendencies and why we desire certain fetishes. I like learning where they come from and why some people get turned on by bondage and others like roleplaying, flogging, or anal." She raised her brow and then grinned. "I'm studying sexual relationships as my major in college."

I giggled with a bit of embarrassment from Stephanie's bold confessions. "I spend a lot of time walking around my loft naked because of you! It's my new favorite thing to do. I do it all the time now!"

"Oh my gosh, girl. I'm so glad you enjoy nakedness alone! You've been a mother for so long that you didn't have time to explore your own sexuality until now. Enjoy every minute of it."

I was fascinated by her taking money for sexual favors. "What's it like to give an ugly guy a blow job for money? Sorry, you don't have to answer. I'm just curious. I couldn't do it."

Stephanie sipped her wine using her tongue to rim the glass for me to notice her motion. "I guess I'm good at psychological play—mind control for myself. I just roleplay and imagine he's Brad Pitt. It's just a job, and I make a lot of money granting wishes. You might say I'm a fairy godmother."

I felt comfortable enough to share some of my deep, dark secrets with her. "My ex-husband number three and his new wife are into swinging. What do you think about that kind of fetish?"

She smiled. "Oh, doll. Look at you…not so innocent after all. Was he really into swinging or cuckolding? You know? When a husband watches his hot wife have sex with someone else but isn't allowed to participate?"

"Cuckolding? I'm not sure. I've never heard of cuckolding!"

She giggled. "It's permission to cheat, basically. Your partner likes to watch you have sex with someone."

Stephanie was serious and suddenly into getting into my head. "Is your ex still into swinging? Do you know what kind of swinging his new wife is into, bi-sexual partners or couples? What was his childhood like? Normal? Just curious. It's great research for me."

I kept talking, willing to share my knowledge. "He was adopted a few days after he was born. He had two great parents and a normal childhood. His new wife, Diane, left her husband for my ex, and they swing with his best friend and his fiancé. I think it's all weird."

Her eyes grew wide, intrigued. "Do you think he would be into me interviewing him privately about his swinging experiences? I want to get inside a swinger's head, get to better understand the desires for my upcoming thesis."

I laughed. "Oh my God, Steph. I could call him right now and ask him, 'Hey. Do you mind if my friend Stephanie comes over to interview you and your wife about fucking your best friend and his fiancé?' I'm sure that would go over well. He'd probably say, 'No worries, Sophia. Send her right over. And why don't you come along?'"

We belly-laughed so loudly that the bartender came over to get in on the conversation. "You girls are having way too much fun. How does a guy like me get in on this girl talk?"

Stephanie acted cocky and got away with it because she was so sexy. "You'll have to pay for that privilege, big time!" She focused back on me. "Are you going to tell me about your cuckolding experience, Sophia? Come on, give it up."

I suddenly felt the blood rush to my face, either from the Opus wine or from Stephanie's persistence in the questioning. "It was a long time ago. I foolishly thought it might save my marriage since my husband begged me to do it. So, I picked up a guy in Vegas."

Her slanted eyes perched as far up on her forehead as they could go. "Ooh la la. Tell me all the juicy details. Was he hung like a horse? What was his fetish? Go on, do tell, Ms. Sophia."

My face was red. I could feel it. "I was attracted to him. He was a captain in the Navy and hadn't been with a woman in two years. So, we had really good sex—fucking while my husband watched. My only complaint was my husband's eyes peering upon our naked bodies. It was awkward at first, but after a while, I forgot he was in the room until he wanted to join us."

Stephanie sipped the Opus wine, hanging on to every word I said. "So, hubby was into men as well as women? There's a plot twist!"

"Yeah. Believe me, I was surprised. I had no idea until that very minute. He was into both men and women. Kinda freaked me out. The captain wasn't into men, so my husband left us alone in the room to finish our passionate lovemaking while he threw his frustrations down at the blackjack table."

She smiled. "Aw, lucky you! Did hubby ask for you to repeat the performance?"

I shook my head up and down, remembering that time in my life as if it were yesterday. "He wanted to watch me have sex with men more often, and I just couldn't do it. Even though the sex was great in Vegas, I hated having my husband in the room."

"Why did it feel so wrong when you say it felt so good to you when it was happening? Did you feel guilty?" She didn't wait for my answer. "Wait, I know the answer—good, old-fashioned Catholic guilt."

Suddenly, I felt ready to release my innermost thoughts on the subject. "Oh God. Hell, yes. Guilt for feeling like I was free to explore my own sexuality, my own selfish needs. My mother did a fine job of raising a totally guilt-ridden daughter. But quite honestly, I didn't really enjoy having someone watch me have sex."

Stephanie called Jules over to clear the empty dinner plates, grabbed the dessert menu, and ordered two of the finest creme brulee desserts with different toppings. "Let's indulge, free from guilt. Let's be sinners tonight, Sophia."

We giggled as we finished the last sips of the bottle of Opus. "See what guilt can do to a girl?"

"Ruins everything," I agreed. "I raised two babies, practically alone, built an empire for my ex-husband, lost it all overnight, and now here I'm starting over again. Guilt is all I have, besides regrets and mistakes."

Stephanie grabbed my arm and squeezed it tight, peering into my eyes like she was about to perform an exorcism. "Let's get rid of these evil spirits inside your soul.

Peace be with you, my child. I order you to a weekend of pure bliss, whatever that looks like to the non-guilty Sophia. A weekend fuck-fest walking around in the nude, or whatever *it* is for you. Men, women, or both. Just go for it. Do you know what it would look like for you?"

I was blown away by the question. I hadn't ever thought about it. A weekend of self-indulging, a guilt-free weekend without regrets. "I have no idea, Steph. No idea."

She smiled, keeping my attention. "But isn't your ex-husband lucky to have discovered and indulged in his *it?* You must admit you might even be jealous of his newfound freedom?"

"I guess, when you put it that way. I'm not jealous of his *it* because it's not my fetish, but I get what you're saying. It's liberating to be in your own freedom zone, doing what pleasures you the most."

"I know what turns me on—intelligence. I love the brain and the way it works. My perfect lover will read medical journals to me while he's fucking me from behind."

She burst out in a big laugh, teasing me with her great sense of humor. I was proud of my ability to keep up to my friend's wit. I covered my mouth when I laughed, so the bartender didn't come back over to quiet us down again.

"So, you're a Sapiosexual. Someone who loves big brains. I love intelligence, but there's nothing like a big dick to finish off a nice, long tongue bath."

We clicked our empty wine glasses. "Touché' to big! Everything big is so much better. Go big or go home!"

Stephanie had a way with words, and tonight was no exception. "I can't wait to get butt-fucked by your friend Gary again so we can continue this sex talk over dinner next week!"

Captivated by our confessions, I exclaimed, "You already have another session scheduled with Gary?"

"Yes, he's back from Chicago on Thursday night and coming over to the loft on Friday afternoon at three. Wanna join us?"

"Hell, no, Steph. I don't wanna watch you spank his ass red with delight or watch him fuck you in the ass. Oh my God, no."

"Relax, doll. I was joking; besides, you'll be starting your weekend of bliss next Friday around three, right?"

"Maybe. I gotta figure out what a weekend of bliss is for me first, and that could take a week!"

Stephanie slipped a little white pill into my hand. "Take this little baby, and let your mind relax. You'll know what your bliss is within an hour. Here's what to do—take off all your clothes, slip the pill on your tongue wash it down with a big gulp of red wine, then relax on your bed. In a few minutes, you'll be ready to write down your ideas in a journal. Your mind will thank you. It's harmless, I promise. Just a Vicodin. A low dose. You need to chill, girl. Were you always this fucking responsible?"

I took the pill and tucked it into my bag. "Girl, I had a baby at nineteen, divorced by twenty, another baby at twenty-five, divorced twice by twenty-six. I've been raped and beaten, but none of the bastards could keep me down. So, yes, I've always been fucking responsible."

She grinned. "Jesus, Sophia. We need to pick up exactly where we left off. Promise me! I want inside your head, promise. I gotta meet a redneck millionaire who gets his rocks off by jerking off into cobb salads. I'm not kidding!"

I giggled, continuing to relish her sense of humor. "Gross! A redneck? Really, Steph? You gotta be kidding me!"

Stephanie got serious for a minute as she stopped in the crosswalk, waiting for the light to turn green. "I wish I was kidding; money doesn't buy class, love. I gotta pay for my books for next semester, so baby gotta do what baby gotta do!" We walked hand-in-hand down the busy street.

Stephanie turned heads wherever she went. Her beauty was exotic and rare, but she hardly noticed.

"What a truly beautiful night. Isn't it, Sophia?"

"Yes, it sure is beautiful. We share such a beautiful city life. Don't we, Steph?"

We side-kissed and walked our separate ways. I stepped inside my loft and immediately took off all my clothes. I hung my dress on a soft, velvet hanger inside my closet and placed my shoes inside their appropriate shoebox. I laughed while I talked to myself as I searched for my journal.

You silly girl. You're always so fucking responsible, even when you're alone. Next time, throw your clothes all over the floor, kick off your shoes, and let them fall wherever.

You're home.

◆

I woke to the sound of my alarm, city horns, and the buzzing of cars driving by.

Love the sounds of the city traffic. I'm such a lucky girl.

My wardrobe resembled a well-stocked boutique filled with all the bobbles from the latest designers. It was obvious that no man lived here. My closets were full.

I love my life right now.

I had a hot date for dinner with Shawn. I wondered what special surprise he had waiting for me, as he always had a plan.

How'd I manage to attract such a wonderful lover? It's been so long since passion played a part in my life.

Maybe last weekend was my weekend of bliss. I enjoyed my time with Shawn. This weekend of bliss idea weighed heavy on my mind.

I touched my favorite bottle of perfume; Jo Malone, a crisp, zesty, citrus scent. I smiled, recalling how he remarked on my scent when I wore it.

My little peach with a slice of citrus, juicy, delicious.

My phone rang, surprising me out of my wet fantasy. My ex-husband number three was calling me after years of not speaking a word to each other. Strange how we were just talking about him last night.

I hope he's not calling because someone overheard my story at the restaurant. Oh, God!

I answered without thinking too deeply about it. "Hey, what's up?"

His voice was quivering. "Diane died yesterday. She fell down on the floor in the garage while she was packing the car to go to the airport for a girls' golf trip in Florida. She had a stroke."

I didn't know what to say. Diane had pursued my husband like a dog tracks blood in the woods, following the scent to trap her kill. "Oh my God, I'm so sorry."

He started to cry hysterically, his dog barking in the background. "She was the love of my life, Sophia. I can't go on without her. What will I do? God, I just can't believe it."

I placed my phone down on my dresser and put him on speaker while I walked toward the tall window overlooking the street with the smokestacks in the distance.

Why the fuck did you just call me after all these years? Just to tell me your dead wife was the love of your life. Why the hell did I give you fifteen years of my life? To be second best?

I answered him anyway, staring out into the distance and watching the smoke fade out into the sky. "I'm so sorry. It's hard losing everything you cherish. I do understand the pain."

He sensed my comparison to loss, and his tone quickly changed with me. "I thought you could let my son know his stepmother has died. I should have known you would be a bitch about Diane. You probably used one of those evil curses on her, knowing you and your friends."

"I'm truly sorry for your loss. Really, I am. I'll let our son know. I hope you find peace."

And just like that, we said goodbye and hung up the phone. Silence permeated throughout the loft as I continued to get dressed for my day and my date with Shawn.

I felt disbelief as I peered off into the distance, imagining ex-husband number three finding his wife dead on the garage floor next to her golf bag. For one split second, I worried about my full moon wish for karma. I felt guilty for wishing bad karma on them.

Do I have special powers to deliver karma to those who deserve it? I can't be a witch. If I was, I want to be a good witch, not a bad one. Oh, God!

I called Leanne on my walk to the store, passing by my favorite bakery while I talked. I stepped inside to grab a sesame bagel with cream cheese. I was starving. "What's up, girl? I haven't talked to you in forever. How's Boca, Mouth of the Rat?"

Leanne was on fire as she relayed how she had just finished a long, hard workout with her personal trainer, who handed her an overdue country club invoice. "Fucking Markus claimed his accountant was paying all these bills. I had to find out otherwise by being embarrassed at the club today. He's such a fucking asshole."

"Well, it could be worse. He could fuck you over and leave you without any money to pay it. I would love for someone to have my back when I fall down."

I paused and sighed. "I just fall to the fucking floor, and there's nobody there to catch me. Speaking of falling to the floor—you won't believe why I called you."

She shouted, "Tell me already!"

"I called to tell you that my ex-husband number three's wife, Diane, died. Remember we did the full moon wish a few months ago? Shit, girl. We killed the bitch!"

"Really? Are you fucking kidding me? You're lying. We can't be witches. I fucked a vampire. Does that make me a witch?" She sounded shocked and couldn't stop talking. "What the fuck, Sophia? We're evil witches! Fuck."

"Come on, Lea. You don't really think we have that kind of power? Do we? I feel guilty as fuck. Jesus, Lea. I gotta go home and throw out all that delicious chicken soup. We might be criminals! She's really dead. I looked it up on the internet. She really died yesterday!"

Leanne was walking and talking, so she was out of breath. "Jesus, Sophia. Did you call your son yet? He's not been a fan of his new stepmother, but he needs to know. Don't tell him about our wish. Oh, God. I still can't believe it."

My heart raced thinking about the full moon wish and the soup jarred with 02.14 on it. "I gotta give that soup away today. I'll call Aaron later. I know I gotta call him before we leave for the weekend. Shawn has a weekend planned for us."

"Things are getting a little serious with the doc, huh? Sophia's falling in love, again…oh, God! You better get your ass to Boca so I can get you a one-night stand to get outta this love bullshit!"

I knew changing the subject was my only way to escape the love talk with Leanne. "We're going to Helen's restaurant in Seven Springs. Remember when we all went there for your birthday a few years ago?"

"Oh my God, girl. We were so bad." Leanne was screaming with laughter as she recalled the night. "I had so many dirty martinis we closed the bar down at the resort. My husband was so pissed. What's new? I truly hope he gets fucked in the ass by some big gorilla in prison. Maybe he'll drop the soap in the shower and, whoopsie-daisy, up the poop chute."

We belly-laughed as I moved quickly about my store preparing for the day.

Leanne screamed at her son, "Sit down and eat your breakfast, young man! Where's my fucking nanny? She's just so worthless. I guess your ex-husband number three will get his karma now. Big man on campus can't get a hard-on unless his wife is fucking another man. No more of that shit now! I guess his new nickname will be Mr. Slinky!"

I laughed, flipped on my lights, and turned the closed sign to open on the front door. "Maybe we should brew a full moon stew for your husband, Mr. Hair Pie, next month? Maybe a poop chute lover for him while he's in the lockup?"

She screamed. "Fuck, yeah! I'll look at flights to visit. I need to visit my dad, so it's a great idea! The evil witches strike again!"

I checked the register for internet connection and turned on the music for the day, switching the CD from Ronnie's to Norah Jones. I was in that kinda mood. "I gotta run, girl. I gotta long day at the store, and then Shawn's sending a car for me. Chow."

Chapter Ten

Sinners & Saints

Shawn's driver was right on time. He stepped out of the black Escalade to open the back door for me, saying, "Let me help you with your bag." He took my Louis Vuitton duffle bag and put it in the far back seat. Gazing at the bag, my mind raced back to the day I had bought the new piece to add to my collection. I had just received my first big commission check for a job for The Art Institutes International. I was so proud of myself. I felt like a male peacock with glorious tailfeathers spread wide.

I called my father to share my good news with him about my earnings. He answered without emotion and interrupted me to tell me something. "We gave you a check for three hundred dollars for your birthday. Why did you cash it if you're a millionaire?"

I thought it was an odd question. I didn't know how to answer him. "I don't understand, Dad. Why did you give me the check if you didn't want me to cash it? Was it a test? I thought it was a gift."

The memory haunted me like Jacob Marley in *A Christmas Carol* where he must wear and drag heavy chains that symbolized his greed. Jacob Marley represented Scrooge's possible fate. If Scrooge did not change, he would become a ghost who must also wander the Earth while pondering his sin.

Am I the greedy one?

I longed for answers. I longed for a father who loved me, who was proud of me. I pushed the feelings down deeper to rid myself of the awful feeling.

The driver leaned back, startling me out of my thoughts. His black cap suddenly reminded me of my rockstar's driver on the most memorable night of my life. "I put some bottled water back there for you, Sophia. It's a bit of a drive to the airport, so kick back and relax."

My eyes grew big and round. "The airport? I thought we were going to Helen's restaurant in Seven Springs?"

"I'm not sure, miss. I'm just the driver. There's a phone back there, in the center console, if you want to use it."

I used the time to call my son. I dreaded the call but knew I had to do it. "It's not good news. Diane died suddenly yesterday. Your dad's a wreck, of course. You better call him." I felt an odd sense of relief, yet sadness crept into my heart for ex-husband number three. I hated to think he was suffering, and I felt guilty for our full moon wish.

It was an awful wish. We have to ask for forgiveness.

I quietly said five Hail Marys and five Our Fathers, hoping my sins would be forgiven.

We drove for about an hour until we arrived at a local airport.

Shawn stood on the runway in front of a small aircraft. He beamed and took my hand. "Hi, beautiful. How are you?"

While I kissed him on the lips, he grabbed my ass softly with both hands, pulling me closer to him. "You look amazing." He let his gaze wander over my entire frame, like an art connoisseur appraising a famous painting. "Let's get going. There's a dirty martini waiting for us at the bar."

Shawn had arranged for a helicopter ride to the restaurant in the mountains. The beauty of the fall leaves starting to change into hues of burnt orange and yellow mesmerized me. A rich scent of autumn perfumed the air.

Such a perfect time to be flying over the forest.

"You think of everything. I don't know what I've done to deserve you."

He lightly touched the side of my cheek with his fingertips, letting me know he was simply here to create happiness for me. "You deserve it, for no other reason than I love to please you."

The helicopter landed right in the resort. The pilot bowed his head and said, "Thank you, sir, for trusting me with the flight. Have a great weekend."

Shawn helped me out and took my bag. "Whatcha got in here, girl? It weighs at least twenty pounds. I hope it's something sexy."

I grinned as I recalled what I packed inside before I left the city. "I guess you'll have to wait to see, won't you?"

Shawn arranged for the resort limo to transport us to the restaurant. As we climbed into the huge interior, he whispered, "Let's stop at the house before we go to Helen's." He took my hand while he leaned forward and said to the driver, "It's the big house on the left there, on Woodland Lane. Number 106."

I gasped, feeling shocked beyond words. "What are you up to now, Shawn? Are you holding me hostage? Where are we going?"

He turned to me and whispered, "Shhhh, just wait."

The limo pulled up to a wrought-iron gate nestled behind huge pine trees lining the driveway. There was a call box set at the gate. Shawn pressed the code into the red buttons on the box, and the gate slid open. "Welcome to

Woodland Lane, Sophia. My friend owns this place and offered me the keys for the weekend."

He grinned like a Cheshire cat. "I wanted to surprise you, so I just said we were going to Helen's so you could pack accordingly."

I smiled from ear to ear, knowing I was in for a treat. "You're too much, Shawn. Whatever I did to deserve all this royal treatment, I'm grateful."

The double front doors, oak stained with a cherry finish, opened to an expansive, sunken living room with two oversized sectional sofas covered in white, cotton fabric anchored by king-sized chairs. There was a massive stone fireplace with multiple hues of brown, bronze, orange, and yellow ochre. The natural beauty took my breath away, especially how the earthy, brown tones blended with the soft, wood floors.

What perfect, exquisite décor!

I marveled at the mosaic of color reflecting in the flickering firelight with a pitch-perfect resonance. It felt musical—like a symphony of color.

A Van Gogh room!

Shawn walked me to the bedroom he had chosen for the stay. "I've stayed alone in this room many times before, dreaming of lying next to a sexy woman like you."

I followed him in. "We're never leaving this place. Promise me."

He smiled. "Let's go to Helen's for a martini. We have the entire weekend here, so why not? It's still early, and I'm starving. Aren't you?"

I grabbed my Louis Vuitton bag and opened it so he could see inside. "I brought a few toys. Stephanie gave me these the last time I was over to see her—do you like?"

He grinned. "'Do *you* like?' is really the question. Come on, we'll play later."

I walked back outside with him, hand in hand. The limo driver was still waiting, so I suspected he was up to something else. "You're always up to something…what's next?"

He wasn't giving in to my request to reveal his secrets. "I guess you just have to wait and see." He threw me a mischievous grin. "I'm not telling you any of my secrets, not tonight!"

We walked into the restaurant—an elegant log cabin in the woods. The heavy furniture matched the interior. Bleached, white logs covered in cool hues of green mixed with amber shades of orange, like the autumn leaves.

I forgot how much I loved this place, and I gazed around, mesmerized by its beauty.

I heard voices coming from a table in the back and as we walked closer to the group, I spotted my friends. I looked at Shawn with total surprise in my eyes and covered my mouth with my hands. "Oh my God! Shawn! What the…"

He laughed, pulling me close to kiss me as he gleamed with pleasure. "I wanted you to be with your friends tonight!"

I was smiling from ear to ear. Nobody had ever thrown a surprise party for me. I recognized Helena first and her new racecar driver boyfriend, Brian. They were quite the item since they arrived back from a month in Italy where he had been racing. Jayne and Clinton stood up and clapped! Violet stepped away from her chair, ran over to me, and reached for a hug. "Happy Birthday, Sophia! I love you, beautiful lady!" And Ronnie smiled, stayed seated, and continued to sing with the group.

Stephanie was there with her steady boyfriend, Allen. "Surprise! Ms. Sophia!"

She looked pretty tonight, less seductive, wearing a floral-print dress cinched at the waist. Her hair was pulled back neatly into a bun. Her boyfriend was a used car salesman with a slightly greased-back hairstyle that dated him far past his age. He was handsome, with a Johnny Dangerous kind of look.

He must be hung like a horse. I giggled to myself.

I leaned in, whispering to Shawn, "You invited Helena? Oh my God, I can't believe she actually came to my birthday dinner party. Did she bring a camera crew? Wonder what's on her agenda. Must be more going on here than just my party...."

He smirked. "Be nice, Sophia. She likes you. Maybe that's all it is. Be nice."

As I walked through the room, everyone greeted me, "Happy Birthday! Surprise! Happy Birthday!"

I felt shocked beyond belief. He managed to collect my friends' phone numbers and invited them all to join him for my special fortieth birthday celebration. "How on earth did you pull this off, Shawn? You're crazy!"

"I'm sneaky. I just wanted you to celebrate with your friends. I invited them all to stay overnight tonight at the house with us. Their bags are already there; that's why I wanted to get you out of the house before we opened your bag of toys!"

The dinner was an assortment of all types of pasta, a spread of cheeses and Italian meats, breads, and desserts. Shawn insisted the party was his treat. He made a toast to the group. "You're all so kind for joining me tonight to wish this special lady a happy birthday! Thank you for coming!"

Ronnie stood up and started to sing "Happy Birthday" in a way that only she could sing the lyrics, a mix of rock and roll and the blues. A tear rolled down my face. I stood after she finished the song. "I'm so grateful for your friendships." I scanned all the loving faces. "I love each of you so much, except for Allen, as we just met."

Everyone laughed.

I paused, waiting for silence, then continued, "Allen, you're the luckiest man in the world, for you have Stephanie. If you hurt her, I'll cast a spell on you!"

Helena stood up next and flicked her long, black hair back twice and then a third time as she pursed her lips to make a kiss for me. "I love Bob Dylan's song that reminds us if we're not busy living, we're busy dying. Let's live like there's no tomorrow! Happy Birthday, Cupcake!" She smiled, proud of her wonderful little speech. Then she kissed Brian on the lips for all of us to see that her new lover was her finest adornment.

We never stopped laughing.

Jayne was happier than any of them. She came twirling up to me. She wanted to spend the night at the Woodland House with us. "Come on, Clinton, let's stay overnight, wake up with them, and have coffee together." Jayne insisted the girls go into the bar while the men enjoyed bourbon and cigars. "Let's dance in the bar. I love the music in there."

Clinton frowned like he didn't want to stay, but he nodded. "Okay, baby, whatever makes you happy. I'll stay as long as you know we have to get back to the city right after coffee. I have to work." He told me earlier in the night, he loved the way Jayne forgot her keys, poured her coffee, and sipped her martinis. His eyes were illuminated like a crystal chandelier lighting up an entire room with his dazzling light. He watched her every move.

Helena and Brian decided to drive back to the city. Shawn tried to convince them to stay. But, Helena insisted, "I really need to get back. I've been in Italy for a month, Cupcake. I need to wake up in my own bed. You must understand. We would really love to stay with you two lovebirds, but we must go. Thank you for inviting us to your wonderful celebration." They kissed everyone good night and headed down the mountain on a two-and-a-half-hour journey back to the city.

When my phone rang at three a.m., I had a pounding headache from all the cosmopolitans and the red wine mix. My lover slept next to me.

"Hello, Helena? Is that you? What's wrong?"

Helena was crying hysterically, and she couldn't catch her breath. "It's Brian. He didn't make it. He's gone, Sophia."

I shook Shawn's naked body, trying to wake him from a deep sleep. "Shawn, get up. I need you to talk to Helena. She isn't making any sense."

He took the phone to his ear and then decided to put it on speaker. "Helena. It's Shawn. What's wrong? What's going on?"

She burst into tears.

We could hear noise in the background, like an announcement. Realizing she was in the emergency room, we glanced at each other with concern.

"We were in an accident. Our car went over the hillside. We rolled over and over down a big hill. He died, Shawn. Brian's dead." Shawn looked at me with disbelief in his eyes. He held my hand.

Helen told us she was about to go into surgery for the broken leg she got in the accident. When the car rolled over, she was crushed between the front seat and the front end, forcing her leg to snap back. "The doctors aren't promising they can save the leg, but they were optimistic." She sighed.

"Oh my God, honey. I'm so sorry. Is there anything I can do to help?"

"I must go now. Pray for me, Sophia. I'm so scared. I don't want to lose my leg. I lost Brian. I just can't believe it. My mom's here. I'll ask her to call you tomorrow."

"I'm praying for you. I'm so sorry. We love you. Good luck."

Shawn got out of bed and tied his plaid, flannel robe around his waist. He was so sexy. He walked out of the bedroom. I hung my head in disbelief. *They were just here, alive and well.* I found my robe and gently tossed my hair before I looked in the mirror. Mascara was smeared across my cheeks from my tears. I walked into the kitchen to find Shawn making coffee.

"I just can't believe it, Sophia." He sighed heavily.

I comforted him with a hug. I sensed he felt guilty for not forcing them to stay the night. "It's not your fault, sexy. Truly it's not."

His deep frown told me he felt awful about the accident. "I feel so responsible for not forcing them to stay here last night. Wasn't Brian a race car driver? How did he go off the road?" He looked down at the floor. "I just don't understand what happened."

"It's not your fault, Shawn. Helena's a big girl. She decided to go home. And, yes, Brian was a race car driver. We don't know the details…I didn't have the courage to ask her."

Jayne came out to the kitchen with Clinton, packed and dressed to leave as planned. "What's up, chick-EE birthday girl?"

Shawn told Jayne the story about Helena and Brian.

Ronnie walked in. "I can't take any more grief. My heart is broken." Ronnie stood near the large window, peering out into the forest. "Did you know leaves are very sensitive to changes in their environment? I'm so inspired here in the woods. I gotta rent a place here to write songs."

Violet was crying.

Stephanie came into the kitchen wearing cute pink and white flannel pajamas. She looked so different without her makeup on. She was still pretty but more average in appearance. "What's on the menu for breakfast? Want me to whip something up for us?"

Shawn glanced at me, then proceeded to share the horrible news with her. "We had a terrible call last night. Brian and Helena had an accident on the way down the mountain. Brian died. Helena is in surgery now."

"Oh, God, no. Jesus."

Everyone stared at each other in total disbelief, seeming unsure what to say.

Stephanie spoke up first. "I think we're going to go. It's not the time to party. I'm so sorry, Sophia."

They all left at the same time. Shawn agreed with the decision, nodding and saying, "Stay in touch with us. Please be careful going down the mountain, and call me when you're back in the city, please."

Shawn knew exactly how I liked my coffee. He had created the cup of joe for me so many times before. He ground the fresh beans, added steamed almond milk with a frothy top, and let it cool down for exactly six minutes before serving it to me. It was the little things that he remembered.

He insisted I take my cup of coffee into the living room while he made us some breakfast. He planned to create my favorite eggs benedict with spinach and creamy hollandaise sauce, just the way I liked it.

I cried, unable to disguise my grief, feeling like an ocean was rolling over my head. "Life changes so fast. I'm so tired of all the changes."

The rest of the day lingered on slowly. We sat in silence, watching the clock tick the minutes by until the night air enlightened our senses with our new reality. We sat still as we savored the red wine Shawn had carried with him to the mountain retreat.

"I wanted you to have a special birthday, Sophia. I feel so guilty about what happened to Brian. I hope you don't carry it with you."

I genuinely cared for him, and I wanted him to know how much I appreciated his efforts to create a wonderful memory for my birthday. "You're a special person, and I'll never forget your birthday gift to me."

He must have felt my urgency for tenderness, as he said, "I want to make passionate love to you—a night of total fantasy, the way you've always dreamed of being with a man. That's my birthday gift to you."

I leaned my head back to gaze up at the stars shining brightly in the night sky. "Let's make love without talking. No words, only motions—just our bodies continuously in motion until we can't fuck anymore."

Shawn and I were bound together forever by the tragedy of Helena's accident—a birthday I would not easily forget, for so many reasons. Our lovemaking was poignant with a mix of passion and grief, like mist and steam merging. We made love for hours in complete silence. His strong, surgical hands moved along my curves without hesitation, following my movements without a whisper. I marveled at how we were in sync.

That brisk fall morning, the road seemed to reach up and grab us as we drove through the winding, country paths in silence. I held on to his strong, lean thigh, listening to him and hoping to find strength in his words.

"I'm taking the longer route back to the city to avoid the accident area. I can't bear to see it roped off."

I trusted his instincts and needed his guidance right then. "I trust you. Thank you for being so kind to me. I so love spending time with you."

The city traffic seemed louder, the smells were stronger, and the lights were much brighter due to the way shock and grief propel one into the present moment. I grew acutely aware of everything around me. It felt like being on drugs, somehow. Intense awareness permeated my consciousness all day.

I had dinner plans with Stephanie and was looking forward to my friend's words of wisdom and her talk with me about her regular butt client, Gary's, afternoon delight.

I texted her: *Hey, Steph, we still on for six at Morton's Steak House for tonight?*

Stephanie texted back: *Oh, hell yeah. I'll meet you at the bar. I'll be coming from a class so can't walk with you.*

I prepared the last-minute details for the fashion show on the river. Several retail stores were in the show and competing for a prize for the best overall theme. I confirmed the models and the stylists for the models' hair and makeup. I decided to create the Garden of Eden on the runway, rolling out a green Astro-turf catwalk and dressing the models in sexy loincloths made from a soft, buttery-yellow skin.

I felt guilty for being so excited about creating a fashion show when someone just died, so I called Helena to check on her recovery in the hospital. I left a message. "Call me when you can. I'm thinking of you."

Chapter Eleven

Hail Mary

orton's Steak House wasn't busy when I arrived at the bar a little before six. I needed a martini before Stephanie got there, just to calm me down, and I knew this place made the best stuffed olives. "I'll have a Grey Goose dirty martini with blue cheese olives."

The gentleman next to me signaled for the bartender. "Put the lady's drink on my tab, Patty. It's on me."

I hadn't paid attention, but now I turned to see he was someone Leanne had introduced me to the previous summer. She had asked me to tag along to a potential design job she was bidding on, and we ended up in his penthouse for hours, talking about everything except his desire to renovate the already decadent bachelor pad. "Thank you! Oh my God, Kevin. How are you? I didn't see you there. I'm sorry."

Kevin was one of the wealthiest forty-something-year-olds in the city. His father owned a large steel manufacturing business, which Kevin was fortunate enough to inherit. Although he allowed a board of directors to operate the fifty-year-old business, he stayed actively involved in the day-to-day operations.

How lucky is he to inherit his wealth and power? Jealousy nagged on the edge of my consciousness like waves tickling the shore.

He was a short, pudgy man with a receding hairline. I pondered on the fact that he was not granted good looks, unlike his brother, who had been disinherited before their father passed away.

Kevin overworked his charm to make up for his lack of height. He always went out of his way to buy drinks and dinner for the single ladies. He was recently divorced from his wife, Mary—a Catholic girl who had walked away from the fortune just to save her sanity. *She was admired by everyone in the city when they married.* She claimed she couldn't stay in the marriage due to her husband's addiction to porn being too much for her religious beliefs, but we all knew Kellie's cousin Monique was having an affair with Kevin. That was the real reason Mary left him.

I envy these women and their ability to snag a wealthy man.

I wondered how they ever ended up together, let alone married to each other. They had drastically different personalities. Mary was such a snob, even though she came from a very poor family. She always had her nose up in the air.

I figured she was desperately jealous of the remarkable beauty of her recent competition, as Monique was exceptionally pretty, although she risks so much to enhance her beauty through surgery.

Kevin was gregarious, and he was so generous that most people never realized he was the son of a billionaire.

Kevin leaned in to talk to me, sliding my martini closer. "Whatcha up to, Sophia? Are you married, divorced, or single and loving it?"

I smiled back at his curiosity. I didn't mind catching up with him. "I'm single and living in Shadyside. I opened a retail store. You should come to my fashion show on Friday."

Kevin thanked me for the invitation with a beaming smile. "I'll let you know. I might be headed to Vail to ski for the weekend. Plans are still up in the air, but if I'm in town, I'll stop by."

We tapped our martini glasses, and Kevin made the toast. "Cheers to a successful fashion show, and cheers to being single in the city."

I smiled, and he continued to talk while I quietly sipped the martini, in need of some headspace.

"You know, Mary and I finally got divorced a few months ago. She was fucking bat shit crazy."

I nodded. I wasn't aware but suddenly felt jealous of his soon-to-be ex-wife's position as a marital settlement was certainly in her near future. *Lucky girl.*

Kevin wasn't shy, and he didn't care who heard what he had to say. "She was so cheap, she refused to throw away our cat's food cans. She wanted to reuse them for some stupid idea of hers."

I laughed, hoping he was joking, but I didn't want to be rude. He went on and on.

It was obvious I wasn't going to get a minute of silence, so I joined in, saying, "She came from a very poor family. Do you think that's why she was so conservative?"

Kevin laughed and threw his head back as he looked at me. "She was worse than conservative. She was downright cheap, nothing else. She rolled toilet paper into long tubes to use during her period because she said tampons were too expensive. I can't make this shit up, Sophia. I know it's gross to tell you this shit, but it's the truth. She was cheap. I swear she would eat her own shit for breakfast if she learned a recipe for it."

We giggled.

My mind raced. I tried to focus on Kevin's conversation while suppressing the thoughts of selfishness and jealousy.

It was obvious Kevin might have had one too many martinis before I got there. "I'm having dinner with my friend Stephanie tonight. She'll be here any minute. I better grab a table. Thanks for the drink but excuse me."

Kevin wasn't going to let me get away that easy, and he waved down the bartender. "Hey, Patty. Can you reserve my private dining room for me and my girlfriends for dinner tonight? And open my wine locker, so we can get a nice bottle of red for the table."

I didn't want to have dinner with him because I couldn't wait to see Stephanie and catch up with her in private. "Oh, Kevin. Please don't do anything special for us. We get together for girls' talk every week. We can take care of ourselves but thank you."

There's no way I'll be getting away from him tonight.

He continued to push. "I insist, Sophia. You girls can catch up any time. Come on, let's celebrate your new life in the city. It's on me. I need some fun in my life. I start my day with Captain Crunch and end my day with Captain Morgan. Apparently, I want to be a pirate! What else do I have to spend money on? Come on!"

Stephanie walked in dressed as casually as I had ever seen her before. She was wearing a light-blue, velvet, zip-up hoodie by Juicy Couture with matching bell-bottom pants. Her huge breasts were bulging out of the low-zipped hoodie.

I envied her carefree attitude. She wasn't concerned about what others thought of her appearance. *She's amazing.*

She carried a Chanel tote bag stuffed with books, notepads, and a variety of girly makeup bags.

I was so jealous; I wanted a golden pussy like hers but couldn't get a man to buy me a paper bag, let alone a Chanel tote.

"Sophia, I'm so sorry I'm late. My professor kept me after class to review my thesis idea, and I lost track of the time. I was hoping to go home to change first, but I didn't have time."

Stephanie kissed me on the lips and hugged me as tightly as she could, then she placed her heavy bag on the seat next to her.

I leaned in to whisper in her ear. "I can't get rid of him. He's been telling me all these dirty little secrets about his ex-wife, Mary. It's been so annoying, and now he reserved his private dining room for us to have dinner with him."

She didn't mind, and she threw him a beaming smile. Inwardly, I marveled at how she always went with the flow of even the most radical changes.

Wish I could be more like that. Guess I'll be listening to the male point of view on love and sex tonight.

I recently made so many changes in my life that I liked when usual things happened as expected.

Stephanie placed her warm hand on my arm. "It's fine, girl. Let's see what he has to say. I like hearing about the fucked-up lives of the rich and famous. He'll be pure entertainment and research."

I felt disappointed but nodded. "I know. I was just looking forward to our girl talk. And I wanna hear all about your session with Gary this week." I was so jealous of her sexual freedom.

"We'll catch up tomorrow night instead. Let's go have a bite with Kevin in his private dining room. I've never been in one of those rooms, believe it or not."

Kevin had the bartender carry our dirty martinis into the room and set the table with white linens. In the center, she placed a beautiful bouquet of low-cut flowers around a musky-scented candle.

Stephanie was in professional mode. I think she wanted to impress Kevin. She exclaimed, "I love the cherrywood panels in this room. It's so elegant yet warm and inviting. Makes me want to write."

Kevin immediately loved Stephanie. And I bet it's especially her long, flowing hair and breasts to match. Suddenly, I felt like a third wheel on a date. "Let's order. I'm starving. I waited to eat, knowing we were coming here tonight."

Kevin nodded.

I smiled. *He definitely needs to get some food to tame the beast.*

"I'm starving. I came straight to the bar from my attorney's office, having signed the last of my divorce settlement to Mary today."

I'll bet that cheap-ass Catholic girl is getting a million bucks, she fell into the candy store!

Stephanie picked up on the opportunity to gain a new client. "Aw, so sorry to hear about your divorce, baby. Are you okay? If you require any help getting over it, here's my number." She reached inside her bag, pulled out her business card, and stuffed it in the pocket of his starched, button-up shirt.

"I'll certainly take you up on your offer, Stephanie. Thanks. Now, let's get some food on this table." Kevin took the liberty of ordering for everyone. Obviously, he had done this many times before. He waved down the waiter. "Have the butcher hand-cut one of the twenty-four-day dry-aged steaks."

He looked at both of us with a huge grin on his face, "You gotta try it! It's a steak meant for royalty."

He continued to order, not asking for our input. "Also, bring a side of mushrooms and baked potatoes—and bring us one of the bottles of Chateau Rayas 2003 from my wine locker."

Kevin obviously had an extensive education in the menu. His knowledge was undeniably fueled by years of fancy dinners. My heart panged with the yearning to know more. I wanted to be in his seat.

I felt uncomfortable and ever so guilty, but Stephanie gave me an understanding look from across the table.

"Stop feeling guilty about everything. You deserve to be treated like a queen." She winked.

Kevin filled Stephanie in on his wife's nasty habits, poking fun at her lack of class and inability to step into the royal lifestyle he had thought she was capable of handling. "She pretended to be a sophisticated woman. She acted like she was used to the high society lifestyle we were going to have to uphold my family's traditions, but she was just a peasant in reality."

I love the idea of family traditions. I imagined being surrounded by family who wanted to celebrate every holiday together, setting the table with the finest crystal and real silverware meant for kings and queens.

I added very little to the conversation, as I thought I was just a mere peasant myself. I sipped the wine, thinking I didn't know the difference between this bottle and the bottle I bought at the store for twelve bucks a few days ago, but I acted like it was the best wine I ever tasted. "Oh my gosh. It is so delicious. Thank you so much."

The evening went as slow as molasses dripping out of a bottle. Kevin bragged about all of his wealth and power, telling us about a judge he had in his pocket. "I gotta have these kinds of people in my circle to get things done to my advantage. You'd be surprised how many favors a guy can get when he sends a nine-hundred-dollar bottle of wine to a table of judges."

Stephanie swung swords with him, comparing notes on how to get what you want from people with power. "I have a judge in my pocket as a regular client. No need to send her wine. I just let her lick my pussy and breastfeed on my tits until she comes."

She laughed hysterically as she held up her glass of wine to cheer the table. "She just got me out of a speeding ticket and said I was such a naughty girl, then she bought me this Chanel bag." She held up her beautiful Chanel tote bag and smiled from ear to ear, knowing she just topped Kevin's story.

The jealousy between them was comparable to kings fighting over their lovers; their swords were blood-soaked and filled with passion.

I was out of my element, but I joined the conversation anyway. "So, the moral of the story is simple. You can either inherit a billion dollars or let a judge breastfeed on your tits to get what you want in life. Seems pretty simple to me."

Kevin grinned at my sassy tongue and flirted with me as he poured the last of the wine into my glass. "Drink up, lady. You're finally getting it. The women who work hard to be successful are doing it all wrong. Just fuck your way through life. You'll get so much more that way. At least with me, anyways, and my friends."

I was only joking, but I played along, knowing I had no chance of winning with these two sharks. "So, I should keep on fucking my very young boyfriend while I'm married to an old boring fucker like the judge? Just asking for a friend."

Stephanie laughed and joined in with her own point of view on the subject. "I say absolutely. Women need a good fuck buddy, and they need financial security. Why can't we have it all? Right, Kevin?"

Kevin smiled at his new friend and appeared eager to learn more about her. "So, what do you charge for a session of ass whipping and breastfeeding?"

She was fast in her response. "Oh, doll. I don't talk money at the dinner table. Besides, if you have to ask, you can't afford it."

She's such a fierce opponent. I could learn so much from her; sassy and feisty!

I felt nervous about them working together but kept quiet.

The night ended with another bottle of wine from Kevin's wine locker. I left most of mine in my glass while Stephanie finished the rest of the bottle. "I'll plan to see you at my loft on Sunday afternoon, baby. So nice meeting you, and thanks for dinner."

The rich and sexy always come out on top.

She gave Kevin a side kiss on each cheek, and we walked hand in hand down the street. I couldn't wait to download all the conversation about the dinner talk. "Well, Sophia. I've gotta take you out more often to find me new clients. You've sent me two great regulars in a week. You're my new pimp. Well, actually, you'll be my first pimp since I've never had one! I didn't even get the time to tell you about my session with Gary."

I didn't want credit for finding her clients. I just knew a lot of people after working in the city for three decades. "Oh, God, girl. I'm not your pimp, but you can take me to dinner tomorrow night to thank me. Let's go somewhere quiet where nobody knows us."

As if on cue, she giggled as we passed by a new cigar lounge. "Oh my God, Sophia, let's go inside! I got tickets for this opening last week but forgot. They'll let us in. I know the bouncer!" She grinned.

I said, "Of course you do!"

We walked up closer to the front doors. "I don't feel dressed for a party!"

She shrugged it off, Stephanie couldn't care less about the attire. "Hey, boys! How are ya?" She winked at the handsome, young gentleman standing at the door. "Is Rocky here tonight?"

He sassed her back, "Who wants to know?"

She grinned. "I do. Yes or no, silly boy!" She grabbed her phone from her bag where she snapped the picture of her private invitation and showed it to the young man. "My VIP invite."

He scanned it. "Go on, Miss Stephanie. Enjoy!"

We walked hand in hand inside the new Rocky Patel cigar lounge. *It's as sexy as she is.*

The atmosphere was welcoming with comfortable furniture and a relaxing vibe. Dim lighting and soothing background music played throughout the place. A stunning view of the city captured my attention immediately.

Stephanie nestled herself up to the bar to order an after-dinner drink. "I'll have an espresso martini, and my girlfriend will have a white Russian." She giggled; she liked being in charge.

The liquor stung the back of my throat and we peered around the room, silently enjoying the environment and watching circles of cigar smoke wander up against the well-vented wood-paneled walls. She finished her drink with one big gulp. "Let's get outta here, Sophia. I've had enough for one night. You?"

I smiled, tossing mine back. "I thought you would never ask!"

Stephanie's scent was intoxicating. Her eyes twinkled under the moonlit sky as she leaned in to whisper in my ear. "Let's cook dinner together in your loft tomorrow night. Nobody will know us there, and we can share naughty sex stories all night!"

I could tell she was tipsy from all the wine. She flirted with me, and a couple passing by stared at us as we giggled like schoolgirls. "I'll shop for all the yummiest ingredients to make linguine and my famous Bolognese sauce. Let's do it, love, please!"

How can I say no? I was so envious of her ability to be free and easygoing.

She was so convincing and so delightful. "I would love that, Steph. You and me in my sexy, little city loft, brewing up a stew together and talkin' dirty!"

She laughed, unzipping her velvet hoodie to expose her breasts to the moonlight. "Let's make a full moon wish, girl! Oh, mister moon, moon, bright and shiny moon, won't you please shine down on me!"

I had no choice but to look at her beautiful round breasts; they were perfect. I wanted to have breasts like hers.

I gently pushed her into the alleyway and covered her nipples with the palms of my hands. I hoped nobody was going to witness her public display of nudity. The streets were alive with music, and businesses were still open. "You crazy woman! Are you looking for more clients? We better get home before the city sees you naked in the streets!"

"Silly girl. I gotta judge in my bed. I can do whatever I please in this city! My titties needed a lil' moonlight, that's all! I want you to meet my girlfriend. I think that's exactly what you need, a little girl-on-girl action!"

I knew she was tipsy; she was sexy no matter what though. *She couldn't be ugly if she tried.*

We finally stepped inside the building and pushed the elevator button to our floor. Stephanie stepped out first. "See you later, alligator. After a while, crocodile." She zipped down her hoodie to expose her perfect breasts for me to see again.

I laughed. "Sleep tight, sweet pea."

◆

Stephanie left the bags at the concierge desk, and Dino called me when the groceries arrived. He gave me his usual smile. "Steph said she's running late, but the bags are here. Want me to bring them up?"

I was finalizing the last-minute details for the fashion show. "Yes, thank you, Dino. I'll prop my door open. Come inside. I made homemade chicken soup, and I have a jar of it waiting for you!" I reached inside my pantry and pulled out two mason jars of the full moon wish soup Leanne and I brewed for my ex-husband number three. The evil soup that killed his wife. We had marked the soup Kill Bill 02.14. It had to go.

I gotta get rid of this soup and pass it on to someone who appreciates the kind gesture without the evil spell attached to it. I'll release the bad karma. I hated ex-husband number three, but I didn't want to be responsible for killing his wife. I'm not that evil.

Shawn left me a voicemail. "I'll be back from my medical conference tomorrow afternoon. Wanna meet for happy hour? So much to talk to you about. Miss you."

I smiled, knowing I was in just the right place and time in my life. I texted him back with: *I miss you. Yes, tomorrow at four is perfect. Let's go to Casbah.*

Stephanie arrived right on time. She was carrying two bottles of Opus and a bottle of champagne—Cristal of course. "Let's pop the bubbly first to celebrate my new regulars. Thanks to you!" She popped the cork and sipped right out of the bottle. I followed her lead.

"What a night we had last night!"

Stephanie walked around my loft looking at all of my things and commenting on my design style. "I love these glasses—so sexy, girl. I love your view. It's so much better than mine." She was wearing a worn-out pair of loose-fitting jeans and a simple white t-shirt hugged her curvy body perfectly. She touched the vintage glasses on my bar. "I love these precious gems. You have great taste." She grinned. "And, I bet you taste good, too!" She giggled, flirting with me.

I smiled as she went on.

"I want you to re-design my loft. Will you do it for me, love? I'll pay you, of course. I appreciate your talents and your time."

I smiled. "Maybe that should be my weekend of bliss! You know I will. I would love to do it, especially your boudoir. Ooh la la."

She giggled, her smile illuminated by her perfectly white teeth. "No, that won't be your weekend of bliss. A weekend of bliss doesn't include work, silly girl. Let me tell you about my session with Gary. He's so kinky!"

I started taking the groceries out of the bag and reached for the largest pot for the pasta. Stephanie grabbed the pot for me, then smacked my ass with her full hand open, laughing. "That's just a love tap compared to what I do to Gary. He's really fun to play with. I'm exhausted, and I took a two-hour nap today!"

I filled the pot with water, turned the stove on high, and started to pour more champagne into a glass. "I wonder why he needs to have his ass beaten to get an erection. Have you done any research on it? I'm just so curious."

Stephanie started to prepare the ingredients for her sauce, tying an apron around her t-shirt while she looked at me with her slanted, brown eyes and a big smile on her face. "He likes the pain and humiliation. He said it's the extreme sensations he experiences when he relinquishes control. He's in a control position at work, so it's tough for him to let go unless he's dominated by me."

I carefully listened to her talk, and my mind raced with curiosity. "I prefer to be the submissive one. I like my lovers to take control, so I guess I understand."

Stephanie stirred her sauce and sipped the rest of the champagne left in the bottle. "Maybe your weekend of bliss should be an experience where you take control of your lover. I'm sure Shawn would be open to it. He seems pretty into you and willing to do anything for you. Change it up a bit. You know, for research purposes!"

I raised an eyebrow. I felt a gnawing ache in the pit of my stomach. "I doubt Shawn will be here in the city much longer. He's probably going to accept the partnership offer in South Carolina." I had an empty void inside my chest, like a deep chasm in the Grand Canyon. I knew the day would come sooner than I wanted it to arrive.

She turned away from the stove to console me. "Aw, honey. I'm so sorry. Would you ever consider going with him? I'm sure he'll ask you."

I struggled to answer. "It's fine. Shawn is young and has his whole life ahead of him. It's time." I wanted to change the subject. "Get back to the spanking with Gary. Tell me more about your riding crop!"

She giggled. "I know the more powerful the man is in his normal life, the more he wants to be submissive in the bedroom, especially if he is constantly holding the flame for everyone in his life. Gary said his wife never worked a day in her life, and now he's taking care of his two adult children as well. He has a lot on his plate."

I opened the bottle of wine and stirred the water on the stove. "I guess my sex life is boring. I do love to fuck, but I am not into beating or getting beaten. I had enough abuse in my real life. And Shawn's into pleasing me, but I'm not offering him closet space, for Christ's sake!"

Stephanie walked over to hug me. "Sorry about your friend, Helena's, boyfriend. It's so sad. How's Helena doing?"

I sipped my wine and nervously tucked my hair behind my ears. "I just can't believe it. Helena's okay. They saved her leg. She has months of rehab, but she'll be out and about party-hopping before you know it. She's probably laying in the hospital bed planning her next vacation to some exotic land with a new boyfriend."

She nodded in agreement as she chopped the fresh parsley.

I continued, "You know her husband just went to prison for mail fraud? I think he got five years. Don't you think it's kinda strange that I have two friends with husbands in prison right now? What's that say about me, Ms. Therapist?"

She opened the pantry door to look for something while she turned to me. "Hybristophilia is having a strong preference for someone who commits a criminal act. Maybe you want to be a criminal, Sophia. Ever want to rob a bank?" Stephanie giggled while she added more spices to her sauce. "You wanna get fucked by a guy who robbed a bank?"

"Jesus, Steph, it's not me. It's my two friends, Leanne and Helena, who both married criminals. Just think it's weird to have two friends at the same time who are both married to men in prison."

Stephanie placed the lid on the sauce pot and then walked over to my collection of matches sitting in a large, turquoise bowl—an ornate clay vessel from Italy. "You have such interesting pieces in your castle. If you dare, share this secret fetish of yours—a collection of matchbooks? Do tell."

I smiled. "I'll tell you anything, Steph. Just ask! I started that collection right after divorce number three. When Leanne and I would go out, I'd grab a book of matches to remind me where we went, and the number grew as we traveled!"

She stirred the collection with her hands as though it were sand on the beach. "You must have two or three hundred in here! Jesus, Sophia! The stories are endless! Thank you for inviting me into your magical world!"

I was always amazed by Stephanie's perception of my life. "Oh, God. I'm like a magician all right. I wish I could have made myself disappear into thin air, but I never mastered that trick! Well, not yet anyway!"

I stepped closer to her, searching through the collection, and pulled out one from South Beach. "This one's custom-made—a box filled with gold-tipped wooden sticks." I twirled it in my hand and smiled at the memory. "I got it from the private party on South Beach's Ocean Drive, where we met P. Diddy and Lenny Kravitz!"

She gasped. "I must hear this story. Do tell. I know, let's have a matchbook party! Promise me!"

I laughed. "I promise I'll tell you all about it! This bowl is filled with great stories. You're right!"

I preferred keeping these bowls in sight to enjoy the memories of those streets along the Arno and Peso Rivers, just west of Florence, where Montelupo Florentino, Tuscany's ceramic capital, is nestled. The hills were covered with cypresses, olive groves, and vineyards. The towers of San Gemignani, an old medieval town, dominated the whole valley.

Stephanie's voice startled me back into reality. "You are such an interesting woman with so many secrets. Did you plan your weekend of bliss yet? Pop that Vicodin and be honest with yourself?"

"I'm glad we're friends, Steph. You have such an interesting perception of life, and you're a good influence on me! I'm gonna do my weekend of bliss right after my fashion show. I pinky promise!"

"I love that, Sophia! Good for you! Remind me to give you something before your weekend of bliss. It'll be a surprise you'll always remember."

We finished cooking the sauce and served ourselves two huge helpings of the bolognese.

I took a bite and said, "This is so good. We should do this cooking thing more often!"

She grinned.

The timer went off in the oven. "I can't believe I forgot the bread! I asked Enrico to give me an unbaked loaf this afternoon while I was shopping! It's going to be delicious!" I walked to the oven and pulled the fresh loaf out. "I love living in the city, girl. It's so awesome to be able to walk to specialty markets to collect yummy treats!"

Stephanie smiled as we tore open the bread and put butter all over it while it was hot. "I keep thinking about dinner with Kevin last night. He was into confessing all his dirty, little secrets about his ex-wife, Mary."

I watched her as she swished the hot bread into the melted butter on an Italian plate I found at the thrift store down the street last week. I said, "He doesn't know that I know his girlfriend, Monique. She had way too much champagne at the VIP party and told me her lover has a dick the size of a Gherkin pickle. Oh my God! I hate knowing!"

She gasped, "Oh no!"

I laughed, knowing I had to share the secret with her. "I kept staring at his crotch last night. Did you notice? I'm so glad I told you though! Tag, you're it!"

She giggled while we continued to eat the steaming, hot bread and twirling the pasta around our forks while we gossiped about our dinner. "Oh, shit. I have a session with a Gherkin pickle in two days. Oh, well. I sure hope he likes to eat pussy, or I'm gonna have to upcharge him for lack of size!"

I belly laughed, coaxing her to go on by staying focused.

She said, "Of course, he confessed his shady sides. Everyone likes confessing their dirty, little secrets! Thanks for this new client; we might have to go to Chick-fil-A instead of Capital Grille though…just kidding!"

"Oh my God, Steph! Size does matter! You know it does. I know damn well it does. Eat pussy or not, I couldn't fuck a Gherkin. I gotta have size, you know, one of those monster ones! My ex-husband number three had a limp dick. I called it the slinky!" I snorted. "Limp is even worse than a Gherkin, right?"

"Shit, girl. Limp is really bad. Did he watch porn to try to get it hard? Oh wait, he's the one that loved to watch you fuck other men. He got hard from watching…still, limp is limp. Sorry!"

We continued to devour the hot, steamy bread, laughing like two high school teenagers who just got away with sneaking out after midnight to drink beer with their friends. I watched her lick her fingers, savoring all the butter and garlic. She was sexier than a movie star on the red carpet; even in jeans, she had *it. Just like my rockstar, they both had it.*

She gasped, startling me out of my seat. "Oh my God, Sophia. I forgot to tell you something super juicy!"

I moved toward the bar and poured the last of the wine into our glasses. "What? You scared the shit out of me, Steph. Forgot to tell me what?"

She faced me. "My regular Wednesday client, you know, my judge friend, Patricia. We had time to chat today before her driver came to pick her up. She told me to stop seeing Junior, my silver-spoon baby."

I felt my eyes open as far as they could go. "Do you mean your girl on girl? The one who helped you with medical school, right? What's going on?"

She grabbed my hand and squeezed it tight. "Patty said he's being indicted for mortgage fraud. His file came across her desk again this morning. Daddy isn't going to be able to save him from this one. She wants me to stay clear of him. Thank God she has my back! I ignored at least four calls from Junior today!"

"Oh shit, Steph. I hope his wife, Taylor, is going to be okay. They have three young children."

Stephanie opened the second bottle of Opus wine. "He's definitely going to go to prison! His wife and children will be fine. I'm sure his rich daddy will take care of them while he's scrambling to survive behind bars! He's gonna have a tough time being poor in prison."

I shook my head in agreement with her. "He better watch his ass. Don't drop the soap, Junior!" We belly laughed. I snorted then said, "Oh, I forgot to tell you, Junior's wife, Taylor, was in the dressing room next to you the morning you came in to shop with me. Remember?"

She poured the wine into both of our glasses. "Oh God, Sophia. I had no idea. It's been a while since I went to Vegas with Junior, at least six weeks now."

I sipped my wine and felt the warmth of it fill my belly and soothe my mind. "She heard every word you said, and because she realized you were talking about her soon-to-be ex-husband, she bought a ton of stuff from me. She charged it on his daddy's credit card and told me to thank you for giving her the courage to tell his daddy to go fuck himself! She went to Naples with a hot, young stud that weekend!"

"Wow! I inspired another woman to get fucked by a stud while I fucked her husband. Interesting. See why I'm studying this subject of sexual relationships? It's a never-ending story, and there's a continuous need for my services. Both types—sex worker and med student!"

We laughed hysterically. "Next time you surprise me, Steph, bring a cake and some candles too. Christ, I'm in shock! Junior is going to the pokey!"

I sipped the wine and walked our plates to the sink. I started to load the dishwasher, licking the last of the bread around the plate of melted butter. "Jesus, Steph. Thank God you have the judge."

Stephanie handed me the rest of the dishes. We closed the dishwasher and started it. "I love the art of living without guilt. I'm trying! You taught me that, Steph. Thank you!"

She smiled, rubbing her face next to mine. "I want you to live like this every day! Let the world say you're crazy, then you're free to do what you want! You'll remember that, right?"

I nodded.

It was close to midnight but neither one of us was ready to end the night. "Let's sit on the sofa facing the moon! I want to tell you something…"

Stephanie walked toward the window ledge and traced her finger where the word love was carved into the windowsill. "You know how proud I am of you, Sophia? I know it was hard to share all those past experiences with me. I believe that to move forward, you gotta look back. I'll set up a meeting with the judge—a happy hour—so you can meet her."

I leaned back on the sofa, looking up at the concrete ceiling and admiring the beauty of my castle. Stephanie talked as she peered out the window. "By the way, my pet name for the judge is Peppermint Patty. She loves it when I whisper it in her ear when we're making mad, passionate love."

I admired her honesty. I secretly wanted to know every last detail about her sexual romps with her Peppermint Patty, a girl-on-girl story I would hopefully hear one day. I giggled. I had liquid courage. "Get the sensation! I get the wildest sensation when I take a bite of my Peppermint Patty! Ooh la la."

Her sense of humor was as insanely witty as mine. "Sometimes you feel like a nut, sometimes you don't!"

I laughed, enjoying our time together. "They're magically delicious!"

I stood up and moved next to her, touching the graffiti on the windowsill and glancing up at her. "Love comes in such a variety pack!"

She smiled, reminding me of her need to please me. "I can't wait for you to meet Patty. She's smart and sexy!"

My thoughts ran rampant, like a team of wild horses galloping across the plains. "I can't wait to meet your Peppermint Patty!"

She swished the last few sips of her wine. "I better go, love. I have a long day of thesis research tomorrow. This was so much fun!" She put the cork in the bottle of wine. "Save this for tomorrow!" She kissed me on both cheeks. I locked my door, walked into my bedroom, and stripped off my clothes, allowing them to fall to the floor next to my bed. I crawled in between the luxurious sheets, naked and enjoying the sensation of the cool crisp linens.

I was startled out of a deep sleep when my phone rang at two o'clock in the morning, my head pounding with the red wine hangover. I regretted devouring the Opus wine the night before with Stephanie. I stumbled into the bathroom to toss two aspirin down with a huge gulp of water. I looked down at my phone.

The missed call was from an old friend, Emma Lou, whom I hadn't heard from in a few years. We had lost touch after she moved to Fort Lauderdale. I got divorced shortly afterward and moved out of the dreadful country club where we first met. I rang her back. No answer. I tried again. No answer.

Emma Lou was the only woman at that awful country club who had made me feel welcome. *God, I can't believe I lived there for so long.* She ran right up to me on the first night William and I walked into the bar for happy hour, and said, "Come out on the patio and sit next to me!"

She was easy to love. She was down to earth. She was honest to a fault. I loved her enthusiasm for life. Sixteen country club members were sitting around a large table, all of them dressed in golf attire. I immediately felt out of place wearing my black Prada suit with a crisp white tank underneath, my favorite turquoise medallion nestled tight against my neck. She shouted to the group, her voice loud and shrill, "Meet my new friends, Sophia and William. Isn't Sophia beautiful? Let's do shots of tequila to welcome our new neighbors!"

We connected, snapping together just like Lego blocks perfectly fit into a shape.

She reminded me of Goldie Hawn, especially when she played stupid, hiding behind a mask to disguise her brilliance—as if brains were not attractive. Her giggle. Her thin blonde hair parted perfectly down the middle. She recently cut bangs to cover her slightly wrinkled forehead, but she was beautiful either way. She was a little rough around the edges. I remember her saying, "I'm willing to take it up the poop chute for the right guy!"

Emma Lou's giggles were like bubbles bursting out of a big bubble gun on a hot summer day.

I tried her phone again, now nervous about her situation. *Why's she calling me so late at night? She's a night owl.* She had trouble sleeping. She had demons. An ex-husband in prison for murder. A mysterious past of frequent lovers. She did not answer. I lay back and stared at the ceiling, contemplating Emma's unique life.

She enjoyed having sex with random strangers before her marriage to Jack. She loved bragging about it to me. She once said, "I tried writing the names down of all my lovers but ran out of paper! I think I'm a whore!" Emma giggled, and it was clear she didn't really care. "I had a busy life! I did a lotta things—some good, some bad!"

Jack wasn't the most exciting lover Emma Lou ever had. He was a small-town man. He was hot in a different sort of way. He was a gifted hunter, both big game and women. She liked that about him. Jack was gruff. He chain-smoked and was always complaining about something. Emma cheered him up, bringing a smile to his face with her slutty attitude.

One of her most memorable phrases, which she said often, was, "Dust settles, I don't!"

My mind kept dwelling on memories. I recalled how Emma Lou revealed to me how she realized that being difficult offered her plenty of attention. She told her husband one day that she hated the small town they lived in and suggested they move to Fort Lauderdale, where there's plenty of wealth, so they could double their insurance business.

She had laughed telling me how Jack dragged his muddy cowboy boots across the floor, a trail of dirt left behind. His coughing reminded her of his need to quit smoking, and he responded, "I hate Florida. You know I hate the humidity."

Before the leaves fell to the ground, Emma Lou had convinced her husband to take a chance on her brilliant idea. She would go down without him. She would rent an office and a house while he stayed put to oversee their already established business.

Before she left, she had thrown herself a going away happy hour at the club, where she said, "Come to visit me, Sophia!" She kissed me on both cheeks, we clicked our martini glasses. "I'm going to miss you, girl."

There was no doubt in everyone's mind that Emma Lou was sharp as a tack with business, clients loved working alongside her, and she captured new policies just as easily as taking candy from a baby. *I watched her as she schmoozed potential clients without mentioning the word insurance.*

When the news spread all over the country club gossip circle that Emma Lou successfully won an account that would land their company in the Billion Dollar Club, I wasn't surprised.

Jack flew to Fort Lauderdale to join her for a few months. Her son, Donald, and new daughter-in-law, Jaclyn, would join them as well. She needed the extra help, and she knew she could trust her family the most.

Finally, hours later, my phone rang, and Emma Lou was crying so hysterically I couldn't understand a word she was saying.

"So-ph-ia. I can't be-lieve it. He's such a bastard. An evil bastard."

I screamed at her, "Stop Emma, what's going on? Is Jack there? Let me talk to him."

She stayed mute.

My heart was skipping a mile a minute. "Emma. Please. Who's there with you? What's going on?"

She hung up the phone. I dialed her back. She didn't answer. I tried again. No answer. I fell asleep with the volume set on high and the phone under my pillow.

The sunrise came through my window early. I dialed her number while I laid in bed.

She answered, screaming and crying endlessly. "He's such a bastard. A dirty rotten bastard!"

"Start at the beginning." I used an even voice to try and calm her down. "What's going on?"

"I came home from work early yesterday." Emma's voice was quivering. "I walked in on them. I shocked the fuck out of them." She sniffled. "They were fucking in our bed."

My heart sank. I had a feeling Emma gagged, as I could hear her vomiting in the toilet. "What the fuck is going on there?" I screamed.

She cried. "He fucked Jaclyn. He fucked my daughter-in-law. What am I going to tell my son?"

I jumped out of bed, grabbed my robe and tied it around my nakedness, and walked into the kitchen to start the coffee maker. "Are you fucking kidding me? You can't be serious."

She couldn't keep her composure long enough to complete a sentence. "I-I-I just don't know what…what will I tell Don about his wife? They're newlyweds, Christ!"

My brain was numb to the story. "Jesus! He would never do that! Really?" I blankly gazed out my bedroom window to the flowing river below. I was in total disbelief. *This tragic story has to be the worst confession I've heard.*

Chapter Twelve

My Last Confession

The rest of the day passed by quickly. I had a dinner date with Stephanie's girl lover, Judge Patricia, her Peppermint Patty. We invited Violet. A most unusual plot twist, for me, allowing another woman to enter our private girl talk, but Stephanie was insistent about the invitation. "Just trust me, Sophia. I want Violet to be there tonight."

Stephanie goes on and on, sharing her lover's secrets with me. "I overheard Peppermint Patty's conversation with the lead attorney on a case." She smiled. "I know he's a cop, but he broke the law. He's been hiding this prostitution ring for a year."

My heart raced hearing Stephanie sharing the rest of the story. "Your friend Violet was right. Her partner, Kennedy, is tied into the cop's trouble. She gave him her credit card to use for the girls' rental cars. She's going to be questioned."

Kennedy's cop lover was in big trouble. The attorney had just enough evidence to charge him with the crime but wanted a key witness. An arrest warrant was already issued for him. He would be picked up later that day. The judge wanted to make an example of the cop since he was using criminal records from the prostitute's arrest sheets to gain access to their personal information.

Stephanie relayed all the details to me so vividly, that I could envision the scene in my mind's eye like a screenplay coming to life as a film.

Patty looked at Stephanie with a guilty glance. "These girls are underprivileged, most of them down and out, and he took advantage of them."

Stephanie nodded, agreeing to help her lover. "I know, Pep, I know. I'm lucky to have you in my life. I'm so grateful." She knew their sexual romps kept her safe from harm. Stephanie studied the tension in Patty's face, knowing exactly how to relieve her stress.

She was relentless in her pursuit to bring the judge to an orgasm. Forcefully throwing her legs above her head, around her shoulders so that her pussy was right up in Stephanie's face. She felt her spasms, and Patty screamed for release as she came inside her mouth. "Oh, baby. I could never live without you in my life."

Stephanie had been completely satisfied with her performance and responded, "Same love. Same." She wiped the love juice from her plump lips with her tongue and she kissed her gently, sharing the scent with her lover.

Patty had walked into the shower, still talking as she lathered her tomboy-like shape with the lavender-scented body wash. "Bring your friends over to my place tonight. We'll have privacy there. I'll ask my favorite chef to deliver us some delicious nosh."

Stephanie, standing naked against the wall, had answered, "Okay, love. Sounds good to me. What about hubby?"

She laughed. "He's out of town at a conference this week. You should spend the night; I'll reciprocate your tongue-lashing after our dinner. Make my baby come in my mouth. Would you like that, sweetness?"

Stephanie smiled. "I love that idea, Pep."

I felt like a peeping Tom hearing all their love talk, but it excited me.

Hours later, I met Violet at my loft. She was dressed in a pair of old denim jeans with a brown leather belt that was fastened with a turquoise chip inlay belt buckle from the Aztec Mayan Warriors in Mexico. I loved that buckle.

She greeted me with a huge smile on her face. "Hey, girl. What's this dinner all about? You're not telling me everything!"

I hugged her tight. "Just enjoy the night, you'll love my friend Stephanie. I haven't met Patty yet, myself, so we'll do this together."

I knew Violet was not into meeting new people. She was shy. She kept a small circle of friends. She protected her time. "I'll drive my own car, just in case I gotta leave early. My boys are home alone."

I agreed by shaking my head. "I gotcha girl, I understand."

The gates slowly opened as I approached, parking behind Stephanie's little red Mercedes in the circular driveway. The architectural elegance of Patty's Babcock Mansion was absolutely breathtaking. I couldn't wait to get inside. I had only dreamed of viewing the interior beauty of the mansion on Ellsworth Avenue. "Come on, Violet! I can't wait to see this place!"

She parked across the street and ran through the gates to catch up to me. "Oh my God, Sophia. This place is amazing! It's like a princess's castle in a fairytale! Wow!"

We rang the doorbell.

Patty was a slender woman. She wore a loose-fitting white blouse that was tucked into a pair of skinny black leggings; the top revealed her perky breasts slightly hanging open for us to see she wasn't wearing a bra. She had beautifully manicured toes. She welcomed me with a hug. "Hello! You must be Sophia!"

We side-kissed, and I said, "Yes, hello Patty! What a gorgeous home!"

Violet stood next to me. She stuck out her hand. "Hi, I'm Violet." Her tone and expression seemed nervous.

The music was coming from a piano in the distance. "Come in. Come in, girls. What can I get you both to drink?" We followed her through to an expansive kitchen to find Stephanie opening a bottle of Opus. "I'll skip the wine. How about a martini?"

She grinned. "Yes. I'll join you!"

Patty was in charge of the room and the conversation. "Sit, girls. Let's get right to the reason we are all here. Oh, please enjoy the nosh—Chef Jordan is fabulous. Have a bite while I explain why I wanted to meet you in person."

She went on while I peered over the spread of fancy appetizers. "Violet, your partner is in some hot water with the law. Did you know she gave her credit card to her lover, Mike?"

Violet turned as red as a beet. "Oh God. I just knew the Twinkie was in trouble. Sorry, I mean Kennedy."

Stephanie poured the Opus into a long-stemmed glass for herself. She mixed three martinis and handed them to us, positioning herself next to Patty. I could tell they were lovers.

"My goal is to keep you safe and away from this case, Violet. You can thank your friend Sophia for protecting you. And Stephanie for telling me the truth. But I'll need something from you."

Violet moved around the kitchen counter; she looked pale and suddenly washed out. "I'm sick. I think I'm going to throw up."

She held her stomach. She drank her martini with one big gulp, going to the bar to pour another. "Do you mind?"

Patty nodded with her approval. "Of course not, help yourself."

Violet rambled on, "I warned her about him. I just had a feeling. Nothing added up, to me. She was always making excuses as to why she was at his house; it's such a shithole."

Stephanie leaned in to hug Violet. "Don't worry, Violet. We're going to help you. Listen to Patty, and everything will work out."

Patty pulled a folder out of the drawer in the kitchen. She stood next to Violet to open it. "This is my file on Mike, the cop; it's pretty substantial. He's being arrested as we speak. Your partner is going to be brought in for questioning."

She sipped on her martini, then continued, "I'm hoping the credit card she gave him was personal and not a business card. It will make a difference for you, Violet. Can you check your business statements online for any car rentals? That way I'll know what to do before we get the subpoena out to her in the morning."

There was a frosty silence as Violet tried to get the words out of her mouth. She opened her phone to log in to her business account, scrolling through the list of transactions. "I pray to God she didn't use our card. I'm so sick in my stomach. I can't think straight."

My eyes met Stephanie's, and we glanced over at Patty, who took the lead again. "I'm going to help you, Violet. I'll do my very best to keep you and your partner out of the newspapers and, most importantly, out of trouble with the law."

I popped a crab-stuffed mushroom into my mouth. I felt nervous, not to mention starving, and I wanted to enjoy the food spread.

Patty walked over to Violet, rubbing her shoulders as she asked her more questions. "There's a paper trail of messages back and forth from Kennedy to Mike over the course of five or six months. She had to know what his side hustle was, since she was in and out of his house, which is where some of the girls were meeting their johns. Do you know anything else, Violet? If you do, I need to know."

She wept. "I have no idea. I only know they were fucking in the store. I hate that guy. I hated him from the start."

The piano music stopped playing and we all looked at each other at the same time. I noticed the full moon beaming through the large kitchen window. Violet reminded me of the topic, interrupting my peaceful moment. "I can't find any charges for rental cars on our business account. Thank fucking God."

I forgot tonight was a full moon!

Patty brought out a platter of fillet strips with dipping sauces. "Get some food in your belly, Violet. You can't be getting sick. We need you to be strong. It's gonna be a long couple of months, I'm afraid. This news will hit the papers first thing tomorrow morning."

Stephanie scrolled through her phone, answering messages and rolling her eyes every time her eyes met mine. Violet excused herself; she looked like she had just seen a ghost, she was so pale. "I really need to get home to my boys. I'm glad you told me. I'll let you know if I find out anything else. I'll totally cooperate."

I walked Violet out to the porch and hugged her as tight as I could to reassure her that everything was going to be all right. "Text me when you're home. Pinky promise me."

She agreed. I walked back inside to find Patty and Stephanie in a passionate kiss. "Whoops! Sorry! I gotta go as well. I'll catch up with you girls tomorrow!"

Patty stopped me. She walked closer to me. "Stay a minute, Sophia. There's something else."

She handed me the rest of my martini. "I've told Stephanie, but I want you to hear this straight from my lips. Junior's being investigated for mortgage fraud. I've warned Steph to keep her distance, but I know his wife, Taylor, is your customer. Be careful. My hubby is the District Attorney, and that's all I can really say right now."

I stayed for another hour, until I felt uncomfortable, like a third wheel on a date. "I gotta run. It's been a long day, and Shawn's coming over tomorrow night, so I need the rest! I think he's going to take the partnership and move to South Carolina."

Stephanie pouted like a kid. "Don't worry, honey. Patty and I will keep you company. Oh my God! That reminds me! I want to introduce you to Patty's friend, Roxie. Can you meet us for happy hour this week?" I nodded. "I would love that, thanks girl."

❖

The evening was brisk, but I loved driving slowly through the city streets with my convertible top down and the radio volume up. "Come Away with Me" by Nora Jones was playing on the radio, and I turned it up.

I leaned back to enjoy the crisp winter air blowing through my curly locks. It was refreshing on my face. The busy city seemed alive with twinkling lights and red ribbons, holiday music, and traditions. *I miss my children.*

As my foot hit the brakes for a red light, I checked my phone. I had six missed calls.

Leanne had left a frantic message. "I need your help so bad. Markus wants me to move a million dollars from his business account to buy a house in Boca immediately. He's up to something."

I called her back, pulling away from the intersection slowly. "Don't forget to make your full moon wish tonight!" I could tell she was running on her treadmill, out of breath. "You have to help me! Can you come?"

I parked my car on the rooftop of my open-air garage and left the top down to gaze up at the moon while we caught up, pulling my scarf tighter around my neck to shake off the brisk breeze rolling through. "I can't come this weekend. Shawn's leaving for South Carolina, and I have a lot on my plate at the store, it's holiday time—my busiest time. Maybe a quick overnight one night next week. I gotta play it by ear, though."

Leanne cranked the speed down on her machine. "Okay, girl, I understand. I just gotta sift through his financial documents; he's finally giving me the key to his credenza. His attorney's dropping it off on Friday."

I pondered on the idea of not knowing his financial situation until five years after their marriage. "Jesus, Leanne. That's a big deal. You'll have a field day inside that cabinet full of secrets! I want the cliff notes. We could write a book about the criminal mind—a sexy Jackie Collins novel."

She giggled like a schoolgirl. "Yeah! But you'll insist I include my romps with my young boy toys, and I'm not ready to give up those dirty little secrets just yet! I'll have to fuck with another detective!"

I hit the switch to bring the top back up. I was frozen to the bone but the time under the moon was worth it.

I walked and listened, while she huffed, "Can you believe my fucking husband insisted on having his three teenage daughters visit me in Boca last week? Those fucking cunts threw my Christmas tree out on the lawn and busted every bulb on the tree while my son stood there crying and screaming!"

Who does that to someone?

My heart hurt for her, but she signed on for it. "I met those girls once, for a minute; it was obvious they were little bitches. Jesus, Leanne, I'm sorry." I could see the scene playing out in my mind: *They're already in training for the high society rich bitch club!*

She snapped back at me, "Yeah, all three of them are fucking bitches. I told Markus, never again. It took my housekeeper five fucking hours to clean up the mess, and the gardener had to blow the glass into a special bag to get it all off the grass. I had to shop for hours to buy all new ornaments. I hate those cunts! My full moon wish is going to be evil tonight!"

I giggled. "Don't waste your wish on them. You need to wish for something for yourself, maybe you need to wish for peace!"

She laughed. "Yeah. I'll wish for a piece, a piece of young ass that is!"

We shared our sense of humor. "I love you, girl. You always make me smile!"

The other message was from Shawn. I rang him back as I walked closer to my front door, greeted by a smile from my concierge.

"What's up, sexy man?"

He laughed. I could tell he was driving his sexy little red Porsche and the top was down. *We're so alike.* "I'm thinking back to the night you drove my car, *topless*. God, I loved sitting in the passenger seat watching you take the curves like a pro."

I smiled and took a seat in front of the fireplace in the lobby, warming my hands near the flames, recalling that glorious night with him. "What a great night that was!"

Shawn never hesitated to ask for whatever he wanted, and tonight was no exception. "I can't wait to see you, lick your juicy peach. Mmmm…. I was thinking about our first date, when I licked peach juice from your peach. I was having a difficult time hiding my hardness while the movers packed my boxes!"

I smiled from ear to ear, feeling the warmth of the fireplace fill my heart with sadness. "I can't wait to see you as well, doc. I need you to leave me one thing."

He charmed me. "What's that, sugar?"

I smiled. "I need the scent of your beard after a lovemaking session with me!"

He reassured me. "I wish you would run away with me, peaches. We can open a fruit stand in the countryside. Spend our lives eating peaches and baking pies! You can write a juicy novel about all your dressing room confessions!"

I choked back the tears, full of heartache and wanting to wash away the all-too-familiar pain. "I know, sexy, I know. You'll find a young, ripe peach to take a bite out of soon enough and forget about this old rotten peach! Let's enjoy our last night alone tomorrow. No goodbyes, just see you later, alligator—promise me!" He had an irresistible grin; I couldn't wait to see it one last time.

He played with me. "I want to make you come tonight. Play sex-texting games with me later; text me when you're lying in your bed. I'll wait up for you."

A tear dropped out of my right eye. I sat by the fire for a minute, checking my other messages and peering out through the factory windows at the full moon glistening in the sky. I was going to miss him terribly but envied him for chasing his dreams. *Nothing good ever lasts forever.*

I had two voicemails from an unknown number. I listened to the voice, unrecognizable to me. The deep, sultry voice captivated me. "Kellie gave me your number. Hope you don't mind. I want to take you to dinner, Saturday night. Call me." There was a second message from this mystery man. "Oh, by the way, it's Tom. My friends call me Tommy D. Call me back, please!"

How dare that cockroach give a stranger my private number!

Violet had called and left a message. She would have to wait. I listened as I walked toward the elevator and pressed the button to my floor. "I just can't believe it, Sophia. Meet me for breakfast tomorrow, if you can. Call me."

I texted her back. *Let's meet at ten for coffee, our usual place.*

Stephanie left me a voicemail. "Pep said you're extremely smart. She loved you and said you should consider dating her girlfriend, Roxie. I've met Roxie. She's hot stuff, and smart, just like you like your lovers. Hot and smart! Call me."

I giggled. She rang me again while I was on the elevator. "Pick up, girlfriend. Call me back, please, it's important!"

I walked inside my loft, pulled my boots off, and stripped my jeans and t-shirt away, allowing them to fall to the floor. I walked to the window to take in the energy of the moon, savoring every ounce of the magical mist of the illumination.

My phone lit up with another missed call from Stephanie. "What's up, Steph? I'm just soaking up the moon dust!"

She giggled. "I just had to tell you a little secret while Pep's in the shower."

I snarled, "Another secret. Jesus! So many shady sides. So many secrets. Now what?"

She sounded muffled by her hand covering the phone. "I just can't believe it. Junior's wife, Taylor, just called me. She wants to meet me for lunch tomorrow."

I heard a knock at my door and glanced at the clock; it was midnight. "Stephanie, someone's knocking at my door. Who on earth would be here so late? How did they get past the concierge?" She whispered like she was next to me, "Don't answer it, Sophia."

I tip-toed closer and peeped through the keyhole to see only a man's back in the distance. He was casually dressed. I pushed my soft, leopard chair against the door, walked back into my bedroom, and paced nervously back and forth. "He's still out there. I'm going to call the front desk." I tip-toed back to the peephole, and the stranger was gone. "He's gone, Steph; how creepy!"

The rush of adrenaline ran through my veins. Shawn texted me: *In the mood for a little sex-texting peaches? A new way for us to play while I'm away...*

I texted him back quickly because I needed the comfort: *Oh yes, please!* I pulled back my luxurious white sheets, exposing my leopard undies to the moonlit sky.

He answered: *Tell me what you're wearing. Touch your peach for me, baby.*

I made my full moon wish after I made myself come using his playful words to ease me into a calm, yet furious orgasm. I placed the full moon wish under a glass of milk next to the windowpane to collect all the magic overnight. I wished for abundance.

In the morning, I made coffee in the nude, sank into my luxurious leopard chair, and marveled, as I did several times a day, at what my life had become. I was a store owner, with the help of my close girlfriends, Leanne and Violet. They were so close, in fact, that I allowed Leanne to bring out the best of my naughty side. And I was a feisty single woman living in the city with the help of my most unexpected friend, Stephanie. She was teaching me how to be my authentic self, whatever that meant to me. I was still studying, exploring all the possibilities!

My phone lit up with a message from Stephanie: *Join me for lunch. I'm meeting Taylor, she asked me to invite you. Why? I've no idea. I'm not telling Pep. Join me!*

I texted her back: *I'll be there. Our usual place?*

She answered quickly: *Yes! The hotel where you lost your virginity!*

Acknowledgments

To my publishing advisor, Tim Jacobs, who kept me connected to the team and the goal to bring this book series to life.

To my editor, Nina L. Marshall, the greatest partner and teammate. Thank you for bringing my truths out, extracting my thoughts and the cold hard facts.

To my book project manager, Susie Schaefer, you are simply the best in the business. To me, you symbolize unwavering dedication and willingness to surmount obstacles to flourish.

To my special friend, Evelyn Leamon. Thank you for creating our group, The Lovely Literary Ladies Book Club of Naples, Florida. Each and every one of you have inspired me to share my stories and continue to write!

The journey into my shady sides and yours, this is just the beginning.

About the Author

Cyndi Stuart has been an entrepreneur for as long as she can remember, finding a profound sense of accomplishment in creating new businesses. This passion for building something from nothing inspired her to write her first novel, *Dressing Room Confessions* and she thrives in the conceptualizing phase, deeply grateful for her creative gift.

Cyndi's journey in the entertainment industry began humbly, answering phones at a small production company. Her dedication and talent led to over a decade of work on notable films such as *Silence of the Lambs* and *Kingpin*.

Her production company, Northcoast, Inc. earned numerous American Advertising Awards and Telly Awards for their television commercials. Recognized as visionaries, they were among the first five production houses to adopt animation software. This innovation resulted in the unique mouth manipulation technique for Taco Bell's famous Chihuahua, "Yo Quiero Taco Bell," created by the ad agency Chiat Day.

Years later, Cyndi's extensive knowledge of behind-the-scenes and client needs culminated in designing a state-of-the-art film studio, Studio C, which still operates in Pittsburgh, Pennsylvania.

In the literary world, Cyndi Stuart shines as a luminary, crafting stories that captivate and ignite passions. Specializing in Erotic Romance, where love and desire blend in a symphony of emotions. Her vivid characters and intricate plots create an immersive experience, leaving readers spellbound and eager for more. Cyndi's storytelling mastery transforms words into a journey through the depths of human longing.

To learn more, visit: MidnightInkPublishing.com

www.ingramcontent.com/pod-product-compliance
Lightning Source LLC
Chambersburg PA
CBHW022102310726
48972CB00007B/1850